THE TAPESTRIED CHAMBER
AND
THE LEGEND OF MONTROSE

SIR WALTER SCOTT

THE TAPESTRIED CHAMBER
AND
THE LEGEND OF MONTROSE

BIBLIOBAZAAR

THE TAPESTRIED CHAMBER

AND

THE LEGEND OF MONTROSE

CONTENTS

THE TAPESTRIED CHAMBER...9

DEATH OF THE LAIRD'S JOCK 29

A LEGEND OF MONTROSE
    I.   Introduction to
        A LEGEND OF MONTROSE.............................41
    II.   Introduction (Supplement)
        Sergeant More M'Alpin. 53
    III. Main text of A LEGEND OF MONTROSE. 59
    IV. Appendix.. 279
        No. I Clan Alpin's Vow 279
        No. II The Children of the Mist................................280
    V. Notes. 283
    Note I.— Fides et Fiducia sunt relativa. 283
    Note II.— Wraiths. 283

THE TAPESTRIED CHAMBER;
OR,
THE LADY IN THE SACQUE.

INTRODUCTION.

This is another little story from The Keepsake of 1828. It was told to me many years ago by the late Miss Anna Seward, who, among other accomplishments that rendered her an amusing inmate in a country house, had that of recounting narratives of this sort with very considerable effect—much greater, indeed, than any one would be apt to guess from the style of her written performances. There are hours and moods when most people are not displeased to listen to such things; and I have heard some of the greatest and wisest of my contemporaries take their share in telling them.

AUGUST 1831

* * * * *

The following narrative is given from the pen, so far as memory permits, in the same character in which it was presented to the author's ear; nor has he claim to further praise, or to be more deeply censured, than in proportion to the good or bad judgment which he has employed in selecting his materials, as he has studiously avoided any attempt at ornament which might interfere with the simplicity of the tale.

At the same time, it must be admitted that the particular class of stories which turns on the marvellous possesses a stronger influence when told than when committed to print. The volume taken up at noonday, though rehearsing the same incidents, conveys a much more feeble impression than is achieved by the voice of the speaker on a circle of fireside auditors, who hang upon the narrative as the narrator details the minute incidents which serve to give it authenticity, and lowers his voice with an affectation of mystery while he approaches the fearful and wonderful part. It was with such advantages that the present writer heard the following events related, more than twenty years since, by the celebrated Miss Seward of Litchfield, who, to her numerous accomplishments, added, in a remarkable degree, the power of narrative in private conversation. In its present form the tale must necessarily lose all the interest which was attached to it by the flexible voice and intelligent features of the gifted narrator. Yet still, read aloud to an undoubting audience by the doubtful light of the closing evening, or in silence by a decaying taper, and amidst the solitude of a half-lighted apartment, it may redeem its character as a good ghost story. Miss Seward always affirmed that she had derived her information from an authentic source, although she suppressed the names of the two persons chiefly concerned. I will not avail myself of any particulars I may have since received concerning the localities of the detail, but suffer them to rest under the same general description in which they were first related to me; and for the same reason I will not add to or diminish the narrative by any circumstance, whether more or less material, but simply rehearse, as I heard it, a story of supernatural terror.

About the end of the American war, when the officers of Lord Cornwallis's army, which surrendered at Yorktown, and others, who had been made prisoners during the impolitic and ill-fated controversy, were returning to their own country, to relate their adventures, and repose themselves after their fatigues, there was amongst them a general officer, to whom Miss S. gave the name of Browne, but merely, as I understood, to save the inconvenience of introducing a nameless agent in the narrative. He was an officer of merit, as well as a gentleman of high consideration for family and attainments.

Some business had carried General Browne upon a tour through the western counties, when, in the conclusion of a morning stage, he found himself in the vicinity of a small country town, which presented a scene of uncommon beauty, and of a character peculiarly English.

The little town, with its stately old church, whose tower bore testimony to the devotion of ages long past, lay amidst pastures and cornfields of small extent, but bounded and divided with hedgerow timber of great age and size. There were few marks of modern improvement. The environs of the place intimated neither the solitude of decay nor the bustle of novelty; the houses were old, but in good repair; and the beautiful little river murmured freely on its way to the left of the town, neither restrained by a dam nor bordered by a towing-path.

Upon a gentle eminence, nearly a mile to the southward of the town, were seen, amongst many venerable oaks and tangled thickets, the turrets of a castle as old as the walls of York and Lancaster, but which seemed to have received important alterations during the age of Elizabeth and her successor, It had not been a place of great size; but whatever accommodation it formerly afforded was, it must be supposed, still to be obtained within its walls. At least, such was the inference which General Browne drew from observing the smoke arise merrily from several of the ancient wreathed and carved chimney-stalks. The wall of the park ran alongside of the highway for two or three hundred yards; and through the different points by which the eye found glimpses into the woodland scenery, it seemed to be well stocked. Other points of view opened in succession—now a full one of the front of the old castle, and now a side glimpse at its particular towers, the former rich in all the bizarrerie of the Elizabethan school, while the simple and solid strength of other parts of the building seemed to show that they had been raised more for defence than ostentation.

Delighted with the partial glimpses which he obtained of the castle through the woods and glades by which this ancient feudal fortress was surrounded, our military traveller was determined to inquire whether it might not deserve a nearer view, and whether it contained family pictures or other objects of curiosity worthy of a stranger's visit, when, leaving the vicinity of the park, he rolled through a clean and well-paved street, and stopped at the door of a well-frequented inn.

Before ordering horses, to proceed on his journey, General Browne made inquiries concerning the proprietor of the chateau which had so attracted his admiration, and was equally surprised and pleased at hearing in reply a nobleman named, whom we shall call Lord Woodville. How fortunate! Much of Browne's early recollections, both at school and at college, had been connected with young Woodville, whom, by a few questions, he now ascertained to be the same with the owner of this fair domain. He had been raised to the peerage by the decease of his father a few months before, and, as the General learned from the landlord, the term of mourning being ended, was now taking possession of his paternal estate in the jovial season of merry, autumn, accompanied by a select party of friends, to enjoy the sports of a country famous for game.

This was delightful news to our traveller. Frank Woodville had been Richard Browne's fag at Eton, and his chosen intimate at Christ Church; their pleasures and their tasks had been the same; and the honest soldier's heart warmed to find his early friend in possession of so delightful a residence, and of an estate, as the landlord assured him with a nod and a wink, fully adequate to maintain and add to his dignity. Nothing was more natural than that the traveller should suspend a journey, which there was nothing to render hurried, to pay a visit to an old friend under such agreeable circumstances.

The fresh horses, therefore, had only the brief task of conveying the General's travelling carriage to Woodville Castle. A porter admitted them at a modern Gothic lodge, built in that style to correspond with the castle itself, and at the same time rang a bell to give warning of the approach of visitors. Apparently the sound of the bell had suspended the separation of the company, bent on the various amusements of the morning; for, on entering the court of the chateau, several young men were lounging about in their sporting dresses, looking at and criticizing the dogs which the keepers held in readiness to attend their pastime. As General Browne alighted, the young lord came to the gate of the hall, and for an instant gazed, as at a stranger, upon the countenance of his friend, on which war, with its fatigues and its wounds, had made a great alteration. But the uncertainty lasted no longer than till the visitor had spoken, and the hearty greeting which followed was such as can only be exchanged betwixt those who have passed together the merry days of careless boyhood or early youth.

"If I could have formed a wish, my dear Browne," said Lord Woodville, "it would have been to have you here, of all men, upon this occasion, which my friends are good enough to hold as a sort of holiday. Do not think you have been unwatched during the years you have been absent from us. I have traced you through your dangers, your triumphs, your misfortunes, and was delighted to see that, whether in victory or defeat, the name of my old friend was always distinguished with applause."

The General made a suitable reply, and congratulated his friend on his new dignities, and the possession of a place and domain so beautiful.

"Nay, you have seen nothing of it as yet," said Lord Woodville, "and I trust you do not mean to leave us till you are better acquainted with it. It is true, I confess, that my present party is pretty large, and the old house, like other places of the kind, does not possess so much accommodation as the extent of the outward walls appears to promise. But we can give you a comfortable old-fashioned room, and I venture to suppose that your campaigns have taught you to be glad of worse quarters."

The General shrugged his shoulders, and laughed. "I presume," he said, "the worst apartment in your chateau is considerably superior to the old tobacco-cask in which I was fain to take up my night's lodging when I was in the Bush, as the Virginians call it, with the light corps. There I lay, like Diogenes himself, so delighted with my covering from the elements, that I made a vain attempt to have it rolled on to my next quarters; but my commander for the time would give way to no such luxurious provision, and I took farewell of my beloved cask with tears in my eyes."

"Well, then, since you do not fear your quarters," said Lord Woodville, "you will stay with me a week at least. Of guns, dogs, fishing-rods, flies, and means of sport by sea and land, we have enough and to spare—you cannot pitch on an amusement but we will find the means of pursuing it. But if you prefer the gun and pointers, I will go with you myself, and see whether you have mended your shooting since you have been amongst the Indians of the back settlements."

The General gladly accepted his friendly host's proposal in all its points. After a morning of manly exercise, the company met at dinner, where it was the delight of Lord Woodville to conduce to the display of the high properties of his recovered friend, so as to recommend him to his guests, most of whom were persons of distinction. He led General Browne to speak of the scenes he had witnessed; and as every word marked alike the brave officer and the sensible man, who retained possession of his cool judgment under the most imminent dangers, the company looked upon the soldier with general respect, as on one who had proved himself possessed of an uncommon portion of personal courage—that attribute of all others of which everybody desires to be thought possessed.

The day at Woodville Castle ended as usual in such mansions. The hospitality stopped within the limits of good order. Music, in which the young lord was a proficient, succeeded to the circulation of the bottle; cards and billiards, for those who preferred such amusements, were in readiness; but the exercise of the morning required early hours, and not long after eleven o'clock the guests began to retire to their several apartments.

The young lord himself conducted his friend, General Browne, to the chamber destined for him, which answered the description he had given of it, being comfortable, but old-fashioned, The bed was of the massive form used in the end of the seventeenth century, and the curtains of faded silk, heavily trimmed with tarnished gold. But then the sheets, pillows, and blankets looked delightful to the campaigner, when he thought of his "mansion, the cask." There was an air of gloom in the tapestry hangings, which, with their worn-out graces, curtained the walls of the little chamber, and gently undulated as the autumnal breeze found its way through the ancient lattice window, which pattered and whistled as the air gained entrance. The toilet, too, with its mirror, turbaned after the manner of the beginning of the century, with a coiffure of murrey-coloured silk, and its hundred strange-shaped boxes, providing for arrangements which had been obsolete for more than fifty years, had an antique, and in so far a melancholy, aspect. But nothing could blaze more brightly and cheerfully than the two large wax candles; or if aught could rival them, it was the flaming, bickering fagots in the chimney, that sent at once their gleam and their warmth through the snug apartment, which, notwithstanding the general antiquity of its appearance, was not wanting in the least convenience that modern habits rendered either necessary or desirable.

"This is an old-fashioned sleeping apartment, General," said the young lord; "but I hope you find nothing that makes you envy your old tobacco-cask."

"I am not particular respecting my lodgings," replied the General; "yet were I to make any choice, I would prefer this chamber by many degrees to the gayer and more modern rooms of your family mansion. Believe me that, when I unite its modern air of comfort with its venerable antiquity, and recollect that it is your lordship's property, I shall feel in better quarters here than if I were in the best hotel London could afford."

"I trust—I have no doubt—that you will find yourself as comfortable as I wish you, my dear General," said the young nobleman; and once more bidding his guest good-night, he shook him by the hand, and withdrew.

The General once more looked round him, and internally congratulating himself on his return to peaceful life, the comforts of which were endeared by the recollection of the hardships and dangers he had lately sustained, undressed himself, and prepared for a luxurious night's rest.

Here, contrary to the custom of this species of tale, we leave the General in possession of his apartment until the next morning.

The company assembled for breakfast at an early hour, but without the appearance of General Browne, who seemed the guest that Lord Woodville was desirous of honouring above all whom his hospitality had assembled around him. He more than once expressed surprise at the General's absence, and at length sent a servant to make inquiry after him. The man brought back information that General Browne had been walking abroad since an early hour of the morning, in defiance of the weather, which was misty and ungenial.

"The custom of a soldier," said the young nobleman to his friends. "Many of them acquire habitual vigilance, and cannot sleep after the early hour at which their duty usually commands them to be alert."

Yet the explanation which Lord Woodville thus offered to the company seemed hardly satisfactory to his own mind, and it was in a fit of silence and abstraction that he waited the return of the General. It took place near an hour after the breakfast bell had rung. He looked fatigued and feverish. His hair, the powdering and arrangement of which was at this time one of the most important occupations of a man's whole day, and marked his fashion as much as in the present time the tying of a cravat, or the want of one, was dishevelled, uncurled, void of powder, and dank with dew. His clothes were huddled on with a careless negligence, remarkable in a military man, whose real or supposed duties are usually held to include some attention to the toilet; and his looks were haggard and ghastly in a peculiar degree.

"So you have stolen a march upon us this morning, my dear General," said Lord Woodville; "or you have not found your bed so much to your mind as I had hoped and you seemed to expect. How did you rest last night?"

"Oh, excellently well! remarkably well! never better in my life," said General Browne rapidly, and yet with an air of embarrassment which was obvious to his friend. He then hastily swallowed a cup of tea, and neglecting or refusing whatever else was offered, seemed to fall into a fit of abstraction.

"You will take the gun to-day, General?" said his friend and host, but had to repeat the question twice ere he received the abrupt answer, "No, my lord; I am sorry I cannot have the opportunity of spending another day with your lordship; my post horses are ordered, and will be here directly."

All who were present showed surprise, and Lord Woodville immediately replied "Post horses, my good friend! What can you possibly want with them when you promised to stay with me quietly for at least a week?"

"I believe," said the General, obviously much embarrassed, "that I might, in the pleasure of my first meeting with your lordship, have said something about stopping here a few days; but I have since found it altogether impossible."

"That is very extraordinary," answered the young nobleman. "You seemed quite disengaged yesterday, and you cannot have had a summons to-day, for our post has not come up from the town, and therefore you cannot have received any letters."

General Browne, without giving any further explanation, muttered something about indispensable business, and insisted on the absolute necessity of his departure in a manner which silenced all opposition on the part of his host, who saw that his resolution was taken, and forbore all further importunity.

"At least, however," he said, "permit me, my dear Browne, since go you will or must, to show you the view from the terrace, which the mist, that is now rising, will soon display."

He threw open a sash-window, and stepped down upon the terrace as he spoke. The General followed him mechanically, but seemed little to attend to what his host was saying, as, looking across an extended and rich prospect, he pointed out the different objects worthy of observation. Thus they moved on till Lord Woodville had attained his purpose of drawing his guest entirely apart from the rest of the company, when, turning round upon him with an air of great solemnity, he addressed him thus:—

"Richard Browne, my old and very dear friend, we are now alone. Let me conjure you to answer me upon the word of a friend, and the honour of a soldier. How did you in reality rest during last night?"

"Most wretchedly indeed, my lord," answered the General, in the same tone of solemnity—"so miserably, that I would not run the risk of such a second night, not only for all the lands belonging to this castle, but for all the country which I see from this elevated point of view."

"This is most extraordinary," said the young lord, as if speaking to himself; "then there must be something in the reports concerning that apartment." Again turning to the General, he said, "For God's sake, my dear friend, be candid with me, and let me know the disagreeable particulars which have befallen you under a roof, where, with consent of the owner, you should have met nothing save comfort."

The General seemed distressed by this appeal, and paused a moment before he replied. "My dear lord," he at length said, "what happened to me last night is of a nature so peculiar and so unpleasant, that I could hardly bring myself to detail it even to your lordship, were it not that, independent of my wish to gratify any request of yours, I think that sincerity on my part may lead to some explanation about a circumstance equally painful and mysterious. To others, the communication I am about to make, might place me in the light of a weak-minded, superstitious fool, who suffered his own imagination to delude and bewilder him; but you have known me in childhood and youth, and will not suspect me of having adopted in manhood the feelings and frailties from which my early years were free." Here he paused, and his friend replied,—

"Do not doubt my perfect confidence in the truth of your communication, however strange it may be," replied Lord Woodville. "I know your firmness of disposition too well, to suspect you could be made the object of imposition, and am aware that your honour and your friendship will equally deter you from exaggerating whatever you may have witnessed."

"Well, then," said the General, "I will proceed with my story as well as I can, relying upon your candour, and yet distinctly feeling that I would rather face a battery than recall to my mind the odious recollections of last night."

He paused a second time, and then perceiving that Lord Woodville remained silent and in an attitude of attention, he commenced, though not without obvious reluctance, the history of his night's adventures in the Tapestried Chamber.

"I undressed and went to bed so soon as your lordship left me yesterday evening; but the wood in the chimney, which nearly fronted my bed, blazed brightly and cheerfully, and, aided by a hundred exciting recollections of my childhood and youth, which had been recalled by the unexpected pleasure of meeting your lordship, prevented me from falling immediately asleep. I ought, however, to say that these reflections were all of a pleasant and agreeable kind, grounded on a sense of having for a time exchanged the labour, fatigues, and dangers of my profession for the enjoyments of a peaceful life, and the reunion of those friendly and affectionate ties which I had torn asunder at the rude summons of war.

"While such pleasing reflections were stealing over my mind, and gradually lulling me to slumber, I was suddenly aroused by a sound like that of the rustling of a silken gown, and the tapping of a pair of high-heeled shoes, as if a woman were walking in the apartment. Ere I could draw the curtain to see what the matter was, the figure of a little woman passed between the bed and the fire. The back of this form was turned to me, and I could observe, from the shoulders and neck, it was that of an old woman, whose dress was an old-fashioned gown, which I think ladies call a sacque—that is, a sort of robe completely loose in the body, but gathered into broad plaits upon the neck and shoulders, which fall down to the ground, and terminate in a species of train.

"I thought the intrusion singular enough, but never harboured for a moment the idea that what I saw was anything more than the mortal form of some old woman about the establishment, who had a fancy to dress like her grandmother, and who, having perhaps (as your lordship mentioned that you were rather straitened for room) been dislodged from her chamber for my accommodation, had forgotten the circumstance, and returned by twelve to her old haunt. Under this persuasion I moved myself in bed and coughed a little, to make the intruder sensible of my being in possession of the premises. She turned slowly round, but, gracious Heaven! my lord, what a countenance did she display to me! There was no longer any question what she was, or any thought of her being a living being. Upon a face which wore the fixed features of a corpse were imprinted the traces of the vilest and most hideous passions which had animated her while she lived. The body of some atrocious criminal seemed to have been given up from the grave, and the soul restored from the penal fire, in order to form for a space a union with the ancient accomplice of its guilt. I started up in bed, and sat upright, supporting myself on my palms, as I gazed on this horrible spectre. The hag made, as it seemed, a single and swift stride to the bed where I lay, and squatted herself down upon it, in precisely the same attitude which I had assumed in the extremity of horror, advancing her diabolical countenance within half a yard of mine, with a grin which seemed to intimate the malice and the derision of an incarnate fiend."

Here General Browne stopped, and wiped from his brow the cold perspiration with which the recollection of his horrible vision had covered it.

"My lord," he said, "I am no coward, I have been in all the mortal dangers incidental to my profession, and I may truly boast that no man ever knew Richard Browne dishonour the sword he wears; but in these horrible circumstances, under the eyes, and, as it seemed, almost in the grasp of an incarnation of an evil spirit, all firmness forsook me, all manhood melted from me like wax in the furnace, and I felt my hair individually bristle. The current of my life-blood ceased to flow, and I sank back in a swoon, as very a victim to panic terror as ever was a village girl, or a child of ten years old. How long I lay in this condition I cannot pretend to guess.

"But I was roused by the castle clock striking one, so loud that it seemed as if it were in the very room. It was some time before I dared open my eyes, lest they should again encounter the horrible spectacle. When, however, I summoned courage to look up, she was no longer visible. My first idea was to pull my bell, wake the servants, and remove to a garret or a hay-loft, to be ensured against a second visitation. Nay, I will confess the truth that my resolution was altered, not by the shame of exposing myself, but by the fear that, as the bell-cord hung by the chimney, I might, in making my way to it, be again crossed by the fiendish hag, who, I figured to myself, might be still lurking about some corner of the apartment.

"I will not pretend to describe what hot and cold fever-fits tormented me for the rest of the night, through broken sleep, weary vigils, and that dubious state which forms the neutral ground between them. A hundred terrible objects appeared to haunt me; but there was the great difference betwixt the vision which I have described, and those which followed, that I knew the last to be deceptions of my own fancy and over-excited nerves.

"Day at last appeared, and I rose from my bed ill in health and humiliated in mind. I was ashamed of myself as a man and a soldier, and still more so at feeling my own extreme desire to escape from the haunted apartment, which, however, conquered all other considerations; so that, huddling on my clothes with the most careless haste, I made my escape from your lordship's mansion, to seek in the open air some relief to my nervous system, shaken as it was by this horrible rencounter with a visitant, for such I must believe her, from the other world. Your lordship has now heard the cause of my discomposure, and of my sudden desire to leave your hospitable castle. In other places I trust we may often meet, but God protect me from ever spending a second night under that roof!"

Strange as the General's tale was, he spoke with such a deep air of conviction that it cut short all the usual commentaries which are made on such stories. Lord Woodville never once asked him if he was sure he did not dream of the apparition, or suggested any of the possibilities by which it is fashionable to explain supernatural appearances as wild vagaries of the fancy, or deceptions of the optic nerves, On the contrary, he seemed deeply impressed with the truth and reality of what he had heard; and, after a considerable pause regretted, with much appearance of sincerity, that his early friend should in his house have suffered so severely.

"I am the more sorry for your pain, my dear Browne," he continued, "that it is the unhappy, though most unexpected, result of an experiment of my own. You must know that, for my father and grandfather's time, at least, the apartment which was assigned to you last night had been shut on account of reports that it was disturbed by supernatural sights and noises. When I came, a few weeks since, into possession of the estate, I thought the accommodation which the castle afforded for my friends was not extensive enough to permit the inhabitants of the invisible world to retain possession of a comfortable sleeping apartment. I therefore caused the Tapestried Chamber, as we call it, to be opened, and, without destroying its air of antiquity, I had such new articles of furniture placed in it as became the modern times. Yet, as the opinion that the room was haunted very strongly prevailed among the domestics, and was also known in the neighbourhood and to many of my friends, I feared some prejudice might be entertained by the first occupant of the Tapestried Chamber, which might tend to revive the evil report which it had laboured under, and so disappoint my purpose of rendering it a useful part or the house. I must confess, my dear Browne, that your arrival yesterday, agreeable to me for a thousand reasons besides, seemed the most favourable opportunity of removing the unpleasant rumours which attached to the room, since your courage was indubitable, and your mind free of any preoccupation on the subject. I could not, therefore, have chosen a more fitting subject for my experiment."

"Upon my life," said General Browne, somewhat hastily, "I am infinitely obliged to your lordship—very particularly indebted indeed. I am likely to remember for some time the consequences of the experiment, as your lordship is pleased to call it."

"Nay, now you are unjust, my dear friend," said Lord Woodville. "You have only to reflect for a single moment, in order to be convinced that I could not augur the possibility of the pain to which you have been so unhappily exposed. I was yesterday morning a complete sceptic on the subject of supernatural appearances. Nay, I am sure that, had I told you what was said about that room, those very reports would have induced you, by your own choice, to select it for your accommodation. It was my misfortune, perhaps my error, but really cannot be termed my fault, that you have been afflicted so strangely."

"Strangely indeed!" said the General, resuming his good temper; "and I acknowledge that I have no right to be offended with your lordship for treating me like what I used to think myself—a man of some firmness and courage. But I see my post horses are arrived, and I must not detain your lordship from your amusement."

"Nay, my old friend," said Lord Woodville, "since you cannot stay with us another day—which, indeed, I can no longer urge—give me at least half an hour more. You used to love pictures, and I have a gallery of portraits, some of them by Vandyke, representing ancestry to whom this property and castle formerly belonged. I think that several of them will strike you as possessing merit."

General Browne accepted the invitation, though somewhat unwillingly. It was evident he was not to breathe freely or at ease till he left Woodville Castle far behind him. He could not refuse his friend's invitation, however; and the less so, that he was a little ashamed of the peevishness which he had displayed towards his well-meaning entertainer.

The General, therefore, followed Lord Woodville through several rooms into a long gallery hung with pictures, which the latter pointed out to his guest, telling the names, and giving some account of the personages whose portraits presented themselves in progression. General Browne was but little interested in the details which these accounts conveyed to him. They were, indeed, of the kind which are usually found in an old family gallery. Here was a Cavalier who had ruined the estate in the royal cause; there a fine lady who had reinstated it by contracting a match with a wealthy Roundhead. There hung a gallant who had been in danger for corresponding with the exiled Court at Saint Germain's; here one who had taken arms for William at the Revolution; and there a third that had thrown his weight alternately into the scale of Whig and Tory.

While lord Woodville was cramming these words into his guest's ear, "against the stomach of his sense," they gained the middle of the gallery, when he beheld General Browne suddenly start, and assume an attitude of the utmost surprise, not unmixed with fear, as his eyes were suddenly caught and riveted by a portrait of an old lady in a sacque, the fashionable dress of the end of the seventeenth century.

"There she is!" he exclaimed—"there she is, in form and features, though Inferior in demoniac expression to the accursed hag who visited me last night!"

"If that be the case," said the young nobleman, "there can remain no longer any doubt of the horrible reality of your apparition. That is the picture of a wretched ancestress of mine, of whose crimes a black and fearful catalogue is recorded in a family history in my charter-chest. The recital of them would be too horrible; it is enough to say, that in yon fatal apartment incest and unnatural murder were committed. I will restore it to the solitude to which the better judgment of those who preceded me had consigned it; and never shall any one, so long as I can prevent it, be exposed to a repetition of the supernatural horrors which could shake such courage as yours."

Thus the friends, who had met with such glee, parted in a very different mood—Lord Woodville to command the Tapestried Chamber to be unmantled, and the door built up; and General Browne to seek in some less beautiful country, and with some less dignified friend, forgetfulness of the painful night which he had passed in Woodville Castle.

END OF THE TAPESTRIED CHAMBER.

* * * * *

DEATH OF THE LAIRD'S JOCK

[The manner in which this trifle was introduced at the time to Mr. F. M. Reynolds, editor of The Keepsake of 1828, leaves no occasion for a preface.]

AUGUST 1831.

TO THE EDITOR OF THE KEEPSAKE.

You have asked me, sir, to point out a subject for the pencil, and I feel the difficulty of complying with your request, although I am not certainly unaccustomed to literary composition, or a total stranger to the stores of history and tradition, which afford the best copies for the painter's art. But although SICUT PICTURA POESIS is an ancient and undisputed axiom—although poetry and painting both address themselves to the same object of exciting the human imagination, by presenting to it pleasing or sublime images of ideal scenes—yet the one conveying itself through the ears to the understanding, and the other applying itself only to the eyes, the subjects which are best suited to the bard or tale-teller are often totally unfit for painting, where the artist must present in a single glance all that his art has power to tell us. The artist can neither recapitulate the past nor intimate the future. The single NOW is all which he can present; and hence, unquestionably, many subjects which delight us in poetry or in narrative, whether real or fictitious, cannot with advantage be transferred to the canvas.

Being in some degree aware of these difficulties, though doubtless unacquainted both with their extent and the means by which they may be modified or surmounted, I have, nevertheless, ventured to draw up the following traditional narrative as a story in which, when the general details are known, the interest is so much concentrated in one strong moment of agonizing passion, that it can be understood and sympathized with at a single glance. I therefore presume that it may be acceptable as a hint to some one among the numerous artists who have of late years distinguished themselves as rearing up and supporting the British school.

Enough has been said and sung about

> "The well-contested ground,
> The warlike Border-land,"

to render the habits of the tribes who inhabited it before the union of England and Scotland familiar to most of your readers. The rougher and sterner features of their character were softened by their attachment to the fine arts, from which has arisen the saying that on the frontiers every dale had its battle, and every river its song. A rude species of chivalry was in constant use, and single combats were practised as the amusement of the few intervals of truce which suspended the exercise of war. The inveteracy of this custom may be inferred from the following incident:—

Bernard Gilpin, the apostle of the north, the first who undertook to preach the Protestant doctrines to the Border dalesmen, was surprised, on entering one of their churches, to see a gauntlet or mail-glove hanging above the altar. Upon inquiring; the meaning of a symbol so indecorous being displayed in that sacred place, he was informed by the clerk that the glove was that of a famous swordsman, who hung it there as an emblem of a general challenge and gage of battle to any who should dare to take the fatal token down. "Reach it to me," said the reverend churchman. The clerk and the sexton equally declined the perilous office, and the good Bernard Gilpin was obliged to remove the glove with his own hands, desiring those who were present to inform the champion that he, and no other, had possessed himself of the gage of defiance. But the champion was as much ashamed to face Bernard Gilpin as the officials of the church had been to displace his pledge of combat.

The date of the following story is about the latter years of Queen Elizabeth's reign; and the events took place in Liddesdale, a hilly and pastoral district of Roxburghshire, which, on a part of its boundary, is divided from England only by a small river.

During the good old times of RUGGING AND RIVING— that is, tugging and tearing—under which term the disorderly doings of the warlike age are affectionately remembered, this valley was principally cultivated by the sept or clan of the Armstrongs. The chief of this warlike race was the Laird of Mangerton. At the period of which I speak, the estate of Mangerton, with the power and dignity of chief, was possessed by John Armstrong, a man of great size, strength, and courage. While his father was alive, he was distinguished from others of his clan who bore the same name, by the epithet of the LAIRD'S JOCK—that is to say, the Laird's son Jock, or Jack. This name he distinguished by so many bold and desperate achievements, that he retained it even after his father's death, and is mentioned under it both in authentic records and in tradition. Some of his feats are recorded in the minstrelsy of the Scottish Border, and others are mentioned in contemporary chronicles.

At the species of singular combat which we have described the Laird's Jock was unrivalled, and no champion of Cumberland, Westmoreland, or Northumberland could endure the sway of the huge two-handed sword which he wielded, and which few others could even lift. This "awful sword," as the common people term it, was as dear to him as Durindana or Fushberta to their respective masters, and was nearly as formidable to his enemies as those renowned falchions proved to the foes of Christendom. The weapon had been bequeathed to him by a celebrated English outlaw named Hobbie Noble, who, having committed some deed for which he was in danger from justice, fled to Liddesdale, and became a follower, or rather a brother-in-arms, to the renowned Laird's Jock; till, venturing into England with a small escort, a faithless guide, and with a light single-handed sword instead of his ponderous brand, Hobbie Noble, attacked by superior numbers, was made prisoner and executed.

With this weapon, and by means of his own strength and address, the Laird's Jock maintained the reputation of the best swordsman on the Border side, and defeated or slew many who ventured to dispute with him the formidable title.

But years pass on with the strong and the brave as with the feeble and the timid. In process of time the Laird's Jock grew incapable of wielding his weapons, and finally of all active exertion, even of the most ordinary kind. The disabled champion became at length totally bedridden, and entirely dependent for his comfort on the pious duties of an only daughter, his perpetual attendant and companion.

Besides this dutiful child, the Laird's Jock had an only son, upon whom devolved the perilous task of leading the clan to battle, and maintaining the warlike renown of his native country, which was now disputed by the English upon many occasions. The young Armstrong was active, brave, and strong, and brought home from dangerous adventures many tokens of decided success. Still, the ancient chief conceived, as it would seem, that his son was scarce yet entitled by age and experience to be entrusted with the two-handed sword, by the use of which he had himself been so dreadfully distinguished.

At length an English champion, one of the name of Foster (if I rightly recollect), had the audacity to send a challenge to the best swordsman in Liddesdale; and young Armstrong, burning for chivalrous distinction, accepted the challenge.

The heart of the disabled old man swelled with joy when he heard that the challenge was passed and accepted, and the meeting fixed at a neutral spot, used as the place of rencontre upon such occasions, and which he himself had distinguished by numerous victories. He exulted so much in the conquest which he anticipated, that, to nerve his son to still bolder exertions, he conferred upon him, as champion of his clan and province, the celebrated weapon which he had hitherto retained in his own custody.

This was not all. When the day of combat arrived, the Laird's Jock, in spite of his daughter's affectionate remonstrances, determined, though he had not left his bed for two years, to be a personal witness of the duel. His will was still a law to his people, who bore him on their shoulders, wrapped in plaids and blankets, to the spot where the combat was to take place, and seated him on a fragment of rock, which is still called the Laird's Jock's stone. There he remained with eyes fixed on the lists or barrier, within which the champions were about to meet. His daughter, having done all she could for his accommodation, stood motionless beside him, divided between anxiety for his health, and for the event of the combat to her beloved brother. Ere yet the fight began, the old men gazed on their chief, now seen for the first time after several years, and sadly compared his altered features and wasted frame with the paragon of strength and manly beauty which they once remembered. The young men gazed on his large form and powerful make as upon some antediluvian giant who had survived the destruction of the Flood.

But the sound of the trumpets on both sides recalled the attention of every one to the lists, surrounded as they were by numbers of both nations eager to witness the event of the day. The combatants met in the lists. It is needless to describe the struggle: the Scottish champion fell. Foster, placing his foot on his antagonist, seized on the redoubted sword, so precious in the eyes of its aged owner, and brandished it over his head as a trophy of his conquest. The English shouted in triumph. But the despairing cry of the aged champion, who saw his country dishonoured, and his sword, long the terror of their race, in the possession of an Englishman, was heard high above the acclamations of victory. He seemed for an instant animated by all his wonted power; for he started from the rock on which he sat, and while the garments with which he had been invested fell from his wasted frame, and showed the ruins of his strength, he tossed his arms wildly to heaven, and uttered a cry of indignation, horror, and despair, which, tradition says, was heard to a preternatural distance, and resembled the cry of a dying lion more than a human sound.

His friends received him in their arms as he sank utterly exhausted by the effort, and bore him back to his castle in mute sorrow; while his daughter at once wept for her brother, and endeavoured to mitigate and soothe the despair of her father. But this was impossible; the old man's only tie to life was rent rudely asunder, and his heart had broken with it. The death of his son had no part in his sorrow. If he thought of him at all, it was as the degenerate boy through whom the honour of his country and clan had been lost; and he died in the course of three days, never even mentioning his name, but pouring out unintermitted lamentations for the loss of his noble sword.

I conceive that the moment when the disabled chief was roused into a last exertion by the agony of the moment is favourable to the object of a painter. He might obtain the full advantage of contrasting the form of the rugged old man, in the extremity of furious despair, with the softness and beauty of the female form. The fatal field might be thrown into perspective, so as to give full effect to these two principal figures, and with the single explanation that the piece represented a soldier beholding his son slain, and the honour of his country lost, the picture would be sufficiently intelligible at the first glance. If it was thought necessary to show more clearly the nature of the conflict, it might be indicated by the pennon of Saint George being displayed at one end of the lists, and that of Saint Andrew at the other.

I remain, sir,
Your obedient servant,
THE AUTHOR OF WAVERLEY.

A LEGEND OF MONTROSE

I.
INTRODUCTION TO
A LEGEND OF MONTROSE.

The Legend of Montrose was written chiefly with a view to place before the reader the melancholy fate of John Lord Kilpont, eldest son of William Earl of Airth and Menteith, and the singular circumstances attending the birth and history of James Stewart of Ardvoirlich, by whose hand the unfortunate nobleman fell.

Our subject leads us to talk of deadly feuds, and we must begin with one still more ancient than that to which our story relates. During the reign of James IV., a great feud between the powerful families of Drummond and Murray divided Perthshire. The former, being the most numerous and powerful, cooped up eight score of the Murrays in the kirk of Monivaird, and set fire to it. The wives and the children of the ill-fated men, who had also found shelter in the church, perished by the same conflagration. One man, named David Murray, escaped by the humanity of one of the Drummonds, who received him in his arms as he leaped from amongst the flames. As King James IV. ruled with more activity than most of his predecessors, this cruel deed was severely revenged, and several of the perpetrators were beheaded at Stirling. In consequence of the prosecution against his clan, the Drummond by whose assistance David Murray had escaped, fled to Ireland, until, by means of the person whose life he had saved, he was permitted to return to Scotland, where he and his descendants were distinguished by the name of Drummond-Eirinich, or Ernoch, that is, Drummond of Ireland; and the same title was bestowed on their estate.

The Drummond-ernoch of James the Sixth's time was a king's forester in the forest of Glenartney, and chanced to be employed there in search of venison about the year 1588, or early in 1589. This forest was adjacent to the chief haunts of the MacGregors, or a particular race of them, known by the title of MacEagh, or Children of the Mist. They considered the forester's hunting in their vicinity as an aggression, or perhaps they had him at feud, for the apprehension or slaughter of some of their own name, or for some similar reason. This tribe of MacGregors were outlawed and persecuted, as the reader may see in the Introduction to ROB ROY; and every man's hand being against them, their hand was of course directed against every man. In short, they surprised and slew Drummond-ernoch, cut off his head, and carried it with them, wrapt in the corner of one of their plaids.

In the full exultation of vengeance, they stopped at the house of Ardvoirlich and demanded refreshment, which the lady, a sister of the murdered Drummond-ernoch (her husband being absent), was afraid or unwilling to refuse. She caused bread and cheese to be placed before them, and gave directions for more substantial refreshments to be prepared. While she was absent with this hospitable intention, the barbarians placed the head of her brother on the table, filling the mouth with bread and cheese, and bidding him eat, for many a merry meal he had eaten in that house.

The poor woman returning, and beholding this dreadful sight, shrieked aloud, and fled into the woods, where, as described in the romance, she roamed a raving maniac, and for some time secreted herself from all living society. Some remaining instinctive feeling brought her at length to steal a glance from a distance at the maidens while they milked the cows, which being observed, her husband, Ardvoirlich, had her conveyed back to her home, and detained her there till she gave birth to a child, of whom she had been pregnant; after which she was observed gradually to recover her mental faculties.

Meanwhile the outlaws had carried to the utmost their insults against the regal authority, which indeed, as exercised, they had little reason for respecting. They bore the same bloody trophy, which they had so savagely exhibited to the lady of Ardvoirlich, into the old church of Balquidder, nearly in the centre of their country, where the Laird of MacGregor and all his clan being convened for the purpose, laid their hands successively on the dead man's head, and swore, in heathenish and barbarous manner, to defend the author of the deed. This fierce and vindictive combination gave the author's late and lamented friend, Sir Alexander Boswell, Bart., subject for a spirited poem, entitled "Clan-Alpin's Vow," which was printed, but not, I believe, published, in 1811 [See Appendix No. I].

The fact is ascertained by a proclamation from the Privy Council, dated 4th February, 1589, directing letters of fire and sword against the MacGregors [See Appendix No. II]. This fearful commission was executed with uncommon fury. The late excellent John Buchanan of Cambusmore showed the author some correspondence between his ancestor, the Laird of Buchanan, and Lord Drummond, about sweeping certain valleys with their followers, on a fixed time and rendezvous, and "taking sweet revenge for the death of their cousin, Drummond-ernoch." In spite of all, however, that could be done, the devoted tribe of MacGregor still bred up survivors to sustain and to inflict new cruelties and injuries.

[I embrace the opportunity given me by a second mention of this tribe, to notice an error, which imputes to an individual named Ciar Mohr MacGregor, the slaughter of the students at the battle of Glenfruin. I am informed from the authority of John Gregorson, Esq., that the chieftain so named was dead nearly a century before the battle in question, and could not, therefore, have done the cruel action mentioned. The mistake does not rest with me, as I disclaimed being responsible for the tradition while I quoted it, but with vulgar fame, which is always disposed to ascribe remarkable actions to a remarkable name.—See the erroneous passage, ROB ROY, Introduction; and so soft sleep the offended phantom of Dugald Ciar Mohr.

It is with mingled pleasure and shame that I record the more important error, of having announced as deceased my learned acquaintance, the Rev. Dr. Grahame, minister of Aberfoil.—See ROB ROY, p.360. I cannot now recollect the precise ground of my depriving my learned and excellent friend of his existence, unless, like Mr. Kirke, his predecessor in the parish, the excellent Doctor had made a short trip to Fairyland, with whose wonders he is so well acquainted. But however I may have been misled, my regret is most sincere for having spread such a rumour; and no one can be more gratified than I that the report, however I have been induced to credit and give it currency, is a false one, and that Dr. Grahame is still the living pastor of Aberfoil, for the delight and instruction of his brother antiquaries.]

Meanwhile Young James Stewart of Ardvoirlich grew up to manhood uncommonly tall, strong, and active, with such power in the grasp of his hand in particular, as could force the blood from beneath the nails of the persons who contended with him in this feat of strength. His temper was moody, fierce, and irascible; yet he must have had some ostensible good qualities, as he was greatly beloved by Lord Kilpont, the eldest son of the Earl of Airth and Menteith.

This gallant young nobleman joined Montrose in the setting up his standard in 1644, just before the decisive battle at Tippermuir, on the 1st September in that year. At that time, Stewart of Ardvoirlich shared the confidence of the young Lord by day, and his bed by night, when, about four or five days after the battle, Ardvoirlich, either from a fit of sudden fury or deep malice long entertained against his unsuspecting friend, stabbed Lord Kilpont to the heart, and escaped from the camp of Montrose, having killed a sentinel who attempted to detain him. Bishop Guthrie gives us a reason for this villainous action, that Lord Kilpont had rejected with abhorrence a proposal of Ardvoirlich to assassinate Montrose. But it does not appear that there is any authority for this charge, which rests on mere suspicion. Ardvoirlich, the assassin, certainly did fly to the Covenanters, and was employed and promoted by them. He obtained a pardon for the slaughter of Lord Kilpont, confirmed by Parliament in 1634, and was made Major of Argyle's regiment in 1648. Such are the facts of the tale here given as a Legend of Montrose's wars. The reader will find they are considerably altered in the fictitious narrative.

The author has endeavoured to enliven the tragedy of the tale by the introduction of a personage proper to the time and country. In this he has been held by excellent judges to have been in some degree successful. The contempt of commerce entertained by young men having some pretence to gentility, the poverty of the country of Scotland, the national disposition to wandering and to adventure, all conduced to lead the Scots abroad into the military service of countries which were at war with each other. They were distinguished on the Continent by their bravery; but in adopting the trade of mercenary soldiers, they necessarily injured their national character. The tincture of learning, which most of them possessed, degenerated into pedantry; their good breeding became mere ceremonial; their fear of dishonour no longer kept them aloof from that which was really unworthy, but was made to depend on certain punctilious observances totally apart from that which was in itself deserving of praise. A cavalier of honour, in search of his fortune, might, for example, change his service as he would his shirt, fight, like the doughty Captain Dalgetty, in one cause after another, without regard to the justice of the quarrel, and might plunder the peasantry subjected to him by the fate of war with the most unrelenting rapacity; but he must beware how he sustained the slightest reproach, even from a clergyman, if it had regard to neglect on the score of duty. The following occurrence will prove the truth of what I mean:—

"Here I must not forget the memory of one preacher, Master William Forbesse, a preacher for souldiers, yea, and a captaine in neede to leade souldiers on a good occasion, being full of courage, with discretion and good conduct, beyond some captaines I have knowne, that were not so capable as he. At this time he not onely prayed for us, but went on with us, to remarke, as I thinke, men's carriage; and having found a sergeant neglecting his dutie and his honour at such a time (whose name I will not expresse), having chidden him, did promise to reveale him unto me, as he did after their service. The sergeant being called before me, and accused, did deny his accusation, alleaging, if he were no pasteur that had alleaged it, he would not lie under the injury, The preacher offered to fight with him, [in proof] that it was truth he had spoken of him; whereupon I cashiered the sergeant, and gave his place to a worthier, called Mungo Gray, a gentleman of good worth, and of much courage. The sergeant being cashiered, never called Master William to account, for which he was evill thought of; so that he retired home, and quit the warres."

The above quotation is taken from a work which the author repeatedly consulted while composing the following sheets, and which is in great measure written in the humour of Captain Dugald Dalgetty. It bears the following formidable title:—"MONRO his Expedition with the worthy Scots Regiment, called MacKeye's Regiment, levied in August 1626, by Sir Donald MacKeye Lord Rees Colonel, for his Majestie's service of Denmark, and reduced after the battle of Nerling, in September 1634, at Wormes, in the Palz: Discharged in several duties and observations of service, first, under the magnanimous King of Denmark, during his wars against the Empire; afterwards under the invincible King of Sweden, during his Majestie's lifetime; and since under the Director-General, the Rex-Chancellor Oxensterne, and his Generals: collected and gathered together, at spare hours, by Colonel Robert Monro, as First Lieutenant under the said Regiment, to the noble and worthy Captain Thomas MacKenzie of Kildon, brother to the noble Lord, the Lord Earl of Seaforth, for the use of all noble Cavaliers favouring the laudable profession of arms. To which is annexed, the Abridgement of Exercise, and divers Practical Observations for the Younger Officer, his consideration. Ending with the Soldier's Meditations on going on Service."—London, 1637.

Another worthy of the same school, and nearly the same views of the military character, is Sir James Turner, a soldier of fortune, who rose to considerable rank in the reign of Charles II., had a command in Galloway and Dumfries-shire, for the suppression of conventicles, and was made prisoner by the insurgent Covenanters in that rising which was followed by the battle of Pentland. Sir James is a person even of superior pretensions to Lieutenant-Colonel Monro, having written a Military Treatise on the Pike-Exercise, called "Pallas Armata." Moreover, he was educated at Glasgow College, though he escaped to become an Ensign in the German wars, instead of taking his degree of Master of Arts at that learned seminary.

In latter times, he was author of several discourses on historical and literary subjects, from which the Bannatyne Club have extracted and printed such passages as concern his Life and Times, under the title of SIR JAMES TURNER'S MEMOIRS. From this curious book I extract the following passage, as an example of how Captain Dalgetty might have recorded such an incident had he kept a journal, or, to give it a more just character, it is such as the genius of De Foe would have devised, to give the minute and distinguishing features of truth to a fictitious narrative:—

"Heere I will set doun ane accident befell me; for thogh it was not a very strange one, yet it was a very od one in all its parts. My tuo brigads lay in a village within halfe a mile of Applebie; my own quarter was in a gentleman's house, ho was a Ritmaster, and at that time with Sir Marmaduke; his wife keepd her chamber readie to be brought to bed. The castle being over, and Lambert farre enough, I resolved to goe to bed everie night, haveing had fatigue enough before. 'The first night I sleepd well enough; and riseing nixt morning, I misd one linnen stockine, one halfe silke one, and one boothose, the accoustrement under a boote for one leg; neither could they be found for any search. Being provided of more of the same kind, I made myselfe reddie, and rode to the head-quarters. At my returne, I could heare no news of my stockins. That night I went to bed, and nixt morning found myselfe just so used; missing the three stockins for one leg onlie, the other three being left intire as they were the day before. A narrower search then the first was made, bot without successe. I had yet in reserve one paire of whole stockings, and a paire of boothose, greater then the former. These I put on my legs. The third morning I found the same usage, the stockins for one leg onlie left me. It was time for me then, and my servants too, to imagine it must be rats that had shard my stockins so inequallie with me; and this the mistress of the house knew well enough, but would not tell it me. The roome, which was a low parlour, being well searched with candles, the top of my great boothose was found at a hole, in which they had drawne all the rest. I went abroad and ordered the boards to be raised, to see how the rats had disposed of my moveables. The mistress sent a servant of her oune to be present at this action, which she knew concerned her. One board being bot a litle opend, a litle boy of mine thrust in his hand, and fetchd with him foure and tuentie old peeces of gold, and one angell. The servant of the house affirmed it appertained to his mistres. The boy bringing the gold to me, I went immediatlie to the gentlewomans chamber, and told her, it was probable Lambert haveing quarterd in that house, as indeed he had, some of his servants might have hid that gold; and if so, it was lawfullie mine; bot if she could make it appeare it belongd to her, I should immediatlie give it her. The poore gentlewoman told me with many teares, that her husband being none of the frugallest men (and indeed he was a spendthrift), she had hid that gold without his, knowledge, to make use of it as she had occasion, especiallie when she lay in; and conjured me, as I lovd the King (for whom her husband and she had suffered much), not to detaine her gold. She said, if there was either more or lesse then foure and tuentie whole peeces, and two halfe ones, it sould be none of hers; and that they were put by her in a red velvet purse. After I had given her assureance of her gold, a new search is made, the other angell is found, the velvet purse all gnawd in bits, as my stockins were, and the gold instantlie restord to the gentlewoman. I have often heard that the eating or gnawing of cloths by rats is ominous, and portends some mischance to fall on those to whom the cloths belong. I thank God I was never addicted to such divinations, or heeded them. It is true, that more misfortunes then one fell on me shortlie after; bot I am sure I could have better forseene them myselfe then rats or any such vermine, and yet did it not. I have heard indeed many fine stories told of rats, how they abandon houses and ships, when the first are to be burnt and the second dround. Naturalists say they are very sagacious creatures, and I beleeve they are so; bot I shall never be of the opinion they can forsee future contingencies, which I suppose the divell himselfe can neither forknow nor fortell; these being things which the Almightie hath keepd hidden in the bosome of his divine prescience. And whither the great God hath preordained or predestinated these things, which to us are contingent, to fall out by ane uncontrollable and unavoidable necessitie, is a question not yet decided." [SIR JAMES TURNER'S MEMOIRS, Bannatyne edition, p. 59.]

In quoting these ancient authorities, I must not forget the more modern sketch of a Scottish soldier of the old fashion, by a masterhand, in the character of Lesmahagow, since the existence of that doughty Captain alone must deprive the present author of all claim to absolute originality. Still Dalgetty, as the production of his own fancy, has been so far a favourite with its parent, that he has fallen into the error of assigning to the Captain too prominent a part in the story. This is the opinion of a critic who encamps on the highest pinnacles of literature; and the author is so far fortunate in having incurred his censure, that it gives his modesty a decent apology for quoting the praise, which it would have ill-befited him to bring forward in an unmingled state. The passage occurs in the EDINBURGH REVIEW, No. 55, containing a criticism on IVANHOE:—

"There is too much, perhaps, of Dalgetty,—or, rather, he engrosses too great a proportion of the work,—for, in himself, we think he is uniformly entertaining;—and the author has nowhere shown more affinity to that matchless spirit who could bring out his Falstaffs and his Pistols, in act after act, and play after play, and exercise them every time with scenes of unbounded loquacity, without either exhausting their humour, or varying a note from its characteristic tone, than in his large and reiterated specimens of the eloquence of the redoubted Ritt-master. The general idea of the character is familiar to our comic dramatists after the Restoration—and may be said in some measure to be compounded of Captain Fluellen and Bobadil;—but the ludicrous combination of the SOLDADO with the Divinity student of Mareschal-College, is entirely original; and the mixture of talent, selfishness, courage, coarseness, and conceit, was never so happily exemplified. Numerous as his speeches are, there is not one that is not characteristic—and, to our taste, divertingly ludicrous."

POSTSCRIPT.

While these pages were passing through the press, the author received a letter from the present Robert Stewart of Ardvoirlich, favouring him with the account of the unhappy slaughter of Lord Kilpont, differing from, and more probable than, that given by Bishop Wishart, whose narrative infers either insanity or the blackest treachery on the part of James Stewart of Ardvoirlich, the ancestor of the present family of that name. It is but fair to give the entire communication as received from my respected correspondent, which is more minute than the histories of the period.

"Although I have not the honour of being personally known to you, I hope you will excuse the liberty I now take, in addressing you on the subject of a transaction more than once alluded to by you, in which an ancestor of mine was unhappily concerned. I allude to the slaughter of Lord Kilpont, son of the Earl of Airth and Monteith, in 1644, by James Stewart of Ardvoirlich. As the cause of this unhappy event, and the quarrel which led to it, have never been correctly stated in any history of the period in which it took place, I am induced, in consequence of your having, in the second series of your admirable Tales on the History of Scotland, adopted Wishart's version of the transaction, and being aware that your having done so will stamp it with an authenticity which it does not merit, and with a view, as far as possible, to do justice to the memory of my unfortunate ancestor, to send you the account of this affair as it has been handed down in the family.

"James Stewart of Ardvoirlich, who lived in the early part of the 17th century, and who was the unlucky cause of the slaughter of Lord Kilpont, as before mentioned, was appointed to the command of one of several independent companies raised in the Highlands at the commencement of the troubles in the reign of Charles I.; another of these companies was under the command of Lord Kilpont, and a strong intimacy, strengthened by a distant relationship, subsisted between them. When Montrose raised the royal standard, Ardvoirlich was one of the first to declare for him, and is said to have been a principal means of bringing over Lord Kilpont to the same cause; and they accordingly, along with Sir John Drummond and their respective followers, joined Montrose, as recorded by Wishart, at Buchanty. While they served together, so strong was their intimacy, that they lived and slept in the same tent.

"In the meantime, Montrose had been joined by the Irish under the command of Alexander Macdonald; these, on their march to join Montrose, had committed some excesses on lands belonging to Ardvoirlich, which lay in the line of their march from the west coast. Of this Ardvoirlich complained to Montrose, who, probably wishing as much as possible to conciliate his new allies, treated it in rather an evasive manner. Ardvoirlich, who was a man of violent passions, having failed to receive such satisfaction as he required, challenged Macdonald to single combat. Before they met, however, Montrose, on the information and by advice, as it is said, of Kilpont, laid them both under arrest. Montrose, seeing the evils of such a feud at such a critical time, effected a sort of reconciliation between them, and forced them to shake hands in his presence; when, it was said, that Ardvoirlich, who was a very powerful man, took such a hold of Macdonald's hand as to make the blood start from his fingers. Still, it would appear, Ardvoirlich was by no means reconciled.

"A few days after the battle of Tippermuir, when Montrose with his army was encamped at Collace, an entertainment was given by him to his officers, in honour of the victory he had obtained, and Kilpont and his comrade Ardvoirlich were of the party. After returning to their quarters, Ardvoirlich, who seemed still to brood over his quarrel with Macdonald, and being heated with drink, began to blame Lord Kilpont for the part he had taken in preventing his obtaining redress, and reflecting against Montrose for not allowing him what he considered proper reparation. Kilpont of course defended the conduct of himself and his relative Montrose, till their argument came to high words; and finally, from the state they were both in, by an easy transition, to blows, when Ardvoirlich, with his dirk, struck Kilpont dead on the spot. He immediately fled, and under the cover of a thick mist escaped pursuit, leaving his eldest son Henry, who had been mortally wounded at Tippermuir, on his deathbed.

"His followers immediately withdrew from Montrose, and no course remained for him but to throw himself into the arms of the opposite faction, by whom he was well received. His name is frequently mentioned in Leslie's campaigns, and on more than one occasion he is mentioned as having afforded protection to several of his former friends through his interest with Leslie, when the King's cause became desperate.

"The foregoing account of this unfortunate transaction, I am well aware, differs materially from the account given by Wishart, who alleges that Stewart had laid a plot for the assassination of Montrose, and that he murdered Lord Kilpont in consequence of his refusal to participate in his design. Now, I may be allowed to remark, that besides Wishart having always been regarded as a partial historian, and very questionable authority on any subject connected with the motives or conduct of those who differed from him in opinion, that even had Stewart formed such a design, Kilpont, from his name and connexions, was likely to be the very last man of whom Stewart would choose to make a confidant and accomplice. On the other hand, the above account, though never, that I am aware, before hinted at, has been a constant tradition in the family; and, from the comparative recent date of the transaction, and the sources from which the tradition has been derived, I have no reason to doubt its perfect authenticity. It was most circumstantially detailed as above, given to my father, Mr. Stewart, now of Ardvoirlich, many years ago, by a man nearly connected with the family, who lived to the age of 100. This man was a great-grandson of James Stewart, by a natural son John, of whom many stories are still current in this country, under his appellation of JOHN DHU MHOR. This John was with his father at the time, and of course was a witness of the whole transaction; he lived till a considerable time after the Revolution, and it was from him that my father's informant, who was a man before his grandfather, John dhu Mhor's death, received the information as above stated.

"I have many apologies to offer for trespassing so long on your patience; but I felt a natural desire, if possible, to correct what I conceive to be a groundless imputation on the memory of my ancestor, before it shall come to be considered as a matter of History. That he was a man of violent passions and singular temper, I do not pretend to deny, as many traditions still current in this country amply verify; but that he was capable of forming a design to assassinate Montrose, the whole tenor of his former conduct and principles contradict. That he was obliged to join the opposite party, was merely a matter of safety, while Kilpont had so many powerful friends and connexions able and ready to avenge his death.

"I have only to add, that you have my full permission to make what use of this communication you please, and either to reject it altogether, or allow it such credit as you think it deserves; and I shall be ready at all times to furnish you with any further information on this subject which you may require, and which it may be in my power to afford.

"ARDVOIRLICH, 15TH JANUARY, 1830."

The publication of a statement so particular, and probably so correct, is a debt due to the memory of James Stewart; the victim, it would seem, of his own violent passions, but perhaps incapable of an act of premeditated treachery.

ABBOTSFORD, 1ST AUGUST, 1830.

* * * * *

II. I
NTRODUCTION (SUPPLEMENT).

Sergeant More M'Alpin was, during his residence among us, one of the most honoured inhabitants of Gandercleugh. No one thought of disputing his title to the great leathern chair on the "cosiest side of the chimney," in the common room of the Wallace Arms, on a Saturday evening. No less would our sexton, John Duirward, have held it an unlicensed intrusion, to suffer any one to induct himself into the corner of the left-hand pew nearest to the pulpit, which the Sergeant regularly occupied on Sundays. There he sat, his blue invalid uniform brushed with the most scrupulous accuracy. Two medals of merit displayed at his button-hole, as well as the empty sleeve which should have been occupied by his right arm, bore evidence of his hard and honourable service. His weatherbeaten features, his grey hair tied in a thin queue in the military fashion of former days, and the right side of his head a little turned up, the better to catch the sound of the clergyman's voice, were all marks of his profession and infirmities. Beside him sat his sister Janet, a little neat old woman, with a Highland curch and tartan plaid, watching the very looks of her brother, to her the greatest man upon earth, and actively looking out for him, in his silver-clasped Bible, the texts which the minister quoted or expounded.

I believe it was the respect that was universally paid to this worthy veteran by all ranks in Gandercleugh which induced him to choose our village for his residence, for such was by no means his original intention.

He had risen to the rank of sergeant-major of artillery, by hard service in various quarters of the world, and was reckoned one of the most tried and trusty men of the Scotch Train. A ball, which shattered his arm in a peninsular campaign, at length procured him an honourable discharge. with an allowance from Chelsea, and a handsome gratuity from the patriotic fund. Moreover, Sergeant More M'Alpin had been prudent as well as valiant; and, from prize-money and savings, had become master of a small sum in the three per cent consols.

He retired with the purpose of enjoying this income in the wild Highland glen, in which, when a boy, he had herded black cattle and goats, ere the roll of the drum had made him cock his bonnet an inch higher, and follow its music for nearly forty years. To his recollection, this retired spot was unparalleled in beauty by the richest scenes he had visited in his wanderings. Even the Happy Valley of Rasselas would have sunk into nothing upon the comparison. He came—he revisited the loved scene; it was but a sterile glen, surrounded with rude crags, and traversed by a northern torrent. This was not the worst. The fires had been quenched upon thirty hearths—of the cottage of his fathers he could but distinguish a few rude stones—the language was almost extinguished—the ancient race from which he boasted his descent had found a refuge beyond the Atlantic. One southland farmer, three grey-plaided shepherds, and six dogs, now tenanted the whole glen, which in his youth had maintained, in content, if not in competence, upwards of two hundred inhabitants,

In the house of the new tenant, Sergeant M'Alpin found, however, an unexpected source of pleasure, and a means of employing his social affections. His sister Janet had fortunately entertained so strong a persuasion that her brother would one day return, that she had refused to accompany her kinsfolk upon their emigration. Nay, she had consented, though not without a feeling of degradation, to take service with the intruding Lowlander, who, though a Saxon, she said, had proved a kind man to her. This unexpected meeting with his sister seemed a cure for all the disappointments which it had been Sergeant More's lot to encounter, although it was not without a reluctant tear that he heard told, as a Highland woman alone could ten it, the story of the expatriation of his kinsmen.

She narrated at great length the vain offers they had made of advanced rent, the payment of which must have reduced them to the extremity of poverty, which they were yet contented to face, for permission to live and die on their native soil. Nor did Janet forget the portents which had announced the departure of the Celtic race, and the arrival of the strangers. For two years previous to the emigration, when the night wind howled dawn the pass of Balachra, its notes were distinctly modelled to the tune of "HA TIL MI TULIDH" (we return no more), with which the emigrants usually bid farewell to their native shores. The uncouth cries of the Southland shepherds, and the barking of their dogs, were often heard in the midst of the hills long before their actual arrival. A bard, the last of his race, had commemorated the expulsion of the natives of the glen in a tune, which brought tears into the aged eyes of the veteran, and of which the first stanza may be thus rendered:—

> Woe, woe, son of the Lowlander,
> Why wilt thou leave thine own bonny Border?
> Why comes thou hither, disturbing the Highlander,
> Wasting the glen that was once in fair order?

What added to Sergeant More M'Alpin's distress upon the occasion was, that the chief by whom this change had been effected, was, by tradition and common opinion, held to represent the ancient leaders and fathers of the expelled fugitives; and it had hitherto been one of Sergeant More's principal subjects of pride to prove, by genealogical deduction, in what degree of kindred he stood to this personage. A woful change was now wrought in his sentiments towards him.

"I cannot curse him," he said, as he rose and strode through the room, when Janet's narrative was finished—"I will not curse him; he is the descendant and representative of my fathers. But never shall mortal man hear me name his name again." And he kept his word; for, until his dying day, no man heard him mention his selfish and hard-hearted chieftain.

After giving a day to sad recollections, the hardy spirit which had carried him through so many dangers, manned the Sergeant's bosom against this cruel disappointment. "He would go," he said, "to Canada to his kinsfolk, where they had named a Transatlantic valley after the glen of their fathers. Janet," he said, "should kilt her coats like a leaguer lady; d—n the distance! it was a flea's leap to the voyages and marches he had made on a slighter occasion."

With this purpose he left the Highlands, and came with his sister as far as Gandercleugh, on his way to Glasgow, to take a passage to Canada. But winter was now set in, and as he thought it advisable to wait for a spring passage, when the St. Lawrence should be open, he settled among us for the few months of his stay in Britain. As we said before, the respectable old man met with deference and attention from all ranks of society; and when spring returned, he was so satisfied with his quarters, that he did not renew the purpose of his voyage. Janet was afraid of the sea, and he himself felt the infirmities of age and hard service more than he had at first expected. And, as he confessed to the clergyman, and my worthy principal, Mr. Cleishbotham, "it was better staying with kend friends, than going farther, and faring worse."

He therefore established himself and his domicile at Gandercleugh, to the great satisfaction, as we have already said, of all its inhabitants, to whom he became, in respect of military intelligence, and able commentaries upon the newspapers, gazettes, and bulletins, a very oracle, explanatory of all martial events, past, present, or to come.

It is true, the Sergeant had his inconsistencies. He was a steady jacobite, his father and his four uncles having been out in the forty-five; but he was a no less steady adherent of King George, in whose service he had made his little fortune, and lost three brothers; so that you were in equal danger to displease him, in terming Prince Charles, the Pretender, or by saying anything derogatory to the dignity of King George. Further, it must not be denied, that when the day of receiving his dividends came round, the Sergeant was apt to tarry longer at the Wallace Arms of an evening, than was consistent with strict temperance, or indeed with his worldly interest; for upon these occasions, his compotators sometimes contrived to flatter his partialities by singing jacobite songs, and drinking confusion to Bonaparte, and the health of the Duke of Wellington, until the Sergeant was not only flattered into paying the whole reckoning, but occasionally induced to lend small sums to his interested companions. After such sprays, as he called them, were over, and his temper once more cool, he seldom failed to thank God, and the Duke of York, who had made it much more difficult for an old soldier to ruin himself by his folly, than had been the case in his younger days.

It was not on such occasions that I made a part of Sergeant More M'Alpin's society. But often, when my leisure would permit, I used to seek him, on what he called his morning and evening parade, on which, when the weather was fair, he appeared as regularly as if summoned by tuck of drum. His morning walk was beneath the elms in the churchyard; "for death," he said, "had been his next-door neighbour for so many years, that he had no apology for dropping the acquaintance." His evening promenade was on the bleaching-green by the river-side, where he was sometimes to be seen on an open bench, with spectacles on nose, conning over the newspapers to a circle of village politicians, explaining military terms, and aiding the comprehension of his hearers by lines drawn on the ground with the end of his rattan. On other occasions, he was surrounded by a bevy of school-boys, whom he sometimes drilled to the manual, and sometimes, with less approbation on the part of their parents, instructed in the mystery of artificial fire-works; for in the case of public rejoicings, the Sergeant was pyrotechnist (as the Encyclopedia calls it) to the village of Gandercleugh.

It was in his morning walk that I most frequently met with the veteran. And I can hardly yet look upon the village footpath, overshadowed by the row of lofty elms, without thinking I see his upright form advancing towards me with measured step, and his cane advanced, ready to pay me the military salute—but he is dead, and sleeps with his faithful Janet, under the third of those very trees, counting from the stile at the west corner of the churchyard.

The delight which I had in Sergeant M'Alpin's conversation, related not only to his own adventures, of which he had encountered many in the course of a wandering life, but also to his recollection of numerous Highland traditions, in which his youth had been instructed by his parents, and of which he would in after life have deemed it a kind of heresy to question the authenticity. Many of these belonged to the wars of Montrose, in which some of the Sergeant's ancestry had, it seems, taken a distinguished part. It has happened, that, although these civil commotions reflect the highest honour upon the Highlanders, being indeed the first occasion upon which they showed themselves superior, or even equal to their Low-country neighbours in military encounters, they have been less commemorated among them than any one would have expected, judging from the abundance of traditions which they have preserved upon less interesting subjects. It was, therefore, with great pleasure, that I extracted from my military friend some curious particulars respecting that time; they are mixed with that measure of the wild and wonderful which belongs to the period and the narrator, but which I do not in the least object to the reader's treating with disbelief, providing he will be so good as to give implicit credit to the natural events of the story, which, like all those which I have had the honour to put under his notice, actually rest upon a basis of truth.

* * * * *

III.
A LEGEND OF MONTROSE.

CHAPTER I.

Such as do build their faith upon
The holy text of pike and gun,
Decide all controversies by
Infallible artillery,
And prove their doctrine orthodox,
By apostolic blows and knocks.

—BUTLER.

It was during the period of that great and bloody Civil War which agitated Britain during the seventeenth century, that our tale has its commencement. Scotland had as yet remained free from the ravages of intestine war, although its inhabitants were much divided in political opinions; and many of them, tired of the control of the Estates of Parliament, and disapproving of the bold measure which they had adopted, by sending into England a large army to the assistance of the Parliament, were determined on their part to embrace the earliest opportunity of declaring for the King, and making such a diversion as should at least compel the recall of General Leslie's army out of England, if it did not recover a great part of Scotland to the King's allegiance. This plan was chiefly adopted by the northern nobility, who had resisted with great obstinacy the adoption of the Solemn League and Covenant, and by many of the chiefs of the Highland clans, who conceived their interest and authority to be connected with royalty, who had, besides, a decided aversion to the Presbyterian form of religion, and who, finally, were in that half savage state of society, in which war is always more welcome than peace.

Great commotions were generally expected to arise from these concurrent causes; and the trade of incursion and depredation, which the Scotch Highlanders at all times exercised upon the Lowlands, began to assume a more steady, avowed, and systematic form, as part of a general military system.

Those at the head of affairs were not insensible to the peril of the moment, and anxiously made preparations to meet and to repel it. They considered, however, with satisfaction, that no leader or name of consequence had as yet appeared to assemble an army of royalists, or even to direct the efforts of those desultory bands, whom love of plunder, perhaps, as much as political principle, had hurried into measures of hostility. It was generally hoped that the quartering a sufficient number of troops in the Lowlands adjacent to the Highland line, would have the effect of restraining the mountain chieftains; while the power of various barons in the north, who had espoused the Covenant, as, for example, the Earl Mareschal, the great families of Forbes, Leslie, and Irvine, the Grants, and other Presbyterian clans, might counterbalance and bridle, not only the strength of the Ogilvies and other cavaliers of Angus and Kincardine, but even the potent family of the Gordons, whose extensive authority was only equalled by their extreme dislike to the Presbyterian model.

In the West Highlands the ruling party numbered many enemies; but the power of these disaffected clans was supposed to be broken, and the spirit of their chieftains intimidated, by the predominating influence of the Marquis of Argyle, upon whom the confidence of the Convention of Estates was reposed with the utmost security; and whose power in the Highlands, already exorbitant, had been still farther increased by concessions extorted from the King at the last pacification. It was indeed well known that Argyle was a man rather of political enterprise than personal courage, and better calculated to manage an intrigue of state, than to control the tribes of hostile mountaineers; yet the numbers of his clan, and the spirit of the gallant gentlemen by whom it was led, might, it was supposed, atone for the personal deficiencies of their chief; and as the Campbells had already severely humbled several of the neighbouring tribes, it was supposed these would not readily again provoke an encounter with a body so powerful.

Thus having at their command the whole west and south of Scotland, indisputably the richest part of the kingdom,—Fifeshire being in a peculiar manner their own, and possessing many and powerful friends even north of the Forth and Tay,—the Scottish Convention of Estates saw no danger sufficient to induce them to alter the line of policy they had adopted, or to recall from the assistance of their brethren of the English Parliament that auxiliary army of twenty thousand men, by means of which accession of strength, the King's party had been reduced to the defensive, when in full career of triumph and success.

The causes which moved the Convention of Estates at this time to take such an immediate and active interest in the civil war of England, are detailed in our historians, but may be here shortly recapitulated. They had indeed no new injury or aggression to complain of at the hand of the King, and the peace which had been made between Charles and his subjects of Scotland had been carefully observed; but the Scottish rulers were well aware that this peace had been extorted from the King, as well by the influence of the parliamentary party in England, as by the terror of their own arms. It is true, King Charles had since then visited the capital of his ancient kingdom, had assented to the new organization of the church, and had distributed honours and rewards among the leaders of the party which had shown themselves most hostile to his interests; but it was suspected that distinctions so unwillingly conferred would be resumed as soon as opportunity offered. The low state of the English Parliament was seen in Scotland with deep apprehension; and it was concluded, that should Charles triumph by force of arms against his insurgent subjects of England, he would not be long in exacting from the Scotch the vengeance which he might suppose due to those who had set the example of taking up arms against him. Such was the policy of the measure which dictated the sending the auxiliary army into England; and it was avowed in a manifesto explanatory of their reasons for giving this timely and important aid to the English Parliament. The English Parliament, they said, had been already friendly to them, and might be so again; whereas the King, although he had so lately established religion among them according to their desires, had given them no ground to confide in his royal declaration, seeing they had found his promises and actions inconsistent with each other. "Our conscience," they concluded, "and God, who is greater than our conscience, beareth us record, that we aim altogether at the glory of God, peace of both nations, and honour of the King, in suppressing and punishing in a legal way, those who are the troublers of Israel, the firebrands of hell, the Korahs, the Balaams, the Doegs, the Rabshakehs, the Hamans, the Tobiahs, the Sanballats of our time, which done, we are satisfied. Neither have we begun to use a military expedition to England as a mean for compassing those our pious ends, until all other means which we could think upon have failed us: and this alone is left to us, ULTIMUM ET UNICUM REMEDIUM, the last and only remedy."

Leaving it to casuists to determine whether one contracting party is justified in breaking a solemn treaty, upon the suspicion that, in certain future contingencies, it might be infringed by the other, we shall proceed to mention two other circumstances that had at least equal influence with the Scottish rulers and nation, with any doubts which they entertained of the King's good faith.

The first of these was the nature and condition of their army; headed by a poor and discontented nobility, under whom it was officered chiefly by Scottish soldiers of fortune, who had served in the German wars until they had lost almost all distinction of political principle, and even of country, in the adoption of the mercenary faith, that a soldier's principal duty was fidelity to the state or sovereign from whom he received his pay, without respect either to the justice of the quarrel, or to their own connexion with either of the contending parties. To men of this stamp, Grotius applies the severe character—NULLUM VITAE GENUS ET IMPROBIUS, QUAM EORUM, QUI SINE CAUSAE RESPECTU MERCEDE CONDUCTI, MILITANT. To these mercenary soldiers, as well as to the needy gentry with whom they were mixed in command, and who easily imbibed the same opinions, the success of the late short invasion of England in 1641 was a sufficient reason for renewing so profitable an experiment. The good pay and free quarters of England had made a feeling impression upon the recollection of these military adventurers, and the prospect of again levying eight hundred and fifty pounds a-day, came in place of all arguments, whether of state or of morality.

Another cause inflamed the minds of the nation at large, no less than the tempting prospect of the wealth of England animated the soldiery. So much had been written and said on either side concerning the form of church government, that it had become a matter of infinitely more consequence in the eyes of the multitude than the doctrines of that gospel which both churches had embraced. The Prelatists and Presbyterians of the more violent kind became as illiberal as the Papists, and would scarcely allow the possibility of salvation beyond the pale of their respective churches. It was in vain remarked to these zealots, that had the Author of our holy religion considered any peculiar form of church government as essential to salvation, it would have been revealed with the same precision as under the Old Testament dispensation. Both parties continued as violent as if they could have pleaded the distinct commands of Heaven to justify their intolerance, Laud, in the days of his domination, had fired the train, by attempting to impose upon the Scottish people church ceremonies foreign to their habits and opinions. The success with which this had been resisted, and the Presbyterian model substituted in its place, had endeared the latter to the nation, as the cause in which they had triumphed. The Solemn League and Covenant, adopted with such zeal by the greater part of the kingdom, and by them forced, at the sword's point, upon the others, bore in its bosom, as its principal object, the establishing the doctrine and discipline of the Presbyterian church, and the putting down all error and heresy; and having attained for their own country an establishment of this golden candlestick, the Scots became liberally and fraternally anxious to erect the same in England. This they conceived might be easily attained by lending to the Parliament the effectual assistance of the Scottish forces. The Presbyterians, a numerous and powerful party in the English Parliament, had hitherto taken the lead in opposition to the King; while the Independents and other sectaries, who afterwards, under Cromwell, resumed the power of the sword, and overset the Presbyterian model both in Scotland and England, were as yet contented to lurk under the shelter of the wealthier and more powerful party. The prospect of bringing to a uniformity the kingdoms of England and Scotland in discipline and worship, seemed therefore as fair as it was desirable.

The celebrated Sir Henry Vane, one of the commissioners who negotiated the alliance betwixt England and Scotland, saw the influence which this bait had upon the spirits of those with whom he dealt; and although himself a violent Independent, he contrived at once to gratify and to elude the eager desires of the Presbyterians, by qualifying the obligation to reform the Church of England, as a change to be executed "according to the word of God, and the best reformed churches." Deceived by their own eagerness, themselves entertaining no doubts on the JUS DIVINUM of their own ecclesiastical establishments, and not holding it possible such doubts could be adopted by others, the Convention of Estates and the Kirk of Scotland conceived, that such expressions necessarily inferred the establishment of Presbytery; nor were they undeceived, until, when their help was no longer needful, the sectaries gave them to understand, that the phrase might be as well applied to Independency, or any other mode of worship, which those who were at the head of affairs at the time might consider as agreeable "to the word of God, and the practice of the reformed churches." Neither were the outwitted Scottish less astonished to find, that the designs of the English sectaries struck against the monarchial constitution of Britain, it having been their intention to reduce the power of the King, but by no means to abrogate the office. They fared, however, in this respect, like rash physicians, who commence by over-physicking a patient, until he is reduced to a state of weakness, from which cordials are afterwards unable to recover him.

But these events were still in the womb of futurity. As yet the Scottish Parliament held their engagement with England consistent with justice, prudence, and piety, and their military undertaking seemed to succeed to their very wish. The junction of the Scottish army with those of Fairfax and Manchester, enabled the Parliamentary forces to besiege York, and to fight the desperate action of Long-Marston Moor, in which Prince Rupert and the Marquis of Newcastle were defeated. The Scottish auxiliaries, indeed, had less of the glory of this victory than their countrymen could desire. David Leslie, with their cavalry, fought bravely, and to them, as well as to Cromwell's brigade of Independents, the honour of the day belonged; but the old Earl of Leven, the covenanting general, was driven out of the field by the impetuous charge of

Prince Rupert, and was thirty miles distant, in full flight towards Scotland, when he was overtaken by the news that his party had gained a complete victory.

The absence of these auxiliary troops, upon this crusade for the establishment of Presbyterianism in England, had considerably diminished the power of the Convention of Estates in Scotland, and had given rise to those agitations among the anti-covenanters, which we have noticed at the beginning of this chapter.

CHAPTER II.

His mother could for him as cradle set
Her husband's rusty iron corselet;
Whose jangling sound could hush her babe to rest,
That never plain'd of his uneasy nest;
Then did he dream of dreary wars at hand,
And woke, and fought, and won, ere he could stand
—HALL'S SATIRES

It was towards the close of a summer's evening, during the anxious period which we have commemorated, that a young gentleman of quality, well mounted and armed, and accompanied by two servants, one of whom led a sumpter horse, rode slowly up one of those steep passes, by which the Highlands are accessible from the Lowlands of Perthshire. [The beautiful pass of Leny, near Callander, in Monteith, would, in some respects, answer this description.] Their course had lain for some time along the banks of a lake, whose deep waters reflected the crimson beams of the western sun. The broken path which they pursued with some difficulty, was in some places shaded by ancient birches and oak-trees, and in others overhung by fragments of huge rock. Elsewhere, the hill, which formed the northern side of this beautiful sheet of water, arose in steep, but less precipitous acclivity, and was arrayed in heath of the darkest purple. In the present times, a scene so romantic would have been judged to possess the highest charms for the traveller; but those who journey in days of doubt and dread, pay little attention to picturesque scenery.

The master kept, as often as the wood permitted, abreast of one or both of his domestics, and seemed earnestly to converse with them, probably because the distinctions of rank are readily set aside among those who are made to be sharers of common danger.

The dispositions of the leading men who inhabit this wild country, and the probability of their taking part in the political convulsions that were soon expected, were the subjects of their conversation.

They had not advanced above half way up the lake, and the young gentleman was pointing to his attendants the spot where their intended road turned northwards, and, leaving the verge of the loch, ascended a ravine to the right hand, when they discovered a single horseman coming down the shore, as if to meet them. The gleam of the sunbeams upon his head-piece and corslet showed that he was in armour, and the purpose of the other travellers required that he should not pass unquestioned. "We must know who he is," said the young gentleman, "and whither he is going." And putting spurs to his horse, he rode forward as fast as the rugged state of the road would permit, followed by his two attendants, until he reached the point where the pass along the side of the lake was intersected by that which descended from the ravine, securing thus against the possibility of the stranger eluding them, by turning into the latter road before they came up with him.

The single horseman had mended his pace, when he first observed the three riders advance rapidly towards him; but when he saw them halt and form a front, which completely occupied the path, he checked his horse, and advanced with great deliberation; so that each party had an opportunity to take a full survey of the other. The solitary stranger was mounted upon an able horse, fit for military service, and for the great weight which he had to carry, and his rider occupied his demipique, or war-saddle, with an air that showed it was his familiar seat. He had a bright burnished head-piece, with a plume of feathers, together with a cuirass, thick enough to resist a musket-ball, and a back-piece of lighter materials. These defensive arms he wore over a buff jerkin, along with a pair of gauntlets, or steel gloves, the tops of which reached up to his elbow, and which, like the rest of his armour, were of bright steel. At the front of his military saddle hung a case of pistols, far beyond the ordinary size, nearly two feet in length, and carrying bullets of twenty to the pound. A buff belt, with a broad silver buckle, sustained on one side a long straight double-edged broadsword, with a strong guard, and a blade calculated either to strike or push. On the right side hung a dagger of about eighteen inches in length; a shoulder-belt sustained at his back a musketoon or blunderbuss, and was crossed by a bandelier containing his charges of ammunition. Thigh-pieces of steel, then termed taslets, met the tops of his huge jack-boots, and completed the equipage of a well-armed trooper of the period.

The appearance of the horseman himself corresponded well with his military equipage, to which he had the air of having been long inured. He was above the middle size, and of strength sufficient to bear with ease the weight of his weapons, offensive and defensive. His age might be forty and upwards, and his countenance was that of a resolute weather-beaten veteran, who had seen many fields, and brought away in token more than one scar. At the distance of about thirty yards he halted and stood fast, raised himself on his stirrups, as if to reconnoitre and ascertain the purpose of the opposite party, and brought his musketoon under his right arm, ready for use, if occasion should require it. In everything but numbers, he had the advantage of those who seemed inclined to interrupt his passage.

The leader of the party was, indeed, well mounted and clad in a buff coat, richly embroidered, the half-military dress of the period; but his domestics had only coarse jackets of thick felt, which could scarce be expected to turn the edge of a sword, if wielded by a strong man; and none of them had any weapons, save swords and pistols, without which gentlemen, or their attendants, during those disturbed times, seldom stirred abroad.

When they had stood at gaze for about a minute, the younger gentleman gave the challenge which was then common in the mouth of all strangers who met in such circumstances—"For whom are you?"

"Tell me first," answered the soldier, "for whom are you?—the strongest party should speak first."

"We are for God and King Charles," answered the first speaker.—" Now tell your faction, you know ours."

"I am for God and my standard," answered the single horseman.

"And for which standard?" replied the chief of the other party—"Cavalier or Roundhead, King or Convention?"

"By my troth, sir," answered the soldier, "I would be loath to reply to you with an untruth, as a thing unbecoming a cavalier of fortune and a soldier. But to answer your query with beseeming veracity, it is necessary I should myself have resolved to whilk of the present divisions of the kingdom I shall ultimately adhere, being a matter whereon my mind is not as yet preceesely ascertained."

"I should have thought," answered the gentleman, "that, when loyalty and religion are at stake, no gentleman or man of honour could be long in choosing his party."

"Truly, sir," replied the trooper, "if ye speak this in the way of vituperation, as meaning to impugn my honour or genteelity, I would blithely put the same to issue, venturing in that quarrel with my single person against you three. But if you speak it in the way of logical ratiocination, whilk I have studied in my youth at the Mareschal-College of Aberdeen, I am ready to prove to ye LOGICE, that my resolution to defer, for a certain season, the taking upon me either of these quarrels, not only becometh me as a gentleman and a man of honour, but also as a person of sense and prudence, one imbued with humane letters in his early youth, and who, from thenceforward, has followed the wars under the banner of the invincible Gustavus, the Lion of the North, and under many other heroic leaders, both Lutheran and Calvinist, Papist and Arminian."

After exchanging a word or two with his domestics, the younger gentleman replied, "I should be glad, sir, to have some conversation with you upon so interesting a question, and should be proud if I can determine you in favour of the cause I have myself espoused. I ride this evening to a friend's house not three miles distant, whither, if you choose to accompany me, you shall have good quarters for the night, and free permission to take your own road in the morning, if you then feel no inclination to join with us."

"Whose word am I to take for this?" answered the cautious soldier—"A man must know his guarantee, or he may fall into an ambuscade."

"I am called," answered the younger stranger, "the Earl of Menteith, and, I trust, you will receive my honour as a sufficient security."

"A worthy nobleman," answered the soldier, "whose parole is not to be doubted." With one motion he replaced his musketoon at his back, and with another made his military salute to the young nobleman, and continuing to talk as he rode forward to join him—

"And, I trust," said he, "my own assurance, that I will be BON CAMARADO to your lordship in peace or in peril, during the time we shall abide together, will not be altogether vilipended in these doubtful times, when, as they say, a man's head is safer in a steel-cap than in a marble palace."

"I assure you, sir," said Lord Menteith, "that to judge from your appearance, I most highly value the advantage of your escort; but, I trust, we shall have no occasion for any exercise of valour, as I expect to conduct you to good and friendly quarters."

"Good quarters, my lord," replied the soldier, "are always acceptable, and are only to be postponed to good pay or good booty,—not to mention the honour of a cavalier, or the needful points of commanded duty. And truly, my lord, your noble proffer is not the less welcome, in that I knew not preceesely this night where I and my poor companion" (patting his horse) "were to find lodgments."

"May I be permitted to ask, then," said Lord Menteith, "to whom I have the good fortune to stand quarter-master?"

"Truly, my lord," said the trooper, "my name is Dalgetty— Dugald Dalgetty, Ritt-master Dugald Dalgetty of Drumthwacket, at your honourable service to command. It is a name you may have seen in GALLO BELGICUS, the SWEDISH INTELLIGENCER, or, if you read High Dutch, in the FLIEGENDEN MERCOEUR of Leipsic. My father, my lord, having by unthrifty courses reduced a fair patrimony to a nonentity, I had no better shift, when I was eighteen years auld, than to carry the learning whilk I had acquired at the Mareschal-College of Aberdeen, my gentle bluid and designation of Drumthwacket, together with a pair of stalwarth arms, and legs conform, to the German wars, there to push my way as a cavalier of fortune. My lord, my legs and arms stood me in more stead than either my gentle kin or my book-lear, and I found myself trailing a pike as a private gentleman under old Sir Ludovick Leslie, where I learned the rules of service so tightly, that I will not forget them in a hurry. Sir, I have been made to stand guard eight hours, being from twelve at noon to eight o'clock of the night, at the palace, armed with back and breast, head-piece and bracelets, being iron to the teeth, in a bitter frost, and the ice was as hard as ever was flint; and all for stopping an instant to speak to my landlady, when I should have gone to roll-call."

"And, doubtless, sir," replied Lord Menteith, "you have gone through some hot service, as well as this same cold duty you talk of?"

"Surely, my lord, it doth not become me to speak; but he that hath seen the fields of Leipsic and of Lutzen, may be said to have seen pitched battles. And one who hath witnessed the intaking of Frankfort, and Spanheim, and Nuremberg, and so forth, should know somewhat about leaguers, storms, onslaughts and outfalls."

"But your merit, sir, and experience, were doubtless followed by promotion?"

"It came slow, my lord, dooms slow," replied Dalgetty; "but as my Scottish countrymen, the fathers of the war, and the raisers of those valorous Scottish regiments that were the dread of Germany, began to fall pretty thick, what with pestilence and what with the sword, why we, their children, succeeded to their inheritance. Sir, I was six years first private gentleman of the company, and three years lance speisade; disdaining to receive a halberd, as unbecoming my birth. Wherefore I was ultimately promoted to be a fahndragger, as the High Dutch call it (which signifies an ancient), in the King's Leif Regiment of Black-Horse, and thereafter I arose to be lieutenant and ritt-master, under that invincible monarch, the bulwark of the Protestant faith, the Lion of the North, the terror of Austria, Gustavus the Victorious."

"And yet, if I understand you, Captain Dalgetty,—I think that rank corresponds with your foreign title of ritt-master—"

"The same grade preceesely," answered Dalgetty; "ritt-master signifying literally file-leader."

"I was observing," continued Lord Menteith, "that, if I understood you right, you had left the service of this great Prince."

"It was after his death—it was after his death, sir," said Dalgetty, "when I was in no shape bound to continue mine adherence. There are things, my lord, in that service, that cannot but go against the stomach of any cavalier of honour. In especial, albeit the pay be none of the most superabundant, being only about sixty dollars a-month to a ritt-master, yet the invincible Gustavus never paid above one-third of that sum, whilk was distributed monthly by way of loan; although, when justly considered, it was, in fact, a borrowing by that great monarch of the additional two-thirds which were due to the soldier. And I have seen some whole regiments of Dutch and Holsteiners mutiny on the field of battle, like base scullions, crying out Gelt, gelt, signifying their desire of pay, instead of falling to blows like our noble Scottish blades, who ever disdained, my lord, postponing of honour to filthy lucre."

"But were not these arrears," said Lord Menteith, "paid to the soldiery at some stated period?"

"My lord," said Dalgetty, "I take it on my conscience, that at no period, and by no possible process, could one creutzer of them ever be recovered. I myself never saw twenty dollars of my own all the time I served the invincible Gustavus, unless it was from the chance of a storm or victory, or the fetching in some town or doorp, when a cavalier of fortune, who knows the usage of wars, seldom faileth to make some small profit."

"I begin rather to wonder, sir," said Lord Menteith, "that you should have continued so long in the Swedish service, than that you should have ultimately withdrawn from it."

"Neither I should," answered the Ritt-master; "but that great leader, captain, and king, the Lion of the North, and the bulwark of the Protestant faith, had a way of winning battles, taking towns, over-running countries, and levying contributions, whilk made his service irresistibly delectable to all true-bred cavaliers who follow the noble profession of arms. Simple as I ride here, my lord, I have myself commanded the whole stift of Dunklespiel on the Lower Rhine, occupying the Palsgrave's palace, consuming his choice wines with my comrades, calling in contributions, requisitions, and caduacs, and not failing to lick my fingers, as became a good cook. But truly all this glory hastened to decay, after our great master had been shot with three bullets on the field of Lutzen; wherefore, finding that Fortune had changed sides, that the borrowings and lendings went on as before out of our pay, while the caduacs and casualties were all cut off, I e'en gave up my commission, and took service with Wallenstein, in Walter Butler's Irish regiment."

"And may I beg to know of you," said Lord Menteith, apparently interested in the adventures of this soldier of fortune, "how you liked this change of masters?"

"Indifferent well," said the Captain—"very indifferent well. I cannot say that the Emperor paid much better than the great Gustavus. For hard knocks, we had plenty of them. I was often obliged to run my head against my old acquaintances, the Swedish feathers, whilk your honour must conceive to be double-pointed stakes, shod with iron at each end, and planted before the squad of pikes to prevent an onfall of the cavalry. The whilk Swedish feathers, although they look gay to the eye, resembling the shrubs or lesser trees of ane forest, as the puissant pikes, arranged in battalia behind them, correspond to the tall pines thereof, yet, nevertheless, are not altogether so soft to encounter as the plumage of a goose. Howbeit, in despite of heavy blows and light pay, a cavalier of fortune may thrive indifferently well in the Imperial service, in respect his private casualties are nothing so closely looked to as by the Swede; and so that an officer did his duty on the field, neither Wallenstein nor Pappenheim, nor old Tilly before them, would likely listen to the objurgations of boors or burghers against any commander or soldado, by whom they chanced to be somewhat closely shorn. So that an experienced cavalier, knowing how to lay, as our Scottish phrase runs, 'the head of the sow to the tail of the grice,' might get out of the country the pay whilk he could not obtain from the Emperor."

"With a full hand, sir, doubtless, and with interest," said Lord Menteith.

"Indubitably, my lord," answered Dalgetty, composedly; "for it would be doubly disgraceful for any soldado of rank to have his name called in question for any petty delinquency."

"And pray, Sir," continued Lord Menteith, "what made you leave so gainful a service?"

"Why, truly, sir," answered the soldier, "an Irish cavalier, called O'Quilligan, being major of our regiment, and I having had words with him the night before, respecting the worth and precedence of our several nations, it pleased him the next day to deliver his orders to me with the point of his batoon advanced and held aloof, instead of declining and trailing the same, as is the fashion from a courteous commanding officer towards his equal in rank, though, it may be, his inferior in military grade. Upon this quarrel, sir, we fought in private rencontre; and as, in the perquisitions which followed, it pleased Walter Butler, our oberst, or colonel, to give the lighter punishment to his countryman, and the heavier to me, whereupon, ill-stomaching such partiality, I exchanged my commission for one under the Spaniard."

"I hope you found yourself better off by the change?" said Lord Menteith.

"In good sooth," answered the Ritt-master, "I had but little to complain of. The pay was somewhat regular, being furnished by the rich Flemings and Waloons of the Low Country. The quarters were excellent; the good wheaten loaves of the Flemings were better than the Provant rye-bread of the Swede, and Rhenish wine was more plenty with us than ever I saw the black-beer of Rostock in Gustavus's camp. Service there was none, duty there was little; and that little we might do, or leave undone, at our pleasure; an excellent retirement for a cavalier somewhat weary of field and leaguer, who had purchased with his blood as much honour as might serve his turn, and was desirous of a little ease and good living."

"And may I ask," said Lord Menteith, "why you, Captain, being, as I suppose, in the situation you describe, retired from the Spanish service also?"

"You are to consider, my lord, that your Spaniard," replied Captain Dalgetty, "is a person altogether unparalleled in his own conceit, where-through he maketh not fit account of such foreign cavaliers of valour as are pleased to take service with him. And a galling thing it is to every honourable soldado, to be put aside, and postponed, and obliged to yield preference to every puffing signor, who, were it the question which should first mount a breach at push of pike, might be apt to yield willing place to a Scottish cavalier. Moreover, sir, I was pricked in conscience respecting a matter of religion."

"I should not have thought, Captain Dalgetty," said the young nobleman, "that an old soldier, who had changed service so often, would have been too scrupulous on that head."

"No more I am, my lord," said the Captain, "since I hold it to be the duty of the chaplain of the regiment to settle those matters for me, and every other brave cavalier, inasmuch as he does nothing else that I know of for his pay and allowances. But this was a particular case, my lord, a CASUS IMPROVISUS, as I may say, in whilk I had no chaplain of my own persuasion to act as my adviser. I found, in short, that although my being a Protestant might be winked at, in respect that I was a man of action, and had more experience than all the Dons in our TERTIA put together, yet, when in garrison, it was expected I should go to mass with the regiment. Now, my lord, as a true Scottish man, and educated at the Mareschal-College of Aberdeen, I was bound to uphold the mass to be an act of blinded papistry and utter idolatry, whilk I was altogether unwilling to homologate by my presence. True it is, that I consulted on the point with a worthy countryman of my own, one Father Fatsides, of the Scottish Covenant in Wurtzburg—"

"And I hope," observed Lord Menteith, "you obtained a clear opinion from this same ghostly father?"

"As clear as it could be," replied Captain Dalgetty, "considering we had drunk six flasks of Rhenish, and about two mutchkins of Kirchenwasser. Father Fatsides informed me, that, as nearly as he could judge for a heretic like myself, it signified not much whether I went to mass or not, seeing my eternal perdition was signed and sealed at any rate, in respect of my impenitent and obdurate perseverance in my damnable heresy. Being discouraged by this response, I applied to a Dutch pastor of the reformed church, who told me, he thought I might lawfully go to mass, in respect that the prophet permitted Naaman, a mighty man of valour, and an honourable cavalier of Syria, to follow his master into the house of Rimmon, a false god, or idol, to whom he had vowed service, and to bow down when the king was leaning upon his hand. But neither was this answer satisfactory to me, both because there was an unco difference between an anointed King of Syria and our Spanish colonel, whom I could have blown away like the peeling of an ingan, and chiefly because I could not find the thing was required of me by any of the articles of war; neither was I proffered any consideration, either in perquisite or pay, for the wrong I might thereby do to my conscience."

"So you again changed your service?" said Lord Menteith.

"In troth did I, my lord; and after trying for a short while two or three other powers, I even took on for a time with their High Mightinesses the States of Holland."

"And how did their service jump with your humour?" again demanded his companion.

"O! my lord," said the soldier, in a sort of enthusiasm, "their behaviour on pay-day might be a pattern to all Europe—no borrowings, no lendings, no offsets no arrears—all balanced and paid like a banker's book. The quarters, too, are excellent, and the allowances unchallengeable; but then, sir, they are a preceese, scrupulous people, and will allow nothing for peccadilloes. So that if a boor complains of a broken head, or a beer-seller of a broken can, or a daft wench does but squeak loud enough to be heard above her breath, a soldier of honour shall be dragged, not before his own court-martial, who can best judge of and punish his demerits, hut before a base mechanical burgo-master, who shall menace him with the rasp-house, the cord, and what not, as if he were one of their own mean, amphibious, twenty-breeched boors. So not being able to dwell longer among those ungrateful plebeians, who, although unable to defend themselves by their proper strength, will nevertheless allow the noble foreign cavalier who engages with them nothing beyond his dry wages, which no honourable spirit will put in competition with a liberal license and honourable countenance, I resolved to leave the service of the Mynheers. And hearing at this time, to my exceeding satisfaction, that there is something to be doing this summer in my way in this my dear native country, I am come hither, as they say, like a beggar to a bridal, in order to give my loving countrymen the advantage of that experience which I have acquired in foreign parts. So your lordship has an outline of my brief story, excepting my deportment in those passages of action in the field, in leaguers, storms, and onslaughts, whilk would be wearisome to narrate, and might, peradventure, better befit any other tongue than mine own."

CHAPTER III.

For pleas of right let statesmen vex their head,
Battle's my business, and my guerdon bread;
And, with the sworded Switzer, I can say,
The best of causes is the best of pay.

—DONNE.

The difficulty and narrowness of the road had by this time become such as to interrupt the conversation of the travellers, and Lord Menteith, reining back his horse, held a moment's private conversation with his domestics. The Captain, who now led the van of the party, after about a quarter of a mile's slow and toilsome advance up a broken and rugged ascent, emerged into an upland valley, to which a mountain stream acted as a drain, and afforded sufficient room upon its greensward banks for the travellers to pursue their journey in a more social manner.

Lord Menteith accordingly resumed the conversation, which had been interrupted by the difficulties of the way. "I should have thought," said he to Captain Dalgetty, "that a cavalier of your honourable mark, who hath so long followed the valiant King of Sweden, and entertains such a suitable contempt for the base mechanical States of Holland, would not have hesitated to embrace the cause of King Charles, in preference to that of the low-born, roundheaded, canting knaves, who are in rebellion against his authority?"

"Ye speak reasonably, my lord," said Dalgetty, "and, CAETERIS PARIBUS, I might be induced to see the matter in the same light. But, my lord, there is a southern proverb, fine words butter no parsnips. I have heard enough since I came here, to satisfy me that a cavalier of honour is free to take any part in this civil embroilment whilk he may find most convenient for his own peculiar. Loyalty is your pass-word, my lord—Liberty, roars another chield from the other side of the strath—the King, shouts one war-cry—the Parliament, roars another—Montrose, for ever, cries Donald, waving his bonnet—Argyle and Leven, cries a south-country Saunders, vapouring with his hat and feather. Fight for the bishops, says a priest, with his gown and rochet—Stand stout for the Kirk, cries a minister, in a Geneva cap and band.—Good watchwords all—excellent watchwords. Whilk cause is the best I cannot say. But sure am I, that I have fought knee-deep in blood many a day for one that was ten degrees worse than the worst of them all."

"And pray, Captain Dalgetty," said his lordship, "since the pretensions of both parties seem to you so equal, will you please to inform us by what circumstances your preference will be determined?"

"Simply upon two considerations, my lord," answered the soldier. "Being, first, on which side my services would be in most honourable request;—And, secondly, whilk is a corollary of the first, by whilk party they are likely to be most gratefully requited. And, to deal plainly with you, my lord, my opinion at present doth on both points rather incline to the side of the Parliament."

"Your reasons, if you please," said Lord Menteith, "and perhaps I may be able to meet them with some others which are more powerful."

"Sir, I shall be amenable to reason," said Captain Dalgetty, "supposing it addresses itself to my honour and my interest. Well, then, my lord, here is a sort of Highland host assembled, or expected to assemble, in these wild hills, in the King's behalf. Now, sir, you know the nature of our Highlanders. I will not deny them to be a people stout in body and valiant in heart, and courageous enough in their own wild way of fighting, which is as remote from the usages and discipline of war as ever was that of the ancient Scythians, or of the salvage Indians of America that now is, They havena sae mickle as a German whistle, or a drum, to beat a march, an alarm, a charge, a retreat, a reveille, or the tattoo, or any other point of war; and their damnable skirlin' pipes, whilk they themselves pretend to understand, are unintelligible to the ears of any cavaliero accustomed to civilised warfare. So that, were I undertaking to discipline such a breechless mob, it were impossible for me to be understood; and if I were understood, judge ye, my lord, what chance I had of being obeyed among a band of half salvages, who are accustomed to pay to their own lairds and chiefs, allenarly, that respect and obedience whilk ought to be paid to commissionate officers. If I were teaching them to form battalia by extracting the square root, that is, by forming your square battalion of equal number of men of rank and file, corresponding to the square root of the full number present, what return could I expect for communicating this golden secret of military tactic, except it may be a dirk in my wame, on placing some M'Alister More M'Shemei or Capperfae, in the flank or rear, when he claimed to be in the van?—Truly, well saith holy writ, 'if ye cast pearls before swine, they will turn again and rend ye.'"

"I believe, Anderson," said Lord Menteith, looking back to one of his servants, for both were close behind him, "you can assure this gentleman, we shall have more occasion for experienced officers, and be more disposed to profit by their instructions, than he seems to be aware of."

"With your honour's permission," said Anderson, respectfully raising his cap, "when we are joined by the Irish infantry, who are expected, and who should be landed in the West Highlands before now, we shall have need of good soldiers to discipline our levies."

"And I should like well—very well, to be employed in such service," said Dalgetty; "the Irish are pretty fellows—very pretty fellows—I desire to see none better in the field. I once saw a brigade of Irish, at the taking of Frankfort upon the Oder, stand to it with sword and pike until they beat off the blue and yellow Swedish brigades, esteemed as stout as any that fought under the immortal Gustavus. And although stout Hepburn, valiant Lumsdale, courageous Monroe, with myself and other cavaliers, made entry elsewhere at point of pike, yet, had we all met with such opposition, we had returned with great loss and little profit. Wherefore these valiant Irishes, being all put to the sword, as is usual in such cases, did nevertheless gain immortal praise and honour; so that, for their sakes, I have always loved and honoured those of that nation next to my own country of Scotland."

"A command of Irish," said Menteith, "I think I could almost promise you, should you be disposed to embrace the royal cause."

"And yet," said Captain Dalgetty, "my second and greatest difficulty remains behind; for, although I hold it a mean and sordid thing for a soldado to have nothing in his mouth but pay and gelt, like the base cullions, the German lanz-knechts, whom I mentioned before; and although I will maintain it with my sword, that honour is to be preferred before pay, free quarters, and arrears, yet, EX CONTRARIO, a soldier's pay being the counterpart of his engagement of service, it becomes a wise and considerate cavalier to consider what remuneration he is to receive for his service, and from what funds it is to be paid. And truly, my lord, from what I can see and hear, the Convention are the purse-masters. The Highlanders, indeed, may be kept in humour, by allowing them to steal cattle; and for the Irishes, your lordship and your noble associates may, according to the practice of the wars in such cases, pay them as seldom or as little as may suit your pleasure or convenience; but the same mode of treatment doth not apply to a cavalier like me, who must keep up his horses, servants, arms, and equipage, and who neither can, nor will, go to warfare upon his own charges."

Anderson, the domestic who had before spoken now respectfully addressed his master.—"I think, my lord," he said, "that, under your lordship's favour, I could say something to remove Captain Dalgetty's second objection also. He asks us where we are to collect our pay; now, in my poor mind, the resources are as open to us as to the Covenanters. They tax the country according to their pleasure, and dilapidate the estates of the King's friends; now, were we once in the Lowlands, with our Highlanders and our Irish at our backs, and our swords in our hands, we can find many a fat traitor, whose ill-gotten wealth shall fill our military chest and satisfy our soldiery. Besides, confiscations will fall in thick; and, in giving donations of forfeited lands to every adventurous cavalier who joins his standard, the King will at once reward his friends and punish his enemies. In short, he that joins these Roundhead dogs may get some miserable pittance of pay—he that joins our standard has a chance to be knight, lord, or earl, if luck serve him."

"Have you ever served, my good friend?" said the Captain to the spokesman.

"A little, sir, in these our domestic quarrels," answered the man, modestly.

"But never in Germany or the Low Countries?" said Dalgetty.

"I never had the honour," answered Anderson.

"I profess," said Dalgetty, addressing Lord Menteith, "your lordship's servant has a sensible, natural, pretty idea of military matters; somewhat irregular, though, and smells a little too much of selling the bear's skin before he has hunted him.—I will take the matter, however, into my consideration."

"Do so, Captain," said Lord Menteith; "you will have the night to think of it, for we are now near the house, where I hope to ensure you a hospitable reception."

"And that is what will be very welcome," said the Captain, "for I have tasted no food since daybreak but a farl of oatcake, which I divided with my horse. So I have been fain to draw my sword-belt three bores tighter for very extenuation, lest hunger and heavy iron should make the gird slip."

CHAPTER IV.

Once on a time, no matter when,
Some Glunimies met in a glen;
As deft and tight as ever wore
A durk, a targe, and a claymore,
Short hose, and belted plaid or trews,
In Uist, Lochaber, Skye, or Lewes,
Or cover'd hard head with his bonnet;
Had you but known them, you would own it.
—MESTON.

A hill was now before the travellers, covered with an ancient forest of Scottish firs, the topmost of which, flinging their scathed branches across the western horizon, gleamed ruddy in the setting sun. In the centre of this wood rose the towers, or rather the chimneys, of the house, or castle, as it was called, destined for the end of their journey.

As usual at that period, one or two high-ridged narrow buildings, intersecting and crossing each other, formed the CORPS DE LOGIS. A protecting bartizan or two, with the addition of small turrets at the angles, much resembling pepper-boxes, had procured for Darnlinvarach the dignified appellation of a castle. It was surrounded by a low court-yard wall, within which were the usual offices.

As the travellers approached more nearly, they discovered marks of recent additions to the defences of the place, which had been suggested, doubtless, by the insecurity of those troublesome times. Additional loop-holes for musketry were struck out in different parts of the building, and of its surrounding wall. The windows had just been carefully secured by stancheons of iron, crossing each other athwart and end-long, like the grates of a prison.

The door of the court-yard was shut; and it was only after cautious challenge that one of its leaves was opened by two domestics, both strong Highlanders, and both under arms, like Bitias and Pandarus in the AEneid, ready to defend the entrance if aught hostile had ventured an intrusion.

When the travellers were admitted into the court, they found additional preparations for defence. The walls were scaffolded for the use of fire-arms, and one or two of the small guns, called sackers, or falcons, were mounted at the angles and flanking turrets.

More domestics, both in the Highland and Lowland dress, instantly rushed from the anterior of the mansion, and some hastened to take the horses of the strangers, while others waited to marshal them a way into the dwelling-house. But Captain Dalgetty refused the proffered assistance of those who wished to relieve him of the charge of his horse. "It is my custom, my friends, to see Gustavus (for so I have called him, after my invincible master) accommodated myself; we are old friends and fellow-travellers, and as I often need the use of his legs, I always lend him in my turn the service of my tongue, to call for whatever he has occasion for;" and accordingly he strode into the stable after his steed without farther apology.

Neither Lord Menteith nor his attendants paid the same attention to their horses, but, leaving them to the proffered care of the servants of the place, walked forward into the house, where a sort of dark vaulted vestibule displayed, among other miscellaneous articles, a huge barrel of two-penny ale, beside which were ranged two or three wooden queichs, or bickers, ready, it would appear, for the service of whoever thought proper to employ them. Lord Menteith applied himself to the spigot, drank without ceremony, and then handed the stoup to Anderson, who followed his master's example, but not until he had flung out the drop of ale which remained, and slightly rinsed the wooden cup.

"What the deil, man," said an old Highland servant belonging to the family, "can she no drink after her ain master without washing the cup and spilling the ale, and be tamned to her!"

"I was bred in France," answered Anderson, "where nobody drinks after another out of the same cup, unless it be after a young lady."

"The teil's in their nicety!" said Donald; "and if the ale be gude, fat the waur is't that another man's beard's been in the queich before ye?"

Anderson's companion drank without observing the ceremony which had given Donald so much offence, and both of them followed their master into the low-arched stone hall, which was the common rendezvous of a Highland family. A large fire of peats in the huge chimney at the upper end shed a dim light through the apartment, and was rendered necessary by the damp, by which, even during the summer, the apartment was rendered uncomfortable. Twenty or thirty targets, as many claymores, with dirks, and plaids, and guns, both match-lock and fire-lock, and long-bows, and cross-bows, and Lochaber axes, and coats of plate armour, and steel bonnets, and headpieces, and the more ancient habergeons, or shirts of reticulated mail, with hood and sleeves corresponding to it, all hung in confusion about the walls, and would have formed a month's amusement to a member of a modern antiquarian society. But such things were too familiar, to attract much observation on the part of the present spectators.

There was a large clumsy oaken table, which the hasty hospitality of the domestic who had before spoken, immediately spread with milk, butter, goat-milk cheese, a flagon of beer, and a flask of usquebae, designed for the refreshment of Lord Menteith; while an inferior servant made similar preparations at the bottom of the table for the benefit of his attendants. The space which intervened between them was, according to the manners of the times, sufficient distinction between master and servant, even though the former was, as in the present instance, of high rank. Meanwhile the guests stood by the fire—the young nobleman under the chimney, and his servants at some little distance.

"What do you think, Anderson," said the former, "of our fellow-traveller?"

"A stout fellow," replied Anderson, "if all be good that is upcome. I wish we had twenty such, to put our Teagues into some sort of discipline."

"I differ from you, Anderson," said Lord Menteith; "I think this fellow Dalgetty is one of those horse-leeches, whose appetite for blood being only sharpened by what he has sucked in foreign countries, he is now returned to batten upon that of his own. Shame on the pack of these mercenary swordmen! they have made the name of Scot through all Europe equivalent to that of a pitiful mercenary, who knows neither honour nor principle but his month's pay, who transfers his allegiance from standard to standard, at the pleasure of fortune or the highest bidder; and to whose insatiable thirst for plunder and warm quarters we owe much of that civil dissension which is now turning our swords against our own bowels. I had scarce patience with the hired gladiator, and yet could hardly help laughing at the extremity of his impudence."

"Your lordship will forgive me," said Anderson, "if I recommend to you, in the present circumstances, to conceal at least a part of this generous indignation; we cannot, unfortunately, do our work without the assistance of those who act on baser motives than our own. We cannot spare the assistance of such fellows as our friend the soldado. To use the canting phrase of the saints in the English Parliament, the sons of Zeruiah are still too many for us."

"I must dissemble, then, as well as I can," said Lord Menteith, "as I have hitherto done, upon your hint. But I wish the fellow at the devil with all my heart."

"Ay, but still you must remember, my lord," resumed Anderson, "that to cure the bite of a scorpion, you must crush another scorpion on the wound—But stop, we shall be overheard."

From a side-door in the hall glided a Highlander into the apartment, whose lofty stature and complete equipment, as well as the eagle's feather in his bonnet, and the confidence of his demeanour, announced to be a person of superior rank. He walked slowly up to the table, and made no answer to Lord Menteith, who, addressing him by the name of Allan, asked him how he did.

"Ye manna speak to her e'en now," whispered the old attendant.

The tall Highlander, sinking down upon the empty settle next the fire, fixed his eyes upon the red embers and the huge heap of turf, and seemed buried in profound abstraction. His dark eyes, and wild and enthusiastic features, bore the air of one who, deeply impressed with his own subjects of meditation, pays little attention to exterior objects. An air of gloomy severity, the fruit perhaps of ascetic and solitary habits, might, in a Lowlander, have been ascribed to religious fanaticism; but by that disease of the mind, then so common both in England and the Lowlands of Scotland, the Highlanders of this period were rarely infected. They had, however, their own peculiar superstitions, which overclouded the mind with thick-coming fancies, as completely as the puritanism of their neighbours.

"His lordship's honour," said the Highland servant sideling up to Lord Menteith, and speaking in a very low tone, "his lordship manna speak to Allan even now, for the cloud is upon his mind."

Lord Menteith nodded, and took no farther notice of the reserved mountaineer.

"Said I not," asked the latter, suddenly raising his stately person upright, and looking at the domestic—"said I not that four were to come, and here stand but three on the hall floor?"

"In troth did ye say sae, Allan," said the old Highlander, "and here's the fourth man coming clinking in at the yett e'en now from the stable, for he's shelled like a partan, wi' airn on back and breast, haunch and shanks. And am I to set her chair up near the Menteith's, or down wi' the honest gentlemen at the foot of the table?"

Lord Menteith himself answered the enquiry, by pointing to a seat beside his own.

"And here she comes," said Donald, as Captain Dalgetty entered the hall; "and I hope gentlemens will all take bread and cheese, as we say in the glens, until better meat be ready, until the Tiernach comes back frae the hill wi' the southern gentlefolk, and then Dugald Cook will show himself wi' his kid and hill venison."

In the meantime, Captain Dalgetty had entered the apartment, and walking up to the seat placed next Lord Menteith, was leaning on the back of it with his arms folded. Anderson and his companion waited at the bottom of the table, in a respectful attitude, until they should receive permission to seat themselves; while three or four Highlanders, under the direction of old Donald, ran hither and thither to bring additional articles of food, or stood still to give attendance upon the guests.

In the midst of these preparations, Allan suddenly started up, and snatching a lamp from the hand of an attendant, held it close to Dalgetty's face, while he perused his features with the most heedful and grave attention.

"By my honour," said Dalgetty, half displeased, as, mysteriously shaking his head, Allan gave up the scrutiny—"I trow that lad and I will ken each other when we meet again."

Meanwhile Allan strode to the bottom of the table, and having, by the aid of his lamp, subjected Anderson and his companion to the same investigation, stood a moment as if in deep reflection; then, touching his forehead, suddenly seized Anderson by the arm, and before he could offer any effectual resistance, half led and half dragged him to the vacant seat at the upper end, and having made a mute intimation that he should there place himself, he hurried the soldado with the same unceremonious precipitation to the bottom of the table. The Captain, exceedingly incensed at this freedom, endeavoured to shake Allan from him with violence; but, powerful as he was, he proved in the struggle inferior to the gigantic mountaineer, who threw him off with such violence, that after reeling a few paces, he fell at full length, and the vaulted hall rang with the clash of his armour. When he arose, his first action was to draw his sword and to fly at Allan, who, with folded arms, seemed to await his onset with the most scornful indifference. Lord Menteith and his attendants interposed to preserve peace, while the Highlanders, snatching weapons from the wall, seemed prompt to increase the broil.

"He is mad," whispered Lord Menteith, "he is perfectly mad; there is no purpose in quarrelling with him."

"If your lordship is assured that he is NON COMPOS MENTIS," said Captain Dalgetty, "the whilk his breeding and behaviour seem to testify, the matter must end here, seeing that a madman can neither give an affront, nor render honourable satisfaction. But, by my saul, if I had my provstnt and a bottle of Rhenish under my belt, I should hive stood otherways up to him. And yet it's a pity he should be sae weak in the intellectuals, being a strong proper man of body, fit to handle pike, morgenstern, or any other military implement whatsoever." [This was a sort of club or mace, used in the earlier part of the seventeenth century in the defence of breaches and walls. When the Germans insulted a Scotch regiment then besieged in Trailsund, saying they heard there was a ship come from Denmark to them laden with tobacco pipes, "One of our soldiers," says Colonel Robert Munro, "showing them over the work a morgenstern, made of a large stock banded with iron, like the shaft of a halberd, with a round globe at the end with cross iron pikes, saith, 'Here is one of the tobacco pipes, wherewith we will beat out your brains when you intend to storm us.'"]

Peace was thus restored, and the party seated themselves agreeably to their former arrangement, with which Allan, who had now returned to his settle by the fire, and seemed once more immersed in meditation, did not again interfere. Lord Menteith, addressing the principal domestic, hastened to start some theme of conversation which might obliterate all recollection of the fray that had taken place. "The laird is at the hill then, Donald, I understand, and some English strangers with him?"

"At the hill he is, an it like your honour, and two Saxon calabaleros are with him sure eneugh; and that is Sir Miles Musgrave and Christopher Hall, both from the Cumraik, as I think they call their country."

"Hall and Musgrave?" said Lord Menteith, looking at his attendants, "the very men that we wished to see."

"Troth," said Donald, "an' I wish I had never seen them between the een, for they're come to herry us out o' house and ha'."

"Why, Donald," said Lord Menteith, "you did not use to be so churlish of your beef and ale; southland though they be, they'll scarce eat up all the cattle that's going on the castle mains."

"Teil care an they did," said Donald, "an that were the warst o't, for we have a wheen canny trewsmen here that wadna let us want if there was a horned beast atween this and Perth. But this is a warse job—it's nae less than a wager."

"A wager!" repeated Lord Menteith, with some surprise.

"Troth," continued Donald, to the full as eager to tell his news as Lord Menteith was curious to hear them, "as your lordship is a friend and kinsman o' the house, an' as ye'll hear eneugh o't in less than an hour, I may as weel tell ye mysell. Ye sall be pleased then to know, that when our Laird was up in England where he gangs oftener than his friends can wish, he was biding at the house o' this Sir Miles Musgrave, an' there was putten on the table six candlesticks, that they tell me were twice as muckle as the candlesticks in Dunblane kirk, and neither airn, brass, nor tin, but a' solid silver, nae less;—up wi' their English pride, has sae muckle, and kens sae little how to guide it! Sae they began to jeer the Laird, that he saw nae sic graith in his ain poor country; and the Laird, scorning to hae his country put down without a word for its credit, swore, like a gude Scotsman, that he had mair candlesticks, and better candlesticks, in his ain castle at hame, than were ever lighted in a hall in Cumberland, an Cumberland be the name o' the country."

"That was patriotically said," observed Lord Menteith.

"Fary true," said Donald; "but her honour had better hae hauden her tongue: for if ye say ony thing amang the Saxons that's a wee by ordinar, they clink ye down for a wager as fast as a Lowland smith would hammer shoon on a Highland shelty. An' so the Laird behoved either to gae back o' his word, or wager twa hunder merks; and sa he e'en tock the wager, rather than be shamed wi' the like o' them. And now he's like to get it to pay, and I'm thinking that's what makes him sae swear to come hame at e'en."

"Indeed," said Lord Menteith, "from my idea of your family plate, Donald, your master is certain to lose such a wager."

"Your honour may swear that; an' where he's to get the siller I kenna, although he borrowed out o' twenty purses. I advised him to pit the twa Saxon gentlemen and their servants cannily into the pit o' the tower till they gae up the bagain o' free gude-will, but the Laird winna hear reason."

Allan here started up, strode forward, and interrupted the conversation, saying to the domestic in a voice like thunder, "And how dared you to give my brother such dishonourable advice? or how dare you to say he will lose this or any other wager which it is his pleasure to lay?"

"Troth, Allan M'Aulay," answered the old man, "it's no for my father's son to gainsay what your father's son thinks fit to say, an' so the Laird may no doubt win his wager. A' that I ken against it is, that the teil a candlestick, or ony thing like it, is in the house, except the auld airn branches that has been here since Laird Kenneth's time, and the tin sconces that your father gard be made by auld Willie Winkie the tinkler, mair be token that deil an unce of siller plate is about the house at a', forby the lady's auld posset dish, that wants the cover and ane o' the lugs."

"Peace, old man!" said Allan, fiercely; "and do you, gentlemen, if your refection is finished, leave this apartment clear; I must prepare it for the reception of these southern guests."

"Come away," said the domestic, pulling Lord Menteith by the sleeve; "his hour is on him," said he, looking towards Allan, "and he will not be controlled."

They left the hall accordingly, Lord Menteith and the Captain being ushered one way by old Donald, and the two attendants conducted elsewhere by another Highlander. The former had scarcely reached a sort of withdrawing apartment ere they were joined by the lord of the mansion, Angus M'Aulay by name, and his English guests. Great joy was expressed by all parties, for Lord Menteith and the English gentlemen were well known to each other; and on Lord Menteith's introduction, Captain Dalgetty was well received by the Laird. But after the first burst of hospitable congratulation was over, Lord Menteith could observe that there was a shade of sadness on the brow of his Highland friend.

"You must have heard," said Sir Christopher Hall, "that our fine undertaking in Cumberland is all blown up. The militia would not march into Scotland, and your prick-ear'd Covenanters have been too hard for our friends in the southern shires. And so, understanding there is some stirring work here, Musgrave and I, rather than sit idle at home, are come to have a campaign among your kilts and plaids."

"I hope you have brought arms, men, and money with you," said Lord Menteith, smiling.

"Only some dozen or two of troopers, whom we left at the last Lowland village," said Musgrave, "and trouble enough we had to get them so far."

"As for money," said his companion, "We expect a small supply from our friend and host here."

The Laird now, colouring highly, took Menteith a little apart, and expressed to him his regret that he had fallen into a foolish blunder.

"I heard it from Donald," said Lord Menteith, scarce able to suppress a smile.

"Devil take that old man," said M'Aulay, "he would tell every thing, were it to cost one's life; but it's no jesting matter to you neither, my lord, for I reckon on your friendly and fraternal benevolence, as a near kinsman of our house, to help me out with the money due to these pock-puddings; or else, to be plain wi' ye, the deil a M'Aulay will there be at the muster, for curse me if I do not turn Covenanter rather than face these fellows without paying them; and, at the best, I shall be ill enough off, getting both the scaith and the scorn."

"You may suppose, cousin," said Lord Menteith, "I am not too well equipt just now; but you may be assured I shall endeavour to help you as well as I can, for the sake of old kindred, neighbourhood, and alliance."

"Thank ye—thank ye—thank ye," reiterated M'Aulay; "and as they are to spend the money in the King's service, what signifies whether you, they, or I pay it?—we are a' one man's bairns, I hope? But you must help me out too with some reasonable excuse, or else I shall be for taking to Andrew Ferrara; for I like not to be treated like a liar or a braggart at my own board-end, when, God knows, I only meant to support my honour, and that of my family and country.

Donald, as they were speaking, entered, with rather a blither face than he might have been expected to wear, considering the impending fate of his master's purse and credit. "Gentlemens, her dinner is ready, and HER CANDLES ARE LIGHTED TOO," said Donald, with a strong guttural emphasis on the last clause of his speech.

"What the devil can he mean?" said Musgrave, looking to his countryman.

Lord Menteith put the same question with his eyes to the Laird, which M'Aulay answered by shaking his head.

A short dispute about precedence somewhat delayed their leaving the apartment. Lord Menteith insisted upon yielding up that which belonged to his rank, on consideration of his being in his own country, and of his near connexion with the family in which they found themselves. The two English strangers, therefore, were first ushered into the hall, where an unexpected display awaited them. The large oaken table was spread with substantial joints of meat, and seats were placed in order for the guests. Behind every seat stood a gigantic Highlander, completely dressed and armed after the fashion of his country, holding in his right hand his drawn sword, with the point turned downwards, and in the left a blazing torch made of the bog-pine. This wood, found in the morasses, is so full of turpentine, that, when split and dried, it is frequently used in the Highlands instead of candles. The unexpected and somewhat startling apparition was seen by the red glare of the torches, which displayed the wild features, unusual dress, and glittering arms of those who bore them, while the smoke, eddying up to the roof of the hall, over-canopied them with a volume of vapour. Ere the strangers had recovered from their surprise, Allan stept forward, and pointing with his sheathed broadsword to the torch-bearers, said, in a deep and stern tone of voice, "Behold, gentlemen cavaliers, the chandeliers of my brother's house, the ancient fashion of our ancient name; not one of these men knows any law but their Chiefs command—Would you dare to compare to THEM in value the richest ore that ever was dug out of the mine? How say you, cavaliers?—is your wager won or lost?"

"Lost; lost," said Musgrave, gaily—"my own silver candlesticks are all melted and riding on horseback by this time, and I wish the fellows that enlisted were half as trusty as these.—Here, sir," he added to the Chief, "is your money; it impairs Hall's finances and mine somewhat, but debts of honour must be settled."

"My father's curse upon my father's son," said Allan, interrupting him, "if he receive from you one penny! It is enough that you claim no right to exact from him what is his own."

Lord Menteith eagerly supported Allan's opinion, and the elder M'Aulay readily joined, declaring the whole to be a fool's business, and not worth speaking more about. The Englishmen, after some courteous opposition, were persuaded to regard the whole as a joke.

"And now, Allan," said the Laird, "please to remove your candles; for, since the Saxon gentlemen have seen them, they will eat their dinner as comfortably by the light of the old tin sconces, without scomfishing them with so much smoke."

Accordingly, at a sign from Allan, the living chandeliers, recovering their broadswords, and holding the point erect, marched out of the hall, and left the guests to enjoy their refreshment. [Such a bet as that mentioned in the text is said to have been taken by MacDonald of Keppoch, who extricated himself in the manner there narrated.]

CHAPTER V.

Thareby so fearlesse and so fell he grew,
That his own syre and maister of his guise
Did often tremble at his horrid view;
And if for dread of hurt would him advise,
The angry beastes not rashly to despise,
Nor too much to provoke; for he would learne
The lion stoup to him in lowly wise,
(A lesson hard,) and make the libbard sterne
Leave roaring, when in rage he for revenge did earne.
—SPENSER.

Notwithstanding the proverbial epicurism of the English,—proverbial, that is to say, in Scotland at the period,—the English visitors made no figure whatever at the entertainment, compared with the portentous voracity of Captain Dalgetty, although that gallant soldier had already displayed much steadiness and pertinacity in his attack upon the lighter refreshment set before them at their entrance, by way of forlorn hope. He spoke to no one during the time of his meal; and it was not until the victuals were nearly withdrawn from the table, that he gratified the rest of the company, who had watched him with some surprise, with an account of the reasons why he ate so very fast and so very long.

"The former quality," he said, "he had acquired, while he filled a place at the bursar's table at the Mareschal-College of Aberdeen; when," said he; "if you did not move your jaws as fast as a pair of castanets, you were very unlikely to get any thing to put between them. And as for the quantity of my food, be it known to this honourable company," continued the Captain, "that it's the duty of every commander of a fortress, on all occasions which offer, to secure as much munition and vivers as their magazines can possibly hold, not knowing when they may have to sustain a siege or a blockade. Upon which principle, gentlemen," said he, "when a cavalier finds that provant is good and abundant, he will, in my estimation, do wisely to victual himself for at least three days, as there is no knowing when he may come by another meal."

The Laird expressed his acquiescence in the prudence of this principle, and recommended to the veteran to add a tass of brandy and a flagon of claret to the substantial provisions he had already laid in, to which proposal the Captain readily agreed.

When dinner was removed, and the servants had withdrawn, excepting the Laird's page, or henchman, who remained in the apartment to call for or bring whatever was wanted, or, in a word, to answer the purposes of a modern bell-wire, the conversation began to turn upon politics, and the state of the country; and Lord Menteith enquired anxiously and particularly what clans were expected to join the proposed muster of the King's friends.

"That depends much, my lord, on the person who lifts the banner," said the Laird; "for you know we Highlanders, when a few clans are assembled, are not easily commanded by one of our own Chiefs, or, to say the truth, by any other body. We have heard a rumour, indeed, that Colkitto—that is, young Colkitto, or Alaster M'Donald, is come over the Kyle from Ireland, with a body of the Earl of Antrim's people, and that they had got as far as Ardnamurchan. They might have been here before now, but, I suppose, they loitered to plunder the country as they came along."

"Will Colkitto not serve you for a leader, then?" said Lord Menteith.

"Colkitto?" said Allan M'Aulay, scornfully; "who talks of Colkitto?—There lives but one man whom we will follow, and that is Montrose."

"But Montrose, sir," said Sir Christopher Hall, "has not been heard of since our ineffectual attempt to rise in the north of England. It is thought he has returned to the King at Oxford for farther instructions."

"Returned!" said Allan, with a scornful laugh; "I could tell ye, but it is not worth my while; ye will know soon enough."

"By my honour, Allan," said Lord Menteith, "you will weary out your friends with this intolerable, froward, and sullen humour—

But I know the reason," added he, laughing; "you have not seen Annot Lyle to-day."

"Whom did you say I had not seen?" said Allan, sternly.

"Annot Lyle, the fairy queen of song and minstrelsy," said Lord Menteith.

"Would to God I were never to see her again," said Allan, sighing, "On condition the same weird were laid on you!"

"And why on me?" said Lord Menteith, carelessly.

"Because," said Allan, "it is written on your forehead, that you are to be the ruin of each other." So saying, he rose up and left the room.

"Has he been long in this way?" asked Lord Menteith, addressing his brother.

"About three days," answered Angus; "the fit is wellnigh over, he will be better to-morrow.—But come, gentlemen, don't let the tappit-hen scraugh to be emptied. The King's health, King Charles's health! and may the covenanting dog that refuses it, go to Heaven by the road of the Grassmarket!"

The health was quickly pledged, and as fast succeeded by another, and another, and another, all of a party cast, and enforced in an earnest manner. Captain Dalgetty, however, thought it necessary to enter a protest.

"Gentlemen cavaliers," he said, "I drink these healths, PRIMO, both out of respect to this honourable and hospitable roof-tree, and, SECUNDO, because I hold it not good to be preceese in such matters, INTER POCULA; but I protest, agreeable to the warrandice granted by this honourable lord, that it shall be free to me, notwithstanding my present complaisance, to take service with the Covenanters to-morrow, providing I shall be so minded."

M'Aulay and his English guests stared at this declaration, which would have certainly bred new disturbance, if Lord Menteith had not taken up the affair, and explained the circumstances and conditions. "I trust," he concluded, "we shall be able to secure Captain Dalgetty's assistance to our own party."

"And if not," said the Laird, "I protest, as the Captain says, that nothing that has passed this evening, not even his having eaten my bread and salt, and pledged me in brandy, Bourdeaux, or usquebaugh, shall prejudice my cleaving him to the neck-bone."

"You shall be heartily welcome," said the Captain, "providing my sword cannot keep my head, which it has done in worse dangers than your fend is likely to make for me."

Here Lord Menteith again interposed, and the concord of the company being with no small difficulty restored, was cemented by some deep carouses. Lord Menteith, however, contrived to break up the party earlier than was the usage of the Castle, under pretence of fatigue and indisposition. This was somewhat to the disappointment of the valiant Captain, who, among other habits acquired in the Low countries, had acquired both a disposition to drink, and a capacity to bear, an exorbitant quantity of strong liquors.

Their landlord ushered them in person to a sort of sleeping gallery, in which there was a four-post bed, with tartan curtains, and a number of cribs, or long hampers, placed along the wall, three of which, well stuffed with blooming heather, were prepared for the reception of guests.

"I need not tell your lordship," said M'Aulay to Lord Menteith, a little apart, "our Highland mode of quartering. Only that, not liking you should sleep in the room alone with this German land-louper, I have caused your servants' beds to be made here in the gallery. By G—d, my lord, these are times when men go to bed with a throat hale and sound as ever swallowed brandy, and before next morning it may be gaping like an oyster-shell."

Lord Menteith thanked him sincerely, saying, "It was just the arrangement he would have requested; for, although he had not the least apprehension of violence from Captain Dalgetty, yet Anderson was a better kind of person, a sort of gentleman, whom he always liked to have near his person."

"I have not seen this Anderson," said M'Aulay; "did you hire him in England?"

"I did so," said Lord Menteith; "you will see the man to-morrow; in the meantime I wish you good-night."

His host left the apartment after the evening salutation, and was about to pay the same compliment to Captain Dalgetty, but observing him deeply engaged in the discussion of a huge pitcher filled with brandy posset, he thought it a pity to disturb him in so laudable an employment, and took his leave without farther ceremony.

Lord Menteith's two attendants entered the apartment almost immediately after his departure. The good Captain, who was now somewhat encumbered with his good cheer, began to find the undoing of the clasps of his armour a task somewhat difficult, and addressed Anderson in these words, interrupted by a slight hiccup,—"Anderson, my good friend, you may read in Scripture, that he that putteth off his armour should not boast himself like he that putteth it on—I believe that is not the right word of command; but the plain truth of it is, I am like to sleep in my corslet, like many an honest fellow that never waked again, unless you unloose this buckle."

"Undo his armour, Sibbald," said Anderson to the other servant.

"By St. Andrew!" exclaimed the Captain, turning round in great astonishment, "here's a common fellow—a stipendiary with four pounds a-year and a livery cloak, thinks himself too good to serve Ritt-master Dugald Dalgetty of Drumthwacket, who has studied humanity at the Mareschal-College of Aberdeen, and served half the princes of Europe!"

"Captain Dalgetty," said Lord Menteith, whose lot it was to stand peacemaker throughout the evening, "please to understand that Anderson waits upon no one but myself; but I will help Sibbald to undo your corslet with much pleasure."

"Too much trouble for you, my lord," said Dalgetty; "and yet it would do you no harm to practise how a handsome harness is put on and put off. I can step in and out of mine like a glove; only to-night, although not EBRIUS, I am, in the classic phrase, VINO CIBOQUE GRAVATUS."

By this time he was unshelled, and stood before the fire musing with a face of drunken wisdom on the events of the evening. What seemed chiefly to interest him, was the character of Allan M'Aulay. "To come over the Englishmen so cleverly with his Highland torch-bearers—eight bare-breeched Rories for six silver candlesticks!—it was a master-piece—a TOUR DE PASSE—it was perfect legerdemain—and to be a madman after all!—I doubt greatly, my lord" (shaking his head), "that I must allow him, notwithstanding his relationship to your lordship, the privileges of a rational person, and either baton him sufficiently to expiate the violence offered to my person, or else bring it to a matter of mortal arbitrement, as becometh an insulted cavalier."

"If you care to hear a long story," said Lord Menteith, at this time of night, I can tell you how the circumstances of Allan's birth account so well for his singular character, as to put such satisfaction entirely out of the question."

"A long story, my lord," said Captain Dalgetty, "is, next to a good evening draught and a warm nightcap, the best shoeinghorn for drawing on a sound sleep. And since your lordship is pleased to take the trouble to tell it, I shall rest your patient and obliged auditor."

"Anderson," said Lord Menteith, "and you, Sibbald, are dying to hear, I suppose, of this strange man too! and I believe I must indulge your curiosity, that you may know how to behave to him in time of need. You had better step to the fire then."

Having thus assembled an audience about him, Lord Menteith sat down upon the edge of the four-post bed, while Captain Dalgetty, wiping the relics of the posset from his beard and mustachoes, and repeating the first verse of the Lutheran psalm, ALLE GUTER GEISTER LOBEN DEN HERRN, etc. rolled himself into one of the places of repose, and thrusting his shock pate from between the blankets, listened to Lord Menteith's relation in a most luxurious state, between sleeping and waking.

"The father," said Lord Menteith, "of the two brothers, Angus and Allan M'Aulay, was a gentleman of consideration and family, being the chief of a Highland clan, of good account, though not numerous; his lady, the mother of these young men, was a gentlewoman of good family, if I may be permitted to say so of one nearly connected with my own. Her brother, an honourable and spirited young man, obtained from James the Sixth a grant of forestry, and other privileges, over a royal chase adjacent to this castle; and, in exercising and defending these rights, he was so unfortunate as to involve himself in a quarrel with some of our Highland freebooters or caterans, of whom I think, Captain Dalgetty, you must have heard."

"And that I have," said the Captain, exerting himself to answer the appeal. "Before I left the Mareschal-College of Aberdeen, Dugald Garr was playing the devil in the Garioch, and the Farquharsons on Dee-side, and the Clan Chattan on the Gordons' lands, and the Grants and Camerons in Moray-land. And since that, I have seen the Cravats and Pandours in Pannonia and Transylvania, and the Cossacks from the Polish frontier, and robbers, banditti, and barbarians of all countries besides, so that I have a distinct idea of your broken Highlandmen."

"The clan," said Lord Menteith, "with whom the maternal uncle of the M'Aulays had been placed in feud, was a small sept of banditti, called, from their houseless state, and their incessantly wandering among the mountains and glens, the Children of the Mist. They are a fierce and hardy people, with all the irritability, and wild and vengeful passions, proper to men who have never known the restraint of civilized society. A party of them lay in wait for the unfortunate Warden of the Forest, surprised him while hunting alone and unattended, and slew him with every circumstance of inventive cruelty. They cut off his head, and resolved, in a bravado, to exhibit it at the castle of his brother-in-law. The laird was absent, and the lady reluctantly received as guests, men against whom, perhaps, she was afraid to shut her gates. Refreshments were placed before the Children of the Mist, who took an opportunity to take the head of their victim from the plaid in which it was wrapt, placed it on the table, put a piece of bread between the lifeless jaws, bidding them do their office now, since many a good meal they had eaten at that table. The lady, who had been absent for some household purpose, entered at this moment, and, upon beholding her brother's head, fled like an arrow out of the house into the woods, uttering shriek upon shriek. The ruffians, satisfied with this savage triumph, withdrew. The terrified menials, after overcoming the alarm to which they had been subjected, sought their unfortunate mistress in every direction, but she was nowhere to be found. The miserable husband returned next day, and, with the assistance of his people, undertook a more anxious and distant search, but to equally little purpose. It was believed universally, that, in the ecstasy of her terror, she must either have thrown herself over one of the numerous precipices which overhang the river, or into a deep lake about a mile from the castle. Her loss was the more lamented, as she was six months advanced in her pregnancy; Angus M'Aulay, her eldest son, having been born about eighteen months before.—But I tire you, Captain Dalgetty, and you seem inclined to sleep."

"By no means," answered the soldier; "I am no whit somnolent; I always hear best with my eyes shut. It is a fashion I learned when I stood sentinel."

"And I daresay," said Lord Menteith, aside to Anderson, "the weight of the halberd of the sergeant of the rounds often made him open them."

Being apparently, however, in the humour of story-telling, the young nobleman went on, addressing himself chiefly to his servants, without minding the slumbering veteran.

"Every baron in the country," said he, "now swore revenge for this dreadful crime. They took arms with the relations and brother-in-law of the murdered person, and the Children of the Mist were hunted down, I believe, with as little mercy as they had themselves manifested. Seventeen heads, the bloody trophies of their vengeance, were distributed among the allies, and fed the crows upon the gates of their castles. The survivors sought out more distant wildernesses, to which they retreated."

"To your right hand, counter-march and retreat to your former ground," said Captain Dalgetty; the military phrase having produced the correspondent word of command; and then starting up, professed he had been profoundly atttentive to every word that had been spoken.

"It is the custom in summer," said Lord Menteith, without attending to his apology, "to send the cows to the upland pastures to have the benefit of the grass; and the maids of the village, and of the family, go there to milk them in the morning and evening. While thus employed, the females of this family, to their great terror, perceived that their motions were watched at a distance by a pale, thin, meagre figure, bearing a strong resemblance to their deceased mistress, and passing, of course, for her apparition. When some of the boldest resolved to approach this faded form, it fled from them into the woods with a wild shriek. The husband, informed of this circumstance, came up to the glen with some attendants, and took his measures so well as to intercept the retreat of the unhappy fugitive, and to secure the person of his unfortunate lady, though her intellect proved to be totally deranged. How she supported herself during her wandering in the woods could not be known— some supposed she lived upon roots and wild-berries, with which the woods at that season abounded; but the greater part of the vulgar were satisfied that she must have subsisted upon the milk of the wild does, or been nourished by the fairies, or supported in some manner equally marvellous. Her re-appearance was more easily accounted for. She had seen from the thicket the milking of the cows, to superintend which had been her favourite domestic employment, and the habit had prevailed even in her deranged state of mind.

"In due season the unfortunate lady was delivered of a boy, who not only showed no appearance of having suffered from his mother's calamities, but appeared to be an infant of uncommon health and strength. The unhappy mother, after her confinement, recovered her reason—at least in a great measure, but never her health and spirits. Allan was her only joy. Her attention to him was unremitting; and unquestionably she must have impressed upon his early mind many of those superstitious ideas to which his moody and enthusiastic temper gave so ready a reception. She died when he was about ten years old. Her last words were spoken to him in private; but there is little doubt that they conveyed an injunction of vengeance upon the Children of the Mist, with which he has since amply complied.

"From this moment, the habits of Allan M'Aulay were totally changed. He had hitherto been his mother's constant companion, listening to her dreams, and repeating his own, and feeding his imagination, which, probably from the circumstances preceding his birth, was constitutionally deranged, with all the wild and terrible superstitions so common to the mountaineers, to which his unfortunate mother had become much addicted since her brother's death. By living in this manner, the boy had gotten a timid, wild, startled look, loved to seek out solitary places in the woods, and was never so much terrified, as by the approach of children of the same age. I remember, although some years younger, being brought up here by my father upon a visit, nor can I forget the astonishment with which I saw this infant-hermit shun every attempt I made to engage him in the sports natural to our age. I can remember his father bewailing his disposition to mine, and alleging, at the same time, that it was impossible for him to take from his wife the company of the boy, as he seemed to be the only consolation that remained to her in this world, and as the amusement which Allan's society afforded her seemed to prevent the recurrence, at least in its full force, of that fearful malady by which she had been visited. But, after the death of his mother, the habits and manners of the boy seemed at once to change. It is true he remained as thoughtful and serious as before; and long fits of silence and abstraction showed plainly that his disposition, in this respect, was in no degree altered. But at other times, he sought out the rendezvous of the youth of the c]an, which he had hitherto seemed anxious to avoid. He took share in all their exercises; and, from his very extraordinary personal strength, soon excelled his brother and other youths, whose age considerably exceeded his own. They who had hitherto held him in contempt, now feared, if they did not love him; and, instead of Allan's being esteemed a dreaming, womanish, and feeble-minded boy, those who encountered him in sports or military exercise, now complained that, when heated by the strife, he was too apt to turn game into earnest, and to forget that he was only engaged in a friendly trial of strength.—But I speak to regardless ears," said Lord Menteith, interrupting himself, for the Captain's nose now gave the most indisputable signs that he was fast locked in the arms of oblivion.

"If you mean the ears of that snorting swine, my lord," said Anderson, "they are, indeed, shut to anything that you can say; nevertheless, this place being unfit for more private conference, I hope you will have the goodness to proceed, for Sibbald's benefit and for mine. The history of this poor young fellow has a deep and wild interest in it."

"You must know, then," proceeded Lord Menteith, "that Allan continued to increase in strength and activity, till his fifteenth year, about which time he assumed a total independence of character, and impatience of control, which much alarmed his surviving parent. He was absent in the woods for whole days and nights, under pretence of hunting, though he did not always bring home game. His father was the more alarmed, because several of the Children of the Mist, encouraged by the increasing troubles of the state, had ventured back to their old haunts, nor did he think it altogether safe to renew any attack upon them. The risk of Allan, in his wanderings, sustaining injury from these vindictive freebooters, was a perpetual source of apprehension.

"I was myself upon a visit to the castle when this matter was brought to a crisis. Allan had been absent since day-break in the woods, where I had sought for him in vain; it was a dark stormy night, and he did not return. His father expressed the utmost anxiety, and spoke of detaching a party at the dawn of morning in quest of him; when, as we were sitting at the supper-table, the door suddenly opened, and Allan entered the room with a proud, firm, and confident air. His intractability of temper, as well as the unsettled state of his mind, had such an influence over his father, that he suppressed all other tokens of displeasure, excepting the observation that I had killed a fat buck, and had returned before sunset, while he supposed Allan, who had been on the hill till midnight, had returned with empty hands. 'Are you sure of that?' said Allan, fiercely; 'here is something will tell you another tale.'

"We now observed his hands were bloody, and that there were spots of blood on his face, and waited the issue with impatience; when suddenly, undoing the comer of his plaid, he rolled down on the table a human head, bloody and new severed, saying at the same time, 'Lie thou where the head of a better man lay before ye.' From the haggard features, and matted red hair and beard, partly grizzled with age, his father and others present recognised the head of Hector of the Mist, a well-known leader among the outlaws, redoubted for strength and ferocity, who had been active in the murder of the unfortunate Forester, uncle to Allan, and had escaped by a desperate defence and extraordinary agility, when so many of his companions were destroyed. We were all, it may be believed, struck with surprise, but Allan refused to gratify our curiosity; and we only conjectured that he must have overcome the outlaw after a desperate struggle, because we discovered that he had sustained several wounds from the contest. All measures were now taken to ensure him against the vengeance of the freebooters; but neither his wounds, nor the positive command of his father, nor even the locking of the gates of the castle and the doors of his apartment, were precautions adequate to prevent Allan from seeking out the very persons to whom he was peculiarly obnoxious. He made his escape by night from the window of the apartment, and laughing at his father's vain care, produced on one occasion the head of one, and upon another those of two, of the Children of the Mist. At length these men, fierce as they were, became appalled by the inveterate animosity and audacity with which Allan sought out their recesses. As he never hesitated to encounter any odds, they concluded that he must bear a charmed life, or fight under the guardianship of some supernatural influence. Neither gun, dirk, nor dourlach [DOURLACH—quiver; literally, satchel—of arrows.], they said, availed aught against him. They imputed this to the remarkable circumstances under which he was born; and at length five or six of the stoutest caterans of the Highlands would have fled at Allan's halloo, or the blast of his horn.

"In the meanwhile, however, the Children of the Mist carried on their old trade, and did the M'Aulays, as well as their kinsmen and allies, as much mischief as they could. This provoked another expedition against the tribe, in which I had my share; we surprised them effectually, by besetting at once the upper and under passes of the country, and made such clean work as is usual on these occasions, burning and slaying right before us. In this terrible species of war, even the females and the helpless do not always escape. One little maiden alone, who smiled upon Allan's drawn dirk, escaped his vengeance upon my earnest entreaty. She was brought to the castle, and here bred up under the name of Annot Lyle, the most beautiful little fairy certainly that ever danced upon a heath by moonlight. It was long ere Allan could endure the presence of the child, until it occurred to his imagination, from her features perhaps, that she did not belong to the hated blood of his enemies, but had become their captive in some of their incursions; a circumstance not in itself impossible, but in which he believes as firmly as in holy writ. He is particularly delighted by her skill in music, which is so exquisite, that she far exceeds the best performers in this country in playing on the clairshach, or harp. It was discovered that this produced upon the disturbed spirits of Allan, in his gloomiest moods, beneficial effects, similar to those experienced by the Jewish monarch of old; and so engaging is the temper of Annot Lyle, so fascinating the innocence and gaiety of her disposition, that she is considered and treated in the castle rather as the sister of the proprietor, than as a dependent upon his charity. Indeed, it is impossible for any one to see her without being deeply interested by the ingenuity, liveliness, and sweetness of her disposition."

"Take care, my lord," said Anderson, smiling; "there is danger in such violent commendations. Allan M'Aulay, as your lordship describes him, would prove no very safe rival."

"Pooh! pooh!" said Lord Menteith, laughing, yet blushing at the same time; "Allan is not accessible to the passion of love; and for myself," said he, more gravely; "Annot's unknown birth is a sufficient reason against serious designs, and her unprotected state precludes every other."

"It is spoken like yourself, my lord," said Anderson.—"But I trust you will proceed with your interesting story."

"It is wellnigh finished," said Lord Menteith; "I have only to add, that from the great strength and courage of Allan M'Aulay, from his energetic and uncontrollable disposition, and from an opinion generally entertained and encouraged by himself that he holds communion with supernatural beings, and can predict future events, the clan pay a much greater degree of deference to him than even to his brother, who is a bold-hearted rattling Highlander, but with nothing which can possibly rival the extraordinary character of his younger brother."

"Such a character," said Anderson, "cannot but have the deepest effect on the minds of a Highland host. We must secure Allan, my lord, at all events. What between his bravery and his second sight—"

"Hush!" said Lord Menteith, "that owl is awaking."

"Do you talk of the second sight, or DEUTERO-SCOPIA?" said the soldier; "I remember memorable Major Munro telling me how Murdoch Mackenzie, born in Assint, a private gentleman in a company, and a pretty soldier, foretold the death of Donald Tough, a Lochaber man, and certain other persons, as well as the hurt of the major himself at a sudden onfall at the siege of Trailsund."

"I have often heard of this faculty," observed Anderson, "but I have always thought those pretending to it were either enthusiasts or impostors."

"I should be loath," said Lord Menteith, "to apply either character to my kinsman, Allan M'Aulay. He has shown on many occasions too much acuteness and sense, of which you this night had an instance, for the character of an enthusiast; and his high sense of honour, and manliness of disposition, free him from the charge of imposture."

"Your lordship, then," said Anderson, "is a believer in his supernatural attributes?"

"By no means," said the young nobleman; "I think that he persuades himself that the predictions which are, in reality, the result of judgment and reflection, are supernatural impressions on his mind, just as fanatics conceive the workings of their own imagination to be divine inspiration—at least, if this will not serve you, Anderson, I have no better explanation to give; and it is time we were all asleep after the toilsome journey of the day."

CHAPTER VI.

Coming events cast their shadows before.
                                        —CAMPBELL.

At an early hour in the morning the guests of the castle sprung from their repose; and, after a moment's private conversation with his attendants, Lord Menteith addressed the soldier, who was seated in a corner burnishing his corslet with rot-stone and chamois-leather, while he hummed the old song in honour of the victorious Gustavus Adolphus:—

When cannons are roaring, and bullets are flying,
The lad that would have honour, boys, must never fear dying.

"Captain Dalgetty," said Lord Menteith, "the time is come that we must part, or become comrades in service."

"Not before breakfast, I hope?" said Captain Dalgetty.

"I should have thought," replied his lordship, "that your garrison was victualled for three days at least."

"I have still some stowage left for beef and bannocks," said the Captain; "and I never miss a favourable opportunity of renewing my supplies."

"But," said Lord Menteith, "no judicious commander allows either flags of truce or neutrals to remain in his camp longer than is prudent; and therefore we must know your mind exactly, according to which you shall either have a safe-conduct to depart in peace, or be welcome to remain with us."

"Truly," said the Captain, "that being the case, I will not attempt to protract the capitulation by a counterfeited parley, (a thing excellently practised by Sir James Ramsay at the siege of Hannau, in the year of God 1636,) but I will frankly own, that if I like your pay as well as your provant and your company, I care not how soon I take the oath to your colours."

"Our pay," said Lord Menteith, "must at present be small, since it is paid out of the common stock raised by the few amongst us who can command some funds—As major and adjutant, I dare not promise Captain Dalgetty more than half a dollar a-day."

"The devil take all halves and quarters!" said the Captain; "were it in my option, I could no more consent to the halving of that dollar, than the woman in the Judgment of Solomon to the disseverment of the child of her bowels."

"The parallel will scarce hold, Captain Dalgetty, for I think you would rather consent to the dividing of the dollar, than give it up entire to your competitor. However, in the way of arrears, I may promise you the other half-dollar at the end of the campaign."

"Ah! these arrearages!" said Captain Dalgetty, "that are always promised, and always go for nothing! Spain, Austria, and Sweden, all sing one song. Oh! long life to the Hoganmogans! if they were no officers of soldiers, they were good paymasters.— And yet, my lord, if I could but be made certiorate that my natural hereditament of Drumthwacket had fallen into possession of any of these loons of Covenanters, who could be, in the event of our success, conveniently made a traitor of, I have so much value for that fertile and pleasant spot, that I would e'en take on with you for the campaign."

"I can resolve Captain Dalgetty's question," said Sibbald, Lord Menteith's second attendant; "for if his estate of Drumthwacket be, as I conceive, the long waste moor so called, that lies five miles south of Aberdeen, I can tell him it was lately purchased by Elias Strachan, as rank a rebel as ever swore the Covenant"

"The crop-eared hound!" said Captain Dalgetty, in a rage; "What the devil gave him the assurance to purchase the inheritance of a family of four hundred years standing?—CYNTHIUS AUREM VELLET, as we used to say at Mareschal-College; that is to say, I will pull him out of my father's house by the ears. And so, my Lord Menteith, I am yours, hand and sword, body and soul, till death do us part, or to the end of the next campaign, whichever event shall first come to pass."

"And I," said the young nobleman, "rivet the bargain with a month's pay in advance."

"That is more than necessary," said Dalgetty, pocketing the money however. "But now I must go down, look after my war-saddle and abuilziements, and see that Gustavus has his morning, and tell him we have taken new service."

There goes your precious recruit," said Lord Menteith to Anderson, as the Captain left the room; "I fear we shall have little credit of him."

"He is a man of the times, however," said Anderson; "and without such we should hardly be able to carry on our enterprise."

"Let us go down," answered Lord Menteith, "and see how our muster is likely to thrive, for I hear a good deal of bustle in the castle."

When they entered the hall, the domestics keeping modestly in the background, morning greetings passed between Lord Menteith, Angus M'Aulay, and his English guests, while Allan, occupying the same settle which he had filled the preceding evening, paid no attention whatever to any one. Old Donald hastily rushed into the apartment. "A message from Vich Alister More; [The patronymic of MacDonell of Glengarry.] he is coming up in the evening."

"With how many attendants?" said M'Aulay.

"Some five-and-twenty or thirty," said Donald, "his ordinary retinue."

"Shake down plenty of straw in the great barn," said the Laird.

Another servant here stumbled hastily in, announcing the expected approach of Sir Hector M'Lean, "who is arriving with a large following."

"Put them in the malt-kiln," said M'Aulay; "and keep the breadth of the middenstead between them and the M'Donalds; they are but unfriends to each other."

Donald now re-entered, his visage considerably lengthened— "The tell's i' the folk," he said; "the haill Hielands are asteer, I think. Evan Dhu, of Lochiel, will be here in an hour, with Lord kens how many gillies."

"Into the great barn with them beside the M'Donalds," said the Laird.

More and more chiefs were announced, the least of whom would have accounted it derogatory to his dignity to stir without a retinue of six or seven persons. To every new annunciation, Angus

M'Aulay answered by naming some place of accommodation,—the stables, the loft, the cow-house, the sheds, every domestic office, were destined for the night to some hospitable purpose or other. At length the arrival of M'Dougal of Lorn, after all his means of accommodation were exhausted, reduced him to some perplexity. "What the devil is to be done, Donald?" said he; "the great barn would hold fifty more, if they would lie heads and thraws; but there would be drawn dirks amang them which should lie upper-most, and so we should have bloody puddings before morning!"

"What needs all this?" said Allan, starting up, and coming forward with the stern abruptness of his usual manner; "are the Gael to-day of softer flesh or whiter blood than their fathers were? Knock the head out of a cask of usquebae; let that be their night-gear—their plaids their bed-clothes—the blue sky their canopy, and the heather their couch.—Come a thousand more, and they would not quarrel on the broad heath for want of room!"

"Allan is right," said his brother; "it is very odd how Allan, who, between ourselves," said he to Musgrave, "is a little wowf, [WOWF, i.e. crazed.] seems at times to have more sense than us all put together. Observe him now."

"Yes" continued Allan, fixing his eyes with a ghastly stare upon the opposite side of the hall, "they may well begin as they are to end; many a man will sleep this night upon the heath, that when the Martinmas wind shalt blow shall lie there stark enough, and reck little of cold or lack of covering."

"Do not forespeak us, brother," said Angus; "that is not lucky."

"And what luck is it then that you expect?" said Allan; and straining his eyes until they almost started from their sockets, he fell with a convulsive shudder into the arms of Donald and his brother, who, knowing the nature of his fits, had come near to prevent his fall. They seated him upon a bench, and supported him until he came to himself, and was about to speak.

For God's sake, Allan," said his brother, who knew the impression his mystical words were likely to make on many of the guests, "say nothing to discourage us."

"Am I he who discourages you?" said Allan; "let every man face his weird as I shall face mine. That which must come, will come; and we shall stride gallantly over many a field of victory, ere we reach yon fatal slaughter-place, or tread yon sable scaffolds."

"What slaughter-place? what scaffolds?" exclaimed several voices; for Allan's renown as a seer was generally established in the Highlands.

"You will know that but too soon," answered Allan. "Speak to me no more, I am weary of your questions." He then pressed his hand against his brow, rested his elbow upon his knee, and sunk into a deep reverie.

Send for Annot Lyle, and the harp," said Angus, in a whisper, to his servant; "and let those gentlemen follow me who do not fear a Highland breakfast."

All accompanied their hospitable landlord excepting only Lord Menteith, who lingered in one of the deep embrasures formed by the windows of the hall. Annot Lyle shortly after glided into the room, not ill described by Lord Menteith as being the lightest and most fairy figure that ever trode the turf by moonlight. Her stature, considerably less than the ordinary size of women, gave her the appearance of extreme youth, insomuch, that although she was near eighteen, she might have passed for four years younger. Her figure, hands, and feet, were formed upon a model of exquisite symmetry with the size and lightness of her person, so that Titania herself could scarce have found a more fitting representative. Her hair was a dark shade of the colour usually termed flaxen, whose clustering ringlets suited admirably with her fair complexion, and with the playful, yet simple, expression of her features. When we add to these charms, that Annot, in her orphan state, seemed the gayest and happiest of maidens, the reader must allow us to claim for her the interest of almost all who looked on her. In fact, it was impossible to find a more universal favourite, and she often came among the rude inhabitants of the castle, as Allan himself, in a poetical mood, expressed it, "like a sunbeam on a sullen sea," communicating to all others the cheerfulness that filled her own mind.

Annot, such as we have described her, smiled and blushed, when, on entering the apartment, Lord Menteith came from his place of retirement, and kindly wished her good-morning.

"And good-morning to you, my lord," returned she, extending her hand to her friend; "we have seldom seen you of late at the castle, and now I fear it is with no peaceful purpose."

"At least, let me not interrupt your harmony, Annot," said Lord Menteith, "though my arrival may breed discord elsewhere. My cousin Allan needs the assistance of your voice and music."

"My preserver," said Annot Lyle, "has a right to my poor exertions; and you, too, my lord,—you, too, are my preserver, and were the most active to save a life that is worthless enough, unless it can benefit my protectors."

So saying, she sate down at a little distance upon the bench on which Allan M'Aulay was placed, and tuning her clairshach, a small harp, about thirty inches in height, she accompanied it with her voice. The air was an ancient Gaelic melody, and the words, which were supposed to be very old, were in the same language; but we subjoin a translation of them, by Secundus Macpherson, Esq. of Glenforgen, which, although submitted to the fetters of English rhythm, we trust will be found nearly as genuine as the version of Ossian by his celebrated namesake.

> "Birds of omen dark and foul,
> Night-crow, raven, bat, and owl,
> Leave the sick man to his dream—
> All night long he heard your scream—
> Haste to cave and ruin'd tower,
> Ivy, tod, or dingled bower,
> There to wink and mope, for, hark!
> In the mid air sings the lark.
>
> "Hie to moorish gills and rocks,
> Prowling wolf and wily fox,—
> Hie you fast, nor turn your view,
> Though the lamb bleats to the ewe.
> Couch your trains, and speed your flight,
> Safety parts with parting night;
> And on distant echo borne,
> Comes the hunter's early horn.
>
> "The moon's wan crescent scarcely gleams,
> Ghost-like she fades in morning beams;
> Hie hence each peevish imp and fay,
> That scare the pilgrim on his way:—
> Quench, kelpy! quench, in bog and fen,

Thy torch that cheats benighted men;
Thy dance is o'er, thy reign is done,
For Benyieglo hath seen the sun.

"Wild thoughts, that, sinful, dark, and deep,
O'erpower the passive mind in sleep,
Pass from the slumberer's soul away,
Like night-mists from the brow of day:
Foul hag, whose blasted visage grim
Smothers the pulse, unnerves the limb,
Spur thy dark palfrey, and begone!
Thou darest not face the godlike sun."

As the strain proceeded, Allan M'Aulay gradually gave signs of recovering his presence of mind, and attention to the objects around him. The deep-knit furrows of his brow relaxed and smoothed themselves; and the rest of his features, which had seemed contorted with internal agony, relapsed into a more natural state. When he raised his head and sat upright, his countenance, though still deeply melancholy, was divested of its wildness and ferocity; and in its composed state, although by no means handsome, the expression of his features was striking, manly, and even noble. His thick, brown eyebrows, which had hitherto been drawn close together, were now slightly separated, as in the natural state; and his grey eyes, which had rolled and flashed from under them with an unnatural and portentous gleam, now recovered a steady and determined expression.

"Thank God!" he said, after sitting silent for about a minute, until the very last sounds of the harp had ceased to vibrate, "my soul is no longer darkened—the mist hath passed from my spirit."

"You owe thanks, cousin Allan," said Lord Menteith, coming forward, "to Annot Lyle, as well as to heaven, for this happy change in your melancholy mood."

"My noble cousin Menteith," said Allan, rising and greeting him very respectfully, as well as kindly, "has known my unhappy circumstances so long, that his goodness will require no excuse for my being thus late in bidding him welcome to the castle."

"We are too old acquaintances, Allan," said Lord Menteith, "and too good friends, to stand on the ceremonial of outward greeting; but half the Highlands will be here to-day, and you know, with our mountain Chiefs, ceremony must not be neglected. What will you give little Annot for making you fit company to meet Evan Dhu, and I know not how many bonnets and feathers?"

"What will he give me?" said Annot, smiling; "nothing less, I hope, than the best ribbon at the Fair of Doune."

"The Fair of Doune, Annot?" said Allan sadly; "there will be bloody work before that day, and I may never see it; but you have well reminded me of what I have long intended to do."

Having said this, he left the room.

"Should he talk long in this manner," said Lord Menteith, "you must keep your harp in tune, my dear Annot."

"I hope not," said Annot, anxiously; "this fit has been a long one, and probably will not soon return. It is fearful to see a mind, naturally generous and affectionate, afflicted by this constitutional malady."

As she spoke in a low and confidential tone, Lord Menteith naturally drew close, and stooped forward, that he might the better catch the sense of what she said. When Allan suddenly entered the apartment, they as naturally drew back from each other with a manner expressive of consciousness, as if surprised in a conversation which they wished to keep secret from him. This did not escape Allan's observation; he stopt short at the door of the apartment—his brows were contracted—his eyes rolled; but it was only the paroxysm of a moment. He passed his broad sinewy hand across his brow, as if to obliterate these signs of emotion, and advanced towards Annot, holding in his hand a very small box made of oakwood, curiously inlaid. "I take you to witness," he said, "cousin Menteith, that I give this box and its contents to Annot Lyle. It contains a few ornaments that belonged to my poor mother—of trifling value, you may guess, for the wife of a Highland laird has seldom a rich jewel-casket."

"But these ornaments," said Annot Lyle, gently and timidly refusing the box, "belong to the family—I cannot accept—"

"They belong to me alone, Annot," said Allan, interrupting her; "they were my mother's dying bequest. They are all I can call my own, except my plaid and my claymore. Take them, therefore—they are to me valueless trinkets—and keep them for my sake—should I never return from these wars."

So saying, he opened the case, and presented it to Annot. "If," said he, "they are of any value, dispose of them for your own support, when this house has been consumed with hostile fire, and can no longer afford you protection. But keep one ring in memory of Allan, who has done, to requite your kindness, if not all he wished, at least all he could."

Annot Lyle endeavoured in vain to restrain the gathering tears, when she said, "ONE ring, Allan, I will accept from you as a memorial of your goodness to a poor orphan, but do not press me to take more; for I cannot, and will not, accept a gift of such disproportioned value."

"Make your choice, then," said Allan; "your delicacy may be well founded; the others will assume a shape in which they may be more useful to you."

"Think not of it," said Annot, choosing from the contents of the casket a ring, apparently the most trifling in value which it contained; "keep them for your own, or your brother's bride.—But, good heavens!" she said, interrupting herself, and looking at the ring, "what is this that I have chosen?"

Allan hastened to look upon it, with eyes of gloomy apprehension; it bore, in enamel, a death's head above two crossed daggers. When Allan recognised the device, he uttered a sigh so deep, that she dropped the ring from her hand, which rolled upon the floor. Lord Menteith picked it up, and returned it to the terrified Annot.

"I take God to witness," said Allan, in a solemn tone, "that your hand, young lord, and not mine, has again delivered to her this ill-omened gift. It was the mourning ring worn by my mother in memorial of her murdered brother."

"I fear no omens," said Annot, smiling through her tears; "and nothing coming through the hands of my two patrons," so she was wont to call Lord Menteith and Allan, "can bring bad luck to the poor orphan."

She put the ring on her finger, and, turning to her harp, sung, to a lively air, the following verses of one of the fashionable songs of the period, which had found its way, marked as it was with the quaint hyperbolical taste of King Charles's time, from some court masque to the wilds of Perthshire:—

> "Gaze not upon the stars, fond sage,
> In them no influence lies;
> To read the fate of youth or age,
> Look on my Helen's eyes.
>
> "Yet, rash astrologer, refrain!
> Too dearly would be won
> The prescience of another's pain,
> If purchased by thine own."

"She is right, Allan," said Lord Menteith; "and this end of an old song is worth all we shall gain by our attempt to look into futurity."

"She is WRONG, my lord," said Allan, sternly, "though you, who treat with lightness the warnings I have given you, may not live to see the event of the omen.—laugh not so scornfully," he added, interrupting himself "or rather laugh on as loud and as long as you will; your term of laughter will find a pause ere long."

"I care not for your visions, Allan," said Lord Menteith; however short my span of life, the eye of no Highland seer can see its termination."

"For heaven's sake," said Annot Lyle, interrupting him, "you know his nature, and how little he can endure—"

"Fear me not," said Allan, interrupting her,—"my mind is now constant and calm.—But for you, young lord," said he, turning to Lord Menteith, "my eye has sought you through fields of battle, where Highlanders and Lowlanders lay strewed as thick as ever the rooks sat on those ancient trees," pointing to a rookery which was seen from the window—"my eye sought you, but your corpse was not there—my eye sought you among a train of unresisting and disarmed captives, drawn up within the bounding walls of an ancient and rugged fortress;—flash after flash—platoon after platoon—the hostile shot fell amongst them, They dropped like the dry leaves in autumn, but you were not among their ranks;—scaffolds were prepared—blocks were arranged, saw-dust was spread—the priest was ready with his book, the headsman with his axe—but there, too, mine eye found you not."

"The gibbet, then, I suppose, must be my doom?" said Lord Menteith. "Yet I wish they had spared me the halter, were it but for the dignity of the peerage."

He spoke this scornfully, yet not without a sort of curiosity, and a wish to receive an answer; for the desire of prying into futurity frequently has some influence even on the minds of those who disavow all belief in the possibility of such predictions.

"Your rank, my lord, will suffer no dishonour in your person, or by the manner of your death. Three times have I seen a Highlander plant his dirk in your bosom—and such will be your fate."

"I wish you would describe him to me," said Lord Menteith, "and I shall save him the trouble of fulfilling your prophecy, if his plaid be passible to sword or pistol."

"Your weapons," said Allan, "would avail you little; nor can I give you the information you desire. The face of the vision has been ever averted from me."

"So be it then," said Lord Menteith, "and let it rest in the uncertainty in which your augury has placed it. I shall dine not the less merrily among plaids, and dirks, and kilts to-day."

"It may be so," said Allan; "and, it may be, you do well to enjoy these moments, which to me are poisoned by auguries of future evil. But I," he continued—"I repeat to you, that this weapon—that is, such a weapon as this," touching the hilt of the dirk which he wore, "carries your fate." "In the meanwhile," said Lord Menteith, "you, Allan, have frightened the blood from the cheeks of Annot Lyle—let us leave this discourse, my friend, and go to see what we both understand,—the progress of our military preparations."

They joined Angus M'Aulay and his English guests, and, in the military discussions which immediately took place, Allan showed a clearness of mind, strength of judgment, and precision of thought, totally inconsistent with the mystical light in which his character has been hitherto exhibited.

CHAPTER VII.

When Albin her claymore indignantly draws,
When her bonneted chieftains around her shall crowd,
Clan-Ranald the dauntless, and Moray the proud,
All plaided and plumed in their tartan array
              —LOCHEIL'S WARNING.

Whoever saw that morning, the Castle of Darnlinvarach, beheld a busy and a gallant sight.

The various Chiefs, arriving with their different retinues, which, notwithstanding their numbers, formed no more than their usual equipage and body-guard upon occasions of solemnity, saluted the lord of the castle and each other with overflowing kindness, or with haughty and distant politeness, according to the circumstances of friendship or hostility in which their clans had recently stood to each other. Each Chief, however small his comparative importance, showed the full disposition to exact from the rest the deference due to a separate and independent prince; while the stronger and more powerful, divided among themselves by recent contentions or ancient feuds, were constrained in policy to use great deference to the feelings of their less powerful brethren, in order, in case of need, to attach as many well-wishers as might be to their own interest and standard. Thus the meeting of Chiefs resembled not a little those ancient Diets of the Empire, where the smallest FREY-GRAF, who possessed a castle perched upon a barren crag, with a few hundred acres around it, claimed the state and honours of a sovereign prince, and a seat according to his rank among the dignitaries of the Empire.

The followers of the different leaders were separately arranged and accommodated, as room and circumstances best permitted, each retaining however his henchman, who waited, close as the shadow, upon his person, to execute whatever might be required by his patron.

The exterior of the castle afforded a singular scene. The Highlanders, from different islands, glens, and straths, eyed each other at a distance with looks of emulation, inquisitive curiosity, or hostile malevolence; but the most astounding part of the assembly, at least to a Lowland ear, was the rival performance of the bagpipers. These warlike minstrels, who had the highest opinion, each, of the superiority of his own tribe, joined to the most overweening idea of the importance connected with his profession, at first, performed their various pibrochs in front each of his own clan. At length, however, as the black-cocks towards the end of the season, when, in sportsman's language, they are said to flock or crowd, attracted together by the sound of each others' triumphant crow, even so did the pipers, swelling their plaids and tartans in the same triumphant manner in which the birds ruffle up their feathers, begin to approach each other within such distance as might give to their brethren a sample of their skill. Walking within a short interval, and eyeing each other with looks in which self-importance and defiance might be traced, they strutted, puffed, and plied their screaming instruments, each playing his own favourite tune with such a din, that if an Italian musician had lain buried within ten miles of them, he must have risen from the dead to run out of hearing.

The Chieftains meanwhile had assembled in close conclave in the great hall of the castle. Among them were the persons of the greatest consequence in the Highlands, some of them attracted by zeal for the royal cause, and many by aversion to that severe and general domination which the Marquis of Argyle, since his rising to such influence in the state, had exercised over his Highland neighbours. That statesman, indeed, though possessed of considerable abilities, and great power, had failings, which rendered him unpopular among the Highland chiefs. The devotion which he professed was of a morose and fanatical character; his ambition appeared to be insatiable, and inferior chiefs complained of his want of bounty and liberality. Add to this, that although a Highlander, and of a family distinguished for valour before and since, Gillespie Grumach [GRUMACH—ill-favored.] (which, from an obliquity in his eyes, was the personal distinction he bore in the Highlands, where titles of rank are unknown) was suspected of being a better man in the cabinet than in the field. He and his tribe were particularly obnoxious to the M'Donalds and the M'Leans, two numerous septs, who, though disunited by ancient feuds, agreed in an intense dislike to the Campbells, or, as they were called, the Children of Diarmid.

For some time the assembled Chiefs remained silent, until some one should open the business of the meeting. At length one of the most powerful of them commenced the diet by saying,— "We have been summoned hither, M'Aulay, to consult of weighty matters concerning the King's affairs, and those of the state; and we crave to know by whom they are to be explained to us?"

M'Aulay, whose strength did not lie in oratory, intimated his wish that Lord Menteith should open the business of the council. With great modesty, and at the same time with spirit, that young lord said,"he wished what he was about to propose had come from some person of better known and more established character. Since, however, it lay with him to be spokesman, he had to state to the Chiefs assembled, that those who wished to throw off the base yoke which fanaticism had endeavoured to wreath round their necks, had not a moment to lose. "The Covenanters," he said, "after having twice made war upon their sovereign, and having extorted from him every request, reasonable or unreasonable, which they thought proper to demand—after their Chiefs had been loaded with dignities and favours—after having publicly declared, when his Majesty, after a gracious visit to the land of his nativity, was upon his return to England, that he returned a contented king from a contented people,—after all this, and without even the pretext for a national grievance, the same men have, upon doubts and suspicions, equally dishonourable to the King, and groundless in themselves, detached a strong army to assist his rebels in England, in a quarrel with which Scotland had no more to do than she has with the wars in Germany. It was well," he said, "that the eagerness with which this treasonable purpose was pursued, had blinded the junta who now usurped the government of Scotland to the risk which they were about to incur. The army which they had dispatched to England under old Leven comprehended their veteran soldiers, the strength of those armies which had been levied in Scotland during the two former wars—"

Here Captain Dalgetty endeavoured to rise, for the purpose of explaining how many veteran officers, trained in the German wars, were, to his certain knowledge, in the army of the Earl of Leven. But Allan M'Aulay holding him down in his seat with one hand, pressed the fore-finger of the other upon his own lips, and, though with some difficulty, prevented his interference. Captain Dalgetty looked upon him with a very scornful and indignant air, by which the other's gravity was in no way moved, and Lord Menteith proceeded without farther interruption.

"The moment," he said, "was most favourable for all true-hearted and loyal Scotchmen to show, that the reproach their country had lately undergone arose from the selfish ambition of a few turbulent and seditious men, joined to the absurd fanaticism which, disseminated from five hundred pulpits, had spread like a land-flood over the Lowlands of Scotland. He had letters from the Marquis of Huntly in the north, which he should show to the Chiefs separately. That nobleman, equally loyal and powerful was determined to exert his utmost energy in the common cause, and the powerful Earl of Seaforth was prepared to join the same standard. From the Earl of Airly, and the Ogilvies in Angusshire, he had had communications equally decided; and there was no doubt that these, who, with the Hays, Leiths, Burnets, and other loyal gentlemen, would be soon on horseback, would form a body far more than sufficient to overawe the northern Covenanters, who had already experienced their valour in the well-known rout which was popularly termed the Trot of Turiff. South of Forth and Tay," he said, "the King had many friends, who, oppressed by enforced oaths, compulsory levies, heavy taxes, unjustly imposed and unequally levied, by the tyranny of the Committee of Estates, and the inquisitorial insolence of the Presbyterian divines, waited but the waving of the royal banner to take up arms. Douglas, Traquair, Roxburgh, Hume, all friendly to the royal cause, would counterbalance," he said, "the covenanting interest in the south; and two gentlemen, of name and quality, here present, from the north of England, would answer for the zeal of Cumberland, Westmoreland, and Northumberland. Against so many gallant gentlemen the southern Covenanters could but arm raw levies; the Whigamores of the western shires, and the ploughmen and mechanics of the Low-country. For the West Highlands, he knew no interest which the Covenanters possessed there, except that of one individual, as well known as he was odious. But was there a single man, who, on casting his eye round this hall, and recognising the power, the gallantry, and the dignity of the chiefs assembled, could entertain a moment's doubt of their success against the utmost force which Gillespie Grumach could collect against them? He had only farther to add, that considerable funds, both of money and ammunition, had been provided for the army"—(Here Dalgetty pricked up his ears)—"that officers of ability and experience in the foreign wars, one of whom was now present," (the Captain drew himself up, and looked round,) "had engaged to train such levies as might require to be disciplined;—and that a numerous body of auxiliary forces from Ireland, having been detached from the Earl of Antrim, from Ulster, had successfully accomplished their descent upon the main land, and, with the assistance of Clanranald's people, having taken and fortified the Castle of Mingarry, in spite of Argyle's attempts to intercept them, were in full march to this place of rendezvous. It only remained," he said, "that the noble Chiefs assembled, laying aside every lesser consideration, should unite, heart and hand, in the common cause; send the fiery cross through their clans, in order to collect their utmost force, and form their junction with such celerity as to leave the enemy no time, either for preparation, or recovery from the panic which would spread at the first sound of their pibroch. He himself," he said, "though neither among the richest nor the most powerful of the Scottish nobility, felt that he had to support the dignity of an ancient and honourable house, the independence of an ancient and honourable nation, and to that cause he was determined to devote both life and fortune. If those who were more powerful were equally prompt, he trusted they would deserve the thanks of their King, and the gratitude of posterity."

Loud applause followed this speech of Lord Menteith, and testified the general acquiescence of all present in the sentiments which he had expressed; but when the shout had died away, the assembled Chiefs continued to gaze upon each other as if something yet remained to be settled. After some whispers among themselves, an aged man, whom his grey hairs rendered respectable, although he was not of the highest order of Chiefs, replied to what had been said.

"Thane of Menteith," he said, "you have well spoken; nor is there one of us in whose bosom the same sentiments do not burn like fire. But it is not strength alone that wins the fight; it is the head of the commander, as well as the arm of the soldier, that brings victory. I ask of you who is to raise and sustain the banner under which we are invited to rise and muster ourselves? Will it be expected that we should risk our children, and the flower of our kinsmen, ere we know to whose guidance they are to be intrusted? This were leading those to slaughter, whom, by the laws of God and man, it is our duty to protect. Where is the royal commission, under which the lieges are to be convocated in arms? Simple and rude as we may be deemed, we know something of the established rules of war, as well as of the laws of our country; nor will we arm ourselves against the general peace of Scotland, unless by the express commands of the King, and under a leader fit to command such men as are here assembled."

"Where would you find such a leader," said another Chief, starting up, "saving the representative of the Lord of the Isles, entitled by birth and hereditary descent to lead forth the array of every clan of the Highlands; and where is that dignity lodged, save in the house of Vich Alister More?"

"I acknowledge," said another Chief, eagerly interrupting the speaker, "the truth in what has been first said, but not the inference. If Vich Alister More desires to be held representative of the Lord of the Isles, let him first show his blood is redder than mine."

"That is soon tried," said Vich Alister More, laying his hand upon the basket hilt of his claymore. Lord Menteith threw himself between them, entreating and imploring each to remember that the interests of Scotland, the liberty of their country, and the cause of their King, ought to be superior in their eyes to any personal disputes respecting descent, rank, and precedence. Several of the Highland Chiefs, who had no desire to admit the claims of either chieftain, interfered to the same purpose, and none with more emphasis than the celebrated Evan Dhu.

"I have come from my lakes," he said, "as a stream descends from the hills, not to turn again, but to accomplish my course. It is not by looking back to our own pretensions that we shall serve Scotland or King Charles. My voice shall be for that general whom the King shall name, who will doubtless possess those qualities which are necessary to command men like us. High-born he must be, or we shall lose our rank in obeying him—wise and skilful, or we shall endanger the safety of our people—bravest among the brave, or we shall peril our own honour—temperate, firm, and manly, to keep us united. Such is the man that must command us. Are you prepared, Thane of Menteith, to say where such a general is to be found?"

"There is but ONE," said Allan M'Aulay; "and here," he said, laying his hand upon the shoulder of Anderson, who stood behind Lord Menteith, "here he stands!"

The general surprise of the meeting was expressed by an impatient murmur; when Anderson, throwing back the cloak in which his face was muffled, and stepping forward, spoke thus:— "I did not long intend to be a silent spectator of this interesting scene, although my hasty friend has obliged me to disclose myself somewhat sooner than was my intention. Whether I deserve the honour reposed in me by this parchment will best appear from what I shall be able to do for the King's service. It is a commission under the great seal, to James Graham, Earl of Montrose, to command those forces which are to be assembled for the service of his Majesty in this kingdom."

A loud shout of approbation burst from the assembly. There was, in fact, no other person to whom, in point of rank, these proud mountaineers would have been disposed to submit. His inveterate and hereditary hostility to the Marquis of Argyle insured his engaging in the war with sufficient energy, while his well-known military talents, and his tried valour, afforded every hope of his bringing it to a favourable conclusion.

CHAPTER VIII.

Our plot is a good plot as ever was laid; our friends
true and constant: a good plot, good friends, and full of
expectation: an excellent plot, very good friends.
—HENRY IV Part I.

No sooner had the general acclamation of joyful surprise
subsided, than silence was eagerly demanded for reading the royal
commission; and the bonnets, which hitherto each Chief had worn,
probably because unwilling to be the first to uncover, were now at
once vailed in honour of the royal warrant. It was couched in the
most full and ample terms, authorizing the Earl of Montrose to
assemble the subjects in arms, for the putting down the present
rebellion, which divers traitors and seditious persons had levied
against the King, to the manifest forfaulture, as it stated, of their
allegiance, and to the breach of the pacification between the two
kingdoms. It enjoined all subordinate authorities to be obedient
and assisting to Montrose in his enterprise; gave him the power of
making ordinances and proclamations, punishing misdemeanours,
pardoning criminals, placing and displacing governors and
commanders. In fine, it was as large and full a commission as any
with which a prince could intrust a subject. As soon as it was finished,
a shout burst from the assembled Chiefs, in testimony of their
ready submission to the will of their sovereign. Not contented with
generally thanking them for a reception so favourable, Montrose
hastened to address himself to individuals, The most important
Chiefs had already been long personally known to him, but even
to those of inferior consequence he now introduced himself and
by the acquaintance he displayed with their peculiar designations,
and the circumstances and history of their clans, he showed how

long he must have studied the character of the mountaineers, and prepared himself for such a situation as he now held.

While he was engaged in these acts of courtesy, his graceful manner, expressive features, and dignity of deportment, made a singular contrast with the coarseness and meanness of his dress. Montrose possessed that sort of form and face, in which the beholder, at the first glance, sees nothing extraordinary, but of which the interest becomes more impressive the longer we gaze upon them. His stature was very little above the middle size, but in person he was uncommonly well-built, and capable both of exerting great force, and enduring much fatigue. In fact, he enjoyed a constitution of iron, without which he could not have sustained the trials of his extraordinary campaigns, through all of which he subjected himself to the hardships of the meanest soldier. He was perfect in all exercises, whether peaceful or martial, and possessed, of course, that graceful ease of deportment proper to those to whom habit has rendered all postures easy.

His long brown hair, according to the custom of men of quality among the Royalists, was parted on the top of his head, and trained to hang down on each side in curled locks, one of which, descending two or three inches lower than the others, intimated Montrose's compliance with that fashion against which it pleased Mr. Prynne, the puritan, to write a treatise, entitled, THE UNLOVELINESS OF LOVE-LOCKS. The features which these tresses enclosed, were of that kind which derive their interest from the character of the man, rather than from the regularity of their form. But a high nose, a full, decided, well-opened, quick grey eye, and a sanguine complexion, made amends for some coarseness and irregularity in the subordinate parts of the face; so that, altogether, Montrose might be termed rather a handsome, than a hard-featured man. But those who saw him when his soul looked through those eyes with all the energy and fire of genius—those who heard him speak with the authority of talent, and the eloquence of nature, were impressed with an opinion even of his external form, more enthusiastically favourable than the portraits which still survive would entitle us to ascribe to it. Such, at least, was the impression he made upon the assembled Chiefs of the mountaineers, over whom, as upon all persons in their state of society, personal appearance has no small influence.

In the discussions which followed his discovering himself, Montrose explained the various risks which he had run in his present undertaking. His first attempt had been to assemble a body of loyalists in the north of England, who, in obedience to the orders of the Marquis of Newcastle, he expected would have marched into Scotland; but the disinclination of the English to cross the Border, and the delay of the Earl of Antrim, who was to have landed in the Solway Frith with his Irish army, prevented his executing this design. Other plans having in like manner failed, he stated that he found himself under the necessity of assuming a disguise to render his passage secure through the Lowlands, in which he had been kindly assisted by his kinsman of Menteith. By what means Allan M'Aulay had come to know him, he could not pretend to explain. Those who knew Allan's prophetic pretensions, smiled mysteriously; but he himself only replied, that "the Earl of Montrose need not be surprised if he was known to thousands, of whom he himself could retain no memory."

"By the honour of a cavalier," said Captain Dalgetty, finding at length an opportunity to thrust in his word, "I am proud and happy in having an opportunity of drawing a sword under your lordship's command; and I do forgive all grudge, malecontent, and malice of my heart, to Mr. Allan M'Aulay, for having thrust me down to the lowest seat of the board yestreen. Certes, he hath this day spoken so like a man having full command of his senses, that I had resolved in my secret purpose that he was no way entitled to claim the privilege of insanity. But since I was only postponed to a noble earl, my future commander-in-chief, I do, before you all, recognise the justice of the preference, and heartily salute Allan as one who is to be his BON-CAMARADO."

Having made this speech, which was little understood or attended to, without putting off his military glove, he seized on Allan's hand, and began to shake it with violence, which Allan, with a gripe like a smith's vice, returned with such force, as to drive the iron splents of the gauntlet into the hand of the wearer.

Captain Dalgetty might have construed this into a new affront, had not his attention, as he stood blowing and shaking the injured member, been suddenly called by Montrose himself.

"Hear this news," he said, "Captain Dalgetty—I should say Major Dalgetty,—the Irish, who are to profit by your military experience, are now within a few leagues of us."

"Our deer-stalkers," said Angus M'Aulay, "who were abroad to bring in venison for this honourable party, have heard of a band of strangers, speaking neither Saxon nor pure Gaelic, and with difficulty making themselves understood by the people of the country, who are marching this way in arms, under the leading, it is said, of Alaster M'Donald, who is commonly called Young Colkitto."

"These must be our men," said Montrose; "we must hasten to send messengers forward, both to act as guides and to relieve their wants."

"The last," said Angus M'Aulay, "will be no easy matter; for I am informed, that, excepting muskets and a very little ammunition, they want everything that soldiers should have; and they are particularly deficient in money, in shoes, and in raiment."

"There is at least no use in saying so," said Montrose, "in so loud a tone. The puritan weavers of Glasgow shall provide them plenty of broad-cloth, when we make a descent from the Highlands; and if the ministers could formerly preach the old women of the Scottish boroughs out of their webs of napery, to make tents to the fellows on Dunse Law, [The Covenanters encamped on Dunse Law, during the troubles of 1639.] I will try whether I have not a little interest both to make these godly dames renew their patriotic gift, and the prick-eared knaves, their husbands, open their purses."

"And respecting arms," said Captain Dalgetty, "if your lordship will permit an old cavalier to speak his mind, so that the one-third have muskets, my darling weapon would be the pike for the remainder, whether for resisting a charge of horse, or for breaking the infantry. A common smith will make a hundred pike-heads in a day; here is plenty of wood for shafts; and I will uphold, that, according to the best usages of war, a strong battalion of pikes, drawn up in the fashion of the Lion of the North, the immortal Gustavus, would beat the Macedonian phalanx, of which I used to read in the Mareschal-College, when I studied in the ancient town of Bon-accord; and further, I will venture to predicate—"

The Captain's lecture upon tactics was here suddenly interrupted by Allan M'Aulay, who said, hastily,—"Room for an unexpected and unwelcome guest!"

At the same moment, the door of the hall opened, and a grey-haired man, of a very stately appearance, presented himself to the assembly. There was much dignity, and even authority, in his manner. His stature was above the common size, and his looks such as were used to command. He cast a severe, and almost stern glance upon the assembly of Chiefs. Those of the higher rank among them returned it with scornful indifference; but some of the western gentlemen of inferior power, looked as if they wished themselves elsewhere.

"To which of this assembly," said the stranger, "am I to address myself as leader? or have you not fixed upon the person who is to hold an office at least as perilous as it is honourable?"

"Address yourself to me, Sir Duncan Campbell," said Montrose, stepping forward.

"To you!" said Sir Duncan Campbell, with some scorn.

"Yes,—to me," repeated Montrose,—"to the Earl of Montrose, if you have forgot him."

"I should now, at least," said Sir Duncan Campbell, "have had some difficulty in recognising him in the disguise of a groom.— and yet I might have guessed that no evil influence inferior to your lordship's, distinguished as one who troubles Israel, could have collected together this rash assembly of misguided persons."

"I will answer unto you," said Montrose, "in the manner of your own Puritans. I have not troubled Israel, but thou and thy father's house. But let us leave an altercation, which is of little consequence but to ourselves, and hear the tidings you have brought from your Chief of Argyle; for I must conclude that it is in his name that you have come to this meeting."

"It is in the name of the Marquis of Argyle," said Sir Duncan Campbell,—" in the name of the Scottish Convention of Estates, that I demand to know the meaning of this singular convocation. If it is designed to disturb the peace of the country, it were but acting like neighbours, and men of honour, to give us some intimation to stand upon our guard."

"It is a singular, and new state of affairs in Scotland," said Montrose, turning from Sir Duncan Campbell to the assembly, "when Scottish men of rank and family cannot meet in the house of a common friend without an inquisitorial visit and demand, on the part of our rulers, to know the subject of our conference. Methinks our ancestors were accustomed to hold Highland huntings, or other purposes of meeting, without asking the leave either of the great M'Callum More himself, or any of his emissaries or dependents."

"The times have been such in Scotland," answered one of the Western Chiefs, "and such they will again be, when the intruders on our ancient possessions are again reduced to be Lairds of Lochow instead of overspreading us like a band of devouring locusts."

"Am I to understand, then," said Sir Duncan, that it is against my name alone that these preparations are directed? or are the race of Diarmid only to be sufferers in common with the whole of the peaceful and orderly inhabitants of Scotland?"

"I would ask," said a wild-looking Chief, starting hastily up, "one question of the Knight of Ardenvohr, ere he proceeds farther in his daring catechism.—Has he brought more than one life to this castle, that he ventures to intrude among us for the purposes of insult?"

"Gentlemen," said Montrose, "let me implore your patience; a messenger who comes among us for the purpose of embassy, is entitled to freedom of speech and safe-conduct. And since Sir Duncan Campbell is so pressing, I care not if I inform him, for his guidance, that he is in an assembly of the King's loyal subjects, convoked by me, in his Majesty's name and authority, and as empowered by his Majesty's royal commission."

"We are to have, then, I presume," said Sir Duncan Campbell, "a civil war in all its forms? I have been too long a soldier to view its approach with anxiety; but it would have been for my Lord of Montrose's honour, if, in this matter, he had consulted his own ambition less, and the peace of the country more."

"Those consulted their own ambition and self-interest, Sir Duncan," answered Montrose, "who brought the country to the pass in which it now stands, and rendered necessary the sharp remedies which we are now reluctantly about to use."

"And what rank among these self-seekers," said Sir Duncan Campbell, "we shall assign to a noble Earl, so violently attached to the Covenant, that he was the first, in 1639, to cross the Tyne, wading middle deep at the head of his regiment, to charge the royal forces? It was the same, I think, who imposed the Covenant upon the burgesses and colleges of Aberdeen, at the point of sword and pike."

"I understand your sneer, Sir Duncan," said Montrose, temperately; "and I can only add, that if sincere repentance can make amends for youthful error, and for yielding to the artful representation of ambitious hypocrites, I shall be pardoned for the crimes with which you taunt me. I will at least endeavour to deserve forgiveness, for I am here, with my sword in my hand, willing to spend the best blood of my body to make amends for my error; and mortal man can do no more."

"Well, my lord," said Sir Duncan, "I shall be sorry to carry back this language to the Marquis of Argyle. I had it in farther charge from the Marquis, that, to prevent the bloody feuds which must necessarily follow a Highland war, his lordship will be contented if terms of truce could be arranged to the north of the Highland line, as there is ground enough in Scotland to fight upon, without neighbours destroying each other's families and inheritances."

"It is a peaceful proposal," said Montrose, smiling," such as it should be, coming from one whose personal actions have always been more peaceful than his measures. Yet, if the terms of such a truce could be equally fixed, and if we can obtain security, for that, Sir Duncan, is indispensable,—that your Marquis will observe these terms with strict fidelity, I, for my part, should be content to leave peace behind us, since we must needs carry war before us. But, Sir Duncan, you are too old and experienced a soldier for us to permit you to remain in our leaguer, and witness our proceedings; we shall therefore, when you have refreshed yourself, recommend your speedy return to Inverary, and we shall send with you a gentleman on our part to adjust the terms of the Highland armistice, in case the Marquis shall be found serious in proposing such a measure." Sir Duncan Campbell assented by a bow.

"My Lord of Menteith," continued Montrose, "will you have the goodness to attend Sir Duncan Campbell of Ardenvohr, while we determine who shall return with him to his Chief? M'Aulay will permit us to request that he be entertained with suitable hospitality."

"I will give orders for that," said Allan M'Aulay, rising and coming forward. "I love Sir Duncan Campbell; we have been joint sufferers in former days, and I do not forget it now."

"My Lord of Menteith," said Sir Duncan Campbell, "I am grieved to see you, at your early age, engaged in such desperate and rebellious courses."

"I am young," answered Menteith, "yet old enough to distinguish between right and wrong, between loyalty and rebellion; and the sooner a good course is begun, the longer and the better have I a chance of running it."

"And you too, my friend, Allan M'Aulay," said Sir Duncan, taking his hand, "must we also call each other enemies, that have been so often allied against a common foe?" Then turning round to the meeting, he said, "Farewell, gentlemen; there are so many of you to whom I wish well, that your rejection of all terms of mediation gives me deep affliction. May Heaven," he said, looking upwards, "judge between our motives, and those of the movers of this civil commotion!"

"Amen," said Montrose; "to that tribunal we all submit us."

Sir Duncan Campbell left the hall, accompanied by Allan M'Aulay and Lord Menteith. "There goes a true-bred Campbell," said Montrose, as the envoy departed, "for they are ever fair and false."

"Pardon me, my lord," said Evan Dhu; "hereditary enemy as I am to their name, I have ever found the Knight of Ardenvohr brave in war, honest in peace, and true in council."

"Of his own disposition," said Montrose, "such he is undoubtedly; but he now acts as the organ or mouth-piece of his Chief, the Marquis, the falsest man that ever drew breath. And, M'Aulay," he continued in a whisper to his host, "lest he should make some impression upon the inexperience of Menteith, or the singular disposition of your brother, you had better send music into their chamber, to prevent his inveigling them into any private conference."

"The devil a musician have I," answered M'Aulay, "excepting the piper, who has nearly broke his wind by an ambitious contention for superiority with three of his own craft; but I can send Annot Lyle and her harp." And he left the apartment to give orders accordingly.

Meanwhile a warm discussion took place, who should undertake the perilous task of returning with Sir Duncan to Inverary. To the higher dignitaries, accustomed to consider themselves upon an equality even with M'Callum More, this was an office not to be proposed; unto others who could not plead the same excuse, it was altogether unacceptable. One would have thought Inverary had been the Valley of the Shadow of Death, the inferior chiefs showed such reluctance to approach it. After a considerable hesitation, the plain reason was at length spoken out, namely, that whatever Highlander should undertake an office so distasteful to M'Callum More, he would be sure to treasure the offence in his remembrance, and one day or other to make him bitterly repent of it.

In this dilemma, Montrose, who considered the proposed armistice as a mere stratagem on the part of Argyle, although he had not ventured bluntly to reject it in presence of those whom it concerned so nearly, resolved to impose the danger and dignity upon Captain Dalgetty, who had neither clan nor estate in the Highlands upon which the wrath of Argyle could wreak itself.

"But I have a neck though," said Dalgetty, bluntly; "and what if he chooses to avenge himself upon that? I have known a case where an honourable ambassador has been hanged as a spy before now. Neither did the Romans use ambassadors much more mercifully at the siege of Capua, although I read that they only cut off their hands and noses, put out their eyes, and suffered them to depart in peace."

"By my honour Captain Dalgetty," said Montrose, "should the Marquis, contrary to the rules of war, dare to practise any atrocity against you, you may depend upon my taking such signal vengeance that all Scotland shall ring of it."

"That will do but little for Dalgetty," returned the Captain; "but corragio! as the Spaniard says. With the Land of Promise full in view, the Moor of Drumthwacket, MEA PAUPERA REGNA, as we said at Mareschal-College, I will not refuse your Excellency's commission, being conscious it becomes a cavalier of honour to obey his commander's orders, in defiance both of gibbet and sword."

"Gallantly resolved," said Montrose; "and if you will come apart with me, I will furnish you with the conditions to be laid before M'Callum More, upon which we are willing to grant him a truce for his Highland dominions."

With these we need not trouble our readers. They were of an evasive nature, calculated to meet a proposal which Montrose considered to have been made only for the purpose of gaining time. When he had put Captain Dalgetty in complete possession of his instructions, and when that worthy, making his military obeisance, was near the door of his apartment, Montrose made him a sign to return.

"I presume," said he, "I need not remind an officer who has served under the great Gustavus, that a little more is required of a person sent with a flag of truce than mere discharge of his instructions, and that his general will expect from him, on his return, some account of the state of the enemy's affairs, as far as they come under his observation. In short, Captain Dalgetty, you must be UN PEU CLAIR-VOYANT."

"Ah ha! your Excellency," said the Captain, twisting his hard features into an inimitable expression of cunning and intelligence, "if they do not put my head in a poke, which I have known practised upon honourable soldados who have been suspected to come upon such errands as the present, your Excellency may rely on a preceese narration of whatever Dugald Dalgetty shall hear or see, were it even how many turns of tune there are in M'Callum More's pibroch, or how many checks in the sett of his plaid and trews."

"Enough," answered Montrose; "farewell, Captain Dalgetty: and as they say that a lady's mind is always expressed in her postscript, so I would have you think that the most important part of your commission lies in what I have last said to you."

Dalgetty once more grinned intelligence, and withdrew to victual his charger and himself, for the fatigues of his approaching mission.

At the door of the stable, for Gustavus always claimed his first care,—he met Angus M'Aulay and Sir Miles Musgrave, who had been looking at his horse; and, after praising his points and carriage, both united in strongly dissuading the Captain from taking an animal of such value with him upon his present very fatiguing journey.

Angus painted in the most alarming colours the roads, or rather wild tracks, by which it would be necessary for him to travel into Argyleshire, and the wretched huts or bothies where he would be condemned to pass the night, and where no forage could be procured for his horse, unless he could eat the stumps of old heather. In short, he pronounced it absolutely impossible, that, after undertaking such a pilgrimage, the animal could be in any case for military service. The Englishman strongly confirmed all that Angus had said, and gave himself, body and soul, to the devil, if he thought it was not an act little short of absolute murder to carry a horse worth a farthing into such a waste and inhospitable desert. Captain Dalgetty for an instant looked steadily, first at one of the gentlemen and next at the other, and then asked them, as if in a state of indecision, what they would advise him to do with Gustavus under such circumstances.

"By the hand of my father, my dear friend," answered M'Aulay, "if you leave the beast in my keeping, you may rely on his being fed and sorted according to his worth and quality, and that upon your happy return, you will find him as sleek as an onion boiled in butter."

"Or," said Sir Miles Musgrave, "if this worthy cavalier chooses to part with his charger for a reasonable sum, I have some part of the silver candlesticks still dancing the heys in my purse, which I shall be very willing to transfer to his."

"In brief, mine honourable friends," said Captain Dalgetty, again eyeing them both with an air of comic penetration, "I find it would not be altogether unacceptable to either of you, to have some token to remember the old soldier by, in case it shall please M'Callum More to hang him up at the gate of his own castle. And doubtless it would be no small satisfaction to me, in such an event, that a noble and loyal cavalier like Sir Miles Musgrave, or a worthy and hospitable chieftain like our excellent landlord, should act as my executor."

Both hastened to protest that they had no such object, and insisted again upon the impassable character of the Highland paths. Angus M'Aulay mumbled over a number of hard Gaellic names, descriptive of the difficult passes, precipices, corries, and beals, through which he said the road lay to Inverary, when old Donald, who had now entered, sanctioned his master's account of these difficulties, by holding up his hands, and elevating his eyes, and shaking his head, at every gruttural which M'Aulay pronounced. But all this did not move the inflexible Captain.

"My worthy friends," said he, "Gustavus is not new to the dangers of travelling, and the mountains of Bohemia; and (no disparagement to the beals and corries Mr. Angus is pleased to mention, and of which Sir Miles, who never saw them, confirms the horrors,) these mountains may compete with the vilest roads in

Europe. In fact, my horse hath a most excellent and social quality; for although he cannot pledge in my cup, yet we share our loaf between us, and it will be hard if he suffers famine where cakes or bannocks are to be found. And, to cut this matter short, I beseech you, my good friends, to observe the state of Sir Duncan Campbell's palfrey, which stands in that stall before us, fat and fair; and, in return for your anxiety an my account, I give you my honest asseveration, that while we travel the same road, both that palfrey and his rider shall lack for food before either Gustavus or I."

Having said this he filled a large measure with corn, and walked up with it to his charger, who, by his low whinnying neigh, his pricked ears, and his pawing, showed how close the alliance was betwixt him and his rider. Nor did he taste his corn until he had returned his master's caresses, by licking his hands and face. After this interchange of greeting, the steed began to his provender with an eager dispatch, which showed old military habits; and the master, after looking on the animal with great complacency for about five minutes, said,—"Much good may it do your honest heart, Gustavus;—now must I go and lay in provant myself for the campaign."

He then departed, having first saluted the Englishman and Angus M'Aulay, who remained looking at each other for some time in silence, and then burst out into a fit of laughter.

"That fellow," said Sir Miles Musgrave, "is formed to go through the world."

"I shall think so too," said M'Aulay, "if he can slip through M'Callum More's fingers as easily as he has done through ours."

"Do you think," said the Englishman, "that the Marquis will not respect, in Captain Dalgetty's person, the laws of civilized war?"

"No more than I would respect a Lowland proclamation," said Angus M'Aulay.—"But come along, it is time I were returning to my guests."

CHAPTER IX.

... In a rebellion,
When what's not meet, but what must be, was law,
Then were they chosen, in a better hour,
Let what is meet be said it must be meet,
And throw their power i' the dust.

—CORIOLANUS.

In a small apartment, remote from the rest of the guests assembled at the castle, Sir Duncan Campbell was presented with every species of refreshment, and respectfully attended by Lord Menteith, and by Allan M'Aulay. His discourse with the latter turned upon a sort of hunting campaign, in which they had been engaged together against the Children of the Mist, with whom the Knight of Ardenvohr, as well as the M'Aulays, had a deadly and irreconcilable feud. Sir Duncan, however, speedily endeavoured to lead back the conversation to the subject of his present errand to the castle of Darnlinvarach.

"It grieved him to the very heart," he said, "to see that friends and neighbours, who should stand shoulder to shoulder, were likely to be engaged hand to hand in a cause which so little concerned them. What signifies it," he said, "to the Highland Chiefs, whether King or Parliament got uppermost? Were it not better to let them settle their own differences without interference, while the Chiefs, in the meantime, took the opportunity of establishing their own authority in a manner not to be called in question hereafter by either King or Parliament?" He reminded Allan M'Aulay that the measures taken in the last reign to settle the peace, as was alleged, of the Highlands, were in fact levelled at the patriarchal power of the Chieftains; and he mentioned the celebrated settlement of the Fife Undertakers, as they were called, in the Lewis, as part of a deliberate plan, formed to introduce strangers among the Celtic tribes, to destroy by degrees their ancient customs and mode of government, and to despoil them of the inheritance of their fathers. [In the reign of James VI., an attempt of rather an extraordinary kind was made to civilize the extreme northern part of the Hebridean Archipelago. That monarch granted the property of the Island of Lewis, as if it had been an unknown and savage country, to a number of Lowland gentlemen, called undertakers, chiefly natives of the shire of Fife, that they might colonize and settle there. The enterprise was at first successful, but the natives of the island, MacLeods and MacKenzies, rose on the Lowland adventurers, and put most of them to the sword.] "And yet," he continued, addressing Allan, "it is for the purpose of giving despotic authority to the monarch by whom these designs have been nursed, that so many Highland Chiefs are upon the point of quarrelling with, and drawing the sword against, their neighbours, allies, and ancient confederates." "It is to my brother," said Allan, "it is to the eldest son of my father's house, that the Knight of Ardenvohr must address these remonstrances. I am, indeed, the brother of Angus; but in being so, I am only the first of his clansmen, and bound to show an example to the others by my cheerful and ready obedience to his commands."

"The cause also," said Lord Menteith, interposing, "is far more general than Sir Duncan Campbell seems to suppose it. It is neither limited to Saxon nor to Gael, to mountain nor to strath, to Highlands nor to Lowlands. The question is, if we will continue to be governed by the unlimited authority assumed by a set of persons in no respect superior to ourselves, instead of returning to the natural government of the Prince against whom they have rebelled. And respecting the interest of the Highlands in particular," he added, "I crave Sir Duncan Campbell's pardon for my plainness; but it seems very clear to me, that the only effect produced by the present usurpation, will be the aggrandisement of one overgrown clan at the expense of every independent Chief in the Highlands."

"I will not reply to you, my lord," said Sir Duncan Campbell, "because I know your prejudices, and from whom they are borrowed; yet you will pardon my saying, that being at the head of a rival branch of the House of Graham, I have both read of and known an Earl of Menteith, who would have disdained to have been tutored in politics, or to have been commanded in war, by an Earl of Montrose."

"You will find it in vain, Sir Duncan," said Lord Menteith, haughtily, "to set my vanity in arms against my principles. The King gave my ancestors their title and rank; and these shall never prevent my acting, in the royal cause, under any one who is better qualified than myself to be a commander-in-chief. Least of all, shall any miserable jealousy prevent me from placing my hand and sword under the guidance of the bravest, the most loyal, the most heroic spirit among our Scottish nobility."

"Pity," said Sir Duncan Campbell, "that you cannot add to this panegyric the farther epithets of the most steady, and the most consistent. But I have no purpose of debating these points with you, my lord," waving his hand, as if to avoid farther discussion; "the die is cast with you; allow me only to express my sorrow for the disastrous fate to which Angus M'Aulay's natural rashness, and your lordship's influence, are dragging my gallant friend Allan here, with his father's clan, and many a brave man besides."

"The die is cast for us all, Sir Duncan," replied Allan, looking gloomy, and arguing on his own hypochondriac feelings; "the iron hand of destiny branded our fate upon our forehead long ere we could form a wish, or raise a finger in our own behalf. Were this otherwise, by what means does the Seer ascertain the future from those shadowy presages which haunt his waking and his sleeping eye? Nought can be foreseen but that which is certain to happen."

Sir Duncan Campbell was about to reply, and the darkest and most contested point of metaphysics might have been brought into discussion betwixt two Highland disputants, when the door opened, and Annot Lyle, with her clairshach in her hand, entered the apartment. The freedom of a Highland maiden was in her step and in her eye; for, bred up in the closest intimacy with the Laird of M'Aulay and his brother, with Lord Menteith, and other young men who frequented Darnlinvarach, she possessed none of that timidity which a female, educated chiefly among her own sex, would either have felt, or thought necessary to assume, on an occasion like the present,

Her dress partook of the antique, for new fashions seldom penetrated into the Highlands, nor would they easily have found their way to a castle inhabited chiefly by men, whose sole occupation was war and the chase. Yet Annot's garments were not only becoming, but even rich. Her open jacket, with a high collar, was composed of blue cloth, richly embroidered, and had silver clasps to fasten, when it pleased the wearer. Its sleeves, which were wide, came no lower than the elbow, and terminated in a golden fringe; under this upper coat, if it can be so termed, she wore an under dress of blue satin, also richly embroidered, but which was several shades lighter in colour than the upper garment. The petticoat was formed of tartan silk, in the sett, or pattern, of which the colour of blue greatly predominated, so as to remove the tawdry effect too frequently produced in tartan, by the mixture and strong opposition of colours. An antique silver chain hung round her neck, and supported the WREST, or key, with which she turned her instrument. A small ruff rose above her collar, and was secured by a brooch of some value, an old keepsake from Lord Menteith. Her profusion of light hair almost hid her laughing eyes, while, with a smile and a blush, she mentioned that she had M'Aulay's directions to ask them if they chose music. Sir Duncan Campbell gazed with considerable surprise and interest at the lovely apparition, which thus interrupted his debate with Allan M'Aulay.

"Can this," he said to him in a whisper, "a creature so beautiful and so elegant, be a domestic musician of your brother's establishment?"

"By no means," answered Allan, hastily, yet with some hesitation; "she is a—a—near relation of our family—and treated," he added, more firmly, "as an adopted daughter of our father's house."

As he spoke thus, he arose from his seat, and with that air of courtesy which every Highlander can assume when it suits him to practise it, he resigned it to Annot, and offered to her, at the same time, whatever refreshments the table afforded, with an assiduity which was probably designed to give Sir Duncan an impression of her rank and consequence. If such was Allan's purpose, however, it was unnecessary. Sir Duncan kept his eyes fixed upon Annot with an expression of much deeper interest than could have arisen from any impression that she was a person of consequence. Annot even felt embarrassed under the old knight's steady gaze; and it was not without considerable hesitation, that, tuning her instrument, and receiving an assenting look from Lord Menteith and Allan, she executed the following ballad, which our friend, Mr. Secundus M'Pherson, whose goodness we had before to acknowledge, has thus translated into the English tongue:

THE ORPHAN MAID.

November's hail-cloud drifts away,
November's sunbeam wan
Looks coldly on the castle grey,
When forth comes Lady Anne.

The orphan by the oak was set,
Her arms, her feet, were bare,
The hail-drops had not melted yet,
Amid her raven hair.

"And, Dame," she said, "by all the ties
That child and mother know,
Aid one who never knew these joys,
Relieve an orphan's woe."

The Lady said, "An orphan's state
Is hard and sad to bear;
Yet worse the widow'd mother's fate,
Who mourns both lord and heir.

"Twelve times the rolling year has sped,
Since, when from vengeance wild
Of fierce Strathallan's Chief I fled,
Forth's eddies whelm'd my child."

"Twelve times the year its course has born,"
The wandering maid replied,
"Since fishers on St. Bridget's morn
Drew nets on Campsie side.

"St. Bridget sent no scaly spoil;—
An infant, wellnigh dead,
They saved, and rear'd in want and toil,
To beg from you her bread."

That orphan maid the lady kiss'd—
"My husband's looks you bear;
St. Bridget and her morn be bless'd!
You are his widow's heir."

They've robed that maid, so poor and pale,
In silk and sandals rare;
And pearls, for drops of frozen hail,
Are glistening in her hair.

The admirers of pure Celtic antiquity, notwithstanding the elegance of the above translation, may be desirous to see a literal version from the original Gaelic, which we therefore subjoin; and have only to add, that the original is deposited with Mr. Jedediah Cleishbotham.

LITERAL TRANSLATION.

The hail-blast had drifted away upon the wings of the gale of autumn. The sun looked from between the clouds, pale as the wounded hero who rears his head feebly on the heath when the roar of battle hath passed over him.

Finele, the Lady of the Castle, came forth to see her maidens pass to the herds with their leglins [Milk-pails].

There sat an orphan maiden beneath the old oak-tree of appointment. The withered leaves fell around her, and her heart was more withered than they.

The parent of the ice [poetically taken from the frost] still congealed the hail-drops in her hair; they were like the specks of white ashes on the twisted boughs of the blackened and half-consumed oak that blazes in the hall.

And the maiden said, "Give me comfort, Lady, I am an orphan child." And the Lady replied, "How can I give that which I have not? I am the widow of a slain lord,— the mother of a perished child. When I fled in my fear from the vengeance of my husband's foes, our bark was overwhelmed in the tide, and my infant perished. This was on St. Bridget's morn, near the strong Lyns of Campsie. May ill luck light upon the day." And the maiden answered, "It was on St. Bridget's morn, and twelve harvests before this time, that the fishermen of Campsie drew in their nets neither grilse nor salmon, but an infant half dead, who hath since lived in misery, and must die, unless she is now aided." And the Lady answered, "Blessed be Saint Bridget and her morn, for these are the dark eyes and the falcon look of my slain lord; and thine shall be the inheritance of his widow." And she called for her waiting attendants, and she bade them clothe that maiden in silk, and in samite; and the pearls which they wove among her black tresses, were whiter than the frozen hail-drops.

While the song proceeded, Lord Menteith observed, with some surprise, that it appeared to produce a much deeper effect upon the mind of Sir Duncan Campbell, than he could possibly have anticipated from his age and character. He well knew that the Highlanders of that period possessed a much greater sensibility both for tale and song than was found among their Lowland neighbours; but even this, he thought, hardly accounted for the embarrassment with which the old man withdrew his eyes from the songstress, as if unwilling to suffer them to rest on an object so interesting. Still less was it to be expected, that features which expressed pride, stern common sense, and the austere habit of authority, should have been so much agitated by so trivial a circumstance. As the Chief's brow became clouded, he drooped his large shaggy grey eyebrows until they almost concealed his eyes, on the lids of which something like a tear might be seen to glisten. He remained silent and fixed in the same posture for a minute or two, after the last note had ceased to vibrate. He then raised his head, and having looked at Annot Lyle, as if purposing to speak to her, he as suddenly changed that purpose, and was about to address Allan, when the door opened, and the Lord of the Castle made his appearance.

CHAPTER X.

Dark on their journey lour'd the gloomy day,
Wild were the hills, and doubtful grew the way;
More dark, more gloomy, and more doubtful, show'd
The mansion, which received them from the road.
        —THE TRAVELLERS, A ROMANCE.

Angus M'Aulay was charged with a message which he seemed to find some difficulty in communicating; for it was not till after he had framed his speech several different ways, and blundered them all, that he succeeded in letting Sir Duncan Campbell know, that the cavalier who was to accompany him was waiting in readiness, and that all was prepared for his return to Inverary. Sir Duncan Campbell rose up very indignantly; the affront which this message implied immediately driving out of his recollection the sensibility which had been awakened by the music.

"I little expected this," he said, looking indignantly at Angus M'Aulay. "I little thought that there was a Chief in the West Highlands, who, at the pleasure of a Saxon, would have bid the Knight of Ardenvohr leave his castle, when the sun was declining from the meridian, and ere the second cup had been filled. But farewell, sir, the food of a churl does not satisfy the appetite; when I next revisit Darnlinvarach, it shall be with a naked sword in one hand, and a firebrand in the other."

"And if you so come," said Angus, "I pledge myself to meet you fairly, though you brought five hundred Campbells at your back, and to afford you and them such entertainment, that you shall not again complain of the hospitality of Darnlinvarach."

"Threatened men," said Sir Duncan, "live long. Your turn for gasconading, Laird of M'Aulay, is too well known, that men of honour should regard your vaunts. To you, my lord, and to

Allan, who have supplied the place of my churlish host, I leave my thanks.—And to you, pretty mistress," he said, addressing Annot Lyle, "this little token, for having opened a fountain which hath been dry for many a year." So saying, he left the apartment, and commanded his attendants to be summoned. Angus M'Aulay, equally embarrassed and incensed at the charge of inhospitality, which was the greatest possible affront to a Highlander, did not follow Sir Duncan to the court-yard, where, mounting his palfrey, which was in readiness, followed by six mounted attendants, and accompanied by the noble Captain Dalgetty, who had also awaited him, holding Gustavus ready for action, though he did not draw his girths and mount till Sir Duncan appeared, the whole cavalcade left the castle.

The journey was long and toilsome, but without any of the extreme privations which the Laird of M'Aulay had prophesied. In truth, Sir Duncan was very cautious to avoid those nearer and more secret paths, by means of which the county of Argyle was accessible from the eastward; for his relation and chief, the Marquis, was used to boast, that he would not for a hundred thousand crowns any mortal should know the passes by which an armed force could penetrate into his country.

Sir Duncan Campbell, therefore, rather shunned the Highlands, and falling into the Low-country, made for the nearest seaport in the vicinity, where he had several half-decked galleys, or birlings, as they were called, at his command. In one of these they embarked, with Gustavus in company, who was so seasoned to adventure, that land and sea seemed as indifferent to him as to his master.

The wind being favourable, they pursued their way rapidly with sails and oars; and early the next morning it was announced to Captain Dalgetty, then in a small cabin beneath the hall-deck, that the galley was under the walls of Sir Duncan Campbell's castle.

Ardenvohr, accordingly, rose high above him, when he came upon the deck of the galley. It was a gloomy square tower, of considerable size and great height, situated upon a headland projecting into the salt-water lake, or arm of the sea, which they had entered on the preceding evening. A wall, with flanking towers at each angle, surrounded the castle to landward; but, towards the lake, it was built so near the brink of the precipice as only to leave room for a battery of seven guns, designed to protect the fortress from any insult from that side, although situated too high to be of any effectual use according to the modern system of warfare.

The eastern sun, rising behind the old tower, flung its shadow far on the lake, darkening the deck of the galley, on which Captain Dalgetty now walked, waiting with some impatience the signal to land. Sir Duncan Campbell, as he was informed by his attendants, was already within the walls of the castle; but no one encouraged the Captain's proposal of following him ashore, until, as they stated, they should receive the direct permission or order of the Knight of Ardenvohr.

In a short time afterwards the mandate arrived, while a boat, with a piper in the bow, bearing the Knight of Ardenvohr's crest in silver upon his left arm, and playing with all his might the family march, entitled "The Campbells are coming," approached to conduct the envoy of Montrose to the castle of Ardenvohr. The distance between the galley and the beach was so short as scarce to require the assistance of the eight sturdy rowers, in bonnets, short coats, and trews, whose efforts sent the boat to the little creek in which they usually landed, before one could have conceived that it had left the side of the birling. Two of the boatmen, in spite of Dalgetty's resistance, horsed the Captain on the back of a third Highlander, and, wading through the surf with him, landed him high and dry upon the beach beneath the castle rock. In the face of this rock there appeared something like the entrance of a low-browed cavern, towards which the assistants were preparing to hurry our friend Dalgetty, when, shaking himself loose from them with some difficulty, he insisted upon seeing Gustavus safely landed before he proceeded one step farther. The Highlanders could not comprehend what he meant, until one who had picked up a little English, or rather Lowland Scotch, exclaimed, "Houts! it's a' about her horse, ta useless baste." Farther remonstrance on the part of Captain Dalgetty was interrupted by the appearance of Sir Duncan Campbell himself, from the mouth of the cavern which we have described, for the purpose of inviting Captain Dalgetty to accept of the hospitality of Ardenvohr, pledging his honour, at the same time, that Gustavus should be treated as became the hero from whom he derived his name, not to mention the important person to whom he now belonged. Notwithstanding this satisfactory guarantee, Captain Dalgetty would still have hesitated, such was his anxiety to witness the fate of his companion Gustavus, had not two Highlanders seized him by the arms, two more pushed him on behind, while a fifth exclaimed, "Hout awa wi' the daft Sassenach! does she no hear the Laird bidding her up to her ain castle, wi' her special voice, and isna that very mickle honour for the like o' her?"

Thus impelled, Captain Dalgetty could only for a short space keep a reverted eye towards the galley in which he had left the partner of his military toils. In a few minutes afterwards he found himself involved in the total darkness of a staircase, which, entering from the low-browed cavern we have mentioned, winded upwards through the entrails of the living rock.

"The cursed Highland salvages!" muttered the Captain, half aloud; "what is to become of me, if Gustavus, the namesake of the invincible Lion of the Protestant League, should be lamed among their untenty hands!"

"Have no fear of that," said the voice of Sir Duncan, who was nearer to him than he imagined; "my men are accustomed to handle horses, both in embarking and dressing them, and you will soon see Gustavus as safe as when you last dismounted from his back,"

Captain Dalgetty knew the world too well to offer any farther remonstrance, whatever uneasiness he might suppress within his own bosom. A step or two higher up the stair showed light and a door, and an iron-grated wicket led him out upon a gallery cut in the open face of the rock, extending a space of about six or eight yards, until he reached a second door, where the path re-entered the rock, and which was also defended by an iron portcullis. "An admirable traverse," observed the Captain; "and if commanded by a field-piece, or even a few muskets, quite sufficient to ensure the place against a storming party."

Sir Duncan Campbell made no answer at the time; but, the moment afterwards, when they had entered the second cavern, he struck with the stick which he had in his hand, first on the one side, and then on the other of the wicket, and the sullen ringing sound which replied to the blows, made Captain Dalgetty sensible that there was a gun placed on each side, for the purpose of raking the gallery through which they had passed, although the embrasures, through which they might be fired on occasion, were masked on the outside with sods and loose stones. Having ascended the second staircase, they found themselves again on an open platform and gallery, exposed to a fire both of musketry and wall-guns, if, being come with hostile intent, they had ventured farther. A third flight of steps, cut in the rock like the former, but not caverned over, led them finally into the battery at the foot of the tower. This last stair also was narrow and steep, and, not to mention the fire which might be directed on it from above, one or two resolute men, with pikes and battle-axes, could have made the pass good against hundreds; for the staircase would not admit two persons abreast, and was not secured by any sort of balustrade, or railing, from the sheer and abrupt precipice, on the foot of which the tide now rolled with a voice of thunder. So that, under the jealous precautions used to secure this ancient Celtic fortress, a person of weak nerves, and a brain liable to become dizzy, might have found it something difficult to have achieved the entrance to the castle, even supposing no resistance had been offered.

Captain Dalgetty, too old a soldier to feel such tremors, had no sooner arrived in the court-yard, than he protested to God, the defences of Sir Duncan's castle reminded him more of the notable fortress of Spandau, situated in the March of Brandenburg, than of any place whilk it had been his fortune to defend in the course of his travels. Nevertheless, he criticised considerably the mode of placing the guns on the battery we have noticed, observing, that "where cannon were perched, like to scarts or sea-gulls on the top of a rock, he had ever observed that they astonished more by their noise than they dismayed by the skaith or damage which they occasioned."

Sir Duncan, without replying, conducted the soldier into the tower; the defences of which were a portcullis and ironclenched oaken door, the thickness of the wall being the space between them. He had no sooner arrived in a hall hung with tapestry, than the Captain prosecuted his military criticism. It was indeed suspended by the sight of an excellent breakfast, of which he partook with great avidity; but no sooner had he secured this meal, than he made the tour of the apartment, examining the ground around the Castle very carefully from each window in the room. He then returned to his chair, and throwing himself back into it at his length, stretched out one manly leg, and tapping his jack-boot with the riding-rod which he carried in his hand, after the manner of a half-bred man who affects ease in the society of his betters, he delivered his unasked opinion as follows:—"This house of yours, now, Sir Duncan, is a very pretty defensible sort of a tenement, and yet it is hardly such as a cavaliero of honour would expect to maintain his credit by holding out for many days. For, Sir Duncan, if it pleases you to notice, your house is overcrowed, and slighted, or commanded, as we military men say, by yonder round hillock to the landward, whereon an enemy might stell such a battery of cannon as would make ye glad to beat a chamade within forty-eight hours, unless it pleased the Lord extraordinarily to show mercy."

"There is no road," replied Sir Duncan, somewhat shortly, "by which cannon can be brought against Ardenvohr. The swamps and morasses around my house would scarce carry your horse and yourself, excepting by such paths as could be rendered impassable within a few hours."

"Sir Duncan," said the Captain, "it is your pleasure to suppose so; and yet we martial men say, that where there is a sea-coast there is always a naked side, seeing that cannon and munition, where they cannot be transported by land, may be right easily brought by sea near to the place where they are to be put in action. Neither is a castle, however secure in its situation, to be accounted altogether invincible, or, as they say, impregnable; for I protest t'ye, Sir Duncan, that I have known twenty-five men, by the mere surprise and audacity of the attack, win, at point of pike, as strong a hold as this of Ardenvohr, and put to the sword, captivate, or hold to the ransom, the defenders, being ten times their own number."

Notwithstanding Sir Duncan Campbell's knowledge of the world, and his power of concealing his internal emotion, he appeared piqued and hurt at these reflections, which the Captain made with the most unconscious gravity, having merely selected the subject of conversation as one upon which he thought himself capable of shining, and, as they say, of laying down the law, without exactly recollecting that the topic might not be equally agreeable to his landlord.

"To cut this matter short," said Sir Duncan, with an expression of voice and countenance somewhat agitated, "it is unnecessary for you to tell me, Captain Dalgetty, that a castle may be stormed if it is not valorously defended, or surprised if it is not heedfully watched.

I trust this poor house of mine will not be found in any of these predicaments, should even Captain Dalgetty himself choose to beleaguer it."

"For all that, Sir Duncan," answered the persevering commander, "I would premonish you, as a friend, to trace out a sconce upon that round hill, with a good graffe, or ditch, whilk may be easily accomplished by compelling the labour of the boors in the vicinity; it being the custom of the valorous Gustavus Adolphus to fight as much by the spade and shovel, as by sword, pike, and musket. Also, I would advise you to fortify the said sconce, not only by a foussie, or graffe, but also by certain stackets, or palisades."—(Here Sir Duncan, becoming impatient, left the apartment, the Captain following him to the door, and raising his voice as he retreated, until he was fairly out of hearing.)—"The whilk stackets, or palisades, should be artificially framed with re-entering angles and loop-holes, or crenelles, for musketry, whereof it shall arise that the foeman— The Highland brute! the old Highland brute! They are as proud as peacocks, and as obstinate as tups—and here he has missed an opportunity of making his house as pretty an irregular fortification as an invading army ever broke their teeth upon.—But I see," he continued, looking own from the window upon the bottom of the precipice, "they have got Gustavus safe ashore—Proper fellow! I would know that toss of his head among a whole squadron. I must go to see what they are to make of him."

He had no sooner reached, however, the court to the seaward, and put himself in the act of descending the staircase, than two Highland sentinels, advancing their Lochaber axes, gave him to understand that this was a service of danger.

"Diavolo!" said the soldier, "and I have got no pass-word. I could not speak a syllable of their salvage gibberish, an it were to save me from the provost-marshal."

"I will be your surety, Captain Dalgetty," said Sir Duncan, who had again approached him without his observing from whence; "and we will go together, and see how your favourite charger is accommodated."

He conducted him accordingly down the staircase to the beach, and from thence by a short turn behind a large rock, which concealed the stables and other offices belonging to the castle, Captain Dalgetty became sensible, at the same time, that the side of the castle to the land was rendered totally inaccessible by a ravine, partly natural and partly scarped with great care and labour, so as to be only passed by a drawbridge. Still, however, the Captain insisted, not withstanding the triumphant air with which Sir Duncan pointed out his defences, that a sconce should be erected on Drumsnab, the round eminence to the east of the castle, in respect the house might be annoyed from thence by burning bullets full of fire, shot out of cannon, according to the curious invention of Stephen Bathian, King of Poland, whereby that prince utterly ruined the great Muscovite city of Moscow. This invention, Captain Dalgetty owned, he had not yet witnessed, but observed, "that it would give him particular delectation to witness the same put to the proof against Ardenvohr, or any other castle of similar strength;" observing, "that so curious an experiment could not but afford the greatest delight to all admirers of the military art."

Sir Duncan Campbell diverted this conversation by carrying the soldier into his stables, and suffering him to arrange Gustavus according to his own will and pleasure. After this duty had been carefully performed, Captain Dalgetty proposed to return to the castle, observing, it was his intention to spend the time betwixt this and dinner, which, he presumed, would come upon the parade about noon, in burnishing his armour, which having sustained some injury from the sea-air, might, he was afraid, seem discreditable in the eyes of M'Callum More. Yet, while they were returning to the castle, he failed not to warn Sir Duncan Campbell against the great injury he might sustain by any sudden onfall of an enemy, whereby his horses, cattle, and granaries, might be cut off and consumed, to his great prejudice; wherefore he again strongly conjured him to construct a sconce upon the round hill called Drumsnab, and offered his own friendly services in lining out the same. To this disinterested advice Sir Duncan only replied by ushering his guest to his apartment, and informing him that the tolling of the castle bell would make him aware when dinner was ready.

CHAPTER XI.

Is this thy castle, Baldwin? Melancholy
Displays her sable banner from the donjon,
Darkening the foam of the whole surge beneath.
Were I a habitant, to see this gloom
Pollute the face of nature, and to hear
The ceaseless sound of wave, and seabird's scream,
I'd wish me in the hut that poorest peasant
E'er framed, to give him temporary shelter.

—BROWN.

The gallant Ritt-master would willingly have employed his leisure in studying the exterior of Sir Duncan's castle, and verifying his own military ideas upon the nature of its defences. But a stout sentinel, who mounted guard with a Lochaber-axe at the door of his apartment, gave him to understand, by very significant signs, that he was in a sort of honourable captivity.

It is strange, thought the Ritt-master to himself, how well these salvages understand the rules and practique of war. Who should have pre-supposed their acquaintance with the maxim of the great and godlike Gustavus Adolphus, that a flag of truce should be half a messenger half a spy?—And, having finished burnishing his arms, he sate down patiently to compute how much half a dollar per diem would amount to at the end of a six-months' campaign; and, when he had settled that problem, proceeded to the more abstruse calculations necessary for drawing up a brigade of two thousand men on the principle of extracting the square root.

From his musings, he was roused by the joyful sound of the dinner bell, on which the Highlander, lately his guard, became his gentleman-usher, and marshalled him to the hall, where a table with four covers bore ample proofs of Highland hospitality. Sir Duncan entered, conducting his lady, a tall, faded, melancholy female, dressed in deep mourning. They were followed by a Presbyterian clergyman, in his Geneva cloak, and wearing a black silk skull-cap, covering his short hair so closely, that it could scarce be seen at all, so that the unrestricted ears had an undue predominance in the general aspect. This ungraceful fashion was universal at the time, and partly led to the nicknames of roundheads, prick-eared curs, and so forth, which the insolence of the cavaliers liberally bestowed on their political enemies.

Sir Duncan presented his military guest to his lady, who received his technical salutation with a stiff and silent reverence, in which it could scarce be judged whether pride or melancholy had the greater share. The churchman, to whom he was next presented, eyed him with a glance of mingled dislike and curiosity.

The Captain, well accustomed to worse looks from more dangerous persons, cared very little either for those of the lady or of the divine, but bent his whole soul upon assaulting a huge piece of beef, which smoked at the nether end of the table. But the onslaught, as he would have termed it, was delayed, until the conclusion of a very long grace, betwixt every section of which Dalgetty handled his knife and fork, as he might have done his musket or pike when going upon action, and as often resigned them unwillingly when the prolix chaplain commenced another clause of his benediction. Sir Duncan listened with decency, though he was supposed rather to have joined the Covenanters out of devotion to his chief, than real respect for the cause either of liberty or of Presbytery. His lady alone attended to the blessing, with symptoms of deep acquiescence.

The meal was performed almost in Carthusian silence; for it was none of Captain Dalgetty's habits to employ his mouth in talking, while it could be more profitably occupied. Sir Duncan was absolutely silent, and the lady and churchman only occasionally exchanged a few words, spoken low, and indistinctly.

But, when the dishes were removed, and their place supplied by liquors of various sorts, Captain Dalgetty no longer had, himself, the same weighty reasons for silence, and began to tire of that of the rest of the company. He commenced a new attack upon his landlord, upon the former ground.

"Touching that round monticle, or hill, or eminence, termed Drumsnab, I would be proud to hold some dialogue with you, Sir Duncan, on the nature of the sconce to be there constructed; and whether the angles thereof should be acute or obtuse—anent whilk I have heard the great Velt-Mareschal Bannier hold a learned argument with General Tiefenbach during a still-stand of arms."

"Captain Dalgetty," answered Sir Duncan very dryly, "it is not our Highland usage to debate military points with strangers. This castle is like to hold out against a stronger enemy than any force which the unfortunate gentlemen we left at Darnlinvarach are able to bring against it."

A deep sigh from the lady accompanied the conclusion of her husband's speech, which seemed to remind her of some painful circumstance.

"He who gave," said the clergyman, addressing her in a solemn tone, "hath taken away. May you, honourable lady, be long enabled to say, Blessed be his name!"

To this exhortation, which seemed intended for her sole behoof, the lady answered by an inclination of her head, more humble than Captain Dalgetty had yet observed her make. Supposing he should now find her in a more conversible humour, he proceeded to accost her.

"It is indubitably very natural that your ladyship should be downcast at the mention of military preparations, whilk I have observed to spread perturbation among women of all nations, and almost all conditions. Nevertheless, Penthesilea, in ancient times, and also Joan of Arc, and others, were of a different kidney. And, as I have learned while I served the Spaniard, the Duke of Alva in former times had the leaguer-lasses who followed his camp marshalled into TERTIAS (whilk me call regiments), and officered and commanded by those of their own feminine gender, and regulated by a commander-in chief, called in German Hureweibler, or, as we would say vernacularly, Captain of the Queans. True it is, they were persons not to be named as parallel to your ladyship, being such QUAE QUAESTUM CORPORIBUS FACIEBANT, as we said of Jean Drochiels at Mareschal-College; the same whom the French term CURTISANNES, and we in Scottish—"

"The lady will spare you the trouble of further exposition, Captain Dalgetty," said his host, somewhat sternly; to which the clergyman added, "that such discourse better befitted a watch-tower guarded by profane soldiery than the board of an honourable person, and the presence of a lady of quality."

"Craving your pardon, Dominie, or Doctor, AUT QUOCUNQUE ALIO NOMINE GAUDES, for I would have you to know I have studied polite letters," said the unabashed envoy, filling a great cup of wine, "I see no ground for your reproof, seeing I did not speak of those TURPES PERSONAE, as if their occupation or character was a proper subject of conversation for this lady's presence, but simply PAR ACCIDENS, as illustrating the matter in hand, namely, their natural courage and audacity, much enhanced, doubtless, by the desperate circumstances of their condition."

"Captain Dalgetty," said Sir Duncan Campbell, "to break short this discourse, I must acquaint you, that I have some business to dispatch to-night, in order to enable me to ride with you to-morrow towards Inverary; and therefore—"

"To ride with this person to-morrow!" exclaimed his lady; "such cannot be your purpose, Sir Duncan, unless you have forgotten that the morrow is a sad anniversary, and dedicated to as sad a solemnity."

"I had not forgotten," answered Sir Duncan; "how is it possible I can ever forget? but the necessity of the times requires I should send this officer onward to Inverary, without loss of time."

"Yet, surely, not that you should accompany him in person?" enquired the lady.

"It were better I did," said Sir Duncan; "yet I can write to the Marquis, and follow on the subsequent day.—Captain Dalgetty, I will dispatch a letter for you, explaining to the Marquis of Argyle your character and commission, with which you will please to prepare to travel to Inverary early to-morrow morning."

"Sir Duncan Campbell," said Dalgetty, "I am doubtless at your discretionary disposal in this matter; not the less, I pray you to remember the blot which will fall upon your own escutcheon, if you do in any way suffer me, being a commissionate flag of truce, to be circumvented in this matter, whether CLAM, VI, VEL PRECARIO; I do not say by your assent to any wrong done to me, but even through absence of any due care on your part to prevent the same."

"You are under the safeguard of my honour, sir," answered Sir Duncan Campbell, "and that is more than a sufficient security. And now," continued he, rising, "I must set the example of retiring."

Dalgetty saw himself under the necessity of following the hint, though the hour was early; but, like a skilful general, he availed himself of every instant of delay which circumstances permitted. "Trusting to your honourable parole," said he, filling his cup, "I drink to you, Sir Duncan, and to the continuance of your honourable-house." A sigh from Sir Duncan was the only reply. "Also, madam," said the soldier, replenishing the quaigh with all possible dispatch, "I drink to your honourable health, and fulfilment of all your virtuous desires—and, reverend sir" (not forgetting to fit the action to the words), "I fill this cup to the drowning of all unkindness betwixt you and Captain Dalgetty—I should say Major—and, in respect the flagon contains but one cup more, I drink to the health of all honourable cavaliers and brave soldados—and, the flask being empty, I am ready, Sir Duncan, to attend your functionary or sentinel to my place of private repose."

He received a formal permission to retire, and an assurance, that as the wine seemed to be to his taste, another measure of the same vintage should attend him presently, in order to soothe the hours of his solitude.

No sooner had the Captain reached the apartment than this promise was fulfilled; and, in a short time afterwards, the added comforts of a pasty of red-deer venison rendered him very tolerant both of confinement and want of society. The same domestic, a sort of chamberlain, who placed this good cheer in his apartment, delivered to Dalgetty a packet, sealed and tied up with a silken thread, according to the custom of the time, addressed with many forms of respect to the High and Mighty Prince, Archibald, Marquis of Argyle, Lord of Lorne, and so forth. The chamberlain at the same time apprized the Ritt-master, that he must take horse at an early hour for Inverary, where the packet of Sir Duncan would be at once his introduction and his passport. Not forgetting that it was his object to collect information as well as to act as an envoy, and desirous, for his own sake, to ascertain Sir Duncan's reasons for sending him onward without his personal attendance, the Ritt-master enquired the domestic, with all the precaution that his experience suggested, what were the reasons which detained

Sir Duncan at home on the succeeding day. The man, who was from the Lowlands, replied, "that it was the habit of Sir Duncan and his lady to observe as a day of solemn fast and humiliation the anniversary on which their castle had been taken by surprise, and their children, to the number of four, destroyed cruelly by a band of Highland freebooters during Sir Duncan's absence upon an expedition which the Marquis of Argyle had undertaken against the Macleans of the Isle of Mull."

"Truly," said the soldier, "your lord and lady have some cause for fast and humiliation. Nevertheless, I will venture to pronounce, that if he had taken the advice of any experienced soldier, having skill in the practiques of defending places of advantage, he would have built a sconce upon the small hill which is to the left of the draw-brigg. And this I can easily prove to you, mine honest friend; for, holding that pasty to be the castle—What's your name, friend?"

"Lorimer, sir," replied the man.

"Here is to your health, honest Lorimer.—I say, Lorimer— holding that pasty to be the main body or citadel of the place to be defended, and taking the marrow-bone for the sconce to be erected—"

"I am sorry, sir," said Lorimer, interrupting him, "that I cannot stay to hear the rest of your demonstration; but the bell will presently ring. As worthy Mr. Graneangowl, the Marquis's own chaplain, does family worship, and only seven of our household out of sixty persons understand the Scottish tongue, it would misbecome any one of them to be absent, and greatly prejudice me in the opinion of my lady. There are pipes and tobacco, sir, if you please to drink a whiff of smoke, and if you want anything else, it shall be forthcoming two hours hence, when prayers are over." So saying, he left the apartment.

No sooner was he gone, than the heavy toll of the castle-bell summoned its inhabitants together; and was answered by the shrill clamour of the females, mixed with the deeper tones of the men, as, talking Earse at the top of their throats, they hurried from different quarters by a long but narrow gallery, which served as a communication to many rooms, and, among others, to that in which Captain Dalgetty was stationed. There they go as if they were beating to the roll-call, thought the soldier to himself; if they all attend the parade, I will look out, take a mouthful of fresh air, and make mine own observations on the practicabilities of this place.

Accordingly, when all was quiet, he opened his chamber door, and prepared to leave it, when he saw his friend with the axe advancing towards him from the distant end of the gallery, half whistling, a Gaelic tune. To have shown any want of confidence, would have been at once impolitic, and unbecoming his military character; so the Captain, putting the best face upon his situation he could, whistled a Swedish retreat, in a tone still louder than the notes of his sentinel; and retreating pace by pace, with an air of indifference, as if his only purpose had been to breathe a little fresh air, he shut the door in the face of his guard, when the fellow had approached within a few paces of him.

It is very well, thought the Ritt-master to himself; he annuls my parole by putting guards upon me, for, as we used to say at Mareschal-College, FIDES ET FIDUCIA SUNT RELATIVA [See Note I]; and if he does not trust my word, I do not see how I am bound to keep it, if any motive should occur for my desiring to depart from it. Surely the moral obligation of the parole is relaxed, in as far as physical force is substituted instead thereof.

Thus comforting himself in the metaphysical immunities which he deduced from the vigilance of his sentinel, Ritt-master Dalgetty retired to his apartment, where, amid the theoretical calculations of tactics, and the occasional more practical attacks on the flask and pasty, he consumed the evening until it was time to go to repose. He was summoned by Lorimer at break of day, who gave him to understand, that, when he had broken his fast, for which he produced ample materials, his guide and horse were in attendance for his journey to Inverary. After complying with the hospitable hint of the chamberlain, the soldier proceeded to take horse. In passing through the apartments, he observed that domestics were busily employed in hanging the great hall with black cloth, a ceremony which, he said, he had seen practised when the immortal Gustavus Adolphus lay in state in the Castle of Wolgast, and which, therefore, he opined, was a testimonial of the strictest and deepest mourning.

When Dalgetty mounted his steed, he found himself attended, or perhaps guarded, by five or six Campbells, well armed, commanded by one, who, from the target at his shoulder, and the short cock's feather in his bonnet, as well as from the state which he took upon himself, claimed the rank of a Dunniewassel, or clansman of superior rank; and indeed, from his dignity of deportment, could not stand in a more distant degree of relationship to Sir Duncan, than that of tenth or twelfth cousin at farthest. But it was impossible to extract positive information on this or any other subject, inasmuch as neither this commander nor any of his party spoke English. The Captain rode, and his military attendants walked; but such was their activity, and so numerous the impediments which the nature of the road presented to the equestrian mode of travelling, that far from being retarded by the slowness of their pace, his difficulty was rather in keeping up with his guides. He observed that they occasionally watched him with a sharp eye, as if they were jealous of some effort to escape; and once, as he lingered behind at crossing a brook, one of the gillies began to blow the match of his piece, giving him to understand that he would run some risk in case of an attempt to part company. Dalgetty did not augur much good from the close watch thus maintained upon his person; but there was no remedy, for an attempt to escape from his attendants in an impervious and unknown country, would have been little short of insanity. He therefore plodded patiently on through a waste and savage wilderness, treading paths which were only known to the shepherds and cattle-drivers, and passing with much more of discomfort than satisfaction many of those sublime combinations of mountainous scenery which now draw visitors from every corner of England, to feast their eyes upon Highland grandeur, and mortify their palates upon Highland fare.

At length they arrived on the southern verge of that noble lake upon which Inverary is situated; and a bugle, which the Dunniewassel winded till rock and greenwood rang, served as a signal to a well-manned galley, which, starting from a creek where it lay concealed, received the party on board, including Gustavus; which sagacious quadruped, an experienced traveller both by water and land, walked in and out of the boat with the discretion of a Christian.

Embarked on the bosom of Loch Fine, Captain Dalgetty might have admired one of the grandest scenes which nature affords. He might have noticed the rival rivers Aray and Shiray, which pay tribute to the lake, each issuing from its own dark and wooded retreat. He might have marked, on the soft and gentle slope that ascends from the shores, the noble old Gothic castle, with its varied outline, embattled walls, towers, and outer and inner courts, which, so far as the picturesque is concerned, presented an aspect much more striking than the present massive and uniform mansion. He might have admired those dark woods which for many a mile surrounded this strong and princely dwelling, and his eye might have dwelt on the picturesque peak of Duniquoich, starting abruptly from the lake, and raising its scathed brow into the mists of middle sky, while a solitary watch-tower, perched on its top like an eagle's nest, gave dignity to the scene by awakening a sense of possible danger. All these, and every other accompaniment of this noble scene, Captain Dalgetty might have marked, if he had been so minded. But, to confess the truth, the gallant Captain, who had eaten nothing since daybreak, was chiefly interested by the smoke which ascended from the castle chimneys, and the expectations which this seemed to warrant of his encountering an abundant stock of provant, as he was wont to call supplies of this nature.

The boat soon approached the rugged pier, which abutted into the loch from the little town of Inverary, then a rude assemblage of huts, with a very few stone mansions interspersed, stretching upwards from the banks of Loch Fine to the principal gate of the castle, before which a scene presented itself that might easily have quelled a less stout heart, and turned a more delicate stomach, than those of Ritt-master Dugald Dalgetty, titular of Drumthwacket.

CHAPTER XII.

For close designs and crooked counsels fit,
Sagacious, bold, and turbulent of wit,
Restless, unfix'd in principle and place,
In power unpleased, impatient in disgrace.
　　　　　　—ABSALOM AND ACHITOPHEL.

The village of Inverary, now a neat country town, then partook of the rudeness of the seventeenth century, in the miserable appearance of the houses, and the irregularity of the unpaved street. But a stronger and more terrible characteristic of the period appeared in the market-place, which was a space of irregular width, half way betwixt the harbour, or pier, and the frowning castle-gate, which terminated with its gloomy archway, portcullis, and flankers, the upper end of the vista. Midway this space was erected a rude gibbet, on which hung five dead bodies, two of which from their dress seemed to have been Lowlanders, and the other three corpses were muffled in their Highland plaids. Two or three women sate under the gallows, who seemed to be mourning, and singing the coronach of the deceased in a low voice. But the spectacle was apparently of too ordinary occurrence to have much interest for the inhabitants at large, who, while they thronged to look at the military figure, the horse of an unusual size, and the burnished panoply of Captain Dalgetty, seemed to bestow no attention whatever on the piteous spectacle which their own market-place afforded.

The envoy of Montrose was not quite so indifferent; and, hearing a word or two of English escape from a Highlander of decent appearance, he immediately halted Gustavus and addressed him, "The Provost-Marshal has been busy here, my friend. May I crave of you what these delinquents have been justified for?"

He looked towards the gibbet as he spoke; and the Gael, comprehending his meaning rather by his action than his words, immediately replied, "Three gentlemen caterans,—God sain them" (crossing himself)—"twa Sassenach bits o' bodies, that wadna do something that M'Callum More bade them;" and turning from Dalgetty with an air of indifference, away he walked, staying no farther question.

Dalgetty shrugged his shoulders and proceeded, for Sir Duncan Campbell's tenth or twelfth cousin had already shown some signs of impatience.

At the gate of the castle another terrible spectacle of feudal power awaited him. Within a stockade or palisade, which seemed lately to have been added to the defences of the gate, and which was protected by two pieces of light artillery, was a small enclosure, where stood a huge block, on which lay an axe. Both were smeared with recent blood, and a quantity of saw-dust strewed around, partly retained and partly obliterated the marks of a very late execution.

As Dalgetty looked on this new object of terror, his principal guide suddenly twitched him by the skirt of his jerkin, and having thus attracted his attention, winked and pointed with his finger to a pole fixed on the stockade, which supported a human head, being that, doubtless, of the late sufferer. There was a leer on the Highlander's face, as he pointed to this ghastly spectacle, which seemed to his fellow-traveller ominous of nothing good.

Dalgetty dismounted from his horse at the gateway, and Gustavus was taken from him without his being permitted to attend him to the stable, according to his custom.

This gave the soldier a pang which the apparatus of death had not conveyed.—"Poor Gustavus!" said he to himself, "if anything but good happens to me, I had better have left him at Darnlinvarach than brought him here among these Highland salvages, who scarce know the head of a horse from his tail. But duty must part a man from his nearest and dearest—

"When the cannons are roaring, lads, and the colours are
    flying,
The lads that seek honour must never fear dying;
Then, stout cavaliers, let us toil our brave trade in,
And fight for the Gospel and the bold King of Sweden."

Thus silencing his apprehensions with the but-end of a military ballad, he followed his guide into a sort of guard-room filled with armed Highlanders. It was intimated to him that he must remain here until his arrival was communicated to the Marquis. To make this communication the more intelligible, the doughty Captain gave to the Dunniewassel Sir Duncan Campbell's packet, desiring, as well as he could, by signs, that it should be delivered into the Marquis's own hand. His guide nodded, and withdrew.

The Captain was left about half an hour in this place, to endure with indifference, or return with scorn, the inquisitive, and, at the same time, the inimical glances of the armed Gael, to whom his exterior and equipage were as much subject of curiosity, as his person and country seemed matter of dislike. All this he bore with military nonchalance, until, at the expiration of the above period, a person dressed in black velvet, and wearing a gold chain like a modern magistrate of Edinburgh, but who was, in fact, steward of the household to the Marquis of Argyle, entered the apartment, and invited, with solemn gravity, the Captain to follow him to his master's presence.

The suite of apartments through which he passed, were filled with attendants or visitors of various descriptions, disposed, perhaps, with some ostentation, in order to impress the envoy of Montrose with an idea of the superior power and magnificence belonging to the rival house of Argyle. One ante-room was filled with lacqueys, arrayed in brown and yellow, the colours of the family, who, ranged in double file, gazed in silence upon Captain Dalgetty as he passed betwixt their ranks. Another was occupied by Highland gentlemen and chiefs of small branches, who were amusing themselves with chess, backgammon, and other games, which they scarce intermitted to gaze with curiosity upon the stranger. A third was filled with Lowland gentlemen and officers, who seemed also in attendance; and, lastly, the presence-chamber of the Marquis himself showed him attended by a levee which marked his high importance.

This apartment, the folding doors of which were opened for the reception of Captain Dalgetty, was a long gallery, decorated with tapestry and family portraits, and having a vaulted ceiling of open wood-work, the extreme projections of the beams being richly carved and gilded. The gallery was lighted by long lanceolated Gothic casements, divided by heavy shafts, and filled with painted glass, where the sunbeams glimmered dimly through boars'-heads, and galleys, and batons, and swords, armorial bearings of the powerful house of Argyle, and emblems of the high hereditary offices of Justiciary of Scotland, and Master of the Royal Household, which they long enjoyed. At the upper end of this magnificent gallery stood the Marquis himself, the centre of a splendid circle of Highland and Lowland gentlemen, all richly dressed, among whom were two or three of the clergy, called in, perhaps, to be witnesses of his lordship's zeal for the Covenant.

The Marquis himself was dressed in the fashion of the period, which Vandyke has so often painted, but his habit was sober and uniform in colour, and rather rich than gay. His dark complexion, furrowed forehead, and downcast look, gave him the appearance of one frequently engaged in the consideration of important affairs, and who has acquired, by long habit, an air of gravity and mystery, which he cannot shake off even where there is nothing to be concealed. The cast with his eyes, which had procured him in the Highlands the nickname of Gillespie Grumach (or the grim), was less perceptible when he looked downward, which perhaps was one cause of his having adopted that habit. In person, he was tall and thin, but not without that dignity of deportment and manners, which became his high rank. Something there was cold in his address, and sinister in his look, although he spoke and behaved with the usual grace of a man of such quality. He was adored by his own clan, whose advancement he had greatly studied, although he was in proportion disliked by the Highlanders of other septs, some of whom he had already stripped of their possessions, while others conceived themselves in danger from his future schemes, and all dreaded the height to which he was elevated.

We have already noticed, that in displaying himself amidst his councillors, his officers of the household, and his train of vassals, allies, and dependents, the Marquis of Argyle probably wished to make an impression on the nervous system of Captain Dugald Dalgetty. But that doughty person had fought his way, in one department or another, through the greater part of the Thirty Years' War in Germany, a period when a brave and successful soldier was a companion for princes. The King of Sweden, and, after his example, even the haughty Princes of the Empire, had found themselves fain, frequently to compound with their dignity, and silence, when they could not satisfy the pecuniary claims of their soldiers, by admitting them to unusual privileges and familiarity. Captain Dugald Dalgetty had it to boast, that he had sate with princes at feasts made for monarchs, and therefore was not a person to be brow-beat even by the dignity which surrounded M'Callum More. Indeed, he was naturally by no means the most modest man in the world, but, on the contrary, had so good an opinion of himself, that into whatever company he chanced to be thrown, he was always proportionally elevated in his own conceit; so that he felt as much at ease in the most exalted society as among his own ordinary companions. In this high opinion of his own rank, he was greatly fortified by his ideas of the military profession, which, in his phrase, made a valiant cavalier a camarade to an emperor.

When introduced, therefore, into the Marquis's presence-chamber, he advanced to the upper end with an air of more confidence than grace, and would have gone close up to Argyle's person before speaking, had not the latter waved his hand, as a signal to him to stop short. Captain Dalgetty did so accordingly, and having made his military congee with easy confidence, he thus accosted the Marquis: "Give you good morrow, my lord—or rather I should say, good even; BESO A USTED LOS MANOS, as the Spaniard says."

"Who are you, sir, and what is your business?" demanded the Marquis, in a tone which was intended to interrupt the offensive familiarity of the soldier.

"That is a fair interrogative, my lord," answered Dalgetty, "which I shall forthwith answer as becomes a cavalier, and that PEREMPTORIE, as we used to say at Mareschal-College."

"See who or what he is, Neal," said the Marquis sternly, to a gentleman who stood near him.

"I will save the honourable gentleman the labour of investigation," continued the Captain. "I am Dugald Dalgetty, of Drumthwacket, that should be, late Ritt-master in various services, and now Major of I know not what or whose regiment of Irishes; and I am come with a flag of truce from a high and powerful lord, James Earl of Montrose, and other noble persons now in arms for his Majesty. And so, God save King Charles!"

"Do you know where you are, and the danger of dallying with us, sir," again demanded the Marquis, "that you reply to me as if I were a child or a fool? The Earl of Montrose is with the English malignants; and I suspect you are one of those Irish runagates, who are come into this country to burn and slay, as they did under Sir Phelim O'Neale."

"My lord," replied Captain Dalgetty, "I am no renegade, though a Major of Irishes, for which I might refer your lordship to the invincible Gustavus Adolphus the Lion of the North, to Bannier, to Oxenstiern, to the warlike Duke of Saxe-Weimar, Tilly, Wallenstein, Piccolomini, and other great captains, both dead and living; and touching the noble Earl of Montrose, I pray your lordship to peruse these my full powers for treating with you in the name of that right honourable commander."

The Marquis looked slightingly at the signed and sealed paper which Captain Dalgetty handed to him, and, throwing it with contempt upon a table, asked those around him what he deserved who came as the avowed envoy and agent of malignant traitors, in arms against the state?

"A high gallows and a short shrift," was the ready answer of one of the bystanders.

"I will crave of that honourable cavalier who hath last spoken," said Dalgetty, "to be less hasty in forming his conclusions, and also of your lordship to be cautelous in adopting the same, in respect such threats are to be held out only to base bisognos, and not to men of spirit and action, who are bound to peril themselves as freely in services of this nature, as upon sieges, battles, or onslaughts of any sort. And albeit I have not with me a trumpet, or a white flag, in respect our army is not yet equipped with its full appointments, yet the honourable cavaliers and your lordship must concede unto me, that the sanctity of an envoy who cometh on matter of truth or parle, consisteth not in the fanfare of a trumpet, whilk is but a sound, or in the flap of a white flag, whilk is but an old rag in itself, but in the confidence reposed by the party sending, and the party sent, in the honour of those to whom the message is to be carried, and their full reliance that they will respect the JUS GENTIUM, as weel as the law of arms, in the person of the commissionate."

"You are not come hither to lecture us upon the law of arms, sir," said the Marquis, "which neither does nor can apply to rebels and insurgents; but to suffer the penalty of your insolence and folly for bringing a traitorous message to the Lord Justice General of Scotland, whose duty calls upon him to punish such an offence with death."

"Gentlemen," said the Captain, who began much to dislike the turn which his mission seemed about to take, "I pray you to remember, that the Earl of Montrose will hold you and your possessions liable for whatever injury my person, or my horse, shall sustain by these unseemly proceedings, and that he will be justified in executing retributive vengeance on your persons and possessions."

This menace was received with a scornful laugh, while one of the Campbells replied, "It is a far cry to Lochow;" proverbial expression of the tribe, meaning that their ancient hereditary domains lay beyond the reach of an invading enemy. "But, gentlemen," further urged the unfortunate Captain, who was unwilling to be condemned, without at least the benefit of a full hearing, "although it is not for me to say how far it may be to Lochow, in respect I am a stranger to these parts, yet, what is more to the purpose, I trust you will admit that I have the guarantee of an honourable gentleman of your own name, Sir Duncan Campbell of Ardenvohr, for my safety on this mission; and I pray you to observe, that in breaking the truce towards me, you will highly prejudicate his honour and fair fame."

This seemed to be new information to many of the gentlemen, for they spoke aside with each other, and the Marquis's face, notwithstanding his power of suppressing all external signs of his passions, showed impatience and vexation.

"Does Sir Duncan of Ardenvohr pledge his honour for this person's safety, my lord?" said one of the company, addressing the Marquis.

"I do not believe it," answered the Marquis; "but I have not yet had time to read his letter."

"We will pray your lordship to do so," said another of the Campbells; "our name must not suffer discredit through the means of such a fellow as this."

"A dead fly," said a clergyman, "maketh the ointment of the apothecary to stink."

"Reverend sir," said Captain Dalgetty, "in respect of the use to be derived, I forgive you the unsavouriness of your comparison; and also remit to the gentleman in the red bonnet, the disparaging epithet of FELLOW, which he has discourteously applied to me, who am no way to be distinguished by the same, unless in so far as I have been called fellow-soldier by the great Gustavus Adolphus, the Lion of the North, and other choice commanders, both in Germany and the Low Countries. But, touching Sir Duncan Campbell's guarantee of my safety, I will gage my life upon his making my words good thereanent, when he comes hither to-morrow."

"If Sir Duncan be soon expected, my Lord," said one of the intercessors, "it would be a pity to anticipate matters with this poor man."

"Besides that," said another, "your lordship—I speak with reverence—should, at least, consult the Knight of Ardenvohr's letter, and learn the terms on which this Major Dalgetty, as he calls himself, has been sent hither by him."

They closed around the Marquis, and conversed together in a low tone, both in Gaelic and English. The patriarchal power of the Chiefs was very great, and that of the Marquis of Argyle, armed with all his grants of hereditary jurisdiction, was particularly absolute. But there interferes some check of one kind or other even in the most despotic government. That which mitigated the power of the Celtic Chiefs, was the necessity which they lay under of conciliating the kinsmen who, under them, led out the lower orders to battle, and who formed a sort of council of the tribe in time of peace. The Marquis on this occasion thought himself under the necessity of attending to the remonstrances of this senate, or more properly COUROULTAI, of the name of Campbell, and, slipping out of the circle, gave orders for the prisoner to be removed to a place of security.

"Prisoner!" exclaimed Dalgetty, exerting himself with such force as wellnigh to shake off two Highlanders, who for some minutes past had waited the signal to seize him, and kept for that purpose close at his back. Indeed the soldier had so nearly attained his liberty, that the Marquis of Argyle changed colour, and stepped back two paces, laying, however, his hand on his sword, while several of his clan, with ready devotion, threw themselves betwixt him and the apprehended vengeance of the prisoner. But the Highland guards were too strong to be shaken off, and the unlucky Captain, after having had his offensive weapons taken from him, was dragged off and conducted through several gloomy passages to a small side-door grated with iron, within which was another of wood. These were opened by a grim old Highlander with a long white beard, and displayed a very steep and narrow flight of steps leading downward. The Captain's guards pushed him down two or three steps, then, unloosing his arms, left him to grope his way to the bottom as he could; a task which became difficult and even dangerous, when the two doors being successively locked left the prisoner in total darkness.

CHAPTER XIII.

Whatever stranger visits here,
We pity his sad case,
Unless to worship he draw near
The King of Kings—his Grace.
—BURNS'S EPIGRAM ON A VISIT TO INVERARY.

The Captain, finding himself deprived of light in the manner
we have described, and placed in a very uncertain situation,
proceeded to descend the narrow and broken stair with all the
caution in his power, hoping that he might find at the bottom
some place to repose himself. But with all his care he could not
finally avoid making a false step, which brought him down the
four or five last steps too hastily to preserve his equilibrium. At
the bottom he stumbled over a bundle of something soft, which
stirred and uttered a groan, so deranging the Captain's descent, that
he floundered forward, and finally fell upon his hands and knees on
the floor of a damp and stone-paved dungeon.

When Dalgetty had recovered, his first demand was to know
over whom he had stumbled.

"He was a man a month since," answered a hollow and broken
voice.

"And what is he now, then," said Dalgetty, "that he thinks it
fitting to lie upon the lowest step of the stairs, and clew'd up like
a hurchin, that honourable cavaliers, who chance to be in trouble,
may break their noses over him?"

"What is he now?" replied the same voice; "he is a wretched
trunk, from which the boughs have one by one been lopped away,
and which cares little how soon it is torn up and hewed into billets
for the furnace."

"Friend," said Dalgetty, "I am sorry for you; but PATIENZA, as the Spaniard says. If you had but been as quiet as a log, as you call yourself, I should have saved some excoriations on my hands and knees."

"You are a soldier," replied his fellow-prisoner; "do you complain on account of a fall for which a boy would not bemoan himself?"

"A soldier?" said the Captain; "and how do you know, in this cursed dark cavern, that I am a soldier?"

"I heard your armour clash as you fell," replied the prisoner, "and now I see it glimmer. When you have remained as long as I in this darkness, your eyes will distinguish the smallest eft that crawls on the floor."

"I had rather the devil picked them out!" said Dalgetty; "if this be the case, I shall wish for a short turn of the rope, a soldier's prayer, and a leap from a ladder. But what sort of provant have you got here—what food, I mean, brother in affliction?"

"Bread and water once a day," replied the voice.

"Prithee, friend, let me taste your loaf," said Dalgetty; "I hope we shall play good comrades while we dwell together in this abominable pit."

"The loaf and jar of water," answered the other prisoner, "stand in the corner, two steps to your right hand. Take them, and welcome. With earthly food I have wellnigh done."

Dalgetty did not wait for a second invitation, but, groping out the provisions, began to munch at the stale black oaten loaf with as much heartiness as we have seen him play his part at better viands.

"This bread," he said, muttering (with his mouth full at the same time), "is not very savoury; nevertheless, it is not much worse than that which we ate at the famous leaguer at Werben, where the valorous Gustavus foiled all the efforts of the celebrated Tilly, that terrible old hero, who had driven two kings out of the field—namely, Ferdinand of Bohemia and Christian of Denmark. And anent this water, which is none of the most sweet, I drink in the same to your speedy deliverance, comrade, not forgetting mine own, and devoutly wishing it were Rhenish wine, or humming Lubeck beer, at the least, were it but in honour of the pledge."

While Dalgetty ran on in this way, his teeth kept time with his tongue, and he speedily finished the provisions which the benevolence or indifference of his companion in misfortune had abandoned to his voracity. When this task was accomplished, he wrapped himself in his cloak, and seating himself in a corner of the dungeon in which he could obtain a support on each side (for he had always been an admirer of elbow-chairs, he remarked, even from his youth upward), he began to question his fellow-captive.

"Mine honest friend," said he, "you and I, being comrades at bed and board, should be better acquainted. I am Dugald Dalgetty of Drumthwacket, and so forth, Major in a regiment of loyal Irishes, and Envoy Extraordinary of a High and Mighty Lord, James Earl of Montrose.—Pray, what may your name be?"

"It will avail you little to know," replied his more taciturn companion.

"Let me judge of that matter," answered the soldier.

"Well, then—Ranald MacEagh is my name—that is, Ranald Son of the Mist."

"Son of the Mist!" ejaculated Dalgetty. "Son of utter darkness, say I. But, Ranald, since that is your name, how came you in possession of the provost's court of guard? what the devil brought you here, that is to say?"

"My misfortunes and my crimes," answered Ranald. "Know ye the Knight of Ardenvohr?"

"I do know that honourable person," replied Dalgetty.

"But know ye where he now is?" replied Ranald.

"Fasting this day at Ardenvohr," answered the Envoy, "that he may feast to-morrow at Inverary; in which last purpose if he chance to fail, my lease of human service will be something precarious."

"Then let him know, one claims his intercession, who is his worst foe and his best friend," answered Ranald.

"Truly I shall desire to carry a less questionable message," answered Dalgetty, "Sir Duncan is not a person to play at reading riddles with."

"Craven Saxon," said the prisoner, "tell him I am the raven that, fifteen years since, stooped on his tower of strength and the pledges he had left there—I am the hunter that found out the wolfs den on the rock, and destroyed his offspring—I am the leader of the band which surprised Ardenvohr yesterday was fifteen years, and gave his four children to the sword."

"Truly, my honest friend," said Dalgetty, "if that is your best recommendation to Sir Duncan's favour, I would pretermit my pleading thereupon, in respect I have observed that even the animal creation are incensed against those who intromit with their offspring forcibly, much more any rational and Christian creatures, who have had violence done upon their small family. But I pray you in courtesy to tell me, whether you assailed the castle from the hillock called Drumsnab, whilk I uphold to be the true point of attack, unless it were to be protected by a sconce."

"We ascended the cliff by ladders of withies or saplings," said the prisoner, "drawn up by an accomplice and clansman, who had served six months in the castle to enjoy that one night of unlimited vengeance. The owl whooped around us as we hung betwixt heaven and earth; the tide roared against the foot of the rock, and dashed asunder our skiff. yet no man's heart failed him. In the morning there was blood and ashes, where there had been peace and joy at the sunset."

"It was a pretty camisade, I doubt not, Ranald MacEagh, a very sufficient onslaught, and not unworthily discharged. Nevertheless, I would have pressed the house from that little hillock called Drumsnab. But yours is a pretty irregular Scythian fashion of warfare, Ranald, much resembling that of Turks, Tartars, and other Asiatic people.—But the reason, my friend, the cause of this war—the TETERRIMA CAUSA, as I may say? Deliver me that, Ranald."

"We had been pushed at by the M'Aulays, and other western tribes," said Ranald, "till our possessions became unsafe for us."

"Ah ha!" said Dalgetty; "I have faint remembrance of having heard of that matter. Did you not put bread and cheese into a man's mouth, when he had never a stomach whereunto to transmit the same?"

"You have heard, then," said Ranald, "the tale of our revenge on the haughty forester?"

"I bethink me that I have," said Dalgetty, "and that not of an old date. It was a merry jest that, of cramming the bread into the dead man's mouth, but somewhat too wild and salvage for civilized acceptation, besides wasting the good victuals. I have seen when at a siege or a leaguer, Ranald, a living soldier would have been the better, Ranald, for that crust of bread, whilk you threw away on a dead pow."

"We were attacked by Sir Duncan," continued MacEagh, "and my brother was slain—his head was withering on the battlements which we scaled—I vowed revenge, and it is a vow I have never broken."

"It may be so," said Dalgetty; "and every thorough-bred soldier will confess that revenge is a sweet morsel; but in what manner this story will interest Sir Duncan in your justification, unless it should move him to intercede with the Marquis to change the manner thereof from hanging, or simple suspension, to breaking your limbs on the roue or wheel, with the coulter of a plough, or otherwise putting you to death by torture, surpasses my comprehension. Were I you, Ranald, I would be for miskenning Sir Duncan, keeping my own secret, and departing quietly by suffocation, like your ancestors before you."

"Yet hearken, stranger," said the Highlander. "Sir Duncan of Ardenvohr had four children. Three died under our dirks, but the fourth survives; and more would he give to dandle on his knee the fourth child which remains, than to rack these old bones, which care little for the utmost indulgence of his wrath. One word, if I list to speak it, could turn his day of humiliation and fasting into a day of thankfulness and rejoicing, and breaking of bread. O, I know it by my own heart? Dearer to me is the child Kenneth, who chaseth the butterfly on the banks of the Aven, than ten sons who are mouldering in earth, or are preyed on by the fowls of the air."

"I presume, Ranald," continued Dalgetty, "that the three pretty fellows whom I saw yonder in the market-place, strung up by the head like rizzer'd haddocks, claimed some interest in you?"

There was a brief pause ere the Highlander replied, in a tone of strong emotion,—"They were my sons, stranger—they were my sons!—blood of my blood—bone of my bone!—fleet of foot—unerring in aim—unvanquished by foemen till the sons of Diarmid overcame them by numbers! Why do I wish to survive them? The old trunk will less feel the rending up of its roots, than it has felt the lopping off of its graceful boughs. But Kenneth must be trained to revenge—the young eagle must learn from the old how to stoop on his foes. I will purchase for his sake my life and my freedom, by discovering my secret to the Knight of Ardenvohr."

"You may attain your end more easily," said a third voice, mingling in the conference, "by entrusting it to me."

All Highlanders are superstitious. "The Enemy of Mankind is among us!" said Ranald MacEagh, springing to his feet. His chains clattered as he rose, while he drew himself as far as they permitted from the quarter whence the voice appeared to proceed. His fear in some degree communicated itself to Captain Dalgetty, who began to repeat, in a sort of polyglot gibberish, all the exorcisms he had ever heard of, without being able to remember more than a word or two of each.

"IN NOMINE DOMINI, as we said at Mareschal-College— SANTISSMA MADRE DI DIOS, as the Spaniard has it—ALLE GUTEN GEISTER LOBEN DEN HERRN, saith the blessed Psalmist, in Dr. Luther's translation—"

"A truce with your exorcisms," said the voice they had heard before; "though I come strangely among you, I am mortal like yourselves, and my assistance may avail you in your present streight, if you are not too proud to be counselled."

While the stranger thus spoke, he withdrew the shade of a dark lantern, by whose feeble light Dalgetty could only discern that the speaker who had thus mysteriously united himself to their company, and mixed in their conversation, was a tall man, dressed in a livery cloak of the Marquis. His first glance was to his feet, but he saw neither the cloven foot which Scottish legends assign to the foul fiend, nor the horse's hoof by which he is distinguished in Germany. His first enquiry was, how the stranger had come among them?

"For," said he, "the creak of these rusty bars would have been heard had the door been made patent; and if you passed through the keyhole, truly, sir, put what face you will on it, you are not fit to be enrolled in a regiment of living men."

"I reserve my secret," answered the stranger, "until you shall merit the discovery by communicating to me some of yours. It may be that I shall be moved to let you out where I myself came in."

"It cannot be through the keyhole, then," said Captain Dalgetty, "for my corslet would stick in the passage, were it possible that my head-piece could get through. As for secrets, I have none of my own, and but few appertaining to others. But impart to us what secrets you desire to know; or, as Professor Snufflegreek used to say at the Mareschal-College, Aberdeen, speak that I may know thee."

"It is not with you I have first to do," replied the stranger, turning his light full on the mild and wasted features, and the large limbs of the Highlander, Ranald MacEagh, who, close drawn up against the walls of the dungeon, seemed yet uncertain whether his guest was a living being.

"I have brought you something, my friend," said the stranger, in a more soothing tone, "to mend your fare; if you are to die tomorrow, it is no reason wherefore you should not live to-night."

"None at all—no reason in the creation," replied the ready Captain Dalgetty, who forthwith began to unpack the contents of a small basket which the stranger had brought under his cloak, while the Highlander, either in suspicion or disdain, paid no attention to the good cheer.

"Here's to thee, my friend," said the Captain, who, having already dispatched a huge piece of roasted kid, was now taking a pull at the wine-flask. "What is thy name, my good friend?"

"Murdoch Campbell, sir," answered the servant, "a lackey of the Marquis of Argyle, and occasionally acting as under-warden."

"Then here is to thee once more, Murdoch," said Dalgetty, "drinking to you by your proper name for the better luck sake. This wine I take to be Calcavella. Well, honest Murdoch, I take it on me to say, thou deservest to be upper-warden, since thou showest thyself twenty times better acquainted with the way of victualling honest gentlemen that are under misfortune, than thy principal. Bread and water? out upon him! It was enough, Murdoch, to destroy the credit of the Marquis's dungeon. But I see you would converse with my friend, Ranald MacEagh here. Never mind my presence; I'll get me into this corner with the basket, and I will warrant my jaws make noise enough to prevent my ears from hearing you."

Notwithstanding this promise, however, the veteran listened with all the attention he could to gather their discourse, or, as he described it himself, "laid his ears back in his neck, like Gustavus, when he heard the key turn in the girnell-kist." He could, therefore, owing to the narrowness of the dungeon, easily overhear the following dialogue.

"Are you aware, Son of the Mist," said the Campbell, "that you will never leave this place excepting for the gibbet?"

"Those who are dearest to me," answered MacEagh, "have trode that path before me."

"Then you would do nothing," asked the visitor, "to shun following them?"

The prisoner writhed himself in his chains before returning an answer.

"I would do much," at length he said; "not for my own life, but for the sake of the pledge in the glen of Strath-Aven."

"And what would you do to turn away the bitterness of the hour?" again demanded Murdoch; "I care not for what cause ye mean to shun it."

"I would do what a man might do, and still call himself a man."

"Do you call yourself a man," said the interrogator, "who have done the deeds of a wolf?"

"I do," answered the outlaw; "I am a man like my forefathers—while wrapt in the mantle of peace, we were lambs—it was rent from us, and ye now call us wolves. Give us the huts ye have burned, our children whom ye have murdered, our widows whom ye have starved—collect from the gibbet and the pole the mangled carcasses, and whitened skulls of our kinsmen—bid them live and bless us, and we will be your vassals and brothers—till then, let death, and blood, and mutual wrong, draw a dark veil of division between us."

"You will then do nothing for your liberty," said the Campbell.

"Anything—but call myself the friend of your tribe," answered MacEagh.

"We scorn the friendship of banditti and caterans," retorted Murdoch, "and would not stoop to accept it.—What I demand to know from you, in exchange for your liberty, is, where the daughter and heiress of the Knight of Ardenvohr is now to be found?"

"That you may wed her to some beggarly kinsman of your great master," said Ranald, "after the fashion of the Children of Diarmid! Does not the valley of Glenorquhy, to this very hour, cry shame on the violence offered to a helpless infant whom her kinsmen were conveying to the court of the Sovereign? Were not her escort compelled to hide her beneath a cauldron, round which they fought till not one remained to tell the tale? and was not the girl brought to this fatal castle, and afterwards wedded to the brother of M'Callum More, and all for the sake of her broad lands?" [Such a story is told of the heiress of the clan of Calder, who was made prisoner in the manner described, and afterwards wedded to Sir Duncan Campbell, from which union the Campbells of Cawdor have their descent.]

"And if the tale be true," said Murdoch, "she had a preferment beyond what the King of Scots would have conferred on her. But this is far from the purpose. The daughter of Sir Duncan of Ardenvohr is of our own blood, not a stranger; and who has so good a right to know her fate as M'Callum More, the chief of her clan?"

"It is on his part, then, that you demand it!" said the outlaw. The domestic of the Marquis assented.

"And you will practise no evil against the maiden?—I have done her wrong enough already."

"No evil, upon the word of a Christian man," replied Murdoch.

"And my guerdon is to be life and liberty?" said the Child of the Mist.

"Such is our paction," replied the Campbell.

"Then know, that the child whom I saved out of compassion at the spoiling of her father's tower of strength, was bred as an adopted daughter of our tribe, until we were worsted at the pass of Ballenduthil, by the fiend incarnate and mortal enemy of our tribe, Allan M'Aulay of the Bloody hand, and by the horsemen of Lennox, under the heir of Menteith."

"Fell she into the power of Allan of the Bloody hand," said Murdoch, "and she a reputed daughter of thy tribe? Then her blood has gilded the dirk, and thou hast said nothing to rescue thine own forfeited life."

"If my life rest on hers," answered the outlaw, "it is secure, for she still survives; but it has a more insecure reliance—the frail promise of a son of Diarmid."

"That promise shall not fail you," said the Campbell, "if you can assure me that she survives, and where she is to be found."

"In the Castle of Darlinvarach," said Ranald MacEagh, "under the name of Annot Lyle. I have often heard of her from my kinsmen, who have again approached their native woods, and it is not long since mine old eyes beheld her."

"You!" said Murdoch, in astonishment, "you, a chief among the Children of the Mist, and ventured so near your mortal foe?"

"Son of Diarmid, I did more," replied the outlaw; "I was in the hall of the castle, disguised as a harper from the wild shores of Skianach. My purpose was to have plunged my dirk in the body of the M'Aulay with the Bloody hand, before whom our race trembles, and to have taken thereafter what fate God should send me. But I saw Annot Lyle, even when my hand was on the hilt of my dagger. She touched her clairshach [Harp] to a song of the Children of the Mist, which she had learned when her dwelling was amongst us. The woods in which we had dwelt pleasantly, rustled their green leaves in the song, and our streams were there with the sound of all their waters. My hand forsook the dagger; the fountains of mine eyes were opened, and the hour of revenge passed away.—And now, Son of Diarmid, have I not paid the ransom of my head?"

"Ay," replied Murdoch, "if your tale be true; but what proof can you assign for it?"

"Bear witness, heaven and earth," exclaimed the outlaw, "he already looks how he may step over his word!"

"Not so," replied Murdoch; "every promise shall be kept to you when I am assured you have told me the truth.—But I must speak a few words with your companion in captivity."

"Fair and false—ever fair and false," muttered the prisoner, as he threw himself once more on the floor of his dungeon.

Meanwhile, Captain Dalgetty, who had attended to every word of this dialogue, was making his own remarks on it in private. "What the HENKER can this sly fellow have to say to me? I have no child, either of my own, so far as I know, or of any other person, to tell him a tale about. But let him come on—he will have some manoeuvring ere he turn the flank of the old soldier."

Accordingly, as if he had stood pike in hand to defend a breach, he waited with caution, but without fear, the commencement of the attack.

"You are a citizen of the world, Captain Dalgetty," said Murdoch Campbell, "and cannot be ignorant of our old Scotch proverb, GIF-GAF, [In old English, KA ME KA THEE, i.e.

mutually serving each other.] which goes through all nations and all services."

"Then I should know something of it," said Dalgetty; "for, except the Turks, there are few powers in Europe whom I have not served; and I have sometimes thought of taking a turn either with Bethlem Gabor, or with the Janizaries."

"A man of your experience and unprejudiced ideas, then, will understand me at once," said Murdoch, "when I say, I mean that your freedom shall depend on your true and up right answer to a few trifling questions respecting the gentlemen you have left; their state of preparation; the number of their men, and nature of their appointments; and as much as you chance to know about their plan of operations."

"Just to satisfy your curiosity," said Dalgetty, "and without any farther purpose?"

"None in the world," replied Murdoch; "what interest should a poor devil like me take in their operations?"

"Make your interrogations, then," said the Captain, "and I will answer them PREREMTORIE."

"How many Irish may be on their march to join James Graham the delinquent?"

"Probably ten thousand," said Captain Dalgetty.

"Ten thousand!" replied Murdoch angrily; "we know that scarce two thousand landed at Ardnamurchan."

"Then you know more about them than I do," answered Captain Dalgetty, with great composure. "I never saw them mustered yet, or even under arms."

"And how many men of the clans may be expected?" demanded Murdoch.

"As many as they can make," replied the Captain.

"You are answering from the purpose, sir," said Murdoch "speak plainly, will there be five thousand men?"

"There and thereabouts," answered Dalgetty.

"You are playing with your life, sir, if you trifle with me," replied the catechist; "one whistle of mine, and in less than ten minutes your head hangs on the drawbridge."

"But to speak candidly, Mr. Murdoch," replied the Captain "do you think it is a reasonable thing to ask me after the secrets of our army, and I engaged to serve for the whole campaign? If

I taught you how to defeat Montrose, what becomes of my pay, arrears, and chance of booty?"

"I tell you," said Campbell, "that if you be stubborn, your campaign shall begin and end in a march to the block at the castle-gate, which stands ready for such land-laufers; but if you answer my questions faithfully, I will receive you into my—into the service of M'Callum More."

"Does the service afford good pay?" said Captain Dalgetty.

"He will double yours, if you will return to Montrose and act under his direction."

"I wish I had seen you, sir, before taking on with him," said Dalgetty, appearing to meditate.

"On the contrary, I can afford you more advantageous terms now," said the Campbell; "always supposing that you are faithful."

"Faithful, that is, to you, and a traitor to Montrose," answered the Captain.

"Faithful to the cause of religion and good order," answered Murdoch, "which sanctifies any deception you may employ to serve it."

"And the Marquis of Argyle—should I incline to enter his service, is he a kind master?" demanded Dalgetty.

"Never man kinder," quoth Campbell.

"And bountiful to his officers?" pursued the Captain.

"The most open hand in Scotland," replied Murdoch.

"True and faithful to his engagements?" continued Dalgetty.

"As honourable a nobleman as breathes," said the clansman.

"I never heard so much good of him before," said Dalgetty; "you must know the Marquis well,—or rather you must be the Marquis himself!—Lord of Argyle," he added, throwing himself suddenly on the disguised nobleman, "I arrest you in the name of King Charles, as a traitor. If you venture to call for assistance, I will wrench round your neck."

The attack which Dalgetty made upon Argyle's person was so sudden and unexpected, that he easily prostrated him on the floor of the dungeon, and held him down with one hand, while his right, grasping the Marquis's throat, was ready to strangle him on the slightest attempt to call for assistance.

"Lord of Argyle," he said, "it is now my turn to lay down the terms of capitulation. If you list to show me the private way by which you entered the dungeon, you shall escape, on condition of being my LOCUM TENENS, as we said at the Mareschal-College, until your warder visits his prisoners. But if not, I will first strangle you—I learned the art from a Polonian heyduck, who had been a slave in the Ottoman seraglio—and then seek out a mode of retreat."

"Villain! you would not murder me for my kindness," murmured Argyle.

"Not for your kindness, my lord," replied Dalgetty: "but first, to teach your lordship the JUS GENTIUM towards cavaliers who come to you under safe-conduct; and secondly, to warn you of the danger of proposing dishonourable terms to any worthy soldado, in order to tempt him to become false to his standard during the term of his service."

"Spare my life," said Argyle, "and I will do as you require."

Dalgetty maintained his gripe upon the Marquis's throat, compressing it a little while he asked questions, and relaxing it so far as to give him the power of answering them.

"Where is the secret door into the dungeon?" he demanded.

"Hold up the lantern to the corner on your right hand, you will discern the iron which covers the spring," replied the Marquis.

"So far so good.—Where does the passage lead to?"

"To my private apartment behind the tapestry," answered the prostrate nobleman.

"From thence how shall I reach the gateway?"

"Through the grand gallery, the anteroom, the lackeys' waiting hall, the grand guardroom—"

"All crowded with soldiers, factionaries, and attendants?—that will never do for me, my lord;—have you no secret passage to the gate, as you have to your dungeons? I have seen such in Germany."

"There is a passage through the chapel," said the Marquis, "opening from my apartment."

"And what is the pass-word at the gate?"

"The sword of Levi," replied the Marquis; "but if you will receive my pledge of honour, I will go with you, escort you through every guard, and set you at full liberty with a passport."

"I might trust you, my lord, were your throat not already black with the grasp of my fingers—as it is, BESO LOS MANOS A

USTED, as the Spaniard says. Yet you may grant me a passport;—are there writing materials in your apartment?"

"Surely; and blank passports ready to be signed. I will attend you there," said the Marquis, "instantly."

"It were too much honour for the like of me," said Dalgetty; "your lordship shall remain under charge of mine honest friend Ranald MacEagh; therefore, prithee let me drag you within reach of his chain.—Honest Ranald, you see how matters stand with us. I shall find the means, I doubt not, of setting you at freedom. Meantime, do as you see me do; clap your hand thus on the weasand of this high and mighty prince, under his ruff, and if he offer to struggle or cry out, fail not, my worthy Ranald, to squeeze doughtily; and if it be AD DELIQUIUM, Ranald, that is, till he swoon, there is no great matter, seeing he designed your gullet and mine to still harder usage."

"If he offer at speech or struggle," said Ranald, "he dies by my hand."

"That is right, Ranald—very spirited:—A thorough-going friend that understands a hint is worth a million!"

Thus resigning the charge of the Marquis to his new confederate, Dalgetty pressed the spring, by which the secret door flew open, though so well were its hinges polished and oiled, that it made not the slightest noise in revolving. The opposite side of the door was secured by very strong bolts and bars, beside which hung one or two keys, designed apparently to undo fetterlocks. A narrow staircase, ascending up through the thickness of the castle-wall, landed, as the Marquis had truly informed him, behind the tapestry of his private apartment. Such communications were frequent in old feudal castles, as they gave the lord of the fortress, like a second Dionysius, the means of hearing the conversation of his prisoners, or, if he pleased, of visiting them in disguise, an experiment which had terminated so unpleasantly on the present occasion for Gillespie Grumach. Having examined previously whether there was any one in the apartment, and finding the coast clear, the Captain entered, and hastily possessing himself of a blank passport, several of which lay on the table, and of writing materials, securing, at the same time, the Marquis's dagger, and a silk cord from the hangings, he again descended into the cavern, where, listening a moment at the door, he could hear the half-stifled voice of the Marquis making great proffers to MacEagh, on condition he would suffer him to give an alarm.

"Not for a forest of deer—not for a thousand head of cattle," answered the freebooter; "not for all the lands that ever called a son of Diarmid master, will I break the troth I have plighted to him of the iron-garment!"

"He of the iron-garment," said Dalgetty, entering, "is bounden unto you, MacEagh, and this noble lord shall be bounden also; but first he must fill up this passport with the names of Major Dugald Dalgetty and his guide, or he is like to have a passport to another world."

The Marquis subscribed, and wrote, by the light of the dark lantern, as the soldier prescribed to him.

"And now, Ranald," said Dalgetty, "strip thy upper garment— thy plaid I mean, Ranald, and in it will I muffle the M'Callum More, and make of him, for the time, a Child of the Mist;—Nay, I must bring it over your head, my lord, so as to secure us against your mistimed clamour.—So, now he is sufficiently muffled;—hold down your hands, or, by Heaven, I will stab you to the heart with your own dagger!—nay, you shall be bound with nothing less than silk, as your quality deserves.—So, now he is secure till some one comes to relieve him. If he ordered us a late dinner, Ranald, he is like to be the sufferer;—at what hour, my good Ranald, did the jailor usually appear?"

"Never till the sun was beneath the western wave," said MacEagh. "Then, my friend, we shall have three hours good," said the cautious Captain. "In the meantime, let us labour for your liberation."

To examine Ranald's chain was the next occupation. It was undone by means of one of the keys which hung behind the private door, probably deposited there, that the Marquis might, if he pleased, dismiss a prisoner, or remove him elsewhere without the necessity of summoning the warden. The outlaw stretched his benumbed arms, and bounded from the floor of the dungeon in all the ecstasy of recovered freedom.

"Take the livery-coat of that noble prisoner," said Captain Dalgetty; "put it on, and follow close at my heels."

The outlaw obeyed. They ascended the private stair, having first secured the door behind them, and thus safely reached the apartment of the Marquis.

[The precarious state of the feudal nobles introduced a great deal of espionage into their castles. Sir Robert Carey mentions his having put on the cloak of one of his own wardens to obtain a confession from the mouth of Geordie Bourne, his prisoner, whom he caused presently to be hanged in return for the frankness of his communication. The fine old Border castle of Naworth contains a private stair from the apartment of the Lord William Howard, by which he could visit the dungeon, as is alleged in the preceding chapter to have been practised by the Marquis of Argyle.]

CHAPTER XIV.

This was the entry then, these stairs—but whither after?
Yet he that's sure to perish on the land
May quit the nicety of card and compass,
And trust the open sea without a pilot.
—TRAGEDY OF BENNOVALT.

"Look out for the private way through the chapel, Ranald," said the Captain, "while I give a hasty regard to these matters."

Thus speaking, he seized with one hand a bundle of Argyle's most private papers, and with the other a purse of gold, both of which lay in a drawer of a rich cabinet, which stood invitingly open. Neither did he neglect to possess himself of a sword and pistols, with powder-flask and balls, which hung in the apartment. "Intelligence and booty," said the veteran, as he pouched the spoils, "each honourable cavalier should look to, the one on his general's behalf, and the other on his own. This sword is an Andrew Ferrara, and the pistols better than mine own. But a fair exchange is no robbery. Soldados are not to be endangered, and endangered gratuitously, my Lord of Argyle.—But soft, soft, Ranald; wise Man of the Mist, whither art thou bound?"

It was indeed full time to stop MacEagh's proceedings; for, not finding the private passage readily, and impatient, it would seem, of farther delay, he had caught down a sword and target, and was about to enter the great gallery, with the purpose, doubtless, of fighting his way through all opposition.

"Hold, while you live," whispered Dalgetty, laying hold on him. "We must be perdue, if possible. So bar we this door, that it may be thought M'Callum More would be private—and now let me make a reconnaissance for the private passage."

By looking behind the tapestry in various places, the Captain at length discovered a private door, and behind that a winding passage, terminated by another door, which doubtless entered the chapel. But what was his disagreeable surprise to hear, on the other side of this second door, the sonorous voice of a divine in the act of preaching.

"This made the villain," he said, "recommend this to us as a private passage. I am strongly tempted to return and cut his throat."

He then opened very gently the door, which led into a latticed gallery used by the Marquis himself, the curtains of which were drawn, perhaps with the purpose of having it supposed that he was engaged in attendance upon divine worship, when, in fact, he was absent upon his secular affairs. There was no other person in the seat; for the family of the Marquis,—such was the high state maintained in those days,—sate during service in another gallery, placed somewhat lower than that of the great man himself. This being the case, Captain Dalgetty ventured to ensconce himself in the gallery, of which he carefully secured the door.

Never (although the expression be a bold one) was a sermon listened to with more impatience, and less edification, on the part of one, at least, of the audience. The Captain heard SIXTEENTHLY-SEVENTEENTHLY-EIGHTEENTHLY and TO CONCLUDE, with a sort of feeling like protracted despair. But no man can lecture (for the service was called a lecture) for ever; and the discourse was at length closed, the clergyman not failing to make a profound bow towards the latticed gallery, little suspecting whom he honoured by that reverence. To judge from the haste with which they dispersed, the domestics of the Marquis were scarce more pleased with their late occupation than the anxious Captain Dalgetty; indeed, many of them being Highlandmen, had the excuse of not understanding a single word which the clergyman spoke, although they gave their attendance on his doctrine by the special order of M'Callum More, and would have done so had the preacher been a Turkish Imaum.

But although the congregation dispersed thus rapidly, the divine remained behind in the chapel, and, walking up and down its Gothic precincts, seemed either to be meditating on what he had just been delivering, or preparing a fresh discourse for the next opportunity. Bold as he was, Dalgetty hesitated what he ought to do.

Time, however, pressed, and every moment increased the chance of their escape being discovered by the jailor visiting the dungeon perhaps before his wonted time, and discovering the exchange which had been made there. At length, whispering Ranald, who watched all his motions, to follow him and preserve his countenance, Captain Dalgetty, with a very composed air, descended a flight of steps which led from the gallery into the body of the chapel. A less experienced adventurer would have endeavoured to pass the worthy clergyman rapidly, in hopes to escape unnoticed. But the Captain, who foresaw the manifest danger of failing in such an attempt, walked gravely to meet the divine upon his walk in the midst of the chancel, and, pulling off his cap, was about to pass him after a formal reverence. But what was his surprise to view in the preacher the very same person with whom he had dined in the castle of Ardenvohr! Yet he speedily recovered his composure; and ere the clergyman could speak, was the first to address him. "I could not," he said, "leave this mansion without bequeathing to you, my very reverend sir, my humble thanks for the homily with which you have this evening favoured us."

"I did not observe, sir," said the clergyman, "that you were in the chapel."

"It pleased the honourable Marquis," said Dalgetty, modestly, "to grace me with a seat in his own gallery." The divine bowed low at this intimation, knowing that such an honour was only vouchsafed to persons of very high rank. "It has been my fate, sir," said the Captain, "in the sort of wandering life which I have led, to have heard different preachers of different religions—as for example, Lutheran, Evangelical, Reformed, Calvinistical, and so forth, but never have I listened to such a homily as yours."

"Call it a lecture, worthy sir," said the divine, "such is the phrase of our church."

"Lecture or homily," said Dalgetty, "it was, as the High Germans say, GANZ FORTRE FLICH; and I could not leave this place without testifying unto you what inward emotions I have undergone during your edifying prelection; and how I am touched to the quick, that I should yesterday, during the refection, have seemed to infringe on the respect due to such a person as yourself."

"Alas! my worthy sir," said the clergyman, "we meet in this world as in the Valley of the Shadow of Death, not knowing against whom we may chance to encounter. In truth, it is no matter of marvel, if we sometimes jostle those, to whom, if known, we would yield all respect. Surely, sir, I would rather have taken you for a profane malignant than for such a devout person as you prove, who reverences the great Master even in the meanest of his servants."

"It is always my custom to do so, learned sir," answered Dalgetty; "for in the service of the immortal Gustavus—but I detain you from your meditations,"—his desire to speak of the King of Sweden being for once overpowered by the necessity of his circumstances.

"By no means, my worthy sir," said the clergyman. "What was, I pray you, the order of that great Prince, whose memory is so dear to every Protestant bosom?"

"Sir, the drums beat to prayers morning and evening, as regularly as for parade; and if a soldier passed without saluting the chaplain, he had an hour's ride on the wooden mare for his pains. Sir, I wish you a very good evening—I am obliged to depart the castle under M'Callum More's passport."

"Stay one instant, sir," said the preacher; "is there nothing I can do to testify my respect for the pupil of the great Gustavus, and so admirable a judge of preaching?"

"Nothing, sir," said the Captain, "but to shew me the nearest way to the gate—and if you would have the kindness," he added, with great effrontery, "to let a servant bring my horse with him, the dark grey gelding—call him Gustavus, and he will prick up his ears—for I know not where the castle-stables are situated, and my guide," he added, looking at Ranald, "speaks no English."

"I hasten to accommodate you," said the clergyman; "your way lies through that cloistered passage."

"Now, Heaven's blessing upon your vanity!" said the Captain to himself. "I was afraid I would have had to march off without Gustavus."

In fact, so effectually did the chaplain exert himself in behalf of so excellent a judge of composition, that while Dalgetty was parleying with the sentinels at the drawbridge, showing his passport, and giving the watchword, a servant brought him his horse, ready saddled for the journey. In another place, the Captain's sudden appearance at large after having been publicly sent to prison, might have excited suspicion and enquiry; but the officers and domestics of the Marquis were accustomed to the mysterious policy of their master, and never supposed aught else than that he had been liberated and intrusted with some private commission by their master. In this belief, and having received the parole, they gave him free passage.

Dalgetty rode slowly through the town of Inverary, the outlaw attending upon him like a foot-page at his horse's shoulder. As they passed the gibbet, the old man looked on the bodies and wrung his hands. The look and gesture was momentary, but expressive of indescribable anguish. Instantly recovering himself, Ranald, in passing, whispered somewhat to one of the females, who, like Rizpah the daughter of Aiah, seemed engaged in watching and mourning the victims of feudal injustice and cruelty. The woman started at his voice, but immediately collected herself and returned for answer a slight inclination of the head.

Dalgetty continued his way out of the town, uncertain whether he should try to seize or hire a boat and cross the lake, or plunge into the woods, and there conceal himself from pursuit. In the former event he was liable to be instantly pursued by the galleys of the Marquis, which lay ready for sailing, their long yard-arms pointing to the wind, and what hope could he have in an ordinary Highland fishing-boat to escape from them? If he made the latter choice, his chance either of supporting or concealing himself in those waste and unknown wildernesses, was in the highest degree precarious. The town lay now behind him, yet what hand to turn to for safety he was unable to determine, and began to be sensible, that in escaping from the dungeon at Inverary, desperate as the matter seemed, he had only accomplished the easiest part of a difficult task. If retaken, his fate was now certain; for the personal injury he had offered to a man so powerful and so vindictive, could be atoned for only by instant death. While he pondered these distressing reflections, and looked around with a countenance which plainly expressed indecision, Ranald MacEagh suddenly asked him, "which way he intended to journey?"

"And that, honest comrade," answered Dalgetty, "is precisely the question which I cannot answer you. Truly I begin to hold the opinion, Ranald, that we had better have stuck by the brown loaf and water-pitcher until Sir Duncan arrived, who, for his own honour, must have made some fight for me."

"Saxon," answered MacEagh, "do not regret having exchanged the foul breath of yonder dungeon for the free air of heaven. Above all, repent not that you have served a Son of the Mist. Put yourself under my guidance, and I will warrant your safety with my head."

"Can you guide me safe through these mountains, and back to the army of Montrose?" said Dalgetty.

"I can," answered MacEagh; "there lives not a man to whom the mountain passes, the caverns, the glens, the thickets, and the corries are known, as they are to the Children of the Mist. While others crawl on the level ground, by the sides of lakes and streams, ours are the steep hollows of the inaccessible mountains, the birth-place of the desert springs. Not all the bloodhounds of Argyle can trace the fastnesses through which I can guide you."

"Say'st thou so, honest Ranald?" replied Dalgetty; "then have on with thee; for of a surety I shall never save the ship by my own pilotage."

The outlaw accordingly led the way into the wood, by which the castle is surrounded for several miles, walking with so much dispatch as kept Gustavus at a round trot, and taking such a number of cross cuts and turns, that Captain Dalgetty speedily lost all idea where he might be, and all knowledge of the points of the compass. At length, the path, which had gradually become more difficult, altogether ended among thickets and underwood. The roaring of a torrent was heard in the neighbourhood, the ground became in some places broken, in others boggy, and everywhere unfit for riding.

"What the foul fiend," said Dalgetty, "is to be done here? I must part with Gustavus, I fear."

"Take no care for your horse," said the outlaw; "he shall soon be restored to you."

As he spoke, he whistled in a low tune, and a lad, half-dressed in tartan, half naked, having only his own shaggy hair, tied with a thong of leather, to protect his head and face from sun and weather, lean, and half-starved in aspect, his wild grey eyes appearing to fill up ten times the proportion usually allotted to them in the human face, crept out, as a wild beast might have done, from a thicket of brambles and briars.

"Give your horse to the gillie," said Ranald MacEagh; "your life depends upon it."

"Och! och!" exclaimed the despairing veteran; "Eheu! as we used to say at Mareschal-College, must I leave Gustavus in such grooming!"

"Are you frantic, to lose time thus!" said his guide; "do we stand on friends' ground, that you should part with your horse as if he were your brother? I tell you, you shall have him again; but if you never saw the animal, is not life better than the best colt ever mare foaled?"

"And that is true too, mine honest friend," sighed Dalgetty; "yet if you knew but the value of Gustavus, and the things we two have done and suffered together—See, he turns back to look at me!—Be kind to him, my good breechless friend, and I will requite you well." So saying, and withal sniffling a little to swallow his grief, he turned from the heart-rending spectacle in order to follow his guide.

To follow his guide was no easy matter, and soon required more agility than Captain Dalgetty could master. The very first plunge after he had parted from his charger, carried him, with little assistance from a few overhanging boughs, or projecting roots of trees, eight foot sheer down into the course of a torrent, up which the Son of the Mist led the way. Huge stones, over which they scrambled,—thickets of them and brambles, through which they had to drag themselves,—rocks which were to be climbed on the one side with much labour and pain, for the purpose of an equally precarious descent upon the other; all these, and many such interruptions, were surmounted by the light-footed and half-naked mountaineer with an ease and velocity which excited the surprise and envy of Captain Dalgetty, who, encumbered by his head-piece, corslet, and other armour, not to mention his ponderous jack-boots, found himself at length so much exhausted by fatigue, and the difficulties of the road, that he sate down upon a stone in order to recover his breath, while he explained to Ranald MacEagh the difference betwixt travelling EXPEDITUS and IMPEDITUS, as these two military phrases were understood at Mareschal-College, Aberdeen. The sole answer of the mountaineer was to lay his hand on the soldier's arm, and point backward in the direction of the wind. Dalgetty could spy nothing, for evening was closing fast, and they were at the bottom of a dark ravine. But at length he could distinctly hear at a distance the sullen toll of a large bell.

"That," said he, "must be the alarm—the storm-clock, as the Germans call it."

"It strikes the hour of your death," answered Ranald, "unless you can accompany me a little farther. For every toll of that bell a brave man has yielded up his soul."

"Truly, Ranald, my trusty friend," said Dalgetty, "I will not deny that the case may be soon my own; for I am so forfoughen (being, as I explained to you, IMPEDITUS, for had I been EXPEDITUS, I mind not pedestrian exercise the flourish of a fife), that I think I had better ensconce myself in one of these bushes, and even lie quiet there to abide what fortune God shall send me. I entreat you, mine honest friend Ranald, to shift for yourself, and leave me to my fortune, as the Lion of the North, the immortal Gustavus Adolphus, my never-to-be-forgotten master (whom you must surely have heard of, Ranald, though you may have heard of no one else), said to Francis Albert, Duke of Saxe-Lauenburgh, when he was mortally wounded on the plains of Lutzen. Neither despair altogether of my safety, Ranald, seeing I have been in as great pinches as this in Germany—more especially, I remember me, that at the fatal battle of Nerlingen—after which I changed service—"

"If you would save your father's son's breath to help his child out of trouble, instead of wasting it upon the tales of Seannachies," said Ranald, who now grew impatient of the Captain's loquacity, "or if your feet could travel as fast as your tongue, you might yet lay your head on an unbloody pillow to-night."

"Something there is like military skill in that," replied the Captain, "although wantonly and irreverently spoken to an officer of rank. But I hold it good to pardon such freedoms on a march, in respect of the Saturnalian license indulged in such cases to the troops of all nations. And now, resume thine office, friend Ranald, in respect I am well-breathed; or, to be more plain, I PRAE, SEQUAR, as we used to say at Mareschal-College."

Comprehending his meaning rather from his motions than his language, the Son of the Mist again led the way, with an unerring precision that looked like instinct, through a variety of ground the most difficult and broken that could well be imagined. Dragging along his ponderous boots, encumbered with thigh-pieces, gauntlets, corslet, and back-piece, not to mention the buff jerkin which he wore under all these arms, talking of his former exploits the whole way, though Ranald paid not the slightest attention to him, Captain Dalgetty contrived to follow his guide a considerable space farther, when the deep-mouthed baying of a hound was heard coming down the wind, as if opening on the scent of its prey.

"Black hound," said Ranald, "whose throat never boded good to a Child of the Mist, ill fortune to her who littered thee! hast thou already found our trace? But thou art too late, swart hound of darkness, and the deer has gained the herd."

So saying, he whistled very softly, and was answered in a tone equally low from the top of a pass, up which they had for some time been ascending. Mending their pace, they reached the top, where the moon, which had now risen bright and clear, showed to Dalgetty a party of ten or twelve Highlanders, and about as many women and children, by whom Ranald MacEagh was received with such transports of joy, as made his companion easily sensible that those by whom he was surrounded, must of course be Children of the Mist. The place which they occupied well suited their name and habits. It was a beetling crag, round which winded a very narrow and broken footpath, commanded in various places by the position which they held.

Ranald spoke anxiously and hastily to the children of his tribe, and the men came one by one to shake hands with Dalgetty, while the women, clamorous in their gratitude, pressed round to kiss even the hem of his garment. "They plight their faith to you," said Ranald MacEagh, "for requital of the good deed you have done to the tribe this day."

"Enough said, Ranald," answered the soldier, "enough said— tell them I love not this shaking of hands—it confuses ranks and degrees in military service; and as to kissing of gauntlets, puldrons, and the like, I remember that the immortal Gustavus, as he rode through the streets of Nuremberg, being thus worshipped by the poulace (being doubtless far more worthy of it than a poor though honourable cavalier like myself), did say unto them, in the way of rebuke, 'If you idolize me thus like a god, who shall assure you that the vengeance of Heaven will not soon prove me to be a mortal?'— And so here, I suppose you intend to make a stand against your followers, Ranald—VOTO A DIOS, as the Spaniard says?—a very pretty position—as pretty a position for a small peloton of men as I have seen in my service—no enemy can come towards it by the road without being at the mercy of cannon and musket.—But then, Ranald, my trusty comrade, you have no cannon, I dare to aver, and I do not see that any of these fellows have muskets either. So with what artillery you propose making good the pass, before you come to hand blows, truly, Ranald, it passeth my apprehension."

"With the weapons and with the courage of our fathers," said MacEagh; and made the Captain observe, that the men of his party were armed with bows and arrows.

"Bows and arrows!" exclaimed Dalgetty; "ha! ha! ha! have we Robin Hood and Little John back again? Bows and arrows! why, the sight has not been seen in civilized war for a hundred years. Bows and arrows! and why not weavers' beams, as in the days of Goliah? Ah! that Dugald Dalgetty, of Drumthwacket, should live to see men fight with bows and arrows!—The immortal Gustavus would never have believed it—nor Wallenstein—nor Butler—nor old Tilly,—Well, Ranald, a cat can have but its claws—since bows and arrows are the word, e'en let us make the best of it. Only, as I do not understand the scope and range of such old-fashioned artillery, you must make the best disposition you can out of your own head for MY taking the command, whilk I would have gladly done had you been to fight with any Christian weapons, is out of the question, when you are to combat like quivered Numidians. I will, however, play my part with my pistols in the approaching melley, in respect my carabine unhappily remains at Gustavus's saddle.—My service and thanks to you," he continued, addressing a mountaineer who offered him a bow; "Dugald Dalgetty may say of himself, as he learned at Mareschal-College,

> "Non eget Mauri jaculis, neque arcu,
> Nec venenatis gravida sagittis,
> Fusce, pharetra;

whilk is to say—"

Ranald MacEagh a second time imposed silence on the talkative commander as before, by pulling his sleeve, and pointing down the pass. The bay of the bloodhound was now approaching nearer and nearer, and they could hear the voices of several persons who accompanied the animal, and hallooed to each other as they dispersed occasionally, either in the hurry of their advance, or in order to search more accurately the thickets as they came along. They were obviously drawing nearer and nearer every moment. MacEagh, in the meantime, proposed to Captain Dalgetty to disencumber himself of his armour, and gave him to understand that the women should transport it to a place of safety.

"I crave your pardon, sir," said Dalgetty, "such is not the rule of our foreign service in respect I remember the regiment of Finland cuirassiers reprimanded, and their kettle-drums taken from them, by the immortal Gustavus, because they had assumed the permission to march without their corslets, and to leave them with the baggage. Neither did they strike kettle-drums again at the head of that famous regiment until they behaved themselves so notably at the field of Leipsic; a lesson whilk is not to be forgotten, any more than that exclamation of the immortal Gustavus, 'Now shall I know if my officers love me, by their putting on their armour; since, if my officers are slain, who shall lead my soldiers into victory?' Nevertheless, friend Ranald, this is without prejudice to my being rid of these somewhat heavy boots, providing I can obtain any other succedaneum; for I presume not to say that my bare soles are fortified so as to endure the flints and thorns, as seems to be the case with your followers."

To rid the Captain of his cumbrous greaves, and case his feet in a pair of brogues made out of deerskin, which a Highlander stripped off for his accommodation, was the work of a minute, and Dalgetty found himself much lightened by the exchange. He was in the act of recommending to Ranald MacEagh, to send two or three of his followers a little lower to reconnoitre the pass, and, at the same time, somewhat to extend his front, placing two detached archers at each flank by way of posts of observation, when the near cry of the hound apprised them that the pursuers were at the bottom of the pass. All was then dead silence; for, loquacious as he was on other occasions, Captain Dalgetty knew well the necessity of an ambush keeping itself under covert.

The moon gleamed on the broken pathway, and on the projecting cliffs of rock round which it winded, its light intercepted here and there by the branches of bushes and dwarf-trees, which, finding nourishment in the crevices of the rocks, in some places overshadowed the brow and ledge of the precipice. Below, a thick copse-wood lay in deep and dark shadow, somewhat resembling the billows of a half-seen ocean. From the bosom of that darkness, and close to the bottom of the precipice, the hound was heard at intervals baying fearfully, sounds which were redoubled by the echoes of the woods and rocks around. At intervals, these sunk into deep silence, interrupted only by the plashing noise of a small runnel of water, which partly fell from the rock, partly found a more silent passage to the bottom along its projecting surface. Voices of men were also heard in stifled converse below; it seemed as if the pursuers had not discovered the narrow path which led to the top of the rock, or that, having discovered it, the peril of the ascent, joined to the imperfect light, and the uncertainty whether it might not be defended, made them hesitate to attempt it.

At length a shadowy figure was seen, which raised itself up from the abyss of darkness below, and, emerging into the pale moonlight, began cautiously and slowly to ascend the rocky path. The outline was so distinctly marked, that Captain Dalgetty could discover not only the person of a Highlander, but the long gun which he carried in his hand, and the plume of feathers which decorated his bonnet. "TAUSEND TEIFLEN! that I should say so, and so like to be near my latter end!" ejaculated the Captain, but under his breath, "what will become of us, now they have brought musketry to encounter our archers?"

But just as the pursuer had attained a projecting piece of rock about half way up the ascent, and, pausing, made a signal for those who were still at the bottom to follow him, an arrow whistled from the bow of one of the Children of the Mist, and transfixed him with so fatal a wound, that, without a single effort to save himself, he lost his balance, and fell headlong from the cliff on which he stood, into the darkness below. The crash of the boughs which received him, and the heavy sound of his fall from thence to the ground, was followed by a cry of horror and surprise, which burst from his followers. The Children of the Mist, encouraged in proportion to the alarm this first success had caused among the pursuers, echoed back the clamour with a loud and shrill yell of exultation, and, showing themselves on the brow of the precipice, with wild cries and vindictive gestures, endeavoured to impress on their enemies a sense at once of their courage, their numbers, and their state of defence. Even Captain Dalgetty's military prudence did not prevent his rising up, and calling out to Ranald, more loud than prudence warranted, "CAROCCO, comrade, as the Spaniard says! The long-bow for ever! In my poor apprehension now, were you to order a file to advance and take position—"

"The Sassenach!" cried a voice from beneath, "mark the Sassenach sidier! I see the glitter of his breastplate." At the same time three muskets were discharged; and while one ball rattled against the corslet of proof, to the strength of which our valiant Captain had been more than once indebted for his life, another penetrated the armour which covered the front of his left thigh, and stretched him on the ground. Ranald instantly seized him in his arms, and bore him back from the edge of the precipice, while he dolefully ejaculated, "I always told the immortal Gustavus, Wallenstein, Tilly, and other men of the sword, that, in my poor mind, taslets ought to be made musket-proof."

With two or three earnest words in Gaelic, MacEagh commended the wounded man to the charge of the females, who were in the rear of his little party, and was then about to return to the contest. But Dalgetty detained him, grasping a firm hold of his plaid.—"I know not how this matter may end—but I request you will inform Montrose, that I died like a follower of the immortal Gustavus—and I pray you, take heed how you quit your present strength, even for the purpose of pursuing the enemy, if you gain any advantage—and—and—"

Here Dalgetty's breath and eyesight began to fail him through loss of blood, and MacEagh, availing himself of this circumstance, extricated from his grasp the end of his own mantle, and substituted that of a female, by which the Captain held stoutly, thereby securing, as he conceived, the outlaw's attention to the military instructions which he continued to pour forth while he had any breath to utter them, though they became gradually more and more incoherent—"And, comrade, you will be sure to keep your musketeers in advance of your stand of pikes, Lochaber-axes, and two-handed swords—Stand fast, dragoons, on the left flank!— where was I?—Ay, and, Ranald, if ye be minded to retreat, leave some lighted matches burning on the branches of the trees—it shows as if they were lined with shot—But I forget—ye have no match-locks nor habergeons—only bows and arrows—bows and arrows! ha! ha! ha!"

Here the Captain sunk back in an exhausted condition, altogether unable to resist the sense of the ludicrous which, as a modern man-at-arms, he connected with the idea of these ancient weapons of war. It was a long time ere he recovered his senses; and, in the meantime, we leave him in the care of the Daughters of the Mist; nurses as kind and attentive, in reality, as they were wild and uncouth in outward appearance.

CHAPTER XV.

But if no faithless action stain
Thy true and constant word,
I'll make thee famous by my pen,
And glorious by my sword.

I'll serve thee in such noble ways
As ne'er were known before;
I'll deck and crown thy head with bays,
And love thee more and more.

—MONTROSE'S LINES.

We must now leave, with whatever regret, the valiant Captain Dalgetty, to recover of his wounds or otherwise as fate shall determine, in order briefly to trace the military operations of Montrose, worthy as they are of a more important page, and a better historian. By the assistance of the chieftains whom we have commemorated, and more especially by the junction of the Murrays, Stewarts, and other clans of Athole, which were peculiarly zealous in the royal cause, he soon assembled an army of two or three thousand Highlanders, to whom he successfully united the Irish under Colkitto. This last leader, who, to the great embarrassment of Milton's commentators, is commemorated in one of that great poet's sonnets, was properly named Alister, or Alexander M'Donnell, by birth a Scottish islesman, and related to the Earl of Antrim, to whose patronage he owed the command assigned him in the Irish troops. In many respects he merited this distinction. He was brave to intrepidity, and almost to insensibility; very strong and active in person, completely master of his weapons, and always ready to show the example in the extremity of danger. To counterbalance these good qualities, it must be recorded, that he was inexperienced in military tactics, and of a jealous and presumptuous disposition, which often lost to Montrose the fruits of Colkitto's gallantry. Yet such is the predominance of outward personal qualities in the eyes of a mild people, that the feats of strength and courage shown by this champion, seem to have made a stronger impression upon the minds of the Highlanders, than the military skill and chivalrous spirit of the great Marquis of Montrose. Numerous traditions are still preserved in the Highland glens concerning Alister M'Donnell, though the name of Montrose is rarely mentioned among them.

[Milton's book, entitled TETRACHORDON, had been ridiculed, it would seem, by the divines assembled at Westminster, and others, on account of the hardness of the title; and Milton in his sonnet retaliates upon the barbarous Scottish names which the Civil War had made familiar to English ears:—

> . . . why is it harder, sirs, than Gordon,
> COLKITTO or M'Donald, or Gallasp?
> These rugged names to our like mouths grow sleek,
> That would have made Quintillian stare and gasp.

"We may suppose," says Bishop Newton, "that these were persons of note among the Scotch ministers, who were for pressing and enforcing the Covenant;" whereas Milton only intends to ridicule the barbarism of Scottish names in general, and quotes, indiscriminately, that of Gillespie, one of the Apostles of the Covenant, and those of Colkitto and M'Donnell (both belonging to one person), one of its bitterest enemies.]

The point upon which Montrose finally assembled his little army, was in Strathearn, on the verge of the Highlands of Perthshire, so as to menace the principal town of that county.

His enemies were not unprepared for his reception. Argyle, at the head of his Highlanders, was dogging the steps of the Irish from the west to the east, and by force, fear, or influence, had collected an army nearly sufficient to have given battle to that under Montrose. The Lowlands were also prepared, for reasons which we assigned at the beginning of this tale. A body of six thousand infantry, and six or seven thousand cavalry, which profanely assumed the title of God's army, had been hastily assembled from the shires of Fife, Angus, Perth, Stirling, and the neighbouring counties. A much less force in former times, nay, even in the preceding reign, would have been sufficient to have secured the Lowlands against a more formidable descent of Highlanders, than those united under Montrose; but times had changed strangely within the last half century. Before that period, the Lowlanders were as constantly engaged in war as the mountaineers, and were incomparably better disciplined and armed. The favourite Scottish order of battle somewhat resembled the Macedonian phalanx. Their infantry formed a compact body, armed with long spears, impenetrable even to the men-at-arms of the age, though well mounted, and arrayed in complete proof. It may easily be conceived, therefore, that their ranks could not be broken by the disorderly charge of Highland infantry armed for close combat only, with swords, and ill furnished with missile weapons, and having no artillery whatever.

This habit of fight was in a great measure changed by the introduction of muskets into the Scottish Lowland service, which, not being as yet combined with the bayonet, was a formidable weapon at a distance, but gave no assurance against the enemy who rushed on to close quarters. The pike, indeed, was not wholly disused in the Scottish army; but it was no longer the favourite weapon, nor was it relied upon as formerly by those in whose hands it was placed; insomuch that Daniel Lupton, a tactician of the day, has written a book expressly upon the superiority of the musket. This change commenced as early as the wars of Gustavus Adolphus, whose marches were made with such rapidity, that the pike was very soon thrown aside in his army, and exchanged for fire-arms. A circumstance which necessarily accompanied this change, as well as the establishment of standing armies, whereby war became a trade, was the introduction of a laborious and complicated system of discipline, combining a variety of words of command with corresponding operations and manoeuvres, the neglect of any one of which was sure to throw the whole into confusion. War therefore, as practised among most nations of Europe, had assumed much more than formerly the character of a profession or mystery, to which previous practice and experience were indispensable requisites. Such was the natural consequence of standing armies, which had almost everywhere, and particularly in the long German wars, superseded what may be called the natural discipline of the feudal militia.

The Scottish Lowland militia, therefore, laboured under a double disadvantage when opposed to Highlanders. They were divested of the spear, a weapon which, in the hands of their ancestors, had so often repelled the impetuous assaults of the mountaineer; and they were subjected to a new and complicated species of discipline, well adapted, perhaps, to the use of regular troops, who could be rendered completely masters of it, but tending only to confuse the ranks of citizen soldiers, by whom it was rarely practised, and imperfectly understood. So much has been done in our own time in bringing back tactics to their first principles, and in getting rid of the pedantry of war, that it is easy for us to estimate the disadvantages under which a half-trained militia laboured, who were taught to consider success as depending upon their exercising with precision a system of tactics, which they probably only so far comprehended as to find out when they were wrong, but without the power of getting right again. Neither can it be denied, that, in the material points of military habits and warlike spirit, the Lowlanders of the seventeenth century had sunk far beneath their Highland countrymen.

From the earliest period down to the union of the crowns, the whole kingdom of Scotland, Lowlands as well as Highlands, had been the constant scene of war, foreign and domestic; and there was probably scarce one of its hardy inhabitants, between the age of sixteen and sixty, who was not as willing in point of fact as he was literally bound in law, to assume arms at the first call of his liege lord, or of a royal proclamation. The law remained the same in sixteen hundred and forty-five as a hundred years before, but the race of those subjected to it had been bred up under very different feelings. They had sat in quiet under their vine and under their fig-tree, and a call to battle involved a change of life as new as it was disagreeable. Such of them, also, who lived near unto the Highlands, were in continual and disadvantageous contact with the restless inhabitants of those mountains, by whom their cattle were driven off, their dwellings plundered, and their persons insulted, and who had acquired over them that sort of superiority arising from a constant system of aggression. The Lowlanders, who lay more remote, and out of reach of these depredations, were influenced by the exaggerated reports circulated concerning the Highlanders, whom, as totally differing in laws, language, and dress, they were induced to regard as a nation of savages, equally void of fear and of humanity. These various prepossessions, joined to the less warlike habits of the Lowlanders, and their imperfect knowledge of the new and complicated system of discipline for which they had exchanged their natural mode of fighting, placed them at great disadvantage when opposed to the Highlander in the field of battle. The mountaineers, on the contrary, with the arms and courage of their fathers, possessed also their simple and natural system of tactics, and bore down with the fullest confidence upon an enemy, to whom anything they had been taught of discipline was, like Saul's armour upon David, a hinderance rather than a help, "because they had not proved it."

It was with such disadvantages on the one side, and such advantages on the other, to counterbalance the difference of superior numbers and the presence of artillery and cavalry, that Montrose encountered the army of Lord Elcho upon the field of Tippermuir. The Presbyterian clergy had not been wanting in their efforts to rouse the spirit of their followers, and one of them, who harangued the troops on the very day of battle, hesitated not to say, that if ever God spoke by his mouth, he promised them, in His name, that day, a great and assured victory. The cavalry and artillery were also reckoned sure warrants of success, as the novelty of their attack had upon former occasions been very discouraging to the Highlanders. The place of meeting was an open heath, and the ground afforded little advantage to either party, except that it allowed the horse of the Covenanters to act with effect.

A battle upon which so much depended, was never more easily decided. The Lowland cavalry made a show of charging; but, whether thrown into disorder by the fire of musketry, or deterred by a disaffection to the service said to have prevailed among the gentlemen, they made no impression on the Highlanders whatever, and recoiled in disorder from ranks which had neither bayonets nor pikes to protect them. Montrose saw, and instantly availed himself of this advantage. He ordered his whole army to charge, which they performed with the wild and desperate valour peculiar to mountaineers. One officer of the Covenanters alone, trained in the Italian wars, made a desperate defence upon the right wing. In every other point their line was penetrated at the first onset; and this advantage once obtained, the Lowlanders were utterly unable to contend at close quarters with their more agile and athletic enemies. Many were slain on the held, and such a number in the pursuit, that above one-third of the Covenanters were reported to have fallen; in which number, however, must be computed a great many fat burgesses who broke their wind in the flight, and thus died without stroke of sword. [We choose to quote our authority for a fact so singular:—"A great many burgesses were killed—twenty-five householders in St. Andrews—many were bursten in the flight, and died without stroke."—See Baillie's Letters, vol. ii. page 92.]

The victors obtained possession of Perth, and obtained considerable sums of money, as well as ample supplies of arms and ammunition. But those advantages were to be balanced against an almost insurmountable inconvenience that uniformly attended a Highland army. The clans could be in no respect induced to consider themselves as regular soldiers, or to act as such. Even so late as the year 1745-6, when the Chevalier Charles Edward, by way of making an example, caused a soldier to be shot for desertion, the Highlanders, who composed his army, were affected as much by indignation as by fear. They could not conceive any principle of justice upon which a man's life could be taken, for merely going home when it did not suit him to remain longer with the army. Such had been the uniform practice of their fathers. When a battle was over, the campaign was, in their opinion, ended; if it was lost, they sought safety in their mountains—if won, they returned there to secure their booty. At other times they had their cattle to look after, and their harvests to sow or reap, without which their families would have perished for want. In either case, there was an end of their services for the time; and though they were easily enough recalled by the prospect of fresh adventures and more plunder, yet the opportunity of success was, in the meantime, lost, and could not afterwards be recovered. This circumstance serves to show, even if history had not made us acquainted with the same fact, that the Highlanders had never been accustomed to make war with the view of permanent conquest, but only with the hope of deriving temporary advantage, or deciding some immediate quarrel. It also explains the reason why Montrose, with all his splendid successes, never obtained any secure or permanent footing in the Lowlands, and why even those Lowland noblemen and gentlemen, who were inclined to the royal cause, showed diffidence and reluctance to join an army of a character so desultory and irregular, as might lead them at all times to apprehend that the Highlanders securing themselves by a retreat to their mountains, would leave whatever Lowlanders might have joined them to the mercy of an offended and predominant enemy. The same consideration will also serve to account for the sudden marches which Montrose was obliged to undertake, in order to recruit his army in the mountains, and for the rapid changes of fortune, by which we often find him obliged to retreat from before those enemies over whom he had recently been victorious. If there should be any who read these tales for any further purpose than that of immediate amusement, they will find these remarks not unworthy of their recollection.

It was owing to such causes, the slackness of the Lowland loyalists and the temporary desertion of his Highland followers, that Montrose found himself, even after the decisive victory of Tippermuir, in no condition to face the second army with which Argyle advanced upon him from the westward. In this emergency, supplying by velocity the want of strength, he moved suddenly from Perth to Dundee, and being refused admission into that town, fell northward upon Aberdeen, where he expected to be joined by the Gordons and other loyalists. But the zeal of these gentlemen was, for the time, effectually bridled by a large body of Covenanters, commanded by the Lord Burleigh, and supposed to amount to three thousand men. These Montrose boldly attacked with half their number. The battle was fought under the walls Of the city, and the resolute valour of Montrose's followers was again successful against every disadvantage.

But it was the fate of this great commander, always to gain the glory, but seldom to reap the fruits of victory. He had scarcely time to repose his small army in Aberdeen, ere he found, on the one hand, that the Gordons were likely to be deterred from joining him, by the reasons we have mentioned, with some others peculiar to their chief, the Marquis of Huntly; on the other hand, Argyle, whose forces had been augmented by those of several Lowland noblemen, advanced towards Montrose at the head of an army much larger than he had yet had to cope with. These troops moved, indeed, with slowness, corresponding to the cautious character of their commander; but even that caution rendered Argyle's approach formidable, since his very advance implied, that he was at the head of an army irresistibly superior

There remained one mode of retreat open to Montrose, and he adopted it. He threw himself into the Highlands, where he could set pursuit at defiance, and where he was sure, in every glen, to recover those recruits who had left his standard to deposit their booty in their native fastnesses. It was thus that the singular character of the army which Montrose commanded, while, on the one hand, it rendered his victory in some degree nugatory, enabled him, on the other, under the most disadvantageous circumstances, to secure his retreat, recruit his forces, and render himself more formidable than ever to the enemy, before whom he had lately been unable to make a stand.

On the present occasion he threw himself into Badenoch, and rapidly traversing that district, as well as the neighbouring country of Athole, he alarmed the Covenanters by successive attacks upon various unexpected points, and spread such general dismay, that repeated orders were dispatched by the Parliament to Argyle, their commander, to engage, and disperse Montrose at all rates.

These commands from his superiors neither suited the haughty spirit, nor the temporizing and cautious policy, of the nobleman to whom they were addressed. He paid, accordingly, no regard to them, but limited his efforts to intrigues among Montrose's few Lowland followers, many of whom had become disgusted with the prospect of a Highland campaign, which exposed their persons to intolerable fatigue, and left their estates at the Covenanters' mercy. Accordingly, several of them left Montrose's camp at this period. He was joined, however, by a body of forces of more congenial spirit, and far better adapted to the situation in which he found himself. This reinforcement consisted of a large body of Highlanders, whom Colkitto, dispatched for that purpose, had levied in Argyleshire. Among the most distinguished was John of Moidart, called the Captain of Clan Ranald, with the Stewarts of Appin, the Clan Gregor, the Clan M'Nab, and other tribes of inferior distinction. By these means, Montrose's army was so formidably increased, that Argyle cared no longer to remain in the command of that opposed to him, but returned to Edinburgh, and there threw up his commission, under pretence that his army was not supplied with reinforcements and provisions in the manner in which they ought to have been. From thence the Marquis returned to Inverary, there, in full security, to govern his feudal vassals, and patriarchal followers, and to repose himself in safety on the faith of the Clan proverb already quoted—"It is a far cry to Lochow."

CHAPTER XVI.

Such mountains steep, such craggy hills,
His army on one side enclose:
The other side, great griesly gills
Did fence with fenny mire and moss.

Which when the Earl understood,
He council craved of captains all,
Who bade set forth with mournful mood,
And take such fortune as would fall.
—FLODDEN FIELD, AN ANCIENT POEM.

Montrose had now a splendid career in his view, provided he could obtain the consent of his gallant, but desultory troops, and their independent chieftains. The Lowlands lay open before him without an army adequate to check his career; for Argyle's followers had left the Covenanters' host when their master threw up his commission, and many other troops, tired of the war, had taken the same opportunity to disband themselves. By descending Strath-Tay, therefore, one of the most convenient passes from the Highlands, Montrose had only to present himself in the Lowlands, in order to rouse the slumbering spirit of chivalry and of loyalty which animated the gentlemen to the north of the Forth. The possession of these districts, with or without a victory, would give him the command of a wealthy and fertile part of the kingdom, and would enable him, by regular pay, to place his army on a permanent footing, to penetrate as far as the capital, perhaps from thence to the Border, where he deemed it possible to communicate with the yet unsubdued forces of King Charles.

Such was the plan of operations by which the truest glory was to be acquired, and the most important success insured for the royal cause. Accordingly it did not escape the ambitious and daring spirit of him whose services had already acquired him the title of the Great Marquis. But other motives actuated many of his followers, and perhaps were not without their secret and unacknowledged influence upon his own feelings.

The Western Chiefs in Montrose's army, almost to a man, regarded the Marquis of Argyle as the most direct and proper object of hostilities. Almost all of them had felt his power; almost all, in withdrawing their fencible men from their own glens, left their families and property exposed to his vengeance; all, without exception, were desirous of diminishing his sovereignty; and most of them lay so near his territories, that they might reasonably hope to be gratified by a share of his spoil. To these Chiefs the possession of Inverary and its castle was an event infinitely more important and desirable than the capture of Edinburgh. The latter event could only afford their clansmen a little transitory pay or plunder; the former insured to the Chiefs themselves indemnity for the past, and security for the future. Besides these personal reasons, the leaders, who favoured this opinion, plausibly urged, that though, at his first descent into the Lowlands, Montrose might be superior to the enemy, yet every day's march he made from the hills must diminish his own forces, and expose him to the accumulated superiority of any army which the Covenanters could collect from the Lowland levies and garrisons. On the other hand, by crushing Argyle effectually, he would not only permit his present western friends to bring out that proportion of their forces which they must otherwise leave at home for protection of their families; but farther, he would draw to his standard several tribes already friendly to his cause, but who were prevented from joining him by fear of M'Callum More.

These arguments, as we have already hinted, found something responsive in Montrose's own bosom, not quite consonant with the general heroism of his character. The houses of Argyle and Montrose had been in former times, repeatedly opposed to each other in war and in politics, and the superior advantages acquired by the former, had made them the subject of envy and dislike to the neighbouring family, who, conscious of equal desert, had not been so richly rewarded. This was not all. The existing heads of these rival families had stood in the most marked opposition to each other since the commencement of the present troubles.

Montrose, conscious of the superiority of his talents, and of having rendered great service to the Covenanters at the beginning of the war, had expected from that party the supereminence of council and command, which they judged it safer to intrust to the more limited faculties, and more extensive power, of his rival Argyle. The having awarded this preference, was an injury which Montrose never forgave the Covenanters; and he was still less likely to extend his pardon to Argyle, to whom he had been postponed. He was therefore stimulated by every feeling of hatred which could animate a fiery temper in a fierce age, to seek for revenge upon the enemy of his house and person; and it is probable that these private motives operated not a little upon his mind, when he found the principal part of his followers determined rather to undertake an expedition against the territories of Argyle, than to take the far more decisive step of descending at once into the Lowlands.

Yet whatever temptation Montrose found to carry into effect his attack upon Argyleshire, he could not easily bring himself to renounce the splendid achievement of a descent upon the Lowlands. He held more than one council with the principal Chiefs, combating, perhaps, his own secret inclination as well as theirs. He laid before them the extreme difficulty of marching even a Highland army from the eastward into Argyleshire, through passes scarcely practicable for shepherds and deer-stalkers, and over mountains, with which even the clans lying nearest to them did not pretend to be thoroughly acquainted. These difficulties were greatly enhanced by the season of the year, which was now advancing towards December, when the mountain-passes, in themselves so difficult, might be expected to be rendered utterly impassable by snowstorms. These objections neither satisfied nor silenced the Chiefs, who insisted upon their ancient mode of making war, by driving the cattle, which, according to the Gaelic phrase, "fed upon the grass of their enemy." The council was dismissed late at night, and without coming to any decision, excepting that the Chiefs, who supported the opinion that Argyle should be invaded, promised to seek out among their followers those who might be most capable of undertaking the office of guides upon the expedition.

Montrose had retired to the cabin which served him for a tent, and stretched himself upon a bed of dry fern, the only place of repose which it afforded. But he courted sleep in vain, for the visions of ambition excluded those of Morpheus. In one moment he imagined himself displaying the royal banner from the reconquered Castle of Edinburgh, detaching assistance to a monarch whose crown depended upon his success, and receiving in requital all the advantages and preferments which could be heaped upon him whom a king delighteth to honour. At another time this dream, splendid as it was, faded before the vision of gratified vengeance, and personal triumph over a personal enemy. To surprise Argyle in his stronghold of Inverary—to crush in him at once the rival of his own house and the chief support of the Presbyterians—to show the Covenanters the difference between the preferred Argyle and the postponed Montrose, was a picture too flattering to feudal vengeance to be easily relinquished.

While he lay thus busied with contradictory thoughts and feelings, the soldier who stood sentinel upon his quarters announced to the Marquis that two persons desired to speak with his Excellency.

"Their names?" answered Montrose, "and the cause of their urgency at such a late hour?"

On these points, the sentinel, who was one of Colkitto's Irishmen, could afford his General little information; so that Montrose, who at such a period durst refuse access to no one, lest he might have been neglecting some important intelligence, gave directions, as a necessary precaution, to put the guard under arms, and then prepared to receive his untimely visitors. His groom of the chambers had scarce lighted a pair of torches, and Montrose himself had scarce risen from his couch, when two men entered, one wearing a Lowland dress, of shamoy leather worn almost to tatters; the other a tall upright old Highlander, of a complexion which might be termed iron-grey, wasted and worn by frost and tempest.

"What may be your commands with me, my friends?" said the Marquis, his hand almost unconsciously seeking the but of one of his pistols; for the period, as well as the time of night, warranted suspicions which the good mien of his visitors was not by any means calculated to remove.

"I pray leave to congratulate you," said the Lowlander, "my most noble General, and right honourable lord, upon the great battles which you have achieved since I had the fortune to be detached from you, It was a pretty affair that tuilzie at Tippermuir; nevertheless, if I might be permitted to counsel—"

"Before doing so," said the Marquis, "will you be pleased to let me know who is so kind as to favour me with his opinion?"

"Truly, my lord," replied the man, "I should have hoped that was unnecessary, seeing it is not so long since I took on in your service, under promise of a commission as Major, with half a dollar of daily pay and half a dollar of arrears; and I am to trust your lordship has nut forgotten my pay as well as my person?"

"My good friend, Major Dalgetty," said Montrose, who by this time perfectly recollected his man, "you must consider what important things have happened to put my friends' faces out of my memory, besides this imperfect light; but all conditions shall be kept.—And what news from Argyleshire, my good Major? We have long given you up for lost, and I was now preparing to take the most signal vengeance upon the old fox who infringed the law of arms in your person."

"Truly, my noble lord," said Dalgetty, "I have no desire that my return should put any stop to so proper and becoming an intention; verily it is in no shape in the Earl of Argyle's favour or mercy that I now stand before you, and I shall be no intercessor for him. But my escape is, under Heaven, and the excellent dexterity which, as an old and accomplished cavalier, I displayed in effecting the same,—I say, under these, it is owing to the assistance of this old Highlander, whom I venture to recommend to your lordship's special favour, as the instrument of saving your lordship's to command, Dugald Dalgetty of Drumthwacket."

"A thankworthy service," said the Marquis, gravely, "which shall certainly be requited in the manner it deserves."

"Kneel down, Ranald," said Major Dalgetty (as we must now call him), "kneel down, and kiss his Excellency's hand."

The prescribed form of acknowledgment not being according to the custom of Ranald's country, he contented himself with folding his arms on his bosom, and making a low inclination of his head.

"This poor man, my lord," said Major Dalgetty, continuing his speech with a dignified air of protection towards Ranald M'Eagh, "has strained all his slender means to defend my person from mine enemies, although having no better weapons of a missile sort than bows and arrows, whilk your lordship will hardly believe."

"You will see a great many such weapons in my camp," said Montrose, "and we find them serviceable." [In fact, for the admirers of archery it may be stated, not only that many of the Highlanders in Montrose's army used these antique missiles, but even in England the bow and quiver, once the glory of the bold yeomen of that land, were occasionally used during the great civil wars.]

"Serviceable, my lord!" said Dalgetty; "I trust your lordship will permit me to be surprised—bows and arrows!—I trust you will forgive my recommending the substitution of muskets, the first convenient opportunity. But besides defending me, this honest Highlander also was at the pains of curing me, in respect that I had got a touch of the wars in my retreat, which merits my best requital in this special introduction of him to your lordship's notice and protection."

"What is your name, my friend?" said Montrose, turning to the Highlander.

"It may not be spoken," answered the mountaineer.

"That is to say," interpreted Major Dalgetty, "he desires to have his name concealed, in respect he hath in former days taken a castle, slain certain children, and done other things, whilk, as your good lordship knows, are often practised in war time, but excite no benevolence towards the perpetrator in the friends of those who sustain injury. I have known, in my military experience, many brave cavaliers put to death by the boors, simply for having used military license upon the country."

"I understand," said Montrose: "This person is at feud with some of our followers. Let him retire to the court of guard, and we will think of the best mode of protecting him."

"You hear, Ranald," said Major Dalgetty, with an air of superiority, "his Excellency wishes to hold privy council with me, you must go to the court of guard.—He does not know where that is, poor fellow!—he is a young soldier for so old a man; I will put him under the charge of a sentinel, and return to your lordship incontinent." He did so, and returned accordingly.

Montrose's first enquiry respected the embassy to Inverary; and he listened with attention to Dalgetty's reply, notwithstanding the prolixity of the Major's narrative. It required an effort from the Marquis to maintain his attention; but no one better knew, that where information is to be derived from the report of such agents as Dalgetty, it can only be obtained by suffering them to tell their story in their own way. Accordingly the Marquis's patience was at length rewarded. Among other spoils which the Captain thought himself at liberty to take, was a packet of Argyle's private papers. These he consigned to the hands of his General; a humour of accounting, however, which went no farther, for I do not understand that he made any mention of the purse of gold which he had appropriated at the same time that he made seizure of the papers aforesaid. Snatching a torch from the wall, Montrose was in an instant deeply engaged in the perusal of these documents, in which it is probable he found something to animate his personal resentment against his rival Argyle.

"Does he not fear me?" said he; "then he shall feel me. Will he fire my castle of Murdoch?—Inverary shall raise the first smoke.— O for a guide through the skirts of Strath-Fillan!"

Whatever might be Dalgetty's personal conceit, he understood his business sufficiently to guess at Montrose's meaning. He instantly interrupted his own prolix narration of the skirmish which had taken place, and the wound he had received in his retreat, and began to speak to the point which he saw interested his General.

"If," said he, "your Excellency wishes to make an infall into Argyleshire, this poor man, Ranald, of whom I told you, together with his children and companions, know every pass into that land, both leading from the east and from the north."

"Indeed!" said Montrose; "what reason have you to believe their knowledge so extensive?"

"So please your Excellency," answered Dalgetty, "during the weeks that I remained with them for cure of my wound, they were repeatedly obliged to shift their quarters, in respect of Argyle's repeated attempts to repossess himself of the person of an officer who was honoured with Your Excellency's confidence; so that I had occasion to admire the singular dexterity and knowledge of the face of the country with which they alternately achieved their retreat and their advance; and when, at length, I was able to repair to your Excellency's standard, this honest simple creature, Ranald MacEagh, guided me by paths which my steed Gustavus (which your lordship may remember) trode with perfect safety, so that I said to myself, that where guides, spies, or intelligencers, were required in a Highland campaign in that western country, more expert persons than he and his attendants could not possibly be desired."

"And can you answer for this man's fidelity?" said Montrose; "what is his name and condition?"

"He is an outlaw and robber by profession, something also of a homicide or murderer," answered Dalgetty; "and by name, called Ranald MacEagh; whilk signifies, Ranald, the Son of the Mist."

"I should remember something of that name," said Montrose, pausing: "Did not these Children of the Mist perpetrate some act of cruelty upon the M'Aulays?"

Major Dalgetty mentioned the circumstance of the murder of the forester, and Montrose's active memory at once recalled all the circumstances of the feud.

"It is most unlucky," said Montrose, "this inexpiable quarrel between these men and the M'Aulays. Allan has borne himself bravely in these wars, and possesses, by the wild mystery of his behaviour and language, so much influence over the minds of his countrymen, that the consequences of disobliging him might be serious. At the same time, these men being so capable of rendering useful service, and being as you say, Major Dalgetty, perfectly trustworthy—"

"I will pledge my pay and arrears, my horse and arms, my head and neck, upon their fidelity," said the Major; "and your Excellency knows, that a soldado could say no more for his own father."

"True," said Montrose; "but as this is a matter of particular moment, I would willingly know the grounds of so positive an assurance."

"Concisely then, my lord," said the Major, "not only did they disdain to profit by a handsome reward which Argyle did me the honour to place upon this poor head of mine, and not only did they abstain from pillaging my personal property, whilk was to an amount that would have tempted regular soldiers in any service of Europe; and not only did they restore me my horse, whilk your Excellency knows to be of value, but I could not prevail on them to accept one stiver, doit, or maravedi, for the trouble and expenses of my sick bed. They actually refused my coined money when freely offered,—a tale seldom to be told in a Christian land."

"I admit," said Montrose, after a moment's reflection, "that their conduct towards you is good evidence of their fidelity; but how to secure against the breaking out of this feud?" He paused, and then suddenly added, "I had forgot I have supped, while you, Major, have been travelling by moonlight."

He called to his attendants to fetch a stoup of wine and some refreshments. Major Dalgetty, who had the appetite of a convalescent returned from Highland quarters, needed not any pressing to partake of what was set before him, but proceeded to dispatch his food with such alacrity, that the Marquis, filling a cup of wine, and drinking to his health, could not help remarking, that coarse as the provisions of his camp were, he was afraid Major Dalgetty had fared much worse during his excursion into Argyleshire.

"Your Excellency may take your corporal oath upon that," said the worthy Major, speaking with his mouth full; "for Argyle's bread and water are yet stale and mouldy in my recollection, and though they did their best, yet the viands that the Children of the Mist procured for me, poor helpless creatures as they were, were so unrefreshful to my body, that when enclosed in my armour, whilk I was fain to leave behind me for expedition's sake, I rattled therein like the shrivelled kernel in a nut that hath been kept on to a second Hallowe'en."

"You must take the due means to repair these losses, Major Dalgetty."

"In troth," answered the soldier, "I shall hardly be able to compass that, unless my arrears are to be exchanged for present pay; for I protest to your Excellency, that the three stone weight which I have lost were simply raised upon the regular accountings of the States of Holland."

"In that case," said the Marquis, "you are only reduced to good marching order. As for the pay, let us once have victory—victory, Major, and your wishes, and all our wishes, shall be amply fulfilled. Meantime, help yourself to another cup of wine."

"To your Excellency's health," said the Major, filling a cup to the brim, to show the zeal with which he drank the toast, "and victory over all our enemies, and particularly over Argyle! I hope to twitch another handful from his board myself—I have had one pluck at it already."

"Very true," answered Montrose; "but to return to those men of the Mist. You understand, Dalgetty, that their presence here, and the purpose for which we employ them, is a secret between you and me?"

Delighted, as Montrose had anticipated, with this mark of his General's confidence, the Major laid his hand upon his nose, and nodded intelligence.

"How many may there be of Ranald's followers?" continued the Marquis.

"They are reduced, so far as I know, to some eight or ten men," answered Major Dalgetty, "and a few women and children."

"Where are they now?" demanded Montrose.

"In a valley, at three miles' distance," answered the soldier, "awaiting your Excellency's command; I judged it not fit to bring them to your leaguer without your Excellency's orders."

"You judged very well," said Montrose; "it would be proper that they remain where they are, or seek some more distant place of refuge. I will send them money, though it is a scarce article with me at present."

"It is quite unnecessary," said Major Dalgetty; "your Excellency has only to hint that the M'Aulays are going in that direction, and my friends of the Mist will instantly make volte-face, and go to the right about."

"That were scarce courteous," said the Marquis. "Better send them a few dollars to purchase them some cattle for the support of the women and children."

"They know how to come by their cattle at a far cheaper rate," said the Major; "but let it be as your Excellency wills."

"Let Ranald MacEagh," said Montrose, "select one or two of his followers, men whom he can trust, and who are capable of keeping their own secret and ours; these, with their chief for scout-master-general, shall serve for our guides. Let them be at my tent to-morrow at daybreak, and see, if possible, that they neither guess my purpose, nor hold any communication with each other in private.—This old man, has he any children?"

"They have been killed or hanged," answered the Major, "to the number of a round dozen, as I believe—but he hath left one grand-child, a smart and hopeful youth, whom I have noted to be never without a pebble in his plaid-nook, to fling at whatsoever might come in his way; being a symbol, that, like David, who was accustomed to sling smooth stones taken from the brook, he may afterwards prove an adventurous warrior."

"That boy, Major Dalgetty," said the Marquis, "I will have to attend upon my own person. I presume he will have sense enough to keep his name secret?"

"Your Excellency need not fear that," answered Dalgetty; "these Highland imps, from the moment they chip the shell—"

"Well," interrupted Montrose, "that boy shall be pledge for the fidelity of his parent, and if he prove faithful, the child's preferment shall be his reward.—And now, Major Dalgetty, I will license your departure for the night; tomorrow you will introduce this MacEagh, under any name or character he may please to assume. I presume his profession has rendered him sufficiently expert in all sort of disguises; or we may admit John of Moidart into our schemes, who has sense, practicability, and intelligence, and will probably allow this man for a time to be disguised as one of his followers. For you, Major, my groom of the chambers will be your quarter-master for this evening."

Major Dalgetty took his leave with a joyful heart greatly elated with the reception he had met with, and much pleased with the personal manners of his new General, which, as he explained at great length to Ranald MacEagh, reminded him in many respects of the demeanour of the immortal Gustavus Adolphus, the Lion of the North, and Bulwark of the Protestant Faith.

CHAPTER XVII.

The march begins in military state,
And nations on his eyes suspended wait;
Stern famine guards the solitary coast,
And winter barricades the realms of frost.
He comes,—nor want, nor cold, his course delay.
　　　　　　—VANITY OF HUMAN WISHES.

By break of day Montrose received in his cabin old MacEagh, and questioned him long and particularly as to the means of approaching the country of Argyle. He made a note of his answers, which he compared with those of two of his followers, whom he introduced as the most prudent and experienced. He found them to correspond in all respects; but, still unsatisfied where precaution was so necessary, the Marquis compared the information he had received with that he was able to collect from the Chiefs who lay most near to the destined scene of invasion, and being in all respects satisfied of its accuracy, he resolved to proceed in full reliance upon it.

In one point Montrose changed his mind. Having judged it unfit to take the boy Kenneth into his own service, lest, in case of his birth being discovered, it should be resented as an offence by the numerous clans who entertained a feudal enmity to this devoted family, he requested the Major to take him in attendance upon himself; and as he accompanied this request with a handsome DOUCEUR, under pretence of clothing and equipping the lad, this change was agreeable to all parties.

It was about breakfast-time, when Major Dalgetty, being dismissed by Montrose, went in quest of his old acquaintances, Lord Menteith and the M'Aulays, to whom he longed to communicate his own adventures, as well as to learn from them the particulars of the campaign. It may be imagined he was received with great glee by men to whom the late uniformity of their military life had rendered any change of society an interesting novelty. Allan M'Aulay alone seemed to recoil from his former acquaintance, although, when challenged by his brother, he could render no other reason than a reluctance to be familiar with one who had been so lately in the company of Argyle, and other enemies. Major Dalgetty was a little alarmed by this sort of instinctive consciousness which Allan seemed to entertain respecting the society he had been lately keeping; he was soon satisfied, however, that the perceptions of the seer in this particular were not infallible.

As Ranald MacEagh was to be placed under Major Dalgetty's protection and superintendence, it was necessary he should present him to those persons with whom he was most likely to associate. The dress of the old man had, in the meantime, been changed from the tartan of his clan to a sort of clothing peculiar to the men of the distant Isles, resembling a waistcoat with sleeves, and a petticoat, all made in one piece. This dress was laced from top to bottom in front, and bore some resemblance to that called Polonaise, still worn by children in Scotland of the lower rank. The tartan hose and bonnet completed the dress, which old men of the last century remembered well to have seen worn by the distant Islesmen who came to the Earl of Mar's standard in the year 1715.

Major Dalgetty, keeping his eye on Allan as he spoke, introduced Ranald MacEagh under the fictitious name of Ranald MacGillihuron in Benbecula, who had escaped with him out of Argyle's prison. He recommended him as a person skilful in the arts of the harper and the senachie, and by no means contemptible in the quality of a second-sighted person or seer. While making this exposition, Major Dalgetty stammered and hesitated in a way so unlike the usual glib forwardness of his manner, that he could not have failed to have given suspicion to Allan M'Aulay, had not that person's whole attention been engaged in steadily perusing the features of the person thus introduced to him. This steady gaze so much embarrassed Ranald MacEagh, that his hand was beginning to sink down towards his dagger, in expectation of a hostile assault, when Allan, suddenly crossing the floor of the hut, extended his hand to him in the way of friendly greeting. They sat down side by side, and conversed in a low mysterious tone of voice. Menteith and Angus M'Aulay were not surprised at this, for there prevailed among the Highlanders who pretended to the second-sight, a sort of Freemasonry, which generally induced them, upon meeting, to hold communication with each other on the nature and extent of their visionary experiences.

"Does the sight come gloomy upon your spirits?" said Allan to his new acquaintance.

"As dark as the shadow upon the moon," replied Ranald, "when she is darkened in her mid-course in heaven, and prophets foretell of evil times."

"Come hither," said Allan, "come more this way, I would converse with you apart; for men say that in your distant islands the sight is poured forth with more clearness and power than upon us, who dwell near the Sassenach."

While they were plunged into their mystic conference, the two English cavaliers entered the cabin in the highest possible spirits, and announced to Angus M'Aulay that orders had been issued that all should hold themselves in readiness for an immediate march to the westward. Having delivered themselves of their news with much glee, they paid their compliments to their old acquaintance Major Dalgetty, whom they instantly recognised, and enquired after the health of his charger, Gustavus.

"I humbly thank you, gentlemen," answered the soldier, "Gustavus is well, though, like his master, somewhat barer on the ribs than when you offered to relieve me of him at Darnlinvarach; and let me assure you, that before you have made one or two of those marches which you seem to contemplate with so much satisfaction in prospect, you will leave, my good knights, some of your English beef, and probably an English horse or two, behind you."

Both exclaimed that they cared very little what they found or what they left, provided the scene changed from dogging up and down Angus and Aberdeenshire, in pursuit of an enemy who would neither fight nor run away.

"If such be the case," said Angus M'Aulay, "I must give orders to my followers, and make provision too for the safe conveyance of Annot Lyle; for an advance into M'Callum More's country will be a farther and fouler road than these pinks of Cumbrian knighthood are aware of." So saying, he left the cabin.

"Annot Lyle!" repeated Dalgetty, "is she following the campaign?"

"Surely," replied Sir Giles Musgrave, his eye glancing slightly from Lord Menteith to Allan M'Aulay; "we could neither march nor fight, advance nor retreat, without the influence of the Princess of Harps."

"The Princess of Broadswords and Targets, I say," answered his companion; "for the Lady of Montrose herself could not be more courteously waited upon; she has four Highland maidens, and as many bare-legged gillies, to wait upon her orders."

"And what would you have, gentlemen?" said Allan, turning suddenly from the Highlander with whom he was in conversation; "would you yourselves have left an innocent female, the companion of your infancy, to die by violence, or perish by famine? There is not, by this time, a roof upon the habitation of my fathers—our crops have been destroyed, and our cattle have been driven—and you, gentlemen, have to bless God, that, coming from a milder and more civilized country, you expose only your own lives in this remorseless war, without apprehension that your enemies will visit with their vengeance the defenceless pledges you may have left behind you."

The Englishmen cordially agreed that they had the superiority in this respect; and the company, now dispersing, went each to his several charge or occupation.

Allan lingered a moment behind, still questioning the reluctant Ranald MacEagh upon a point in his supposed visions, by which he was greatly perplexed. "Repeatedly," he said, "have I had the sight of a Gael, who seemed to plunge his weapon into the body of Menteith,—of that young nobleman in the scarlet laced cloak, who has just now left the bothy. But by no effort, though I have gazed till my eyes were almost fixed in the sockets, can I discover the face of this Highlander, or even conjecture who he may be, although his person and air seem familiar to me." [See Note II.—Wraiths.]

"Have you reversed your own plaid," said Ranald, "according to the rule of the experienced Seers in such case?"

"I have," answered Allan, speaking low, and shuddering as if with internal agony.

"And in what guise did the phantom then appear to you?" said Ranald.

"With his plaid also reversed," answered Allan, in the same low and convulsed tone.

"Then be assured," said Ranald, "that your own hand, and none other, will do the deed of which you have witnessed the shadow."

"So has my anxious soul a hundred times surmised," replied Allan. "But it is impossible! Were I to read the record in the eternal book of fate, I would declare it impossible—we are bound by the ties of blood, and by a hundred ties more intimate—we have stood side by side in battle, and our swords have reeked with the blood of the same enemies—it is IMPOSSIBLE I should harm him!"

"That you WILL do so," answered Ranald, "is certain, though the cause be hid in the darkness of futurity. You say," he continued, suppressing his own emotions with difficulty, "that side by side you have pursued your prey like bloodhounds—have you never seen bloodhounds turn their fangs against each other, and fight over the body of a throttled deer?"

"It is false!" said M'Aulay, starting up, "these are not the forebodings of fate, but the temptation of some evil spirit from the bottomless pit!" So saying, he strode out of the cabin.

"Thou hast it!" said the Son of the Mist, looking after him with an air of exultation; "the barbed arrow is in thy side! Spirits of the slaughtered, rejoice! soon shall your murderers' swords be dyed in each other's blood."

On the succeeding morning all was prepared, and Montrose advanced by rapid marches up the river Tay, and poured his desultory forces into the romantic vale around the lake of the same name, which lies at the head of that river. The inhabitants were Campbells, not indeed the vassals of Argyle, but of the allied and kindred house of Glenorchy, which now bears the name of Breadalbane. Being taken by surprise, they were totally unprepared for resistance, and were compelled to be passive witnesses of the ravages which took place among their flocks and herds. Advancing in this manner to the vale of Loch Dochart, and laying waste the country around him, Montrose reached the most difficult point of his enterprise.

To a modern army, even with the assistance of the good military road which now leads up by Teinedrum to the head of Loch Awe, the passage of these extensive wilds would seem a task of some difficulty. But at this period, and for long afterwards, there was no road or path whatsoever; and to add to the difficulty, the mountains were already covered with snow. It was a sublime scene to look up to them, piled in great masses, one upon another, the front rank of dazzling whiteness, while those which arose behind them caught a rosy tint from the setting of a clear wintry sun. Ben Cruachan, superior in magnitude, and seeming the very citadel of the Genius of the Region, rose high above the others, showing his glimmering and scathed peak to the distance of many miles.

The followers of Montrose were men not to be daunted by the sublime, yet terrible prospect before them. Many of them were of that ancient race of Highlanders, who not only willingly made their couch in the snow, but considered it as effeminate luxury to use a snowball for a pillow. Plunder and revenge lay beyond the frozen mountains which they beheld, and they did not permit themselves to be daunted by the difficulty of traversing them. Montrose did not allow their spirits time to subside. He ordered the pipes to play in the van the ancient pibroch entitled, "HOGGIL NAM BO," etc. (that is, We come through snow-drift to drive the prey), the shrilling sounds of which had often struck the vales of the Lennox with terror. [It is the family-march of the M'Farlanes, a warlike and predatory clan, who inhabited the western banks of Loch-Lomond. See WAVERLY, Note XV.] The troops advanced with the nimble alacrity of mountaineers, and were soon involved in the dangerous pass, through which Ranald acted as their guide, going before them with a select party, to track out the way.

The power of man at no time appears more contemptible than when it is placed in contrast with scenes of natural terror and dignity. The victorious army of Montrose, whose exploits had struck terror into all Scotland, when ascending up this terrific pass, seemed a contemptible handful of stragglers, in the act of being devoured by the jaws of the mountain, which appeared ready to close upon them. Even Montrose half repented the boldness of his attempt, as he looked down from the summit of the first eminence which he attained, upon the scattered condition of his small army. The difficulty of getting forward was so great, that considerable gaps began to occur in the line of march, and the distance between the van, centre, and rear, was each moment increased in a degree equally incommodious and dangerous. It was with great apprehension that Montrose looked upon every point of advantage which the hill afforded, in dread it might be found occupied by an enemy prepared for defence; and he often afterwards was heard to express his conviction, that had the passes of Strath-Fillan been defended by two hundred resolute men, not only would his progress have been effectually stopped, but his army must have been in danger of being totally cut off. Security, however, the bane of many a strong country and many a fortress, betrayed, on this occasion, the district of Argyle to his enemies. The invaders had only to contend with the natural difficulties of the path, and with the snow, which, fortunately, had not fallen in any great quantity. The army no sooner reached the summit of the ridge of hills dividing Argyleshire from the district of Breadalbane, than they rushed down upon the devoted vales beneath them with a fury sufficiently expressive of the motives which had dictated a movement so difficult and hazardous.

Montrose divided his army into three bodies, in order to produce a wider and more extensive terror, one of which was commanded by the Captain of Clan Ranald, one intrusted to the leading of Colkitto, and the third remained under his own direction. He was thus enabled to penetrate the country of Argyle at three different points. Resistance there was none. The flight of the shepherds from the hills had first announced in the peopled districts this formidable irruption, and wherever the clansmen were summoned out, they were killed, disarmed, and dispersed, by an enemy who had anticipated their motions. Major Dalgetty, who had been sent forward against Inverary with the few horse of the army that were fit for service, managed his matters so well, that he had very nearly surprised Argyle, as he expressed it, INTER POCULA; and it was only a rapid flight by water which saved that chief from death or captivity. But the punishment which Argyle himself escaped fell heavily upon his country and clan, and the ravages committed by Montrose on that devoted land, although too consistent with the genius of the country and times, have been repeatedly and justly quoted as a blot on his actions and character.

Argyle in the meantime had fled to Edinburgh, to lay his complaints before the Convention of Estates. To meet the exigence of the moment, a considerable army was raised under General Baillie, a Presbyterian officer of skill and fidelity, with whom was joined in command the celebrated Sir John Urrie, a soldier of fortune like Dalgetty, who had already changed sides twice during the Civil War, and was destined to turn his coat a third time before it was ended. Argyle also, burning with indignation, proceeded to levy his own numerous forces, in order to avenge himself of his feudal enemy. He established his head-quarters at Dunbarton, where he was soon joined by a considerable force, consisting chiefly of his own clansmen and dependants. Being there joined by Baillie and Urrie, with a very considerable army of regular forces, he prepared to march into Argyleshire, and chastise the invader of his paternal territories.

But Montrose, while these two formidable armies were forming a junction, had been recalled from that ravaged country by the approach of a third, collected in the north under the Earl of Seaforth, who, after some hesitation, having embraced the side of the Covenanters, had now, with the assistance of the veteran garrison of Inverness, formed a considerable army, with which he threatened Montrose from Inverness-shire. Enclosed in a wasted and unfriendly country, and menaced on each side by advancing enemies of superior force, it might have been supposed that Montrose's destruction was certain. But these were precisely the circumstances under which the active and enterprising genius of the Great Marquis was calculated to excite the wonder and admiration of his friends, the astonishment and terror of his enemies. As if by magic, he collected his scattered forces from the wasteful occupation in which they had been engaged; and scarce were they again united, ere Argyle and his associate generals were informed, that the royalists, having suddenly disappeared from Argyleshire, had retreated northwards among the dusky and impenetrable mountains of Lochaber.

The sagacity of the generals opposed to Montrose immediately conjectured, that it was the purpose of their active antagonist to fight with, and, if possible, to destroy Seaforth, ere they could come to his assistance. This occasioned a corresponding change in their operations. Leaving this chieftain to make the best defence he could, Urrie and Baillie again separated their forces from those of Argyle; and, having chiefly horse and Lowland troops under their command, they kept the southern side of the Grampian ridge, moving along eastward into the county of Angus, resolving from thence to proceed into Aberdeenshire, in order to intercept Montrose, if he should attempt to escape in that direction.

Argyle, with his own levies and other troops, undertook to follow Montrose's march; so that, in case he should come to action either with Seaforth, or with Baillie and Urrie, he might be placed between two fires by this third army, which, at a secure distance, was to hang upon his rear.

For this purpose, Argyle once more moved towards Inverary, having an opportunity, at every step, to deplore the severities which the hostile clans had exercised on his dependants and country. Whatever noble qualities the Highlanders possessed, and they had many, clemency in treating a hostile country was not of the number; but even the ravages of hostile troops combined to swell the number of Argyle's followers. It is still a Highland proverb, He whose house is burnt must become a soldier; and hundreds of the inhabitants of these unfortunate valleys had now no means of maintenance, save by exercising upon others the severities they had themselves sustained, and no future prospect of happiness, excepting in the gratification of revenge. His bands were, therefore, augmented by the very circumstances which had desolated his country, and Argyle soon found himself at the head of three thousand determined men, distinguished for activity and courage, and commanded by gentlemen of his own name, who yielded to none in those qualities. Under himself, he conferred the principal command upon Sir Duncan Campbell of Ardenvohr, and another Sir Duncan Campbell of Auchenbreck, [This last character is historical] an experienced and veteran soldier, whom he had recalled from the wars of Ireland for this purpose. The cold spirit of Argyle himself, however, clogged the military councils of his more intrepid assistants; and it was resolved, notwithstanding their increased force, to observe the same plan of operations, and to follow Montrose cautiously, in whatever direction he should march, avoiding an engagement until an opportunity should occur of falling upon his rear, while he should be engaged with another enemy in front.

CHAPTER XVIII.

Piobracht au Donuil-dhu,
Piobrachet au Donuil,
Piobrachet agus S'breittach
Feacht an Innerlochy.

The war-tune of Donald the Black,
The war-tune of Black Donald,
The pipes and the banner
Are up in the rendezvous of Inverlochy.

The military road connecting the chains of forts, as it is called,
and running in the general line of the present Caledonian Canal,
has now completely opened the great glen, or chasm, extending
almost across the whole island, once doubtless filled by the sea, and
still affording basins for that long line of lakes, by means of which
modern art has united the German and Atlantic Oceans. The paths
or tracks by which the natives traversed this extensive valley, were,
in 1645-6, in the same situation as when they awaked the strain of
an Irish engineer officer, who had been employed in converting
them into practicable military roads, and whose eulogium begins,
and, for aught I know, ends, as follows:

Had you seen but these roads before they were made, You
would have held up your hands and bless'd General Wade.

But, bad as the ordinary paths were, Montrose avoided
them, and led his army, like a herd of wild deer, from mountain
to mountain, and from forest to forest, where his enemies could
learn nothing of his motions, while he acquired the most perfect
knowledge respecting theirs from the friendly clans of Cameron
and M'Donnell, whose mountainous districts he now traversed.
Strict orders had been given that Argyle's advance should be

watched, and that all intelligence respecting his motions should be communicated instantly to the General himself.

It was a moonlight night, and Montrose, worn out by the fatigues of the day, was laid down to sleep in a miserable shieling. He had only slumbered two hours, when some one touched his shoulder. He looked up, and, by the stately form and deep voice, easily recognised the Chief of the Camerons.

"I have news for you," said that leader, "which is worth while to arise and listen to."

"M'Ilduy [Mhich-Connel Dhu, the descendant of Black Donald.] can bring no other," said Montrose, addressing the Chief by his patronymic title—"are they good or bad?"

"As you may take them," said the Chieftain.

"Are they certain?" demanded Montrose.

"Yes," answered M'Ilduy, "or another messenger should have brought them. Know that, tired with the task imposed upon me of accompanying that unhappy Dalgetty and his handful of horse, who detained me for hours on the march at the pace of a crippled badger, I made a stretch of four miles with six of my people in the direction of Inverlochy, and there met with Ian of Glenroy, who had been out for intelligence. Argyle is moving upon Inverlochy with three thousand chosen men, commanded by the flower of the sons of Diarmid.—These are my news—they are certain—it is for you to construe their purport."

"Their purport must be good," answered Montrose, readily and cheerfully; "the voice of M'Ilduy is ever pleasant in the ears of Montrose, and most pleasant when it speaks of some brave enterprise at hand—What are our musters?"

He then called for light, and easily ascertained that a great part of his followers having, as usual, dispersed to secure their booty, he had not with him above twelve or fourteen hundred men.

"Not much above a third," said Montrose, pausing, "of Argyle's force, and Highlanders opposed to Highlanders.—With the blessing of God upon the royal cause, I would not hesitate were the odds but one to two."

"Then do not hesitate," said Cameron; "for when your trumpets shall sound to attack M'Callum More, not a man of these glens will remain deaf to the summons. Glengarry—Keppoch— I myself—would destroy, with fire and sword, the wretch who should remain behind under any pretence whatsoever. To-morrow, or the next day, shall be a day of battle to all who bear the name of M'Donnell or Cameron, whatever be the event."

"It is gallantly said, my noble friend," said Montrose, grasping his hand, "and I were worse than a coward did I not do justice to such followers, by entertaining the most indubitable hopes of success. We will turn back on this M'Callum More, who follows us like a raven to devour the relics of our army, should we meet braver men who may be able to break its strength! Let the Chiefs and leaders be called together as quickly as possible; and you, who have brought us the first news of this joyful event,—for such it shall be,—you, M'Ilduy, shall bring it to a joyful issue, by guiding us the best and nearest road against our enemy."

"That will I willingly do," said M'Ilduy; "if I have shown you paths by which to retreat through these dusky wilds, with far more readiness will I teach you how to advance against your foe."

A general bustle now prevailed, and the leaders were everywhere startled from the rude couches on which they had sought temporary repose.

"I never thought," said Major Dalgetty, when summoned up from a handful of rugged heather roots, "to have parted from a bed as hard as a stable-broom with such bad will; but, indubitably, having but one man of military experience in his army, his Excellency the Marquis may be vindicated in putting him upon hard duty."

So saying, he repaired to the council, where, notwithstanding his pedantry, Montrose seemed always to listen to him with considerable attention; partly because the Major really possessed military knowledge and experience, and often made suggestions which were found of advantage, and partly because it relieved the General from the necessity of deferring entirely to the opinion of the Highland Chiefs, and gave him additional ground for disputing it when it was not agreeable to his own. On the present occasion, Dalgetty joyfully acquiesced in the proposal of marching back and confronting Argyle, which he compared to the valiant resolution of the great Gustavus, who moved against the Duke of Bavaria, and enriched his troops by the plunder of that fertile country, although menaced from the northward by the large army which Wallenstein had assembled in Bohemia.

The Chiefs of Glengarry, Keppoch, and Lochiel, whose clans, equal in courage and military fame to any in the Highlands, lay within the neighbourhood of the scene of action, dispatched the fiery cross through their vassals, to summon every one who could bear arms to meet the King's lieutenant, and to join the standards of their respective Chiefs, as they marched towards Inverlochy. As the order was emphatically given, it was speedily and willingly obeyed. Their natural love of war, their zeal for the royal cause,—for they viewed the King in the light of a chief whom his clansmen had deserted,—as well as their implicit obedience to their own patriarch, drew in to Montrose's army not only all in the neighbourhood who were able to bear arms, but some who, in age at least, might have been esteemed past the use of them. During the next day's march, which, being directed straight through the mountains of Lochaber, was unsuspected by the enemy, his forces were augmented by handfuls of men issuing from each glen, and ranging themselves under the banners of their respective Chiefs. This was a circumstance highly inspiriting to the rest of the army, who, by the time they approached the enemy, found their strength increased considerably more than one-fourth, as had been prophesied by the valiant leader of the Camerons.

While Montrose executed this counter-march, Argyle had, at the head of his gallant army, advanced up the southern side of Loch-Eil, and reached the river Lochy, which combines that lake with Loch-Lochy. The ancient Castle of Inverlochy, once, as it is said, a royal fortress, and still, although dismantled, a place of some strength and consideration, offered convenient head-quarters, and there was ample room for Argyle's army to encamp around him in the valley, where the Lochy joins Loch-Eil. Several barges had attended, loaded with provisions, so that they were in every respect as well accommodated as such an army wished or expected to be. Argyle, in council with Auchenbreck and Ardenvohr, expressed his full confidence that Montrose was now on the brink of destruction; that his troops must gradually diminish as he moved eastward through such uncouth paths; that if he went westward, he must encounter Urrie and Baillie; if northward, fall into the hands of Seaforth; or should he choose any halting-place, he would expose himself to be attacked by three armies at once.

"I cannot rejoice in the prospect, my lord," said Auchebreck, "that James Grahame will be crushed with little assistance of ours. He has left a heavy account in Argyleshire against him, and I long to reckon with him drop of blood for drop of blood. I love not the payment of such debts by third hands."

"You are too scrupulous," said Argyle; "what signifies it by whose hands the blood of the Grahames is spilt? It is time that of the sons of Diarmid should cease to flow.—What say you, Ardenvohr?"

"I say, my lord," replied Sir Duncan, "that I think Auchenbreck will be gratified, and will himself have a personal opportunity of settling accounts with Montrose for his depredations. Reports have reached our outposts that the Camerons are assembling their full strength on the skirts of Ben-Nevis; this must be to join the advance of Montrose, and not to cover his retreat."

"It must be some scheme of harassing and depredation," said Argyle, "devised by the inveterate malignity of M'Ilduy, which he terms loyalty. They can intend no more than an attack on our outposts, or some annoyance to to-morrow's march."

"I have sent out scouts," said Sir Duncan, "in every direction, to procure intelligence; and we must soon hear whether they really do assemble any force, upon what point, or with what purpose."

It was late ere any tidings were received; but when the moon had arisen, a considerable bustle in the camp, and a noise immediately after heard in the castle, announced the arrival of important intelligence. Of the scouts first dispersed by Ardenvohr, some had returned without being able to collect anything, save uncertain rumours concerning movements in the country of the Camerons. It seemed as if the skirts of Ben-Nevis were sending forth those unaccountable and portentous sounds with which they sometimes announce the near approach of a storm. Others, whose zeal carried them farther upon their mission, were entrapped and slain, or made prisoners, by the inhabitants of the fastnesses into which they endeavoured to penetrate. At length, on the rapid advance of Montrose's army, his advanced guard and the outposts of Argyle became aware of each other's presence, and after exchanging a few musket-shots and arrows, fell back to their respective main bodies, to convey intelligence and receive orders.

Sir Duncan Campbell, and Auchenbreck, instantly threw themselves on horseback, in order to visit the state of the outposts; and Argyle maintained his character of commander-in-chief with reputation, by making a respectable arrangement of his forces in the plain, as it was evident that they might now expect a night alarm, or an attack in the morning at farthest. Montrose had kept his forces so cautiously within the defiles of the mountain, that no effort which Auchenbreck or Ardenvohr thought it prudent to attempt, could ascertain his probable strength. They were aware, however, that, at the utmost computation, it must be inferior to their own, and they returned to Argyle to inform him of the amount of their observations; but that nobleman refused to believe that Montrose could be in presence himself. He said, "It was a madness, of which even James Grahame, in his height of presumptuous frenzy, was incapable; and he doubted not that their march was only impeded by their ancient enemies, Glencoe, Keppoch, and Glengarry; and perhaps M'Vourigh, with his M'Phersons, might have assembled a force, which he knew must be greatly inferior in numbers to his own, and whom, therefore, he doubted not to disperse by force, or by terms of capitulation."

The spirit of Argyle's followers was high, breathing vengeance for the disasters which their country had so lately undergone; and the night passed in anxious hopes that the morning might dawn upon their vengeance. The outposts of either army kept a careful watch, and the soldiers of Argyle slept in the order of battle which they were next day to occupy.

A pale dawn had scarce begun to tinge the tops of these immense mountains, when the leaders of both armies prepared for the business of the day. It was the second of February, 1645-6. The clansmen of Argyle were arranged in two lines, not far from the angle between the river and the lake, and made an appearance equally resolute and formidable. Auchenbreck would willingly have commenced the battle by an attack on the outposts of the enemy, but Argyle, with more cautious policy, preferred receiving to making the onset. Signals were soon heard, that they would not long wait for it in vain. The Campbells could distinguish, in the gorge of the mountains, the war-tunes of various clans as they advanced to the onset. That of the Camerons, which bears the ominous words, addressed to the wolves and ravens, "Come to me, and I will give you flesh," was loudly re-echoed from their native glens. In the language of the Highland bards, the war voice of Glengarry was not silent; and the gathering tunes of other tribes could be plainly distinguished, as they successively came up to the extremity of the passes from which they were to descend into the plain.

"You see," said Argyle to his kinsmen, "it is as I said, we have only to deal with our neighbours; James Grahame has not ventured to show us his banner."

At this moment there resounded from the gorge of the pass a lively flourish of trumpets, in that note with which it was the ancient Scottish fashion to salute the royal standard.

"You may hear, my lord, from yonder signal," said Sir Duncan Campbell, "that he who pretends to be the King's Lieutenant, must be in person among these men."

"And has probably horse with him," said Auchenbreck, "which I could not have anticipated. But shall we look pale for that, my lord, when we have foes to fight, and wrongs to revenge?"

Argyle was silent, and looked upon his arm, which hung in a sash, owing to a fall which he had sustained in a preceding march.

"It is true," interrupted Ardenvohr, eagerly, "my Lord of Argyle, you are disabled from using either sword or pistol; you must retire on board the galleys—your life is precious to us as a head—your hand cannot be useful to us as a soldier."

"No," said Argyle, pride contending with irresolution, "it shall never be said that I fled before Montrose; if I cannot fight, I will at least die in the midst of my children."

Several other principal Chiefs of the Campbells, with one voice, conjured and obtested their Chieftain to leave them for that day to the leading of Ardenvohr and Auchenbreck, and to behold the conflict from a distance and in safety.—We dare not stigmatize Argyle with poltroonery; for, though his life was marked by no action of bravery, yet he behaved with so much composure and dignity in the final and closing scene, that his conduct upon the present and similar occasions, should be rather imputed to indecision than to want of courage. But when the small still voice within a man's own breast, which tells him that his life is of consequence to himself, is seconded by that of numbers around him, who assure him that it is of equal advantage to the public, history affords many examples of men more habitually daring than Argyle, who have consulted self-preservation when the temptations to it were so powerfully increased.

"See him on board, if you will, Sir Duncan," said Auchenbreck to his kinsman; "It must be my duty to prevent this spirit from spreading farther among us."

So saying, he threw himself among the ranks, entreating, commanding, and conjuring the soldiers, to remember their ancient fame and their present superiority; the wrongs they had to revenge, if successful, and the fate they had to dread, if vanquished; and imparting to every bosom a portion of the fire which glowed in his own. Slowly, meanwhile, and apparently with reluctance, Argyle suffered himself to be forced by his officious kinsmen to the verge of the lake, and was transported on board of a galley, from the deck of which he surveyed with more safety than credit the scene which ensued.

Sir Duncan Campbell of Ardenvohr, notwithstanding the urgency of the occasion, stood with his eyes riveted on the boat which bore his Chieftain from the field of battle. There were feelings in his bosom which could not be expressed; for the character of a Chief was that of a father, and the heart of a clansman durst not dwell upon his failings with critical severity as upon those of other men. Argyle, too, harsh and severe to others, was generous and liberal among his kinsmen, and the noble heart of, Ardenvohr was wrung with bitter anguish, when he reflected to what interpretation his present conduct might subject him.

"It is better it should be so," said he to himself, devouring his own emotion; "but—of his line of a hundred sires, I know not one who would have retired while the banner of Diarmid waved in the wind, in the face of its most inveterate foes!"

A loud shout now compelled him to turn, and to hasten with all dispatch to his post, which was on the right flank of Argyle's little army.

The retreat of Argyle had not passed unobserved by his watchful enemy, who, occupying the superior ground, could mark every circumstance which passed below. The movement of three or four horsemen to the rear showed that those who retreated were men of rank.

"They are going," said Dalgetty, "to put their horses out of danger, like prudent cavaliers. Yonder goes Sir Duncan Campbell, riding a brown bay gelding, which I had marked for my own second charger."

You are wrong, Major," said Montrose, with a bitter smile, "they are saving their precious Chief—Give the signal for assault instantly—send the word through the ranks.—Gentlemen, noble Chiefs, Glengarry, Keppoch, M'Vourigh, upon them instantly!— Ride to M'Ilduy, Major Dalgetty, and tell him to charge as he loves Lochaber—return and bring our handful of horse to my standard. They shall be placed with the Irish as a reserve."

CHAPTER XIX.

As meets a rock a thousand waves, so Inisfail met Lochlin.
—OSSIAN.

The trumpets and bagpipes, those clamorous harbingers of blood and death, at once united in the signal for onset, which was replied to by the cry of more than two thousand warriors, and the echoes of the mountain glens behind them. Divided into three bodies, or columns, the Highland followers of Montrose poured from the defiles which had hitherto concealed them from their enemies, and rushed with the utmost determination upon the Campbells, who waited their charge with the greatest firmness. Behind these charging columns marched in line the Irish, under Colkitto, intended to form the reserve. With them was the royal standard, and Montrose himself; and on the flanks were about fifty horse, under Dalgetty, which by wonderful exertions had been kept in some sort fit for service.

The right column of Royalists was led by Glengarry, the left by Lochiel, and the centre by the Earl of Menteith, who preferred fighting on foot in a Highland dress to remaining with the cavalry.

The Highlanders poured on with the proverbial fury of their country, firing their guns, and discharging their arrows, at a little distance from the enemy, who received the assault with the most determined gallantry. Better provided with musketry than their enemies, stationary also, and therefore taking the more decisive aim, the fire of Argyle's followers was more destructive than that which they sustained. The royal clans, perceiving this, rushed to close quarters, and succeeded on two points in throwing their enemies into disorder. With regular troops this must have achieved a victory; but here Highlanders were opposed to Highlanders, and the nature of the weapons, as well as the agility of those who wielded them, was equal on both sides.

Their strife was accordingly desperate; and the clash of the swords and axes, as they encountered each other, or rung upon the targets, was mingled with the short, wild, animating shrieks with which Highlanders accompany the battle, the dance, or indeed violent exertion of any kind. Many of the foes opposed were personally acquainted, and sought to match themselves with each other from motives of hatred, or a more generous emulation of valour. Neither party would retreat an inch, while the place of those who fell (and they fell fast on both sides) was eagerly supplied by others, who thronged to the front of danger. A steam, like that which arises from a seething cauldron, rose into the thin, cold, frosty air, and hovered above the combatants.

So stood the fight on the right and the centre, with no immediate consequence, except mutual wounds and death.

On the right of the Campbells, the Knight of Ardenvohr obtained some advantage, through his military skill and by strength of numbers. He had moved forward obliquely the extreme flank of his line at the instant the Royalists were about to close, so that they sustained a fire at once on front and in flank, and, despite the utmost efforts of their leader, were thrown into some confusion. At this instant, Sir Duncan Campbell gave the word to charge, and thus unexpectedly made the attack at the very moment he seemed about to receive it. Such a change of circumstances is always discouraging, and often fatal. But the disorder was remedied by the advance of the Irish reserve, whose heavy and sustained fire compelled the Knight of Ardenvohr to forego his advantage, and content himself with repulsing the enemy. The Marquis of Montrose, in the meanwhile, availing himself of some scattered birch trees, as well as of the smoke produced by the close fire of the Irish musketry, which concealed the operation, called upon Dalgetty to follow him with the horse, and wheeling round so as to gain the right flank and even the rear of the enemy, he commanded his six trumpets to sound the charge. The clang of the cavalry trumpets, and the noise of the galloping of the horse, produced an effect upon Argyle's right wing which no other sounds could have impressed them with. The mountaineers of that period had a superstitious dread of the war-horse, like that entertained by the Peruvians, and had many strange ideas respecting the manner in which that animal was trained to combat. When, therefore, they found their ranks unexpectedly broken, and that the objects of their greatest terror were suddenly in the midst of them, the panic, in spite of Sir Duncan's attempts to stop it, became universal. Indeed, the figure of Major Dalgetty alone, sheathed in impenetrable armour, and making his horse caracole and bound, so as to give weight to every blow which he struck, would have been a novelty in itself sufficient to terrify those who had never seen anything more nearly resembling such a cavalier, than a SHELTY waddling under a Highlander far bigger than itself. The repulsed Royalists returned to the charge; the Irish, keeping their ranks, maintained a fire equally close and destructive. There was no sustaining the fight longer. Argyle's followers began to break and fly, most towards the lake, the remainder in different directions. The defeat of the right wing, of itself decisive, was rendered irreparable by the death of Auchenbreck, who fell while endeavouring to restore order.

The Knight of Ardenvohr, with two or three hundred men, all gentlemen of descent and distinguished gallantry,—for the Campbells are supposed to have had more gentlemen in their ranks than any of the Highland clans, endeavoured, with unavailing heroism, to cover the tumultuary retreat of the common file. Their resolution only proved fatal to themselves, as they were charged again and again by fresh adversaries, and forced to separate from each other, until at length their aim seemed only to be to purchase an honourable death by resisting to the very last.

"Good quarter, Sir Duncan," called out Major Dalgetty, when he discovered his late host, with one or two others, defending himself against several Highlanders; and, to enforce his offer, he rode up to him with his sword uplifted. Sir Duncan's reply was the discharge of a reserved pistol, which took effect not on the person of the rider, but on that of his gallant horse, which, shot through the heart, fell dead under him. Ranald MacEagh, who was one of those who had been pressing Sir Duncan hard, took the opportunity to cut him down with his broadsword, as he turned from him in the act of firing the pistol.

Allan M'Aulay came up at this moment. They were, excepting Ranald, followers of his brother who were engaged on that part of the field, "Villains!" he said, "which of you has dared to do this, when it was my positive order that the Knight of Ardenvohr should be taken alive?"

Half-a-dozen of busy hands, which were emulously employed in plundering the fallen knight, whose arms and accoutrements were of a magnificence befitting his quality, instantly forbore the occupation, and half the number of voices exculpated themselves, by laying the blame on the Skyeman, as they called Ranald MacEagh.

"Dog of an Islander!" said Allan, forgetting, in his wrath, their prophetic brotherhood, "follow the chase, and harm him no farther, unless you mean to die by my hand." They were at this moment left almost alone; for Allan's threats had forced his own clan from the spot, and all around had pressed onwards toward the lake, carrying before them noise, terror, and confusion, and leaving behind only the dead and dying. The moment was tempting to MacEagh's vengeful spirit.—"That I should die by your hand, red as it is with the blood of my kindred," said he, answering the threat of Allan in a tone as menacing as his own, "is not more likely than that you should fall by mine." With that, he struck at M'Aulay with such unexpected readiness, that he had scarce time to intercept the blow with his target.

"Villain!" said Allan, in astonishment, "what means this?"

"I am Ranald of the Mist!" answered the Islesman, repeating the blow; and with that word, they engaged in close and furious conflict. It seemed to be decreed, that in Allan M'Aulay had arisen the avenger of his mother's wrongs upon this wild tribe, as was proved by the issue of the present, as well as of former combats. After exchanging a few blows, Ranald MacEagh was prostrated by a deep wound on the skull; and M'Aulay, setting his foot on him, was about to pass the broadsword through his body, when the point of the weapon was struck up by a third party, who suddenly interposed. This was no other than Major Dalgetty, who, stunned. by the fall, and encumbered by the dead body of his horse, had now recovered his legs and his understanding. "Hold up your sword," said he to M'Aulay, "and prejudice this person no farther, in respect that he is here in my safeconduct, and in his Excellency's service; and in regard that no honourable cavalier is at liberty, by the law martial, to avenge his own private injuries, FLAGRANTE BELLO, MULTO MAJUS FLAGRANTE PRAELIO."

"Fool!" said Allan, "stand aside, and dare not to come between the tiger and his prey!"

But, far from quitting his point, Dalgetty stept across the fallen body of MacEagh, and gave Allan to understand, that if he called himself a tiger, he was likely, at present, to find a lion in his path. There required no more than the gesture and tone of defiance to turn the whole rage of the military Seer against the person who was opposing the course of his vengeance, and blows were instantly exchanged without farther ceremony.

The strife betwixt Allan and MacEagh had been unnoticed by the stragglers around, for the person of the latter was known to few of Montrose's followers; but the scuffle betwixt Dalgetty and him, both so well known, attracted instant attention; and fortunately, among others, that of Montrose himself, who had come for the purpose of gathering together his small body of horse, and following the pursuit down Loch-Eil. Aware of the fatal consequences of dissension in his little army, he pushed his horse up to the spot, and seeing MacEagh on the ground, and Dalgetty in the attitude of protecting him against M'Aulay, his quick apprehension instantly caught the cause of quarrel, and as instantly devised means to stop it. "For shame," he said, "gentlemen cavaliers, brawling together in so glorious a field of victory!—Are you mad? Or are you intoxicated with the glory which you have both this day gained?"

"It is not my fault, so please your Excellency," said Dalgetty. "I have been known a BONUS SOCIUS, A BON CAMARADO, in all the services of Europe; but he that touches a man under my safeguard—"

"And he," said Allan, speaking at the same time, "who dares to bar the course of my just vengeance—"

"For shame, gentlemen!" again repeated Montrose; "I have other business for you both,—business of deeper importance than any private quarrel, which you may easily find a more fitting time to settle. For you, Major Dalgetty, kneel down."

"Kneel!" said Dalgetty; "I have not learned to obey that word of command, saving when it is given from the pulpit. In the Swedish discipline, the front rank do indeed kneel, but only when the regiment is drawn up six file deep."

"Nevertheless," repeated Montrose,—"kneel down, in the name of King Charles and of his representative."

When Dalgetty reluctantly obeyed, Montrose struck him lightly on the neck with the flat of his sword, saying,—"In reward of the gallant service of this day, and in the name and authority of our Sovereign, King Charles, I dub thee knight; be brave, loyal, and fortunate. And now, Sir Dugald Dalgetty, to your duty. Collect what horsemen you can, and pursue such of the enemy as are flying down the side of the lake. Do not disperse your force, nor venture too far; but take heed to prevent their rallying, which very little exertion may do. Mount, then, Sir Dugald, and do your duty."

"But what shall I mount?" said the new-made chevalier. "Poor Gustavus sleeps in the bed of honour, like his immortal namesake! and I am made a knight, a rider, as the High Dutch have it, just when I have not a horse left to ride upon." [In German, as in Latin, the original meaning of the word Ritter, corresponding to Eques, is merely a horseman.]

"That shall not be said," answered Montrose, dismounting; "I make you a present of my own, which has been thought a good one; only, I pray you, resume the duty you discharge so well."

With many acknowledgments, Sir Dugald mounted the steed so liberally bestowed upon him; and only beseeching his Excellency to remember that MacEagh was under his safe-conduct, immediately began to execute the orders assigned to him, with great zeal and alacrity.

"And you, Allan M'Aulay," said Montrose, addressing the Highlander, who, leaning his sword-point on the ground, had regarded the ceremony of his antagonist's knighthood with a sneer of sullen scorn,—"you, who are superior to the ordinary men led by the paltry motives of plunder, and pay, and personal distinction,—you, whose deep knowledge renders you so valuable a counsellor,—is it YOU whom I find striving with a man like Dalgetty, for the privilege of trampling the remains of life out of so contemptible an enemy as lies there? Come, my friend, I have other work for you. This victory, skilfully improved, shall win Seaforth to our party. It is not disloyalty, but despair of the good cause, that has induced him to take arms against us. These arms, in this moment of better augury, he may be brought to unite with ours. I shall send my gallant friend, Colonel Hay, to him, from this very field of battle, but he must be united in commission with a Highland gentleman of rank, befitting that of Seaforth, and of talents and of influence such as may make an impression upon him. You are not only in every respect the fittest for this most important mission, but, having no immediate command, your presence may be more easily spared than that of a Chief whose following is in the field. You know every pass and glen in the Highlands, as well as the manners and customs of every tribe. Go therefore to Hay, on the right wing; he has instructions, and expects you. You will find him with Glenmorrison's men; be his guide, his interpreter, and his colleague."

Allan M'Aulay bent on the Marquis a dark and penetrating glance, as if to ascertain whether this sudden mission was not conferred for some latent and unexplained purpose. But Montrose, skilful in searching the motives of others, was an equal adept in concealing his own. He considered it as of the last consequence, in this moment of enthusiasm and exalted passion, to remove Allan from the camp for a few days, that he might provide, as his honour required, for the safety of those who had acted as his guides, when he trusted the Seer's quarrel with Dalgetty might be easily made up. Allan, at parting, only recommended to the Marquis the care of Sir Duncan Campbell, whom Montrose instantly directed to be conveyed to a place of safety. He took the same precaution for MacEagh, committing the latter, however, to a party of the Irish, with directions that he should be taken care of, but that no Highlander, of any clan, should have access to him.

The Marquis then mounted a led horse, which was held by one of his attendants, and rode on to view the scene of his victory, which was more decisive than even his ardent hopes had anticipated. Of Argyle's gallant army of three thousand men, fully one-half fell in the battle, or in the flight. They had been chiefly driven back upon that part of the plain where the river forms an angle with the lake, so that there was no free opening either for retreat or escape. Several hundreds were forced into the lake and drowned. Of the survivors, about one-half escaped by swimming the river, or by an early flight along the left bank of the lake. The remainder threw themselves into the old Castle of Inverlochy; but being without either provisions or hopes of relief, they were obliged to surrender, on condition of being suffered to return to their homes in peace. Arms, ammunition, standards, and baggage, all became the prey of the conquerors.

This was the greatest disaster that ever befell the race of Diarmid, as the Campbells were called in the Highlands; it being generally remarked that they were as fortunate in the issue of their undertakings, as they were sagacious in planning, and courageous in executing them. Of the number slain, nearly five hundred were dunniwassels, or gentlemen claiming descent from known and respected houses. And, in the opinion of many of the clan, even this heavy loss was exceeded by the disgrace arising from the inglorious conduct of their Chief, whose galley weighed anchor when the day was lost, and sailed down the lake with all the speed to which sails and oars could impel her.

CHAPTER XX.

Faint the din of battle bray'd,
Distant down the hollow wind;
War and terror fled before,
Wounds and death remain'd behind.

—PENROSE.

Montrose's splendid success over his powerful rival was not attained without some loss, though not amounting to the tenth of what he inflicted. The obstinate valour of the Campbells cost the lives of many brave men of the opposite party; and more were wounded, the Chief of whom was the brave young Earl of Menteith, who had commanded the centre. He was but slightly touched, however, and made rather a graceful than a terrible appearance when he presented to his general the standard of Argyle, which he had taken from the standard-bearer with his own hand, and slain him in single combat. Montrose dearly loved his noble kinsman, in whom there was conspicuous a flash of the generous, romantic, disinterested chivalry of the old heroic times, entirely different from the sordid, calculating, and selfish character, which the practice of entertaining mercenary troops had introduced into most parts of Europe, and of which degeneracy Scotland, which furnished soldiers of fortune for the service of almost every nation, had been contaminated with a more than usual share. Montrose, whose native spirit was congenial, although experience had taught him how to avail himself of the motives of others, used to Menteith neither the language of praise nor of promise, but clasped him to his bosom as he exclaimed, "My gallant kinsman!" And by this burst of heartfelt applause was Menteith thrilled with a warmer glow of delight, than if his praises had been recorded in a report of the action sent directly to the throne of his sovereign.

"Nothing," he said, "my lord, now seems to remain in which I can render any assistance; permit me to look after a duty of humanity—the Knight of Ardenvohr, as I am told, is our prisoner, and severely wounded."

"And well he deserves to be so," said Sir Dugald Dalgetty, who came up to them at that moment with a prodigious addition of acquired importance, "since he shot my good horse at the time that I was offering him honourable quarter, which, I must needs say, was done more like an ignorant Highland cateran, who has not sense enough to erect a sconce for the protection of his old hurley-house of a castle, than like a soldier of worth and quality."

"Are we to condole with you then," said Lord Menteith, "upon the loss of the famed Gustavus?"

"Even so, my lord," answered the soldier, with a deep sigh, "DIEM CLAUSIT SUPREMUM, as we said at the Mareschal-College of Aberdeen. Better so than be smothered like a cadger's pony in some flow-moss, or snow-wreath, which was like to be his fate if this winter campaign lasted longer. But it has pleased his Excellency" (making an inclination to Montrose) "to supply his place by the gift of a noble steed, whom I have taken the freedom to name 'LOYALTY'S REWARD,' in memory of this celebrated occasion."

"I hope," said the Marquis, "you'll find Loyalty's Reward, since you call him so, practised in all the duties of the field,—but I must just hint to you, that at this time, in Scotland, loyalty is more frequently rewarded with a halter than with a horse."

"Ahem! your Excellency is pleased to be facetious. Loyalty's Reward is as perfect as Gustavus in all his exercises, and of a far finer figure. Marry! his social qualities are less cultivated, in respect he has kept till now inferior company."

"Not meaning his Excellency the General, I hope," said Lord Menteith. "For shame, Sir Dugald!"

"My lord," answered the knight gravely, "I am incapable to mean anything so utterly unbecoming. What I asseverate is, that his Excellency, having the same intercourse with his horse during his exercise, that he hath with his soldiers when training them, may form and break either to every feat of war which he chooses to practise, and accordingly that this noble charger is admirably managed. But as it is the intercourse of private life that formeth the social character, so I do not apprehend that of the single soldier to be much polished by the conversation of the corporal or the sergeant, or that of Loyalty's Reward to have been much dulcified, or ameliorated, by the society of his Excellency's grooms, who bestow more oaths, and kicks, and thumps, than kindness or caresses, upon the animals intrusted to their charge; whereby many a generous quadruped, rendered as it were misanthropic, manifests during the rest of his life a greater desire to kick and bite his master, than to love and to honour him."

"Spoken like an oracle," said Montrose. "Were there an academy for the education of horses to be annexed to the Mareschal-College of Aberdeen, Sir Dugald Dalgetty alone should fill the chair."

"Because, being an ass," said Menteith, aside to the General, "there would be some distant relation between the professor and the students."

"And now, with your Excellency's permission," said the new-made knight, "I am going to pay my last visit to the remains of my old companion in arms."

"Not with the purpose of going through the ceremonial of interment?" said the Marquis, who did not know how far Sir Dugald's enthusiasm might lead him; "consider our brave fellows themselves will have but a hasty burial."

"Your Excellency will pardon me," said Dalgetty; "my purpose is less romantic. I go to divide poor Gustavus's legacy with the fowls of heaven, leaving the flesh to them, and reserving to myself his hide; which, in token of affectionate remembrance, I purpose to form into a cassock and trowsers, after the Tartar fashion, to be worn under my armour, in respect my nether garments are at present shamefully the worse of the wear.—Alas! poor Gustavus, why didst thou not live at least one hour more, to have borne the honoured weight of knighthood upon thy loins!"

He was now turning away, when the Marquis called after him,—"As you are not likely to be anticipated in this act of kindness, Sir Dugald, to your old friend and companion, I trust," said the Marquis, "you will first assist me, and our principal friends, to discuss some of Argyle's good cheer, of which we have found abundance in the Castle."

"Most willingly, please your Excellency," said Sir Dugald; "as meat and mass never hinder work. Nor, indeed, am I afraid that the wolves or eagles will begin an onslaught on Gustavus to-night, in regard there is so much better cheer lying all around. But," added he, "as I am to meet two honourable knights of England, with others of the knightly degree in your lordship's army, I pray it may be explained to them, that now, and in future, I claim precedence over them all, in respect of my rank as a Banneret, dubbed in a field of stricken battle."

"The devil confound him!" said Montrose, speaking aside; "he has contrived to set the kiln on fire as fast as I put it out.—This is a point, Sir Dugald," said he, gravely addressing him, "which I shall reserve for his Majesty's express consideration; in my camp, all must be upon equality, like the Knights of the Round Table; and take their places as soldiers should, upon the principle of,—first come, first served."

"Then I shall take care," said Menteith, apart to the Marquis, "that Don Dugald is not first in place to-day.—Sir Dugald," added he, raising his voice, "as you say your wardrobe is out of repair, had you not better go to the enemy's baggage yonder, over which there is a guard placed? I saw them take out an excellent buff suit, embroidered in front in silk and silver."

"VOTO A DIOS! as the Spaniard says," exclaimed the Major, "and some beggarly gilly may get it while I stand prating here!"

The prospect of booty having at once driven out of his head both Gustavus and the provant, he set spurs to Loyalty's Reward, and rode off through the field of battle.

"There goes the hound," said Menteith, "breaking the face, and trampling on the body, of many a better man than himself; and as eager on his sordid spoil as a vulture that stoops upon carrion. Yet this man the world calls a soldier—and you, my lord, select him as worthy of the honours of chivalry, if such they can at this day be termed. You have made the collar of knighthood the decoration of a mere bloodhound."

"What could I do?" said Montrose. "I had no half-picked bones to give him, and bribed in some manner he must be,—I cannot follow the chase alone. Besides, the dog has good qualities."

"If nature has given him such," said Menteith, "habit has converted them into feelings of intense selfishness. He may be punctilious concerning his reputation, and brave in the execution of his duty, but it is only because without these qualities he cannot rise in the service;—nay, his very benevolence is selfish; he may defend his companion while he can keep his feet, but the instant he is down, Sir Dugald will be as ready to ease him of his purse, as he is to convert the skin of Gustavus into a buff jerkin."

"And yet, if all this were true, cousin," answered Montrose, "there is something convenient in commanding a soldier, upon whose motives and springs of action you can calculate to a mathematical certainty. A fine spirit like yours, my cousin, alive to a thousand sensations to which this man's is as impervious as his corslet,—it is for such that thy friend must feel, while he gives his advice." Then, suddenly changing his tone, he asked Menteith when he had seen Annot Lyle.

The young Earl coloured deeply, and answered, "Not since last evening,—excepting," he added, with hesitation, "for one moment, about half an hour before the battle began."

"My dear Menteith," said Montrose, very kindly, "were you one of the gay cavaliers of Whitehall, who are, in their way, as great self-seekers as our friend Dalgetty, should I need to plague you with enquiring into such an amourette as this? it would be an intrigue only to be laughed at. But this is the land of enchantment, where nets strong as steel are wrought out of ladies' tresses, and you are exactly the destined knight to be so fettered. This poor girl is exquisitely beautiful, and has talents formed to captivate your romantic temper. You cannot think of injuring her—you cannot think of marrying her?"

"My lord," replied Menteith, "you have repeatedly urged this jest, for so I trust it is meant, somewhat beyond bounds. Annot Lyle is of unknown birth,—a captive,—the daughter, probably, of some obscure outlaw; a dependant on the hospitality of the M'Aulays."

"Do not be angry, Menteith," said the Marquis, interrupting him; "you love the classics, though not educated at Mareschal-College; and you may remember how many gallant hearts captive beauty has subdued:—

Movit Ajacem, Telamone natum,
Forma captivae dominum Tecmessae.

In a word, I am seriously anxious about this—I should not have time, perhaps," he added very gravely, "to trouble you with my lectures on the subject, were your feelings, and those of Annot, alone interested; but you have a dangerous rival in Allan M'Aulay; and there is no knowing to what extent he may carry his resentment. It is my duty to tell you that the King's service may be much prejudiced by dissensions betwixt you."

"My lord," said Menteith, "I know what you mean is kind and friendly; I hope you will be satisfied when I assure you, that Allan M'Aulay and I have discussed this circumstance; and that I have explained to him, that it is utterly remote from my character to entertain dishonourable views concerning this unprotected female; so, on the other hand, the obscurity of her birth prevents my thinking of her upon other terms. I will not disguise from your lordship, what I have not disguised from M'Aulay,—that if Annot Lyle were born a lady, she should share my name and rank; as matters stand, it is impossible. This explanation, I trust, will satisfy your lordship, as it has satisfied a less reasonable person."

Montrose shrugged his shoulders. "And, like true champions in romance," he said, "you have agreed, that you are both to worship the same mistress, as idolaters do the same image, and that neither shall extend his pretensions farther?"

"I did not go so far, my lord," answered Menteith—"I only said in the present circumstances—and there is no prospect of their being changed,—I could, in duty to myself and family, stand in no relation to Annot Lyle, but as that of friend or brother—But your lordship must excuse me; I have," said he, looking at his arm, round which he had tied his handkerchief, "a slight hurt to attend to."

"A wound?" said Montrose, anxiously; "let me see it.—Alas!" he said, "I should have heard nothing of this, had I not ventured to tent and sound another more secret and more rankling one, Menteith; I am sorry for you—I too have known—But what avails it to awake sorrows which have long slumbered!"

So saying, he shook hands with his noble kinsman, and walked into the castle.

Annot Lyle, as was not unusual for females in the Highlands, was possessed of a slight degree of medical and even surgical skill. It may readily be believed, that the profession of surgery, or medicine, as a separate art, was unknown; and the few rude rules which they observed were intrusted to women, or to the aged, whom constant casualties afforded too much opportunity of acquiring experience.

The care and attention, accordingly, of Annot Lyle, her attendants, and others acting under her direction, had made her services extremely useful during this wild campaign. And most readily had these services been rendered to friend and foe, wherever they could be most useful. She was now in an apartment of the castle, anxiously superintending the preparation of vulnerary herbs, to be applied to the wounded; receiving reports from different females respecting those under their separate charge, and distributing what means she had for their relief, when Allan M'Aulay suddenly entered the apartment. She started, for she had heard that he had left the camp upon a distant mission; and, however accustomed she was to the gloom of his countenance, it seemed at present to have even a darker shade than usual. He stood before her perfectly silent, and she felt the necessity of being the first to speak.

"I thought," she said, with some effort, "you had already set out."

"My companion awaits me," said Allan; "I go instantly." Yet still he stood before her, and held her by the arm, with a pressure which, though insufficient to give her pain, made her sensible of his great personal strength, his hand closing on her like the gripe of a manacle.

"Shall I take the harp?" she said, in a timid voice; "is—is the shadow falling upon you?"

Instead of replying, he led her to the window of the apartment, which commanded a view of the field of the slain, with all its horrors. It was thick spread with dead and wounded, and the spoilers were busy tearing the clothes from the victims of war and feudal ambition, with as much indifference as if they had not been of the same species, and themselves exposed, perhaps to-morrow, to the same fate.

"Does the sight please you?" said M'Aulay.

"It is hideous!" said Annot, covering her eyes with her hands; "how can you bid me look upon it?"

"You must be inured to it," said he, "if you remain with this destined host—you will soon have to search such a field for my brother's corpse—for Menteith's—for mine—but that will be a more indifferent task—You do not love me!"

"This is the first time you have taxed me with unkindness," said Annot, weeping. "You are my brother—my preserver—my protector—and can I then BUT love you?—But your hour of darkness is approaching, let me fetch my harp—"

"Remain," said Allan, still holding her fast; "be my visions from heaven or hell, or from the middle sphere of disembodied spirits—or be they, as the Saxons hold, but the delusions of an over-heated fancy, they do not now influence me; I speak the language of the natural, of the visible world.—You love not me, Annot—you love Menteith—by him you are beloved again, and Allan is no more to you than one of the corpses which encumber yonder heath."

It cannot be supposed that this strange speech conveyed any new information to her who was thus addressed. No woman ever lived who could not, in the same circumstances, have discerned long since the state of her lover's mind. But by thus suddenly tearing off the veil, thin as it was, Allan prepared her to expect consequences violent in proportion to the enthusiasm of his character. She made an effort to repel the charge he had stated.

"You forget," she said, "your own worth and nobleness when you insult so very helpless a being, and one whom fate has thrown so totally into your power. You know who and what I am, and how impossible it is that Menteith or you can use language of affection to me, beyond that of friendship. You know from what unhappy race I have too probably derived my existence."

"I will not believe it," said Allan, impetuously; "never flowed crystal drop from a polluted spring."

"Yet the very doubt," pleaded Annot, "should make you forbear to use this language to me."

"I know," said M'Aulay, "it places a bar between us—but I know also that it divides you not so inseparably from Menteith.— Hear me, my beloved Annot!—leave this scene of terrors and danger—go with me to Kintail—I will place you in the house of the noble Lady of Seaforth—or you shall be removed in safety to Icolmkill, where some women yet devote themselves to the worship of God, after the custom of our ancestors."

"You consider not what you ask of me," replied Annot; "to undertake such a journey under your sole guardianship, were to show me less scrupulous than maiden ought. I will remain here, Allan—here under the protection of the noble Montrose; and when his motions next approach the Lowlands, I will contrive some proper means to relieve you of one, who has, she knows not how, become an object of dislike to you."

Allan stood as if uncertain whether to give way to sympathy with her distress, or to anger at her resistance.

"Annot," he said, "you know too well how little your words apply to my feelings towards you—but you avail yourself of your power, and you rejoice in my departure, as removing a spy upon your intercourse with Menteith. But beware both of you," he added, in a stern tone; "for when was it heard that an injury was offered to Allan M'Aulay, for which he exacted not tenfold vengeance?"

So saying, he pressed her arm forcibly, pulled the bonnet over his brows, and strode out of the apartment.

CHAPTER XXI.

—After you're gone,
I grew acquainted with my heart, and search'd,
What stirr'd it so.—Alas! I found it love.
Yet far from lust, for could I but have lived
In presence of you, I had had my end.
                                        —PHILASTER.

Annot Lyle had now to contemplate the terrible gulf which Allan M'Aulay's declaration of love and jealousy had made to open around her. It seemed as if she was tottering on the very brink of destruction, and was at once deprived of every refuge, and of all human assistance. She had long been conscious that she loved Menteith dearer than a brother; indeed, how could it be otherwise, considering their early intimacy, the personal merit of the young nobleman, his assiduous attentions,—and his infinite superiority in gentleness of disposition, and grace of manners, over the race of rude warriors with whom she lived? But her affection was of that quiet, timid, meditative character, which sought rather a reflected share in the happiness of the beloved object, than formed more presumptuous or daring hopes. A little Gaelic song, in which she expressed her feelings, has been translated by the ingenious and unhappy Andrew M'Donald; and we willingly transcribe the lines:—

Wert thou, like me, in life's low vale,
With thee how blest, that lot I'd share;
With thee I'd fly wherever gale
Could waft, or bounding galley bear.
But parted by severe decree,
Far different must our fortunes prove;

May thine be joy—enough for me
To weep and pray for him I love.

The pangs this foolish heart must feel,
When hope shall be forever flown,
No sullen murmur shall reveal,
No selfish murmurs ever own.
Nor will I through life's weary years,
Like a pale drooping mourner move,
While I can think my secret tears
May wound the heart of him I love.

The furious declaration of Allan had destroyed the romantic plan which she had formed, of nursing in secret her pensive tenderness, without seeking any other requital. Long before this, she had dreaded Allan, as much as gratitude, and a sense that he softened towards her a temper so haughty and so violent, could permit her to do; but now she regarded him with unalloyed terror, which a perfect knowledge of his disposition, and of his preceding history, too well authorised her to entertain. Whatever was in other respects the nobleness of his disposition, he had never been known to resist the wilfulness of passion,—he walked in the house, and in the country of his fathers, like a tamed lion, whom no one dared to contradict, lest they should awaken his natural vehemence of passion. So many years had elapsed since he had experienced contradiction, or even expostulation, that probably nothing but the strong good sense, which, on all points, his mysticism excepted, formed the ground of his character, prevented his proving an annoyance and terror to the whole neighbourhood. But Annot had no time to dwell upon her fears, being interrupted by the entrance of Sir Dugald Dalgetty.

It may well be supposed, that the scenes in which this person had passed his former life, had not much qualified him to shine in female society. He himself felt a sort of consciousness that the language of the barrack, guard-room, and parade, was not proper to entertain ladies. The only peaceful part of his life had been spent at Mareschal-College, Aberdeen; and he had forgot the little he had learned there, except the arts of darning his own hose, and dispatching his commons with unusual celerity, both which had since been kept in good exercise by the necessity of frequent practice. Still it was from an imperfect recollection of what he had acquired during this pacific period, that he drew his sources of conversation when in company with women; in other words, his language became pedantic when it ceased to be military.

"Mistress Annot Lyle," said he, upon the present occasion, "I am just now like the half-pike, or spontoon of Achilles, one end of which could wound and the other cure—a property belonging neither to Spanish pike, brown-bill, partizan, halberd, Lochaber-axe, or indeed any other modern staff-weapon whatever." This compliment he repeated twice; but as Annot scarce heard him the first time, and did not comprehend him the second, he was obliged to explain.

"I mean," he said, "Mistress Annot Lyle, that having been the means of an honourable knight receiving a severe wound in this day's conflict,—he having pistolled, somewhat against the law of arms, my horse, which was named after the immortal King of Sweden,—I am desirous of procuring him such solacement as you, madam, can supply, you being like the heathen god Esculapius" (meaning possibly Apollo), "skilful not only in song and in music, but in the more noble art of chirurgery-OPIFERQUE PER ORBEM DICOR."

"If you would have the goodness to explain," said Annot, too sick at heart to be amused by Sir Dugald's airs of pedantic gallantry.

"That, madam," replied the Knight, "may not be so easy, as I am out of the habit of construing—but we shall try. DICOR, supply EGO—I am called,—OPIFER? OPIFER?—I remember SIGNIFER and FURCIFER—but I believe OPIFER stands in this place for M.D., that is, Doctor of Physic."

"This is a busy day with us all," said Annot; "will you say at once what you want with me?"

"Merely," replied Sir Dugald, "that you will visit my brother knight, and let your maiden bring some medicaments for his wound, which threatens to be what the learned call a DAMNUM FATALE."

Annot Lyle never lingered in the cause of humanity. She informed herself hastily of the nature of the injury, and interesting herself for the dignified old Chief whom she had seen at

Darnlinvarach, and whose presence had so much struck her, she hastened to lose the sense of her own sorrow for a time, in the attempt to be useful to another.

Sir Dugald with great form ushered Annot Lyle to the chamber of her patient, in which, to her surprise, she found Lord Menteith. She could not help blushing deeply at the meeting, but, to hide her confusion, proceeded instantly to examine the wound of the Knight of Ardenvohr, and easily satisfied herself that it was beyond her skill to cure it. As for Sir Dugald, he returned to a large outhouse, on the floor of which, among other wounded men, was deposited the person of Ranald of the Mist.

"Mine old friend," said the Knight, "as I told you before, I would willingly do anything to pleasure you, in return for the wound you have received while under my safe-conduct. I have, therefore, according to your earnest request, sent Mrs. Annot Lyle to attend upon the wound of the knight of Ardenvohr, though wherein her doing so should benefit you, I cannot imagine.—I think you once spoke of some blood relationship between them; but a soldado, in command and charge like me, has other things to trouble his head with than Highland genealogies."

And indeed, to do the worthy Major justice, he never enquired after, listened to, or recollected, the business of other people, unless it either related to the art military, or was somehow or other connected with his own interest, in either of which cases his memory was very tenacious.

"And now, my good friend of the Mist," said he, "can you tell me what has become of your hopeful grandson, as I have not seen him since he assisted me to disarm after the action, a negligence which deserveth the strapado?"

"He is not far from hence," said the wounded outlaw—"lift not your hand upon him, for he is man enough to pay a yard of leathern scourge with a foot of tempered steel."

"A most improper vaunt," said Sir Dugald; "but I owe you some favours, Ranald, and therefore shall let it pass."

"And if you think you owe me anything," said the outlaw, "it is in your power to requite me by granting me a boon."

"Friend Ranald," answered Dalgetty, "I have read of these boons in silly story-books, whereby simple knights were drawn into engagements to their great prejudice; wherefore, Ranald, the more prudent knights of this day never promise anything until they know that they may keep their word anent the premises, without any displeasure or incommodement to themselves. It may be, you would have me engage the female chirurgeon to visit your wound; though you ought to consider, Ranald, that the uncleanness of the place where you are deposited may somewhat soil the gaiety of her garments, concerning the preservation of which, you may have observed, women are apt to be inordinately solicitous. I lost the favour of the lady of the Grand Pensionary of Amsterdam, by touching with the sole of my boot the train of her black velvet gown, which I mistook for a foot-cloth, it being half the room distant from her person."

"It is not to bring Annot Lyle hither," answered MacEagh, "but to transport me into the room where she is in attendance upon the Knight of Ardenvohr. Somewhat I have to say of the last consequence to them both."

"It is something out of the order of due precedence," said Dalgetty, "to carry a wounded outlaw into the presence of a knight; knighthood having been of yore, and being, in some respects, still, the highest military grade, independent always of commissioned officers, who rank according to their patents; nevertheless, as your boon, as you call it, is so slight, I shall not deny compliance with the same." So saying, he ordered three files of men to transport MacEagh on their shoulders to Sir Duncan Campbell's apartment, and he himself hastened before to announce the cause of his being brought thither. But such was the activity of the soldiers employed, that they followed him close at the heels, and, entering with their ghastly burden, laid MacEagh on the floor of the apartment. His features, naturally wild, were now distorted by pain; his hands and scanty garments stained with his own blood, and those of others, which no kind hand had wiped away, although the wound in his side had been secured by a bandage.

"Are you," he said, raising his head painfully towards the couch where lay stretched his late antagonist, "he whom men call the Knight of Ardenvohr?"

"The same," answered Sir Duncan,—"what would you with one whose hours are now numbered?"

"My hours are reduced to minutes," said the outlaw; "the more grace, if I bestow them in the service of one, whose hand has ever been against me, as mine has been raised higher against him."

"Thine higher against me!—Crushed worm!" said the Knight, looking down on his miserable adversary.

"Yes," answered the outlaw, in a firm voice, "my arm hath been highest. In the deadly contest betwixt us, the wounds I have dealt have been deepest, though thine have neither been idle nor unfelt.—I am Ranald MacEagh—I am Ranald of the Mist—the night that I gave thy castle to the winds in one huge blaze of fire, is now matched with the day in which you have fallen under the sword of my fathers.—Remember the injuries thou hast done our tribe—never were such inflicted, save by one, beside thee. HE, they say, is fated and secure against our vengeance—a short time will show."

"My Lord Menteith," said Sir Duncan, raising himself out of his bed, "this is a proclaimed villain, at once the enemy of King and Parliament, of God and man—one of the outlawed banditti of the Mist; alike the enemy of your house, of the M'Aulays, and of mine. I trust you will not suffer moments, which are perhaps my last, to be embittered by his barbarous triumph."

"He shall have the treatment he merits," said Menteith; "let him be instantly removed."

Sir Dugald here interposed, and spoke of Ranald's services as a guide, and his own pledge for his safety; but the high harsh tones of the outlaw drowned his voice.

"No," said he, "be rack and gibbet the word! let me wither between heaven and earth, and gorge the hawks and eagles of Ben-Nevis; and so shall this haughty Knight, and this triumphant Thane, never learn the secret I alone can impart; a secret which would make Ardenvohr's heart leap with joy, were he in the death agony, and which the Earl of Menteith would purchase at the price of his broad earldom.—Come hither, Annot Lyle," he said, raising himself with unexpected strength; "fear not the sight of him to whom thou hast clung in infancy. Tell these proud men, who disdain thee as the issue of mine ancient race, that thou art no blood of ours,—no daughter of the race of the Mist, but born in halls as lordly, and cradled on couch as soft, as ever soothed infancy in their proudest palaces."

"In the name of God," said Menteith, trembling with emotion, "if you know aught of the birth of this lady, do thy conscience the justice to disburden it of the secret before departing from this world!"

"And bless my enemies with my dying breath?" said MacEagh, looking at him malignantly.—"Such are the maxims your priests preach—but when, or towards whom, do you practise them? Let me know first the worth of my secret ere I part with it—What would you give, Knight of Ardenvohr, to know that your superstitious fasts have been vain, and that there still remains a descendant of your house?—I pause for an answer—without it, I speak not one word more.

"I could," said Sir Duncan, his voice struggling between the emotions of doubt, hatred, and anxiety—"I could—but that I know thy race are like the Great Enemy, liars and murderers from the beginning—but could it be true thou tellest me, I could almost forgive thee the injuries thou hast done me."

"Hear it!" said Ranald; "he hath wagered deeply for a son of Diarmid—And you, gentle Thane—the report of the camp says, that you would purchase with life and lands the tidings that Annot Lyle was no daughter of proscription, but of a race noble in your estimation as your own—Well—It is for no love I tell you—The time has been that I would have exchanged this secret against liberty; I am now bartering it for what is dearer than liberty or life.—Annot Lyle is the youngest, the sole surviving child of the Knight of Ardenvohr, who alone was saved when all in his halls besides was given to blood and ashes."

"Can this man speak truth?" said Annot Lyle, scarce knowing what she said; "or is this some strange delusion?"

"Maiden," replied Ranald, "hadst thou dwelt longer with us, thou wouldst have better learnt to know how to distinguish the accents of truth. To that Saxon lord, and to the Knight of Ardenvohr, I will yield such proofs of what I have spoken, that incredulity shall stand convinced. Meantime, withdraw—I loved thine infancy, I hate not thy youth—no eye hates the rose in its blossom, though it groweth upon a thorn, and for thee only do I something regret what is soon to follow. But he that would avenge him of his foe must not reck though the guiltless be engaged in the ruin."

"He advises well, Annot," said Lord Menteith; "in God's name retire! if—if there be aught in this, your meeting with Sir Duncan must be more prepared for both your sakes."

"I will not part from my father, if I have found one!" said Annot—"I will not part from him under circumstances so terrible."

"And a father you shall ever find in me," murmured Sir Duncan.

"Then," said Menteith, "I will have MacEagh removed into an adjacent apartment, and will collect the evidence of his tale myself. Sir Dugald Dalgetty will give me his attendance and assistance."

"With pleasure, my lord," answered Sir Dugald.—"I will be your confessor, or assessor—either or both. No one can be so fit, for I had heard the whole story a month ago at Inverary castle—but onslaughts like that of Ardenvohr confuse each other in my memory, which is besides occupied with matters of more importance."

Upon hearing this frank declaration, which was made as they left the apartment with the wounded man, Lord Menteith darted upon Dalgetty a look of extreme anger and disdain, to which the self-conceit of the worthy commander rendered him totally insensible.

CHAPTER XXII.

I am as free as nature first made man,
Ere the base laws of servitude began,
When wild in woods the noble savage ran.
                    —CONQUEST OF GRANADA

The Earl of Menteith, as he had undertaken, so he proceeded to investigate more closely the story told by Ranald of the Mist, which was corroborated by the examination of his two followers, who had assisted in the capacity of guides. These declarations he carefully compared with such circumstances concerning the destruction of his castle and family as Sir Duncan Campbell was able to supply; and it may be supposed he had forgotten nothing relating to an event of such terrific importance. It was of the last consequence to prove that this was no invention of the outlaw's, for the purpose of passing an impostor as the child and heiress of Ardenvohr.

Perhaps Menteith, so much interested in believing the tale, was not altogether the fittest person to be intrusted with the investigation of its truth; but the examinations of the Children of the Mist were simple, accurate, and in all respects consistent with each other. A personal mark was referred to, which was known to have been borne by the infant child of Sir Duncan, and which appeared upon the left shoulder of Annot Lyle. It was also well remembered, that when the miserable relics of the other children had been collected, those of the infant had nowhere been found. Other circumstances of evidence, which it is unnecessary to quote, brought the fullest conviction not only to Menteith, but to the unprejudiced mind of Montrose, that in Annot Lyle, an humble dependant, distinguished only by beauty and talent, they were in future to respect the heiress of Ardenvohr.

While Menteith hastened to communicate the result of these enquiries to the persons most interested, the outlaw demanded to speak with his grandchild, whom he usually called his son. "He would be found," he said, "in the outer apartment, in which he himself had been originally deposited."

Accordingly, the young savage, after a close search, was found lurking in a corner, coiled up among some rotten straw, and brought to his grandsire.

"Kenneth," said the old outlaw, "hear the last words of the sire of thy father. A Saxon soldier, and Allan of the Red-hand, left this camp within these few hours, to travel to the country to Caberfae. Pursue them as the bloodhound pursues the hurt deer—swim the lake-climb the mountain—thread the forest—tarry not until you join them;" and then the countenance of the lad darkened as his grandfather spoke, and he laid his hand upon a knife which stuck in the thong of leather that confined his scanty plaid. "No!" said the old man; "it is not by thy hand he must fall. They will ask the news from the camp—say to them that Annot Lyle of the Harp is discovered to be the daughter of Duncan of Ardenvohr; that the Thane of Menteith is to wed her before the priest; and that you are sent to bid guests to the bridal. Tarry not their answer, but vanish like the lightning when the black cloud swallows it.—And now depart, beloved son of my best beloved! I shall never more see thy face, nor hear the light sound of thy footstep—yet tarry an instant and hear my last charge. Remember the fate of our race, and quit not the ancient manners of the Children of the Mist. We are now a straggling handful, driven from every vale by the sword of every clan, who rule in the possessions where their forefathers hewed the wood, and drew the water for ours. But in the thicket of the wilderness, and in the mist of the mountain, Kenneth, son of Eracht, keep thou unsoiled the freedom which I leave thee as a birthright. Barter it not neither for the rich garment, nor for the stone-roof, nor for the covered board, nor for the couch of down—on the rock or in the valley, in abundance or in famine—in the leafy summer, and in the days of the iron winter—Son of the Mist! be free as thy forefathers. Own no lord—receive no law—take no hire—give no stipend—build no hut—enclose no pasture—sow no grain;—let the deer of the mountain be thy flocks and herds—if these fail thee, prey upon the goods of our oppressors—of the

Saxons, and of such Gael as are Saxons in their souls, valuing herds and flocks more than honour and freedom. Well for us that they do so—it affords the broader scope for our revenge. Remember those who have done kindness to our race, and pay their services with thy blood, should the hour require it. If a MacIan shall come to thee with the head of the king's son in his hand, shelter him, though the avenging army of the father were behind him; for in Glencoe and Ardnamurchan, we have dwelt in peace in the years that have gone by. The sons of Diarmid—the race of Darnlinvarach—the riders of Menteith—my curse on thy head, Child of the Mist, if thou spare one of those names, when the time shall offer for cutting them off! and it will come anon, for their own swords shall devour each other, and those who are scattered shall fly to the Mist, and perish by its Children. Once more, begone—shake the dust from thy feet against the habitations of men, whether banded together for peace or for war. Farewell, beloved! and mayst thou die like thy forefathers, ere infirmity, disease, or age, shall break thy spirit—Begone!—begone!—live free—requite kindness—avenge the injuries of thy race!"

The young savage stooped, and kissed the brow of his dying parent; but accustomed from infancy to suppress every exterior sign of emotion, he parted without tear or adieu, and was soon far beyond the limits of Montrose's camp.

Sir Dugald Dalgetty, who was present during the latter part of this scene, was very little edified by the conduct of MacEagh upon the occasion. "I cannot think, my friend Ranald," said he, "that you are in the best possible road for a dying man. Storms, onslaughts, massacres, the burning of suburbs, are indeed a soldier's daily work, and are justified by the necessity of the case, seeing that they are done in the course of duty; for burning of suburbs, in particular, it may be said that they are traitors and cut-throats to all fortified towns. Hence it is plain, that a soldier is a profession peculiarly favoured by Heaven, seeing that we may hope for salvation, although we daily commit actions of so great violence. But then, Ranald, in all services of Europe, it is the custom of the dying soldier not to vaunt him of such doings, or to recommend them to his fellows; but, on the contrary, to express contrition for the same, and to repeat, or have repeated to him, some comfortable prayer; which, if you please, I will intercede with his Excellency's chaplain to prefer on your account. It is otherwise no point of my duty to put you in mind of those things; only it may be for the ease of your conscience to depart more like a Christian, and less like a Turk, than you seem to be in a fair way of doing."

The only answer of the dying man—(for as such Ranald MacEagh might now be considered)—was a request to be raised to such a position that he might obtain a view from the window of the Castle. The deep frost mist, which had long settled upon the top of the mountains, was now rolling down each rugged glen and gully, where the craggy ridges showed their black and irregular outline, like desert islands rising above the ocean of vapour. "Spirit of the Mist!" said Ranald MacEagh, "called by our race our father, and our preserver—receive into thy tabernacle of clouds, when this pang is over, him whom in life thou hast so often sheltered." So saying, he sunk back into the arms of those who upheld him, spoke no further word, but turned his face to the wall for a short space.

"I believe," said Dalgetty, "my friend Ranald will be found in his heart to be little better than a heathen." And he renewed his proposal to procure him the assistance of Dr. Wisheart, Montrose's military chaplain; "a man," said Sir Dugald, "very clever in his exercise, and who will do execution on your sins in less time than I could smoke a pipe of tobacco."

"Saxon," said the dying man, "speak to me no more of thy priest—I die contented. Hadst thou ever an enemy against whom weapons were of no avail—whom the ball missed, and against whom the arrow shivered, and whose bare skin was as impenetrable to sword and dirk as thy steel garment—Heardst thou ever of such a foe?"

"Very frequently, when I served in Germany," replied Sir Dugald. "There was such a fellow at Ingolstadt; he was proof both against lead and steel. The soldiers killed him with the buts of their muskets."

"This impassible foe," said Ranald, without regarding the Major's interruption, "who has the blood dearest to me upon his hands—to this man I have now bequeathed agony of mind, jealousy, despair, and sudden death,—or a life more miserable than death itself. Such shall be the lot of Allan of the Red-hand, when he learns that Annot weds Menteith and I ask no more than the certainty that it is so, to sweeten my own bloody end by his hand."

"If that be the case," said the Major, "there's no more to be said; but I shall take care as few people see you as possible, for I cannot think your mode of departure can be at all creditable or exemplary to a Christian army." So saying, he left the apartment, and the Son of the Mist soon after breathed his last.

Menteith, in the meanwhile, leaving the new-found relations to their mutual feelings of mingled emotion, was eagerly discussing with Montrose the consequences of this discovery. "I should now see," said the Marquis, "even had I not before observed it, that your interest in this discovery, my dear Menteith, has no small reference to your own happiness. You love this new-found lady,—your affection is returned. In point of birth, no exceptions can be made; in every other respect, her advantages are equal to those which you yourself possess—think, however, a moment. Sir Duncan is a fanatic—Presbyterian, at least—in arms against the King; he is only with us in the quality of a prisoner, and we are, I fear, but at the commencement of a long civil war. Is this a time, think you, Menteith, for you to make proposals for his heiress? Or what chance is there that he will now listen to it ?"

Passion, an ingenious, as well as an eloquent advocate, supplied the young nobleman with a thousand answers to these objections. He reminded Montrose that the Knight of Ardenvohr was neither a bigot in politics nor religion. He urged his own known and proved zeal for the royal cause, and hinted that its influence might be extended and strengthened by his wedding the heiress of Ardenvohr. He pleaded the dangerous state of Sir Duncan's wound, the risk which must be run by suffering the young lady to be carried into the country of the Campbells, where, in case of her father's death, or continued indisposition, she must necessarily be placed under the guardianship of Argyle, an event fatal to his (Menteith's) hopes, unless he could stoop to purchase his favour by abandoning the King's party.

Montrose allowed the force of these arguments, and owned, although the matter was attended with difficulty, yet it seemed consistent with the King's service that it should be concluded as speedily as possible.

"I could wish," said he, "that it were all settled in one way or another, and that this fair Briseis were removed from our camp before the return of our Highland Achilles, Allan M'Aulay.—I fear some fatal feud in that quarter, Menteith—and I believe it would be best that Sir Duncan be dismissed on his parole, and that you accompany him and his daughter as his escort. The journey can be made chiefly by water, so will not greatly incommode his wound— and your own, my friend, will be an honourable excuse for the absence of some time from my camp."

"Never!" said Menteith. "Were I to forfeit the very hope that has so lately dawned upon me, never will I leave your Excellency's camp while the royal standard is displayed. I should deserve that this trifling scratch should gangrene and consume my sword-arm, were I capable of holding it as an excuse for absence at this crisis of the King's affairs."

"On this, then, you are determined?" said Montrose.

"As fixed as Ben-Nevis," said the young nobleman.

"You must, then," said Montrose, "lose no time in seeking an explanation with the Knight of Ardenvohr. If this prove favourable, I will talk myself with the elder M'Aulay, and we will devise means to employ his brother at a distance from the army until he shall be reconciled to his present disappointment. Would to God some vision would descend upon his imagination fair enough to obliterate all traces of Annot Lyle! That perhaps you think impossible, Menteith?—Well, each to his service; you to that of Cupid, and I to that of Mars."

They parted, and in pursuance of the scheme arranged, Menteith, early on the ensuing morning, sought a private interview with the wounded Knight of Ardenvohr, and communicated to him his suit for the hand of his daughter. Of their mutual attachment Sir Duncan was aware, but he was not prepared for so early a declaration on the part of Menteith. He said, at first, that he had already, perhaps, indulged too much in feelings of personal happiness, at a time when his clan had sustained so great a loss and humiliation, and that he was unwilling, therefore, farther to consider the advancement of his own house at a period so calamitous. On the more urgent suit of the noble lover, he requested a few hours to deliberate and consult with his daughter, upon a question so highly important.

The result of this interview and deliberation was favourable to Menteith. Sir Duncan Campbell became fully sensible that the happiness of his new-found daughter depended upon a union with her lover; and unless such were now formed, he saw that Argyle would throw a thousand obstacles in the way of a match in every respect acceptable to himself. Menteith's private character was so excellent, and such was the rank and consideration due to his fortune and family, that they outbalanced, in Sir Duncan's opinion, the difference in their political opinions. Nor could he have resolved, perhaps, had his own opinion of the match been less favourable, to decline an opportunity of indulging the new-found child of his hopes. There was, besides, a feeling of pride which dictated his determination. To produce the Heiress of Ardenvohr to the world as one who had been educated a poor dependant and musician in the family of Darnlinvarach, had something in it that was humiliating. To introduce her as the betrothed bride, or wedded wife, of the Earl of Menteith, upon an attachment formed during her obscurity, was a warrant to the world that she had at all times been worthy of the rank to which she was elevated.

It was under the influence of these considerations that Sir Duncan Campbell announced to the lovers his consent that they should be married in the chapel of the Castle, by Montrose's chaplain, and as privately as possible. But when Montrose should break up from Inverlochy, for which orders were expected in the course of a very few days, it was agreed that the young Countess should depart with her father to his Castle, and remain there until the circumstances of the nation permitted Menteith to retire with honour from his present military employment. His resolution being once taken, Sir Duncan Campbell would not permit the maidenly scruples of his daughter to delay its execution; and it was therefore resolved that the bridal should take place the next evening, being the second after the battle.

CHAPTER XXIII.

My maid—my blue-eyed maid, he bore away,
Due to the toils of many a bloody day.

—ILLIAD.

It was necessary, for many reasons, that Angus M'Aulay, so long the kind protector of Annot Lyle, should be made acquainted with the change in the fortunes of his late protege; and Montrose, as he had undertaken, communicated to him these remarkable events. With the careless and cheerful indifference of his character, he expressed much more joy than wonder at Annot's good fortune; had no doubt whatever she would merit it, and as she had always been bred in loyal principles, would convey the whole estate of her grim fanatical father to some honest fellow who loved the king. "I should have no objection that my brother Allan should try his chance," added he, "notwithstanding that Sir Duncan Campbell was the only man who ever charged Darnlinvarach with inhospitality. Annot Lyle could always charm Allan out of the sullens, and who knows whether matrimony might not make him more a man of this world?" Montrose hastened to interrupt the progress of his castle-building, by informing him that the lady was already wooed and won, and, with her father's approbation, was almost immediately to be wedded to his kinsman, the Earl of Menteith; and that in testimony of the high respect due to M'Aulay, so long the lady's protector, he was now to request his presence at the ceremony. M'Aulay looked very grave at this intimation, and drew up his person with the air of one who thought that he had been neglected.

"He contrived," he said, "that his uniform kind treatment of the young lady, while so many years under his roof, required something more upon such an occasion than a bare compliment of ceremony. He might," he thought, "without arrogance, have expected to have been consulted. He wished his kinsman of Menteith well, no man could wish him better; but he must say he thought he had been hasty in this matter. Allan's sentiments towards the young lady had been pretty well understood, and he, for one, could not see why the superior pretensions which he had upon her gratitude should have been set aside, without at least undergoing some previous discussion."

Montrose, seeing too well where all this pointed, entreated M'Aulay to be reasonable, and to consider what probability there was that the Knight of Ardenvohr could be brought to confer the hand of his sole heiress upon Allan, whose undeniable excellent qualities were mingled with others, by which they were overclouded in a manner that made all tremble who approached him.

"My lord," said Angus M'Aulay, "my brother Allan has, as God made us all, faults as well as merits; but he is the best and bravest man of your army, be the other who he may, and therefore ill deserved that his happiness should have been so little consulted by your Excellency—by his own near kinsman—and by a young person who owes all to him and to his family."

Montrose in vain endeavoured to place the subject in a different view; this was the point in which Angus was determined to regard it, and he was a man of that calibre of understanding, who is incapable of being convinced when he has once adopted a prejudice. Montrose now assumed a higher tone, and called upon Angus to take care how he nourished any sentiments which might be prejudicial to his Majesty's service. He pointed out to him, that he was peculiarly desirous that Allan's efforts should not be interrupted in the course of his present mission; "a mission," he said, "highly honourable for himself, and likely to prove most advantageous to the King's cause. He expected his brother would hold no communication with him upon other subjects, nor stir up any cause of dissension, which might divert his mind from a matter of such importance."

Angus answered somewhat sulkily, that "he was no makebate, or stirrer-up of quarrels; he would rather be a peacemaker. His brother knew as well as most men how to resent his own quarrels—as for Allan's mode of receiving information, it was generally believed he had other sources than those of ordinary couriers. He should not be surprised if they saw him sooner than they expected."

A promise that he would not interfere, was the farthest to which Montrose could bring this man, thoroughly good-tempered as he was on all occasions, save when his pride, interest, or prejudices, were interfered with. And at this point the Marquis was fain to leave the matter for the present.

A more willing guest at the bridal ceremony, certainly a more willing attendant at the marriage feast, was to be expected in Sir Dugald Dalgetty, whom Montrose resolved to invite, as having been a confidant to the circumstances which preceded it. But even Sir Dugald hesitated, looked on the elbows of his doublet, and the knees of his leather breeches, and mumbled out a sort of reluctant acquiescence in the invitation, providing he should find it possible, after consulting with the noble bridegroom. Montrose was somewhat surprised, but scorning to testify displeasure, he left Sir Dugald to pursue his own course.

This carried him instantly to the chamber of the bride-groom, who, amidst the scanty wardrobe which his camp-equipage afforded, was seeking for such articles as might appear to the best advantage upon the approaching occasion. Sir Dugald entered, and paid his compliments, with a very grave face, upon his approaching happiness, which, he said, "he was very sorry he was prevented from witnessing."

"In plain truth," said he, "I should but disgrace the ceremony, seeing that I lack a bridal garment. Rents, and open seams, and tatters at elbows in the apparel of the assistants, might presage a similar solution of continuity in your matrimonial happiness—and to say truth, my lord, you yourself must partly have the blame of this disappointment, in respect you sent me upon a fool's errand to get a buff-coat out of the booty taken by the Camerons, whereas you might as well have sent me to fetch a pound of fresh butter out of a black dog's throat. I had no answer, my lord, but brandished dirks and broadswords, and a sort of growling and jabbering in what they call their language. For my part, I believe these Highlanders to be no better than absolute pagans, and have been much scandalized by the manner in which my acquaintance, Ranald MacEagh, was pleased to beat his final march, a little while since."

In Menteith's state of mind, disposed to be pleased with everything, and everybody, the grave complaint of Sir Dugald furnished additional amusement. He requested his acceptance of a very handsome buff-dress which was lying on the floor. "I had intended it," he said, "for my own bridal-garment, as being the least formidable of my warlike equipments, and I have here no peaceful dress."

Sir Dugald made the necessary apologies—would not by any means deprive—and so forth, until it happily occurred to him that it was much more according to military rule that the Earl should be married in his back and breast pieces, which dress he had seen the bridegroom wear at the union of Prince Leo of Wittlesbach with the youngest daughter of old George Frederick, of Saxony, under the auspices of the gallant Gustavus Adolphus, the Lion of the North, and so forth. The good-natured young Earl laughed, and acquiesced; and thus having secured at least one merry face at his bridal, he put on a light and ornamented cuirass, concealed partly by a velvet coat, and partly by a broad blue silk scarf, which he wore over his shoulder, agreeably to his rank, and the fashion of the times.

Everything was now arranged; and it had been settled that, according to the custom of the country, the bride and bridegroom should not again meet until they were before the altar. The hour had already struck that summoned the bridegroom thither, and he only waited in a small anteroom adjacent to the chapel, for the Marquis, who condescended to act as bride's-man upon the occasion. Business relating to the army having suddenly required the Marquis's instant attention, Menteith waited his return, it may be supposed, in some impatience; and when he heard the door of the apartment open, he said, laughing, "You are late upon parade."

"You will find I am too early," said Allan M'Aulay, who burst into the apartment. "Draw, Menteith, and defend yourself like a man, or die like a dog!"

"You are mad, Allan!" answered Menteith, astonished alike at his sudden appearance, and at the unutterable fury of his demeanour. His cheeks were livid—his eyes started from their sockets—his lips were covered with foam, and his gestures were those of a demoniac.

"You lie, traitor!" was his frantic reply—"you lie in that, as you lie in all you have said to me. Your life is a lie!"

"Did I not speak my thoughts when I called you mad," said Menteith, indignantly, "your own life were a brief one. In what do you charge me with deceiving you?"

"You told me," answered M'Aulay, "that you would not marry Annot Lyle!—False traitor!—she now waits you at the altar."

"It is you who speak false," retorted Menteith. "I told you the obscurity of her birth was the only bar to our union—that is now removed; and whom do you think yourself, that I should yield up my pretensions in your favour?"

"Draw then," said M'Aulay; "we understand each other."

"Not now," said Menteith, "and not here. Allan, you know me well—wait till to-morrow, and you shall have fighting enough."

"This hour—this instant—or never," answered M'Aulay.

"Your triumph shall not go farther than the hour which is stricken. Menteith, I entreat you by our relationship—by our joint conflicts and labours—draw your sword, and defend your life!" As he spoke, he seized the Earl's hand, and wrung it with such frantic earnestness, that his grasp forced the blood to start under the nails. Menteith threw him off with violence, exclaiming, "Begone, madman!"

"Then, be the vision accomplished!" said Allan; and, drawing his dirk, struck with his whole gigantic force at the Earl's bosom. The temper of the corslet threw the point of the weapon upwards, but a deep wound took place between the neck and shoulder; and the force of the blow prostrated the bridegroom on the floor. Montrose entered at one side of the anteroom. The bridal company, alarmed at the noise, were in equal apprehension and surprise; but ere Montrose could almost see what had happened, Allan M'Aulay had rushed past him, and descended the castle stairs like lightning. "Guards, shut the gate!" exclaimed Montrose—"Seize him—kill him, if he resists!—He shall die, if he were my brother!"

But Allan prostrated, with a second blow of his dagger, a sentinel who was upon duty—traversed the camp like a mountain-deer, though pursued by all who caught the alarm—threw himself into the river, and, swimming to the opposite side, was soon lost among the woods. In the course of the same evening, his brother Angus and his followers left Montrose's camp, and, taking the road homeward, never again rejoined him.

Of Allan himself it is said, that, in a wonderfully short space after the deed was committed, he burst into a room in the Castle of Inverary, where Argyle was sitting in council, and flung on the table his bloody dirk.

"Is it the blood of James Grahame?" said Argyle, a ghastly expression of hope mixing with the terror which the sudden apparition naturally excited.

"It is the blood of his minion," answered M'Aulay—"It is the blood which I was predestined to shed, though I would rather have spilt my own."

Having thus spoken, he turned and left the castle, and from that moment nothing certain is known of his fate. As the boy Kenneth, with three of the Children of the Mist, were seen soon afterwards to cross Lochfine, it is supposed they dogged his course, and that he perished by their hand in some obscure wilderness. Another opinion maintains, that Allan M'Aulay went abroad and died a monk of the Carthusian order. But nothing beyond bare presumption could ever be brought in support of either opinion.

His vengeance was much less complete than he probably fancied; for Menteith, though so severely wounded as to remain long in a dangerous state, was, by having adopted Major Dalgetty's fortunate recommendation of a cuirass as a bridal-garment, happily secured from the worst consequences of the blow. But his services were lost to Montrose; and it was thought best, that he should be conveyed with his intended countess, now truly a mourning bride, and should accompany his wounded father-in-law to the castle of Sir Duncan at Ardenvohr. Dalgetty followed them to the water's edge, reminding Menteith of the necessity of erecting a sconce on Drumsnab to cover his lady's newly-acquired inheritance.

They performed their voyage in safety, and Menteith was in a few weeks so well in health, as to be united to Annot in the castle of her father.

The Highlanders were somewhat puzzled to reconcile Menteith's recovery with the visions of the second sight, and the more experienced Seers were displeased with him for not having died. But others thought the credit of the vision sufficiently fulfilled, by the wound inflicted by the hand, and with the weapon, foretold; and all were of opinion, that the incident of the ring, with the death's head, related to the death of the bride's father, who did not survive her marriage many months. The incredulous held, that all this was idle dreaming, and that Allan's supposed vision was but a consequence of the private suggestions of his own passion, which, having long seen in Menteith a rival more beloved than himself, struggled with his better nature, and impressed upon him, as it were involuntarily, the idea of killing his competitor.

Menteith did not recover sufficiently to join Montrose during his brief and glorious career; and when that heroic general disbanded his army and retired from Scotland, Menteith resolved to adopt the life of privacy, which he led till the Restoration. After that happy event, he occupied a situation in the land befitting his rank, lived long, happy alike in public regard and in domestic affection, and died at a good old age.

Our DRAMATIS PERSONAE have been so limited, that, excepting Montrose, whose exploits and fate are the theme of history, we have only to mention Sir Dugald Dalgetty. This gentleman continued, with the most rigorous punctuality, to discharge his duty, and to receive his pay, until he was made prisoner, among others, upon the field of Philiphaugh. He was condemned to share the fate of his fellow-officers upon that occasion, who were doomed to death rather by denunciations from the pulpit, than the sentence either of civil or military tribunal; their blood being considered as a sort of sin-offering to take away the guilt of the land, and the fate imposed upon the Canaanites, under a special dispensation, being impiously and cruelly applied to them.

Several Lowland officers, in the service of the Covenanters, interceded for Dalgetty on this occasion, representing him as a person whose skill would be useful in their army, and who would be readily induced to change his service. But on this point they found Sir Dugald unexpectedly obstinate. He had engaged with the King for a certain term, and, till that was expired, his principles would not permit any shadow of changing. The Covenanters, again, understood no such nice distinction, and he was in the utmost danger of falling a martyr, not to this or that political principle, but merely to his own strict ideas of a military enlistment. Fortunately, his friends discovered, by computation, that there remained but a fortnight to elapse of the engagement he had formed, and to which, though certain it was never to be renewed, no power on earth could make him false. With some difficulty they procured a reprieve for this short space, after which they found him perfectly willing to come under any engagements they chose to dictate. He entered the service of the Estates accordingly, and wrought himself forward to be Major in Gilbert Ker's corps, commonly called the Kirk's Own

Regiment of Horse. Of his farther history we know nothing, until we find him in possession of his paternal estate of Drumthwacket, which he acquired, not by the sword, but by a pacific intermarriage with Hannah Strachan, a matron somewhat stricken in years, the widow of the Aberdeenshire Covenanter.

Sir Dugald is supposed to have survived the Revolution, as traditions of no very distant date represent him as cruising about in that country, very old, very deaf, and very full of interminable stories about the immortal Gustavus Adolphus, the Lion of the North, and the bulwark of the Protestant Faith.

* * * * *

READER! THE TALES OF MY LANDLORD ARE NOW FINALLY CLOSED, closed, and it was my purpose to have addressed thee in the vein of Jedediah Cleishbotham; but, like Horam the son of Asmar, and all other imaginary story-tellers, Jedediah has melted into thin air.

Mr. Cleishbotham bore the same resemblance to Ariel, as he at whose voice he rose doth to the sage Prospero; and yet, so fond are we of the fictions of our own fancy, that I part with him, and all his imaginary localities, with idle reluctance. I am aware this is a feeling in which the reader will little sympathize; but he cannot be more sensible than I am, that sufficient varieties have now been exhibited of the Scottish character, to exhaust one individual's powers of observation, and that to persist would be useless and tedious. I have the vanity to suppose, that the popularity of these Novels has shown my countrymen, and their peculiarities, in lights which were new to the Southern reader; and that many, hitherto indifferent upon the subject, have been induced to read Scottish history, from the allusions to it in these works of fiction.

I retire from the field, conscious that there remains behind not only a large harvest, but labourers capable of gathering it in. More than one writer has of late displayed talents of this description; and if the present author, himself a phantom, may be permitted to distinguish a brother, or perhaps a sister shadow, he would mention, in particular, the author of the very lively work entitled MARRIAGE.

IV.
APPENDIX.

No. I

The scarcity of my late friend's poem may be an excuse for adding the spirited conclusion of Clan Alpin's vow. The Clan Gregor has met in the ancient church of Balquidder. The head of Drummond-Ernoch is placed on the altar, covered for a time with the banner of the tribe. The Chief of the tribe advances to the altar:

And pausing, on the banner gazed;
Then cried in scorn, his finger raised,
"This was the boon of Scotland's king;"
And, with a quick and angry fling,
Tossing the pageant screen away,
The dead man's head before him lay.
Unmoved he scann'd the visage o'er,
The clotted locks were dark with gore,
The features with convulsion grim,
The eyes contorted, sunk, and dim.
But unappall'd, in angry mood,
With lowering brow, unmoved he stood.
Upon the head his bared right hand
He laid, the other grasp'd his brand:
Then kneeling, cried, "To Heaven I swear
This deed of death I own, and share;
As truly, fully mine, as though
This my right hand had dealt the blow:

Come then, our foeman, one, come all;
If to revenge this caitiffs fall
One blade is bared, one bow is drawn,
Mine everlasting peace I pawn,
To claim from them, or claim from him,
In retribution, limb for limb.
In sudden fray, or open strife,
This steel shall render life for life."
He ceased; and at his beckoning nod,
The clansmen to the altar trod;
And not a whisper breathed around,
And nought was heard of mortal sound,
Save from the clanking arms they bore,
That rattled on the marble floor;
And each, as he approach'd in haste,
Upon the scalp his right hand placed;
With livid lip, and gather'd brow,
Each uttered, in his turn, the vow.
Fierce Malcolm watch'd the passing scene,
And search'd them through with glances keen;
Then dash'd a tear-drop from his eye;
Unhid it came—he knew not why.
Exulting high, he towering stood:
"Kinsmen," he cried, "of Alpin's blood,
And worthy of Clan Alpin's name,
Unstain'd by cowardice and shame,
E'en do, spare nocht, in time of ill
Shall be Clan Alpin's legend still!"

No. II.

It has been disputed whether the Children of the Mist were actual MacGregors, or whether they were not outlaws named MacDonald, belonging to Ardnamurchan. The following act of the Privy Council seems to decide the question:—

"Edinburgh, 4th February, 1589.

The same day, the Lords of Secret Council being crediblie informed of ye cruel and mischievous proceeding of ye wicked

Clangrigor, so lang continueing in blood, slaughters, herships, manifest reifts, and stouths committed upon his Hieness' peaceable and good subjects; inhabiting ye countries ewest ye brays of ye Highlands, thir money years bybgone; but specially heir after ye cruel murder of umqll Jo. Drummond of Drummoneyryuch, his Majesties proper tennant and ane of his fosters of Glenartney, committed upon ye day of last bypast, be certain of ye said clan, be ye council and determination of ye haill, avow and to defend ye authors yrof qoever wald persew for revenge of ye same, qll ye said Jo. was occupied in seeking of venison to his Hieness, at command of Pat. Lord Drummond, stewart of Stratharne, and principal forrester of Clenartney; the Queen, his Majesties dearest spouse, being yn shortlie looked for to arrive in this realm. Likeas, after ye murder committed, ye authors yrof cutted off ye said umqll Jo. Drummond's head, and carried the same to the Laird of M'Grigor, who, and the haill surname of M'Grigors, purposely conveined upon the Sunday yrafter, at the Kirk of Buchquhidder; qr they caused ye said umqll John's head to be pnted to ym, and yr avowing ye sd murder to have been committed by yr communion, council, and determination, laid yr hands upon the pow, and in eithnik, and barbarous manner, swear to defend ye authors of ye sd murder, in maist proud contempt of our sovrn Lord and his authoritie, and in evil example to others wicked limmaris to do ye like, give ys sall be suffered to remain unpunished."

Then follows a commission to the Earls of Huntly, Argyle, Athole, Montrose, Pat. Lord Drummond, Ja. Commendator of Incheffray, And. Campbel of Lochinnel, Duncan Campbel of Ardkinglas, Lauchlane M'Intosh of Dunnauchtane, Sir Jo. Murray of Tullibarden, knt., Geo. Buchanan of that Ilk, and And. M'Farlane of Ariquocher, to search for and apprehend Alaster M'Grigor of Glenstre (and a number of others nominatim), "and all others of the said Clangrigor, or ye assistars, culpable of the said odious murther, or of thift, reset of thift, herships, and sornings, qrever they may be apprehended. And if they refuse to he taken, or flees to strengths and houses, to pursue and assege them with fire and sword; and this commission to endure for the space of three years."

Such was the system of police in 1589; and such the state of Scotland nearly thirty years after the Reformation.

* * * * *

V.
NOTES.

Note I.—FIDES ET FIDUCIA SUNT RELATIVA.

The military men of the times agreed upon dependencies of honour, as they called them, with all the metaphysical argumentation of civilians, or school divines.

The English officer, to whom Sir James Turner was prisoner after the rout at Uttoxeter, demanded his parole of honour not to go beyond the wall of Hull without liberty. "He brought me the message himself,—I told him I was ready to do so, provided he removed his guards from me, for FIDES ET FIDUCIA SUNT RELATIVA; and, if he took my word for my fidelity, he was obliged to trust it, otherwise, it was needless for him to seek it, either to give trust to my word, which I would not break, or his own guards, who I supposed would not deceive him. In this manner I dealt with him, because I knew him to be a scholar."—TURNER'S MEMOIRS, p. 80. The English officer allowed the strength of the reasoning; but that concise reasoner, Cromwell, soon put an end to the dilemma: "Sir James Turner must give his parole, or be laid in irons."

Note II.—WRAITHS.

A species of apparition, similar to what the Germans call a Double-Ganger, was believed in by the Celtic tribes, and is still considered as an emblem of misfortune or death. Mr. Kirke (See Note to ROB ROY,), the minister of Aberfoil, who will no doubt be able to tell us more of the matter should he ever come back from Fairy-land, gives us the following:—

"Some men of that exalted sight, either by art or nature, have told me they have seen at these meetings a double man, or the shape of some man in two places, that is, a superterranean and a subterranean inhabitant perfectly resembling one another in all points, whom he, notwithstanding, could easily distinguish one fro another by some secret tokens and operations, and so go speak to the man his neighbour and familiar, passing by the apparition or resemblance of him. They avouch that every element and different state of being have animals resembling those of another element, as there be fishes at sea resembling Monks of late order in all their hoods and dresses, so as the Roman invention of good and bad daemons and guardian angels particularly assigned, is called by them ane ignorant mistake, springing only from this originall. They call this reflex man a Co-Walker, every way like the man, as a twin-brother and companion haunting him as his shadow, as is that seen and known among men resembling the originall, both before and after the originall is dead, and was also often seen of old to enter a hous, by which the people knew that the person of that liknes was to visit them within a few days. This copy, echo, or living picture, goes at last to his own herd. It accompanied that person so long and frequently for ends best known to its selve, whether to guard him from the secret assaults of some of its own folks, or only as an sportfull ape to counterfeit all his actions."

—KIRKE'S SECRET COMMOMWEALTH, p. 3.

The two following apparitions, resembling the vision of Allan M'Aulay in the text, occur in Theophilus Insulanus (Rev. Mr. Fraser's Treatise on the Second Sight, Relations x. and xvii.):—

"Barbara Macpherson, relict of the deceased Mr. Alexander MacLeod, late minister of St. Kilda, informed me the natives of that island had a particular kind of second sight, which is always a forerunner of their approaching end. Some months before they sicken, they are haunted with an apparition, resembling themselves in all respects as to their person, features, or clothing. This image, seemingly animated, walks with them in the field in broad daylight; and if they are employed in delving, harrowing, seed-sowing, or any other occupation, they are at the same time mimicked by this ghostly visitant. My informer added further that having visited a sick person of the inhabitants, she had the curiosity to enquire of him, if at any time he had seen any resemblance of himself as above described; he answered in the affirmative, and told her, that to make farther trial, as he was going out of his house of a morning, he put on straw-rope garters instead of those he formerly used, and having gone to the fields, his other self appeared in such garters. The conclusion was, the sick man died of that ailment, and she no longer questioned the truth of those remarkable presages."

"Margaret MacLeod, an honest woman advanced in years, informed me, that when she was a young woman in the family of Grishornish, a dairy-maid, who daily used to herd the calves in a park close to the house, observed, at different times, a woman resembling herself in shape and attire, walking solitarily at no great distance from her, and being surprised at the apparition, to make further trial, she put the back part of her upper garment foremost, and anon the phantom was dressed in the same manner, which made her uneasy, believing it portended some fatal consequence to herself. In a short time thereafter she was seized with a fever, which brought her to her end, and before her sickness and on her deathbed, declared the second sight to several."

414281

Made in the USA